PRAISE FOR
THE MONARCHS

"Elevated by debut author Mark Sabbas's infectious passion for music, philosophy, and matters of the spirit, *The Monarchs* delivers an uplifting, vividly imagined tale of human potential and the unifying power of empathy and love . . . this is an engaging and moving hero's journey."

—IndieReader

"Mark Sabbas' *The Monarchs* is pure and powerful. He's crafted an unforgettable page-turning novel featuring fascinating characters who live in a vividly described world that I could clearly see in my mind's eye. A must-read for fiction enthusiasts of all ages!"

—Natacha Belair, Award-Winning Author of
A Stellar Purpose trilogy

"A thought-provoking and spiritual dystopian quest."

—*Kirkus Reviews*

"Steeped in fantasy, this is an action-packed romp through time and space. Suitable for the YA market, due to its fantastical elements, the book has echoes of the Harry Potter books and could be easily made into a TV series along the lines of *His Dark Materials*."

—Madison Brightwell, Amazon Best-Selling Author of
The World Beyond the Redbud Tree

The Monarchs
by Mark Sabbas

Published by

köehlerbooks™

3705 Shore Drive
Virginia Beach, VA 23455
800-435-4811
www.koehlerbooks.com

THE MONARCHS

MARK SABBAS

VIRGINIA BEACH
CAPE CHARLES

This book is dedicated to my incredible wife, Stephanie; my parents, who raised me; the rest of my wonderful family; and all others who have supported me throughout this beautiful, exciting, and often very challenging human journey, both seen and unseen.

This book is dedicated to all those who, despite difficulties, choose to embody love each day to the best of their ability, acting as guiding beacons for others, for they know in their hearts that a better world is possible.

This book is dedicated to the children who have entered this world with purity and imagination, their minds unblemished, knowing all things are possible. We have a lot to learn from them.

Lastly, this book is dedicated to all human beings.

"A human being is a part of the whole, called by us 'Universe,' a part limited in time and space. He experiences himself, his thoughts and feelings as something separated from the rest—a kind of optical delusion of his consciousness. The striving to free oneself from this delusion is the one issue of true religion. Not to nourish the delusion but to try to overcome it is the way to reach the attainable measure of peace of mind."

—ALBERT EINSTEIN, letter to a grieving father

CHAPTER 1

For a moment, there was stillness. Then an eye-opening jolt filled my lungs with breath, as if I had spent a lifetime on another plane and were only now awakening to reality. My pupils hastened to adjust to the blinding light. My limbs shook with a force I did not understand. Ghostly whooshing noises echoed through my awareness, like whispers through an ocean wave. All the while, my mind was off somewhere, floating adrift, blissfully half-awake to the current situation yet anxious to tune back in.

"Give me clarity!" I shouted through a mechanism unknown; and suddenly, I was born again.

With the whispers gone and my body still, I found myself facing a white wall in a small, empty room. I knew this room—knew how much I loathed it—yet could barely recognize my own memory. It had been an eerie, disorienting sleep, accompanied by a silence so deafening that I could hear my heart ticking away like a broken clock.

How did I get here? I asked my open palms, if only to distract from the present moment. Breathing once more with meditative grit, I yearned to retain that spotless mind. Yet as my focus calibrated on those scars from hard labor, the veil of amnesia was inevitably ripped away, letting it all flow back through.

The fear. The pain. The guilt. The loneliness. The emotion came bursting from within, clouding my mind with misery, and I dared not dwell on it longer.

Twisting in my chair, I surveyed the windowless walls of this unnerving prison. They were adorned with only an automated door I was unable to open and the portrait of a man whose gaze I could not bear to meet. This was the reality of the white room, as I so cleverly called it. Everything in the labs was colorless, from the walls to our mandatory robes to the emotions of the ones who tested us like rodents. Here was where we were forced to wait; the sun never shined, and I could hardly stand the sight of my own shadow.

The greeting came from somewhere else entirely: "*Welcome to your life, wandering spirit.*"

With that, I was taken out of myself, gazing into my own eyes from a transcendent perspective—eyes that were nearly twice as large as an average human being's, according to Dr. Salazar, and emitted light in a way that made them true windows to the soul. Setting ablaze when properly stimulated, my eyes could penetrate into the essence of matter. And my mind could manipulate matter in ways not considered normal—at least, by a standard definition of physics.

There were dozens of children with eyes like mine at the Facility, and we could all do things considered abnormal. This was why we were being tested. We were fated for this cruelty.

My heart pounded as I was pulled back in, my sweat-laced palms trembling through a head full of curls as I pushed my hair back from my face. *This here—this is me.* I tried to breathe but this time choked on thick air, my repressed dread forever waiting in the wings.

I was amazed at how easily I had dozed off, as if my sleep-deprived brain had enacted a fail-safe before the panic came. It was, after all, a Sunday. And though I was in the labs most days for checkups and exams, it was on Sundays they liked to experiment with my mind. Hurt it. Drug it. Alter it in strange ways until it did strange things.

And it was worse for me than most of the others. Unlike them, I could not consciously control it—whatever *it* was—and neither could my handlers. Even after ten years of pills, injections, and agonizing shock therapy, a monster lay dormant in the back of my brain, one that only awakened when prodded hard enough.

Soon, they would be coming to take me.

For one precious moment, I closed my eyes and imagined disappearing, surrendering to some boundless void as I had often dreamed while at the Facility. It was only for my tutor, Walter, that I subverted this fantasy; he gave me solace in the form of music, wisdom, and philosophy.

And it was only for Evelyn that I reminded myself how beautiful the world could be, despite our daily suffering and the loss of those loved ones who now only lived in our dreams. We were very close in this regard, and even if she didn't have eyes like mine, they were extraordinary nonetheless, an enchanting crystal blue. "The universe can sometimes leave you in the dark," I could hear her saying, "just to bring you closer to those who share common light."

My limbs stopped quivering as I surrendered to reality. I opened my eyes with a sigh, wondering whether true love was just an illusion. But as I stared again at the white wall, I pictured Evelyn's visage looking back at me. The closest candidate for true love's existence, she held my gaze with her smile. And somehow, I smiled right back, my depression dislodged; the whole of my psyche was ensnared in those blue eyes. I knew that even as our reality crumbled, she would dance with me through it.

"There is a better world," I sang in a whisper. "There must be." I didn't know where this thought came from.

A buzzing noise broke my trance. The automated door slid open. A much older woman stepped into the room, her long blond hair splayed across her lab coat. With her burnt eyes and hollow grin, Alice appeared closer to the edge of madness than ever. Perhaps her mind had finally shattered under the mounting pressure to make something out of me. Perhaps her team was being threatened by the higher-ups. Or maybe this was all unrelated, and there was a whole life of hers I could never know, with her own problems and yearnings for liberation.

I might have felt bad if not for what they had done to me. All that was left to me was that look in Alice's eyes and the breath of my name vibrating across unseen strings.

"Samuel."

There was an extended pause where the woman stood staring from the entrance, leaving me questioning if something was truly wrong. "I must again—" She cleared her throat. "I must again apologize for keeping you waiting. Dr. Salazar is ready to see you now."

I nodded with silent scrutiny, perusing the dull flame of memory for anything that could explain her bizarre behavior. I had only just begun to contemplate my amnesia, unaware of how long I had been waiting and how in the world I had fallen asleep. Time was a tricky agent, and my dreams had faded altogether. It was as if I had appeared out of oblivion.

Attempting to stand on my sandal-clad feet, I nearly got sucked back in, struck by a profound dizziness. Only Alice gliding over to grab me by the shoulder prevented my passing out. With that strangely grounding touch, I focused back in on an uneasy grin and eyes that stared with unreal intensity.

"Are you well, Mr. Helen?"

"I'm *fine*," I asserted, quick to brush her off, though my words were contradicted by the fact that it didn't feel like me who was saying them. I was used to this sort of numbness. Walter had told me that dissociation could be a side effect of traumatic experience.

"We only wish to help you," Alice responded, sensing my growing discomfort. "That is all you have to remember."

"I . . ." I trailed off as I looked down at my palms, then back into the eyes of the scientist. Something seemed different, and for a second, I considered making a run for it. But where would I go, exactly? Life was a game of choices, yet for me there was no choice except to walk through the open door.

I shook my head in surrender. "Let's just get this over with."

"Are you afraid, Mr. Helen?" she inquired, and I wondered if I caught a flicker of empathy in her eyes—whether she and the other scientists truly thought they were doing good things, however skewed their reasoning. At the very least, I could see their eyes, unlike those of the soldiers who patrolled the Facility.

"I'm just afraid I can never change," I said honestly.

"You know very well that we're not giving up on you, not after all these years. In fact," she continued with something close to a smile, "I think we may have hit on a breakthrough."

My heart skipped a beat. Having heard those words several times too many, they did nothing but spur me to brace for pain. I felt the monster kick from within before I quivered out, "What are you going to do to me?"

Alice hesitated, probing my eyes with that maddening stare before gesturing for me to follow. "You will be taken care of, Samuel. You must trust it."

It was futile to resist and tiresome to question. I trailed Salazar's head assistant as she exited the white room. But I glanced back at that man on the wall whose eyes I always had trouble meeting. He was the reason I was here—the reason I could never escape. Painted in front of the seven-star flag of the Union, General Mabus flaunted a proud, defiant grin, representative of the increasing military might of a once-decimated nation.

However, behind his gaze, dampened by thick silence, seemed to be a mysterious whispering that could only be picked up by the deeper subconscious. It was as if the man himself were conveying a message to me, one only I could decipher if I listened very, very—

"Samuel?" Alice called from the other side of the door. "Are you coming?"

"Yeah," I grunted, darkly amused by the irony of her question and chalking the whispering up to an imagination disenchanted by a decade of loneliness.

~

The labs consisted of a huge, maze-like complex with white-coated scientists popping in and out of rooms. Some carried smart glass pads that could produce holographic images of our brains. I was unfamiliar with most of the scientists, but as we passed, a few stopped dead in their tracks, inspecting my eyes before continuing on to their own assigned subjects whose minds they handled freely.

These subjects had eyes like mine, yet most of them were years younger, and all of them had better control of their abilities. Within a glass cubicle I noticed Lila, a playful adolescent with purplish hair and an uncanny ability for remote perception. I paused as her handler wrote coordinates on a whiteboard: 02R3-0144, corresponding to a target through mental association. Sitting in front of a Union map, Lila entered a meditative state and pointed toward the sea.

A few rooms down I found little Noah, who was telekinetically revolving an egg around a world globe, much to the intrigue of two scientists. Noah was one of the few children I was close to because of our shared duties working in the fields weekly with Evelyn and the orphans. The bright-eyed twelve-year-old smiled warmly as I passed; the scientists expressed disappointment as he lost focus and the egg fell and cracked on the ground.

Then I passed Maya, Lila's dark-skinned friend of the same age who had the gift of clairvoyance. She went through a deck of cards with extrasensory ease. The man who was testing her revealed a queen and grinned in contentment. Powerful energy surged from an unknown place within, and I averted my eyes before Alice pushed me along.

I did not recognize the others we passed. All of my distinctive comrades had arrived after me, some within the past few weeks. When they first brought me in as a young boy, the Facility was a smaller military base used to construct weapons. With more and more large-eyed, psychic children born across the Union every year, there were now countless numbers of us being tested in the labs each Sunday. They called us the new youth. And we had become their newest weapons. To some, we were the next step in human evolution—to others, nothing more than radiation-afflicted freaks. I was used to this, for I was the one who started it all.

As we passed a boy with a shaved head who couldn't have been older than nine, I was uncomfortably reminded that I had no idea what had happened to their parents. I couldn't ask most of them, as they liked us to interact as little as possible—a safeguard against psychic rebellion. Even with those few exceptions, I was too nervous to bring it up. All I could do was reassure myself that perhaps they were safer here anyway, in one of the rare corners of the earth untouched by disaster and deadly energy.

All at once, alarms blared throughout the building.

Yelling echoed in the distance, and myriad scientists rushed out into the corridor. In their eyes, I saw that they feared the worst: that we were under attack by the enemies of the Union, rising up once more to take what was left of the planet.

For a minute, I was also afraid. Yet a dark part of me hoped for this destruction. It craved it. In my mind's eye, a grim scene showed the labs and the Facility all burning away, and with it the years of traumatic memory. I caught myself smiling.

Then, I spotted Cyrus.

Curiously naked with the exception of his briefs, the burly teenager sprinted around the corner, determined to bulldoze through the crowd of stunned scientists. As he ran and shrieked, it became clear that this wasn't the same Cyrus I had known since we were young. His arms flailed. His enormous eyes were aflame. And his screams were terrifying, louder than the alarms. Gone was my smile as I stared in bewilderment.

What have they done to him?

Before I had time to think, he was headed straight for me. I stood stiff, trapped like Medusa's prey, entranced by the power within those eyes.

"Move!" a man shouted from behind, thrusting me aside with brute force.

I gazed up in horror from the floor at the three soldiers who took my place. Clad with white body armor and helmets concealing their eyes, they pointed their weapons, and time seemed to slow. It took shots from each of them to bring Cyrus to his knees. Tiny darts hit his skin, funneling currents of electricity through his trembling body for several terrible seconds until he passed out.

The spectators gasped, for it was painful to see my benevolent, bushy-haired friend sprawled unconscious across the floor. As part of the first wave of children at the Facility, Cyrus was one of the few close to me in age, closest in unhinged ability, and therefore closest in testing procedure. As the scientists slowly gathered around him, I could do little but pray for my psychic counterpart to keep on breathing.

The soldiers stowed their weapons. The alarms ceased, replaced by quiet murmuring. A few moments later, a slight man with hunched shoulders and a fidgety demeanor wriggled through the crowd.

"Where is he?!" demanded Dr. Salazar, appearing next to Cyrus with eyes wide behind his spectacles. He caught my gaze, giving me a nod before angrily confronting the soldiers. "What have you done?"

They did not react. After all my years at the Facility, I had yet to figure out if they were even fully human.

"On the contrary, Malcolm, what have *you* done to the boy?" challenged another scientist, the one who worked with Noah. "Your reckless experimentation had him screaming like a madman."

"Don't question me, Erwin. If only you had seen the power I unleashed in him! Nasty hallucinations can be a side effect, unfortunately."

"That was more than simply hallucinations. He was clearly in anguish. As usual, it appears you're playing with darkness."

"Sometimes one needs the darkness to recognize the light," Salazar asserted—an interesting sentiment, coming from him—before bending over Cyrus. "Come on now, boy. Wake up," he said to his naked and debilitated subject. An ominous feeling arose within me. Cold sweat dripped down my neck as my heart pounded back to life, intuiting something to come. The soldiers and scientists stood unsettlingly still. Alice was staring in silence. And as I looked around at all the children watching from their cubicles, my awareness wavered in and out of reality.

Something definitely wasn't right.

The eyes of the shaved-headed boy grounded me as I connected with them. Smirking slyly despite being trapped behind those thick glass walls, he mouthed one word to me: "Escape."

More gasps arose as Cyrus twitched on the floor. His eyes opened with a violent snap, and he inhaled. After a moment of stillness, Salazar looked up at the crowd in relief.

"See! He's—"

Before the lead scientist could finish, his body was propelled ten feet down the corridor, cushioned by several others. Immediately, the soldiers pulled their rifles on the telekinetic culprit.

"No!" I heard myself scream as I barged into one of them, pushing him to the ground. Cyrus thrust back the others with a shriek of psychic will. A glance of gratitude was sufficient before he turned and ran. To my utter astonishment, I ran right after him, through the startled scientists and away from the soldiers retrieving their weapons. Bullets sang as we turned the corner, with a plea from Salazar echoing through the commotion.

"Stop! You can't kill him!"

We darted through the labs without time to look back, only pausing to make a choice at each intersection. But the corridors were eerily empty, and there wasn't an end in sight, only more corners. We were rats scurrying through a labyrinth, yet we ran nonetheless. We ran until we were breathless. We ran until we were convinced we were running in circles, for there were no scientists and no exits—not even any doors! Soon, there wasn't a sound but our own heavy breath.

"We need to get out of here!" Cyrus bent over with exhaustion at a four-way intersection. "Where's the way out?"

"I thought you knew," I said, still in disbelief.

"My mind is not right, Samuel. But you've been here the longest." His eyes glowed, a fiery red swirling around his pupils. "Samuel?"

"I . . . I can't remember."

"Come on, Samuel. Trust your gut. It has to be in there somewhere."

I stared at my palms as if they would provide an answer, and remarkably, I felt a sharp tingling in my right as a faint memory emerged through my dazed awareness.

"This way!"

We ran along our chosen path, not knowing where it would lead. But it wasn't long before we noticed an unusual sight along the colorless walls: a blue wooden door, sanctuary from the storm. I wasn't sure if I had ever seen this door, yet a part of me recognized it. I turned the handle; it was open.

"I guess we have no other choice," Cyrus said. Voices and the sound of pounding feet closed in from either direction. I nodded, and we stepped through together.

As the door shut behind us, we found ourselves in what seemed like an old storage room, filled with so many dusty objects that I could barely make out the walls. Hurriedly, I approached a circular stone table sitting near the corner and attempted to drag it to the door. My arms were too weak. I gathered my strength before trying once more.

It lifted into the air with no effort at all. There it remained, levitating.

Eyes ablaze, Cyrus transported the heavy table with his mind alone, a couple of items falling off in the process, and set it down against the door with a thud. This feat left me envious. I had never seen anything like it from him, never mind from myself. He looked at me and seemed to know what I was thinking.

"Our powers can come in handy. But if it weren't for your bravery back there, I might have been killed. Thank you, Samuel."

"I couldn't just sit back and watch," I said, surveying the troubled soul of my friend. "Still, I didn't know you could do something like that."

"Neither did I."

"What did they do to you?" I asked.

"What they're going to do to you."

I felt another stirring from that darker aspect. It led me to thoughts of power—of psychic strength over others. I replayed the scene of Salazar flying through the air and remembered Alice talking about a breakthrough. Within my fractured soul, I was suddenly conflicted.

"Trust me, Samuel," Cyrus warned, reading me with unnerving accuracy. "It's difficult to feel the things I felt in there. And I still feel it."

"What do you feel?"

The force of his stare was hair raising. "Like someone else is in control." As if to show rather than tell, an image began forming in his eyes, rearranging into a pattern resembling stars in the sky. The wonder of it all was spellbinding, and for an extended moment, I was lost for words. He broke the connection when he noticed something in the center of the room.

"Samuel, look!"

I turned to see an object that had fallen off the table—one of those smart glass pads. Resting face down, the device emitted a peculiar light onto the floor. Cyrus flipped it over with a telekinetic touch, and holographic words appeared in the air in front of us:

PROJECT MONARCH

We exchanged perplexed glances, never having heard of anything like this during our years at the Facility. I was ready to write it off as some forgotten government project, but then the words transformed into an immersive movie of a young man with strange eyes.

That young man was me.

My jaw dropped as I watched myself digging holes in the hot sun, drenched in sweat, as part of my duties. I looked pained and exhausted and reached for my flask of water, oblivious to the fact that I was being recorded. And I appeared the same age in the hologram as I did in that moment, setting off alarms in every corner of my mind.

"They're . . . watching me," I whispered.

Cyrus nodded as the hologram transitioned.

The next recording made my heart sink. It came from the perspective of the ceiling of Walter's office, looking down at me and him in the middle of a conversation, presumably about some meaningful philosophy. Walter rose from his chair and combed through his collection of music albums. Although the hologram itself was silent, it was obvious that someone else was listening in.

"Why is it only you?" Cyrus questioned, looking as dumbfounded as I felt.

I shook my head slowly. "I don't know."

When the scene switched once again, every ounce of breath left my lungs. I saw a little boy with the same strange eyes lying in the arms of a beautiful woman, who seemed to be comforting him while he was ill. With this, I gave up questioning and simply observed, tears of stupefaction dripping down my face. It was extraordinary to behold myself around ten years younger—never mind the woman smiling over me as if still alive.

"How is this even possible?" My voice trembled.

There was no time to ponder, for the sounds of soldiers crowding outside the door reached us. Soon, there was a turn of the handle, followed by a forceful push. The door banged against the table. They knew we were in here.

"Samuel, we have to hide!"

I stared at him, then focused again on the hologram, attempting to enter it somehow, to return to a time when everything was better.

"There's an air vent back here," he said, reinforcing the door with his mind. "If I can get it open, maybe we can crawl through!"

A male voice resounded from outside: "Open, or we'll shoot!"

Cyrus shook me by the shoulders in desperation.

"Samuel, they'll kill us!"

Understanding set in, albeit only for an instant. "No. They won't."

I sank into a trance as the hologram morphed into a life-size projection of a girl with rose-red hair and crystal-blue eyes standing before a gorgeous waterfall, recognizing me with a joyful expression. I did not know how it was possible, though I did not care to rationalize. In spite of the calls from Cyrus and the harsh threats from the soldiers, nothing mattered but Evelyn and me together. Tears flooded out; I loved her more than anyone alive.

I then witnessed something remarkable take place: a sudden transformation, quickening the aura around her. Even through the hologram, I was blinded by a flash of boundless light. When I opened my eyes, she was reaching for my hand. Her soul was infinite, and her eyes seemed . . . different.

No sooner had I grazed her fingers than a bullet pierced through the door and punctured the device, deactivating the hologram and sending me back to reality.

As more bullets followed, I looked around for Cyrus. He was nowhere to be found. I shouted his name, then dove behind some old laboratory equipment and curled up in fright. My friend had left me, and with the door breaking open, I knew they would soon come to punish me for my act of defiance—if I even made it out alive. What they had in store, I could not say. I had never dared to flee before an experiment. *What was I thinking?* Escaping the labs was a futile endeavor, much less the entire facility.

Fear gave way to anger as I came to understand how closely I was being monitored. Me and everyone I loved, prey to some wicked game. I hummed an old song to calm myself but was interrupted by gunshots. I tried to picture Evelyn's eyes, but her face was blurred by panic as I wondered if these were my last moments on earth.

"Samuel."

The voice came from inside of my mind, but it belonged to a young woman equipped with a certain familiarity. I thought I was hallucinating until it came again, clear above the ruckus of the outside world.

"Samuel! Over here, silly."

I lifted my head to find something astonishing: a girl with the eyes of a new youth staring from behind a window in the far wall. I blinked, certain that this window had not been there previously. Tapping on the glass, the girl winked flirtatiously. Her luminous gaze and long dark hair were dazzling. The voice in my mind did not come again; rather, she slowly moved her lips. Although I could not hear what she was saying, I felt a commanding chord strike from within, as if my awareness had spontaneously jumped a level.

Her eyes were like a drug, endowed with a hypnotic energy. And suddenly, everything was fine.

The gunshots ceased, and I heard Salazar fiercely scolding the trigger-happy soldiers. Even as they entered the room, I refused to move from this state of stillness, enamored by the familiarity of the girl in the window. I tried reading her lips, for surely it was a message, and that's when I noticed a golden cuff around her wrist.

"Samuel." My name came by spoken word this time. With a surprising amount of effort, I broke eye contact to find Alice kneeling beside me. She appeared concerned. "Samuel, are you hurt?"

I shook my head, releasing the anger at what I had seen and letting the mystery the girl represented wash through me.

"Good." She glanced around the room, which suddenly appeared back in order. "Where's the other one?"

"He isn't here," I said. "What did you do to him?"

"We unlocked a tiny glimpse of the potential you also have within," Salazar interjected. He had entered trailed by the soldiers. Judging by his slight limp, he was shaken from the psychic attack but seemed pleased nonetheless. "Unfortunately for him, the treatment temporarily hindered the rational part of his brain, causing violent tendencies and fantasies of escaping. We know you only wished to help your friend, but it was unwise of you to nourish his delusions."

I stared curiously at him, then at the girl in the window. Still moving her lips, she pointed to her ear, telling me to listen. I turned back to the scientists. "We can never be free from this place, can we?"

Salazar laughed, not unkindly. "Being free is all we want for you, Samuel. Free from yourself—from the chains of your mind. And if this works, my boy, you can be free from this place, too. That is a promise to you. We know of your longings for a true home."

My heart raced while my mind continued to question. Never had they acted with such empathy toward me, and they had certainly never promised my freedom. I switched between the gazes of Alice and Salazar, and however hard it was to trust them, I was struck by a sense of sincerity. Maybe they were just trying to help, after all these years. But I had one more question.

"That girl over there." I gestured to the far wall. "Who is she? She said my name, but it was like she was speaking *through* me."

Salazar looked puzzled before a sly grin spread across his face, unnatural for the stoic scientist. "Be careful with those telepaths, my boy." He pointed to his head. "They can play with your psyche. They can manipulate your mind."

I turned to look, but she was gone. Unbelievably, the window had vanished too, replaced by a shining mirror. Before I could express my bewilderment, the soldiers were on me, pinning me down as Salazar revealed a needle like none that I had ever seen—filled with a black, gooey substance.

"Okay now, just a little pinprick," he sang.

Struggling was useless as he stuck my vein. I felt frightened again, and somewhat betrayed. But it all disappeared as I became lightheaded, hearing the voice of the doctor before losing consciousness.

"Just relax, Samuel. There is no pain. But you may feel a little sick."

The words were oddly familiar.

~

Light streamed through my eyelids, and my head throbbed. I lay on a cold floor, naked and woozy, a caged beast for all to see.

They wanted something supernatural. Something uncanny.

What are they going to do with me?

I sat up to find Salazar and a couple of young assistants staring intently from behind a glass wall, in full view of whatever miracle was set to happen. The assistants perked up when they saw me. Salazar smiled. They seemed yet unaccustomed to seeing humans with my eyes, and I wondered if they were afraid of me—if they believed that I could do the same to them as Cyrus did to their superior.

Maybe if they get me angry enough.

I recalled the escape attempt. The holograms. The black goo injection. With dread, I stared down at the veins on my wrist, a dark, unknown substance running through them. I focused on my breath the way Walter had taught me, trying to calm my racing heart. That's when I noticed someone else in the room, gliding over with a cup of steaming liquid.

"Drink," said Alice.

"Cyrus," I uttered.

"Cyrus is fine. Just getting some rest. It is you we have to worry about." She offered me the cup. It exuded a golden radiance. "Drink, Samuel. It will help you to feel better."

"You're not forcing anything else into me." I glared at her bitterly.

"Very well then. It's your choice whether to take the medicine. Just know that everything we did to you—and will do in the future— is a necessary process."

"Necessary for what?" I asked in frustration.

"For you to fully awaken."

I searched her eyes, futilely trying to discern her intentions. With my mouth dry and my mind still weak, I accepted the cup begrudgingly. The steam felt soothing on my skin, but as I gulped the tea, it tasted undeniably foul.

"What is this?" I asked Alice, gagging.

"A necessary process," she stressed, lifting my hand so that I finished the rest. "Very good. Can you stand up?"

With force of will, I did as she requested, handing her back the cup. I did not know why they had stripped me of my robes, but it was not my first concern. I was used to being treated like an animal. I was more puzzled that none of the usual equipment was in the room—no wires attached to my body and, thankfully, none of the machinery for electroshock therapy. I saw only a small black cube around two feet in length, made of some exotic metal, waiting for me at the other end of the room. As Alice headed for the exit, I was left utterly confused.

"Wait! What should I do?"

To my incredulity, the scientist turned and winked. "You will know," she said before going through the automated door to join the others in the parallel room. They observed from behind unbreakable glass while I was stranded with whatever lay in that cube.

Salazar spoke into a device, his voice tinny. "All right, Samuel. Just nod if you can hear me."

I met his eyes with impatience. "Yes. What do you want from me?"

"All you have to do is focus," he urged. "Tap into that magnificent power of yours."

I stared back disbelievingly. How many times had he used those words, knowing full well the conditions through which it emerged?

However, as my breath deepened, I noticed a peculiar vibration originating at the crown of my head and spreading through the rest of my body. Though not painful, the sensation was unsettling, as if a tremendous energy were knocking at the door of my consciousness.

"Oh, and Samuel," Salazar added with a smirk, "when it comes, I wouldn't fight it. It is best to just let it take you over."

"Let wha—" I suddenly couldn't speak, for the vibrations had become so strong that they shook my mind out of alignment with its body. Just as I was questioning what in the world they had given me, I dropped to my knees, losing all touch with reality. The last thing I felt was my crown cracking open and flooding with energy, allowing cosmic visions to vividly emerge.

Peering down from space, I saw a beautiful planet—then mushroom clouds erupting, devastating her image. I saw silver ships hovering in her orbit, waiting. Subsequently, what seemed like comets began descending, though there was no danger, because they were of pure, white light, and I sensed that they were conscious, filled with life and intelligence.

The next series of images didn't make much sense: an ice cream cone; a flying, black dragon; two robots holding each other, passionately kissing. My mind plunged into eccentricity, and I could only surrender to it. I didn't know how much time had passed when logic fell dead. From what I could tell, I was ten feet tall, then as small as a caterpillar, hanging from a tree next to a river, struggling with all my might to burst from my cocoon.

It all stopped as quickly as it began, and I breathed as if born again.

I didn't stand so much as I floated to my feet with relative ease. Instantly, I knew that my brain was operating at a higher capacity. My senses were elevated, the light of my eyes amplifying to laser-like precision. I felt good—sublime, even—yet my handlers still had me trapped in a cage, like a freak on display.

I realized that I could sense them without even looking at them. I felt their hearts beating, their pulses quickening as I stared each of them down. I knew that they were hiding something.

Salazar grinned when I arrived at him, pleased by my sudden confidence. "Focus!" he said through the intercom. He motioned to the mysterious black cube several feet away, which immediately caught my heightened attention.

There was something living in there, fighting to get out. They would soon let it loose, just as they did with Cyrus. The creature was not very large, but it might still be deadly and would be on me swiftly once that happened. This was the experiment, was it not? They wanted to see how I reacted in the face of fear, with a mind vitalized by psychoactive compounds. Surely they already had an idea of what would happen.

They knew my past, after all.

They knew that I could kill.

And they had in all likelihood been watching me since I was young, according to what I had seen in that hologram. With silent anger, I felt something else taking over.

My heart rate rose with a burst of adrenaline. Sweat seeped out along my bare skin. I wanted to scream—to exemplify my power— and for a moment I wondered if I really was a monster. Regardless, the darkness in that cube would inevitably confront my own. It was not the first time my handlers had engaged me with a mutated creature, though none so vicious that it had to be contained by metal.

I glanced again at Salazar; he nodded slowly, as if he could tell what I was thinking. To his side was Alice, holding her breath. She mouthed two words to me: "Get . . . ready."

I took a step back and inhaled all the air I could muster while the hair on my arms raised instinctively. There was a faint buzzing, and after a few excruciating seconds, the front side of the cube gradually slid open. Emerging from its shadows was a devil of perfect white, crawling out eagerly to meet me in a fight. It was a . . . a . . .

A rabbit?!

At first I thought it was another hallucination, but my discerning eyes could not be mistaken. The innocent little bunny hopped out in front of me, in no way deformed and in no sense malevolent. I looked around, dumbfounded.

"Samuel."

I caught Salazar's eyes gazing into mine and became strangely hypnotized. He spoke his next words with intensive purpose: "Remember who you are and what you are here to accomplish."

A bell chimed below my conscious mind, activating a hidden blueprint and sparking a high-pitched ringing at the center of my brain that sent me screaming to the floor in torment. I clutched my head, feeling as if a nail were being inserted into it. My whole body shook with electricity, its molecular bonds breaking. Finally, my consciousness left entirely, and again I saw the visions. But this time they felt more like live experiences, seen from the eyes of others.

I was my mother, holding the hand of a frightened little boy, telling him about the angels that would always protect him.

I was my father, screaming in rage while the eyes of that same boy turned dangerously red.

I was little Evelyn, approaching the boy now curled up on the grass, seeking to cure his desolation.

Then I became the girl in the window, interacting with myself in the room with the blue door. And she—*I*—was singing beautifully, picking up from a tune I knew intimately:

"Listen carefully to the sound of your loneliness."

As I returned behind my own eyes, my heart sent out a shock wave so mighty that it shattered the glass wall, silencing the ringing. A loving energy wrapped around me, shielding my body from harm, while the rabbit lay stiff in my blurred vision, its spirit released in sacrifice.

I saw a soft blue light before shutting my eyes, and everything felt right.

CHAPTER 2

MY EYES OPENED to the sound of a fading melody along a comforting breeze. The sun shined high in the sky, burning down on my exposed body, which was barely sheltered by the surrounding grass. I had passed out in broad daylight. Oddly, it felt like I had reawakened into a dream.

I sat up in a frenzy, remembering where I was.

"I was wondering when you would wake up." Noah's voice rang with a teasing tone. I turned to find him standing beside me, covered in dirt, shovel in hand. Guilt swept over me as I climbed to my feet, shaking my head in disbelief.

"How long have I been out?"

"Around a half hour. Maybe a bit longer," he said breezily.

Judging by the position of the sun, that was probably a modest estimate. We had started our duties early that morning, and I didn't recall getting much done before I was suddenly ambushed by a wave of exhaustion.

"I'm so sorry, Noah. You know you could've woken me."

"Don't worry. You've been so tired. You needed to rest. Besides." He grinned, gesturing to the soldiers on the perimeter of the field. "They didn't even seem to notice."

"I guess we're lucky." I grabbed my shovel. "That's never happened to me before."

Noah chuckled. "It was probably the ice cream."

It took a second to grasp what he was referring to; then it came like a download as I recalled telling him about the debacle in the labs the day before—how I could hardly remember anything at all, except for breaking a wall of unbreakable glass and the sight of a dead rabbit. Thankfully, I came out unscathed. But they must have felt bad about what happened, because I woke up with an ice cream cone preserved at my bedside, a rare commodity from the old world.

"Yeah, it probably was." I plastered on a smile.

I gazed up the adjacent dirt road toward the gates of the Facility, not daring to ponder. Then we went back to work on digging a hole he had started. We were in the midst of planting long wooden posts as part of a project to rebuild the fence around the horse stable. Glancing at him with appreciation, I realized how lucky I was to have a partner like Noah. We could have gotten in serious trouble, but he was happy to cover for me. Forever optimistic, his eyes were as bright as the sun itself, belying the shadows of his short years before the Facility. He reminded me of a younger version of myself, albeit much more cheerful given our shared situation.

Soon, however, I could tell that something was bothering him. He glanced over his shoulder before speaking in a hushed tone. "Samuel, who's that watching us?"

Even from a distance, our eyes met like magnets. She was an extraordinary-looking girl, sitting back in the grass as if relaxing on a sunny day, her pale skin apparently unbothered by the intensity of the rays. She was a new youth—perhaps among the first, judging by her age—yet I could not recall why I recognized her face.

I turned back to Noah. "How long has she been there?"

"For a while now. She came when you fell asleep. Is she even supposed to be out here?"

Indeed, the girl was adorned with clean white robes, unlike the rags we wore while working in the fields. She waved at us jovially, amused by our attention, and I was struck by the glint of a cuff around her wrist.

"I don't think we should look at her," Noah whispered, averting his eyes. "Whenever I do, weird thoughts come into my mind."

"What kind of thoughts?" I questioned.

"Thoughts that aren't mine."

Against his advice, I scanned her features—long, dark hair, full lips, and giant green eyes. Then it dawned on me, an image slipping through the blockade of memory. *She was there. Watching through a window.* However fleeting the recollection, it was enough to establish that for whatever reason, she had been in the labs at some point during the experiment.

Then came a voice in my head as clear as day. *"That's right, Sammy. And I just want to say, it's pretty messed up what you did to that rabbit."*

My eyes widened. In my experience with telepathy, I had never heard it as pristinely as I did then, simultaneously evoking the image of the ill-fated animal. It baffled me how she even knew my name, never mind the ugly situation I could hardly remember.

I mouthed my response, "How . . . do . . . you . . ."

"I have my ways," she interjected psychically. *"But I'm serious, Sammy. That wasn't very nice. Rabbits are my spirit animal, you know."*

There was an eerie quality about her as she gazed through my soul. I pushed against that mental block, trying to summon my memory, but it was no use. I had so many questions I wanted to communicate. Instead, I just stared.

"Oh God, what have they done to you in this place?" She shook her head, proceeding to get up and yell, "I'm heading back home, honey, but call me if you need me!" We watched in astonishment as she strolled past an oblivious soldier and onto the road leading back to the Facility. She didn't walk very far, however, before she turned and winked, declaring telepathically, *"They're coming."*

"*Who's* coming?" I boldly shouted after her, yet she was already on her way. I sighed, refraining from further questioning. "What a strange girl."

"I told you," said Noah. "But she also must be very powerful. How do you think Mabus got ahold of her?"

"I don't know." I continued staring as she headed toward the gates. "But something tells me she's a willing prisoner."

Right then, a rumble of engines emerged from the other direction. We turned our attention down the road and quickly realized what she was warning us about.

As the only man with eyes uncovered, Lieutenant Hernandez stood out amid the troop of white soldiers riding in the back of the first truck in a speeding convoy. I looked nervously at Noah. Without hesitation, he extended his hand to the stack of posts and, in an act of psychic brilliance, brought one flying in. It halted before us and dove straight into the hole. We hurriedly shoveled in the dirt, doing our best to pretend that we were normal humans hard at work.

I prayed for the convoy to keep going, but as expected, it halted by our location.

The lieutenant hopped out along with several of his men, marching toward us. I didn't have to look to feel him scrutinizing the half-built fence, judging our every move.

"You two aren't *slacking*, are you?"

We planted our shovels as he approached. As the second in command to General Mabus, he possessed a great deal of influence in how the Facility was operated. I could not deny the intimidating influence of his presence, with his rifle at his side and muscles bulging against his uniform. Still, I wasn't afraid to look directly into his eyes.

"We're doing the best we can," I responded, wiping the sweat from my forehead.

He snickered. "Well, the best you can clearly ain't good enough. I can tell by looking at them that those posts aren't anchored in the ground. How do you expect them to contain our horses? Unless you want them to escape again."

I had to restrain myself from shouting at him to give us more than just wood and shovels. It perplexed me why we needed horses in the first place with all the advanced technology in the labs, but outside those walls, I had been told, it was like another world; they did not dare share their innovations with the Union population, nor use them to truly help the children. It was all a tactic of control.

"With all due respect, *sir*," I retorted, "it's very hot out, and we don't have much water."

"It's hot out, is it?" He stomped toward me, pressing his face within inches of mine. "Tell me, boy, have you ever seen someone burned alive? Have you walked the desert wastelands in search of your men, only to find them face down with blistered skin peeled to the bone?"

Shadows crept beneath his eyes, depriving them of life. His putrid breath infiltrated my senses.

"Answer me!"

"No, sir."

He grinned, pleased by my submissiveness. "I know exactly what you are, Samuel Helen." He paused to shift his stare between me and Noah, the poor boy shaking in the sunlight. "Who the hell is supervising these two anyway?"

By the time he turned, his men were already rushing to the perimeter of the field, where the soldiers had formerly stood. My heart leaped out of my chest as I realized that they were all lying in the grass as if they had collapsed from the high temperature—or something more sinister.

"What's going on?!" the lieutenant howled, hatred in his eyes as he turned back to us. "What did *you do*?"

"I . . ." I choked with anxiety. Luckily, I was saved by one of his young cadets running over.

"They were asleep, sir."

"Asleep?!" Hernandez glared at me with suspicion before marching out there himself, yelling up a storm at the soldiers, who thankfully ascended from their stupor. I exchanged glances with Noah, knowing what he was thinking.

Meanwhile, the cadet stood silently in front of us, watching through his tinted helmet. The light of his eyes was purposefully hidden as a sort of psychic protection from telepathic children. That had not stopped the strange girl from, by all appearances, toying with the minds of a few unfortunate men.

Hernandez soon marched back with his face red, fists clenched at his sides. I swore that he would strike me until Noah stepped in, carrying a voice of innocence.

"Neither of us noticed them, sir. We promise."

The lieutenant's fists quivered for a moment before suddenly relaxing, his face softening, and for the first time, I wondered if he had a little son of his own, or perhaps a daughter. "I will return shortly," he said. "If I don't see more progress, you'll get double time tomorrow. And if this turns out to be some kind of voodoo sorcery, you two are as good as dead."

We nodded as he rounded up the others, leaving the trusted cadet to stand guard. As the convoy started toward the Facility, I saw that they were transporting bushels of crops they had presumably wrested from the surrounding villages. The closest one was just down the road, where Evelyn lived with her group of orphans, cherishing the portion of their harvest they could keep to themselves.

I sighed as we continued building the fence, waiting for the cadet to take a break in the nearby shade so that we could converse quietly.

"That was crazy!" said Noah. "It had to be that weird girl. Do you think it was?"

"Probably," I answered, though I was still lost in the distance, focused on another—one I was sure had pure intentions. Noah knew exactly where I was.

"You miss her, huh?"

I nodded. "We'll see her tomorrow. But later today I'm seeing Walter, at least."

Those were the only times Noah got jealous: whenever I mentioned Walter. His tutor followed the lesson plan straight from General Mabus, filled with propaganda and historical cover-ups. Incredibly, Noah was unaware of how the earth used to be— brimming with clear blue skies, bustling cities, and, of course, some amazing music. Moreover, the military was quite honorable before it was hijacked by men who wished to see the world burn, demolishing democracy while plunging society into a state of panic.

Then came the bombings. Radiation and bioweapons, sprayed into the air, pervaded any area formerly inhabitable. The cities were deserted, and vast portions of the sky became filled with toxic mist. As if the earth had finally had enough, her violent fits helped finish the process. Much of the remaining population had since reverted to farming communities, resisting the push to reinstate a worthless currency.

Against what was best for his own safety, Walter told me the truth: that these villages were better off autonomous, without the militarized Union bullying them out of food rations and stealing away children with our eyes.

But I knew what Noah especially envied.

"Maybe I can sneak you into his office sometime," I said reassuringly. "He'd love to show you his albums."

Noah smiled as he started on another hole, but something was still bothering him. "Hey, Samuel. That ice cream they gave you this morning—what flavor was it?"

I was about to answer, yet hesitated when the memory did not surface. Truthfully, I was worried about my amnesic tendencies. The worst part was that I knew there were more important things I was forgetting. I brushed it off with a chuckle. "It was strawberry flavored, but it was made from milk derived from almonds. It tasted *so* good." My voice came out dry, and it only now hit me how parched I was. "Hey, do you really think that girl could put those soldiers to sleep?"

My question went unanswered. Dropping his shovel, Noah pulled a flask from beneath his garments, which he graciously offered.

"You're breathing fire, Samuel. Drink some water."

I hesitated, staring as if it were some holy liquid. "I don't—"

"You need it more than I do," he insisted. "Drink."

Receiving it with gratitude, I put it to my lips, each gulp invigorating me with new life. All the while, Noah's eyes beamed with light. It astounded me how he could be so happy all the time. I was convinced that the boy could smile through the apocalypse.

Then again, there was one stark difference between us: Noah had been abandoned as a toddler and was unable to remember the serenity of his mother's arms. Our slavery was much easier for him to accept, for this was his whole reality.

He picked up his shovel as something caught his attention. "He's coming!"

The lieutenant returned with the soldiers and supervised our work for the next few hours. Driven by fear, we didn't talk again, and Noah—despite being among the most gifted at the Facility—dared not use his telekinesis outside, or he would be punished severely. It was not as if I could control mine, anyway. Whatever new breakthrough they had in the labs clearly hadn't worked; it simply made me forget. I still kept that side of myself caged in the back of my brain.

Alas, I was just a normal human being toiling under the sun, praying for relief. In the distant forest, I heard birds singing, beckoning a better world.

We continued working until we had no water and the skin was peeling from our shoulders.

～

The Facility was made up of several buildings packed together within an enormous, gated area. The most significant portion was devoted to the labs, then barracks for the soldiers and dwellings for the children, scientists, and workers. Walter established his residence near the far corner of the compound.

After washing up in my quarters, eating a supper of lentil soup, and putting on a fresh set of robes, I was on my way to my tutor's home, escorted by two soldiers. My eyes couldn't hide that I was absolutely exhausted and in no way prepared for an intellectual conversation. By the time I arrived, our trusted star was hanging low in the sky.

His door was unlocked, leading to a living area reflective of his eccentric personality. The walls were decorated with surrealist images centered on a tapestry of a prism refracting white light into a spectrum. There were plants and flowers, even some crystals, along with bookcase after bookcase of philosophical and spiritual texts— several of which Walter had written himself during his lonely years on a devastated planet.

I walked down a small corridor to his office door, giving a cordial knock.

"Come in!"

Turning the handle, I found my tutor, a man of at least sixty, scurrying clumsily on his knees, peering at me from behind his desk. He appeared in the process of rearranging the numerous albums scattered across the wooden floor. Walter never failed to amaze me.

"Samuel! It's time already?"

"Yes. It should be." I spotted his clock at a couple of minutes past 5:30.

"I must have lost track. Just give me another minute, will you, kiddo?"

I sat in the armchair facing his desk, and despite my weariness, I couldn't help but laugh. "So, what exactly happened here?"

"Oh, just a small tornado." He shook his head with a playful smile. "Luckily, it gives me a chance to organize my collection."

Walter was a self-proclaimed music aficionado, but for him the draw was more than just the pleasant melodies; the man believed that music held the key to creation itself. Inspired by the teachings of Pythagoras, he was infatuated with what he termed the musical theory of the universe—an idea that the core of reality was composed of a symphony of vibrating strings, resonating at specific bands of frequency, such that all things could be expressed through vibration, sound, and geometry.

Both corners of the far wall contained portraits of beloved musicians, Bob Dylan on the left and Jimi Hendrix on the right. Directly below were shelves for hundreds of vinyl records, now largely dispersed across his office. I scanned the floor for artists I recognized—Outkast, the Doors, Phoenix, Nirvana, and a strange-sounding band with a strange-sounding name that had an album cover of an embryo with angel wings. Although I liked some more than others, I'd learned to appreciate the creative expression in every genre as remnants of a forgotten world.

Between Bob and Jimi was a dull reminder of our unfortunate timeline: General Mabus. It had been years since I had seen him in person, for he preferred to reside in the Union's capital, close to the ocean. Rising from the ashes of a once-great nation, the general vowed to restore our civilization to the militarized might of what it once was, as a show to our apparent adversary. Walter secretly disliked him, but as long as this portrait remained, he was allowed to decorate however he pleased.

As I gazed into Mabus's unflinching eyes, I was suddenly taken to another time. I was only seven years old, traumatized and staring into them with apprehension. A pale, stocky man with a sinister aura about him, he wished to validate the rumors, to have me demonstrate my abilities to an enemy of the Union bound by the chains in front of me. When I wouldn't comply, he shocked me with a weapon. I still remembered his merciless grin as he realized that pain was the trick, leading him to implement a torturous program.

"Samuel, are you okay?"

Walter now sat behind his desk, appearing concerned. He wore robes similar to my own, and his unruly hair might have made it hard for some to take him seriously—even more so his treasured monocle, which he joked helped him see spirits; but beneath was a gaze that was gentle yet incredibly insightful, as if it carried a soul ripened through many lifetimes of experience.

"I'm fine," I told him. "Just had a long day."

"Sorry to have kept you waiting, but it would have been discourteous of me to keep some of the legends on the floor. So, what's going on? You look more tired than usual."

I told him about the craziness of the past couple of days: the experiment I couldn't remember, the ice cream by my bedside— which seemed to intrigue Walter—and the ruthless lieutenant working me and Noah to our limit. I omitted the part about the telepathic girl, however, for fear that she had truly put the soldiers to sleep. They might have been watching us, after all.

Walter was silent when I finished. I would have welcomed words of sympathy, but he merely pulled an apple from his drawer and offered it. When I politely refused, he took a sizable bite and set it awkwardly between his prized figurine of a rainbow Buddha, beaming in bliss, and an old photograph of a gorgeous woman holding a young boy with the same dark skin and gentle eyes as his father.

Finally, he asked, "What is it you're looking for, Samuel?"

"What do you mean?" I replied.

"Are there any questions whose answers you seek?"

"Um, not particularly."

"All men of faith and men of science have their questions," he said with wide eyes. "What's on your mind?"

I was too tired for his riddles but knew I would have to engage eventually.

"Well, I'm seeing Evelyn tomorrow."

"There's a start," he said encouragingly.

"It's all I really look forward to anymore—besides you, of course." I sighed, then gazed at him with sincerity. "I just need to know if they will ever let me be with her so that we can create a life together and both be free. When will they finally be done with me, Walter?"

The normally cheerful man examined my eyes solemnly.

"You have grown so much in the ten years I have known you, but I am so sorry that it had to be in this world. It is very dangerous out there for anybody, but especially for those like you. Unfortunately, I cannot answer that question."

My heart felt like it had been dragged down by weights, and Walter was quick to note my disappointment.

"Do you love her, Samuel?"

"Yes. At least, I think that I do. But how can you tell if love is real? How do you know what love really is?"

"Now, *that's* a good question." He leaned back in contemplation. "I suppose if you truly love someone, you feel connected in ways that the mind can't comprehend. It is a unifying force on a very deep level, found in the silence, more powerful than anything else you can ever experience. You almost wouldn't want to keep living in this world if those you love were no longer there with you." His eyes welled up.

My words slipped out as I glanced at the photograph, "Is that how you felt . . ."

"Yes." Walter nodded. "Yes, I did. But you push through that pain and that loneliness, and you arrive at an understanding greater than yourself. Love is a choice, Samuel. You may choose to act upon it within every decisive moment, adopting it as a state of being. And you may summon it within you in times of need. It is an imperishable fire, burning the most fiercely once we are stripped of everything but our innermost identity—our indestructible soul. You learn to love yourself again and project that onto others who come into your life for a sacred purpose. I know that you too, Samuel, have lost those you held dear." He wiped away tears, then beamed with the Buddha. "Did that answer your question?"

"I think it helped. But honestly, I don't understand how anything is a choice for us, Walter. Not here. It just feels . . ."

"What do you feel?"

"It feels like I have no control over my destiny—that I am on this path that is already written. And every day I'm just going through the motions, killing time instead of living, like a puppet on strings." I shook my head. "I know it sounds crazy."

"It is not crazy at all to question your free will. In fact, it is one of the most contentious topics in all of philosophy. It was Plato who believed that free will was impossible without first cultivating—"

"I don't care about Plato. He lived thousands of years before we destroyed our planet. He could have never stepped into my shoes." I felt bad for interrupting, but a glance down at my calloused hands shored up my conviction. "The effort to be free seems pointless to me."

Walter smiled. "Tell me, Samuel, do you believe in God?"

It was a simple question, though profound in its implications. We had long talked about the concept of God intellectually—studying the writings of Plotinus, Spinoza, Heraclitus, and Avicenna, among others—but never in the decade I had known him had he asked about my belief.

It was tougher than I imagined. I shifted uncomfortably in my seat.

"Hasn't religion faded away since the bombings?"

"Organized religion has indeed dwindled significantly," he said. "That does not mean that God is dead."

"There are many who say there's no evidence, with what we've learned in science."

"I'm asking what *you* think, kiddo."

I paused, deciding whether I should lay it on him. "I think that no God would allow what has become of the earth, the eradication of a majority of the population. As far as I can tell, there is no man in the sky watching over us, listening to our prayers, sending angels to protect us. Or if there is, he must be very cruel to permit such evil."

I thought this would insult Walter, who was clearly a spiritual man, but he remained smiling warmly. He answered, "The greatest secret to the nature of God is that *God* is just a word, Samuel—an indirect symbol that can in no way penetrate its primordial essence, nor can the human mind grasp its full magnificence. So God doesn't have to be a man in the sky, judging and controlling our every action. There are some who see divine intelligence in the miraculous order of the universe, intertwined with the light of a cosmic mind. Others equate God with love itself, and from this perspective, it is love that is real, a singular truth that binds us all. Everything else that we experience, any ripple out of stillness, is the illusion, my young friend, and not the other way around.

"Likewise, you may be misguided about science. The newest breakthroughs have only confirmed what scientists suspected regarding quantum physics. That there is an aspect of consciousness that is fundamental to this universe, perhaps even more so than space and time. There exists a transcendent mind—a soul, as some would say—entangled throughout a unified field of intelligence." He raised his eyebrows. "Then came the new youth."

I had to admit he was right. There were scientists who used to brush off consciousness as some strange accident isolated inside our brains. It was a paradigm that encouraged much greed and division. But after large-eyed children were born, effortlessly bending spoons and perceiving targets halfway across the earth, or even through time, they were forced to rewrite the fundamentals of physics.

"I can believe all of that, for sure," I affirmed. "But that doesn't lead to the same concept of God that has caused so many wars, and not the same science, either."

"Exactly, Samuel! God is not limited to a projection of human prejudice, as we see in the most distorted teachings. I've long believed that a true understanding of spirituality, merged with science, will lead us to the dawn of a new age—an age of peace and prosperity and the realization of oneness. It would be an evolutionary leap in consciousness!"

"Then why isn't this happening?" I grew annoyed. "Just look at where we are. We're living in a military base, for goodness' sake. For all I know, they plan to weaponize us for even more battles, and no God is going to come save us."

"Because God isn't something that is outside of us. The divine will breathes through every living being, steering us onto a collective course. We must take responsibility for the alignment of that course and choose not to repeat mistakes of violence."

"Fair enough," I acknowledged. "That doesn't change the fact that I'm trapped here."

"There is always an opportunity to free your mind, no matter the external conditions. Otherwise, you may indeed find yourself trapped, reliving the same cycles of experience." He leaned in close to emphasize the import of his words. "There is an enlightened version of yourself that evolves beyond that prewritten path, transcending the strings of time itself. You become the creator of your destiny, a god in your own right. But only once you accept accountability for the circumstances of your own life."

"You're holding me accountable?" I exhaled with frustration. "How could you say such a thing? Can't you see that we're prisoners here? Don't you know that I never had a choice?"

"You always have a choice, Samuel. Even if it is a choice from a higher level, incomprehensible to the logic of your conscious mind. But deep inside, you must know you came here for a reason."

I wanted to groan but held my tongue, awaiting his speech about higher selves and soul contracts, which would certainly go right over my head. As much as I admired Walter, his philosophical idealism could be unbearable at times, and I was sure he was self-aware in that regard.

Thankfully, he read my mind. "You know, I prepared a whole lesson on quantum entanglement, but this has already been far too serious. Plus, you look like you've been hit by a truck. How about we learn through a more enjoyable method?"

"Music?" I hazarded with a grin.

"You got it, kiddo!" He stood and perused the records organized under Dylan. "Truthfully, the musicians of the old world were much wiser than the scientists. If humanity had chosen to listen to the messages of Bob Marley and John Lennon, we would not be in this position. We wouldn't have let the earth become so sick. Ah, here it is."

He revealed an album cover with sketches of four men I recognized. The Beatles were among his favorites, after all, and I also was fond of their music, even if it occasionally descended into weirdness. Apparently, they were *the* most famous band of their time, which I found surprising given they were named after an insect.

"I'm sure you know who this is by now." He regarded the album happily. "It is their seventh album, *Revolver*, released nearly a century ago. Have I ever shown you this one?"

"Not that I recall."

"You're in for a treat."

He walked to his record player and spun the disc beneath the needle. Seconds later, sounds of jangling guitars and melodic singing arose out of the memory of a forsaken society.

"This one's by George Harrison," Walter remarked, sitting back in his chair and taking another bite of his apple. "Wonderful musician, and a very thoughtful man."

Although the lyrics were unusual, I greatly enjoyed the melody. The record skipped to a song with a haunting backdrop of strings, this one undoubtedly about human loneliness. It was soon followed by a pleasant tune that had something to do with floating in a dream.

All the while, Walter and I talked amiably. He spoke about how influential the Beatles were, even if they played at a time only his grandparents could remember. He told me how John Lennon was murdered in a now desolate metropolis and that George Harrison was the most spiritual among them, passing away shortly before the first in a series of devastating wars.

Although it was a sad subject, it planted a seed of appreciation for the mere miracle that I was alive in this world—and that I still had people who cared for me.

Two beautiful lines caught my attention, sung by Paul McCartney:

"Each one believing that love never dies,
Watching her eyes and hoping I'm always there."

It had me contemplating what we had talked about earlier, and whom I would see the following morning.

"You like the music, don't you?" Walter observed, catching me smiling.

"It's fantastic," I replied honestly. "Even though I've never heard it before, I feel like it . . . relates to me. I can't say why."

"Every child with your eyes invariably displays a prodigious intelligence, yet none of the others appreciate my records the way you do." He chuckled. "Perhaps they are too young."

"Perhaps." I looked to my tutor with gratitude. After listening together to a childlike sing-along, the album sprang to a more serious tune:

"She said, I know what it's like to be dead,
I know what it is to be sad."

"Walter?"

"Yes?"

"What made you believe in God? Despite everything that happened."

He beamed. "Another excellent question, and there are many ways I could answer. I must caution you, however, to not get so caught up in belief. It is more a matter of recognition."

"Recognition of what?"

"Of your very essence, Samuel. Your inner nature. *You* are the living truth of life—along with everyone you encounter. We can debate all we want, but at the end of the day, there is nothing you need to believe in but yourself. Once you do, you can have anything your heart desires."

"But what if you just desire to be a kid again, with your family? Because don't you miss it, Walter? Your memories of society? The movies? The music? The ice cream?"

"When I was a boy, everything was right," he sang along with John Lennon, winking at the apparent synchronicity. "Believe me, I can go on for hours about memories, but it is fruitless to dwell on the past. We ought to only look ahead, my extraordinary friend, toward the dawn of a new tomorrow and the promise of an enlightened world."

This time, I didn't mind his idealism. The Beatles played, and after a chaotic couple of days, I felt more empowered than I had in a long while. I lost myself in the moment, sensing everything more fully. Even the walls breathed with a hidden geometry.

The music ceased soon after, prompting Walter to walk to his record player with a grin. "I think we're ready for side two."

We stayed there listening until the album descended into more than just weirdness; it became something of a psychedelic experience, with hypnotic drumming and esoteric lyrics, ending with what sounded like the Buddha himself chanting off a high mountain:

"All play the game existence to the end,
Of the beginning

Of the beginning
Of the beginning."

CHAPTER 3

EVELYN AGARTHA WAS the epitome of beauty, her silver robes flowing in the morning wind.

We found ourselves alone, surrounded by stalks of corn, so I had the chance to take it all in: her rose-red hair, saint-like smile, and bright-blue eyes formed a gorgeous visage. Yet her radiant aura of kindness and empathy stood out above any outward features. I realized there was a force connecting our hearts together, so great that I almost wouldn't want to live in this world without her, and from her soul-baring gaze, I trusted that she felt the same.

I must have had baggy eyes from lack of sleep after reflecting on my conversations with Walter, but I felt sustained by this higher energy. Working in the cornfields meant we could afford some privacy, and thankfully, I was allowed my nice white robes, so I led Evelyn into the harvest to talk with her.

For I knew that I loved her. And I was planning to tell her.

"You're blushing, Samuel," she affectionately teased. "What is it you wanted to tell me?"

I could swear that time stopped as I met her eyes. "Well, I was up all night thinking about it, and it's something I just thought you should know. I wanted to tell you that I . . ." I cleared my throat, suddenly overwhelmed with the importance of what I wanted to say. "I wanted to tell you that I—"

She interrupted with a dreadful cough, followed by several more as she was seized by a fit that sometimes lasted for minutes. Worried, I gently rubbed her back. She clung to her golden, heart-shaped locket as she wheezed.

"Breathe, Evelyn. Just breathe."

Evelyn had been sick ever since I could remember. There was a problem with her lungs, though she was never properly diagnosed. I had asked Salazar to examine her countless times, but he continually refused. It simply wasn't his job to work with ordinary humans.

After a horrible few minutes, she was finally able to speak.

"I'm sorry, Samuel. I didn't see that coming."

"Don't be sorry. Are you feeling okay now?"

She nodded, a sparkle forming in her eyes. "So, what was it you were going to tell me?"

"Right. Well, I was going to tell you that . . . I listened to another Beatles album last night. Walter showed me."

I wanted to slap myself. I was up until dawn staring at the ceiling of my quarters, listening to the rain, repeating three words like a crazy person. Yet none of it prepared me for how challenging it was to say those words when it truly mattered.

Still, she smiled. "Oh, was it the one with them crossing a city road? I used to listen to that one with my father. He and Walter would've gotten along. He loved music from that era."

"It was actually called *Revolver*. And I'm sure you would've loved it, too."

I went on to tell her about the experiment I had forgotten, as well as my tiring duties with Noah and how the music instantly made me feel better. It seemed to captivate her. She had not heard recorded music in a long time. All she had left were the birds.

"I've missed you," I said without thinking.

She stroked her hand against my chest, jolting my heart with electricity, and kissed me tenderly on the lips. It was something we had been doing since soon after we hit puberty, and it never failed to invigorate me. "I've missed you too. Now, let's finish this basket and get back to the group."

Harvesting corn was simpler than most crops: we would check for maturity by color, twist the ear off its stalk, cut away silk, and pack it into a bushel basket. Only later would we remove the exterior husk to reveal the sweet kernels inside.

We soon filled our basket. I carried it through thick green stalks still wet with rain, not wanting Evelyn to do anything too strenuous. We quickly arrived at the clearing, where a dozen orphans were gathered, most of them small children.

"Were you guys working hard in there?" asked a lighthearted voice, arousing several giggles. I turned to find Noah—the only new youth who had accompanied me from the Facility—standing beside a girl his age who seemed new to the group and who stared at us with a curious smile. Unlike most others, who were initially frightened of us, she appeared fascinated by our physical abnormalities.

"Settle down, everyone. Let them be the adults they are."

A sturdy, middle-aged woman whom we all admired emerged in her farming attire. Maggie was an honorable steward of the village, attending to the fields and looking after its orphans, including those from unsafe areas. Evelyn had lived under her care for as long as I had been at the Facility. Finding each other had been an apparent stroke of destiny, and we worked together weekly with Maggie's support. In addition to being part of a tribute program for the supposed protection of the military, these outings comprised an experiment in interaction with normal children— one I was grateful for.

"Good morning, Samuel." She greeted me warmly. "Let me give you a hand with that."

Grasping one handle of the basket as I held the other, she helped me toward a caravan so large that it was drawn by four horses. The majestic animals had been tied to a post by the stablemaster, a somewhat hostile man who had never once offered his name. We climbed onto the rear and stacked the basket in the corner next to a few others. It was the first bushel Evelyn and I had harvested, and the day would not end until the space was filled to the brim.

"How is everything going?" the older woman asked in the shade of the caravan's cover. "Are they treating you all right up there?"

"Yeah, they're good to me," I lied. Walter was the only exception.

"You know you can be honest with me."

"Thank you, Maggie, but I'm doing fine. We're having progress with my—"

She sighed. "How long has it been, Samuel?"

"Ten years now. It's okay. I know we're at least safe there."

"Well, if you ever need anything, please let me know." She placed her hand on my shoulder, glancing around to make sure no soldiers were listening. "Anything at all, okay?"

Evelyn stood on the grass nearby, observing me with that same look of concern. I sensed a seed of thought implanting in her mind.

"Samuel?" Maggie inquired.

"Okay. I will."

She gave me a sympathetic pat and hopped off the caravan. "After last night's rain, looks like we've got another bright sun rising! Take your time, you two. Make sure the harvest is ripe. And, of course, don't forget to drink lots of water."

～

Five hours passed, with Evelyn and I only taking breaks to drink out of a shared jug or to wait out her coughing fits. I grew hungry, and the lack of sleep was catching up to me. Although my robes provided shelter from the sweltering sun, my peeling skin stung underneath, and dirt coated my feet and sandals.

I still hadn't worked up the courage to tell Evelyn how I felt. Each additional minute drained more energy from the invisible force that vitalized me.

We talked about trivial things, like the crazy weather and flavors of ice cream, despite each of us sensing that something was missing. I hardly reacted when I gashed open the palm of my hand while cutting silk from an ear of corn. Dropping my knife, I revealed the blood to Evelyn, who rummaged through her bag of equipment, which also carried our water. Luckily, there were bandages. I forgot about the pain as she cleaned and wrapped the wound.

"Walter would say it's karma." I forced a laugh.

"Why is that?" she asked.

"You know how I told you that I can't remember anything from that experiment? Well, it's not entirely true. I have a memory of a dead rabbit in front of me." I paused, my stomach churning with guilt. "I think I killed it."

She smiled softly. "Don't blame yourself, Samuel. I know you. You wouldn't hurt a soul. And what they gave you probably messed with your mind. Now, let me see those eyes of yours."

I met her gaze as she finished with my hand, and she kissed me for the first time since that morning. Still, I could tell the seed kept growing.

~

It wasn't until later that afternoon, when we were close to finishing, that Evelyn started showing more signs of turmoil. We were apart from the group again, filling up a bushel deep within the cornfield, so I finally asked her what was wrong.

With watery eyes, she uttered a simple question: "Are you happy?"

I faltered for a second, trying to find the right words.

"With you I am, Evelyn."

"Samuel, I know that you were lying to Maggie. It's not right for you to be in there! Not after ten years. You understand what she was hinting at, don't you?"

"Please talk quietly. I don't want them to—"

"I don't care if they hear me!" she shouted defiantly. "If they do, all the better. The both of us can't be trapped here forever."

I sighed, caressing her arm with my bandaged hand. "Believe me, I want to get out of here too. But Walter says it's not safe out there. Especially for people like me."

"And have you once stopped to think that Walter might not know what's best for you? He's been great to you, Samuel, but you have to realize that he lives there too. He works for them."

"Walter is the only employee who actually cares about me."

"That may be so, but clearly not enough to want your freedom."

I fell silent with disappointment. I could never be truly angry at Evelyn, but she was making claims about someone she had never even met. And as much as I despised the thought, because she had plenty of her own difficulties, she didn't know what it was like living as part of a group that a good portion of the population believed were actual demons sent to cleanse the earth.

I muttered, "There are dozens of soldiers surrounding these fields who would surely shoot us before they let us escape. How would we possibly get past them?"

"I don't know, but you heard Maggie earlier. Maybe she knows a way to sneak us to the forest. It's dense enough for us to hide, and we don't need to run very far to reach the edge."

"We shouldn't put Maggie at risk."

"We'll find a way, then. We can always find a way." She clutched her locket. "Once we make it, we'll just follow our hearts and trust they will take us someplace safe."

"I'm not sure if there is another place. The earth is sick and covered with radiation."

"Have you ever actually seen any other part of the earth, Samuel? Instead of just believing what they tell you? We'll both be eighteen this year. We have the right to choose our own lives. I'm old enough now that I can leave Maggie's group, but I'm not going anywhere without you by my side."

"And what if Walter is right? That it's dangerous?"

"Then I'd rather find out for myself than stay imprisoned by fear," she asserted. "The earth may be sick, but I know she can heal."

Too many thoughts were competing for space in my mind.

"Let's just finish up, Evelyn. I cut my hand. I killed a rabbit. I couldn't sleep last night. And I feel like I'm about to lose my mind!"

I lifted our basket and began walking away, hating myself for getting frustrated with her like I had Walter. But an inspiring melody was quick to apprehend me:

"Do you realize,
That you have the most beautiful face . . ."

I turned in amazement. Despite the issues with her lungs, Evelyn's voice was as pristine as I remembered. Using all her strength to hold it together, she inhaled sharply before each line.

"Do you realize,
We're floating in space . . ."

As she finished and I put down the basket, her eyes turned a melancholy red. "I couldn't sleep either. I stayed up crying in bed and singing to myself. When things got really bad when I was younger, my parents would sing me that song. It was the only thing that could keep the tears at bay."

"Why were you crying?" I asked, worried.

"You know why I was crying." She stepped forward to take my hand under the drizzle of a passing cloud. "But I'm not sure if you understand how much I care about you. You only see me at my best. I can barely get through the other six days of the week. And my lungs get worse, too. I feel sick all day long from not being with you."

"What about Maggie and the others?"

"Oh, they're kind. They keep me company, and I care for them. But I need something more, Samuel. I need somebody to—" She coughed hoarsely yet still clasped my hand. "All I know is that as long as we're together, we'll be just fine. Because I feel that when I'm with you, everything is all right again with the world. I know it's right."

My mouth fell open, and I pulled back instinctively.

"Are you okay?" She frowned. "Did I say something wrong?"

"It's just that last thing you said. Did you hear that from anywhere?"

She stared, perplexed. "I don't follow."

We were distracted by rustling in the stalks, followed by the sound of children laughing. Noah emerged near where we stood, showing off his telekinetic prowess by juggling ears of corn without touching them. His female companion followed close behind, beaming with wonderment.

He froze when he noticed us, and the corn gave in to gravity. "Sorry. Looks like you two need some more privacy."

"It's okay, Noah." Evelyn sniffled. "We're doing fine."

"All right, well, I just came to tell you that we're leaving soon, Samuel. Maggie's gathering everyone." He turned back around. "We'll see you guys at the—"

"Wait!" The girl stayed put, glancing at the corn and then probing my eyes. "Can you do it too?"

"Not like he can." I managed a smile.

"That's still so cool. My name is Penelope, by the way," she said while Noah flashed me a thumbs-up and dragged her away. "Evelyn talks *so much* about you."

The silence was palpable once we were alone again, and I didn't know what to do except take her hand and tell her the truth, whispering, "Not a day goes by that I don't dream of leaving this place with you, but it's too risky right now, and you're already sick as it is. Trust me that I also care about you. A lot. And I want you to be safe."

She withdrew her hand and lifted the heavy basket on her own, shuffling ahead of me as I followed. She didn't get very far before surrendering to exhaustion, gasping. I quietly took over and gave her what was left of our water. We didn't speak until we were back at the clearing.

Maggie had the orphans huddled together, commending everyone for their hours of labor despite knowing that this harvest wasn't theirs to keep. Bushels of corn filled the caravan, with our last one squeezing into the back. The stablemaster prepared the horses as soldiers hopped into their trucks to escort us to the Facility.

We had a few minutes to say our goodbyes, with some children feeling comfortable enough to approach and give me a high-five. To everyone's amusement, Noah's face flushed with embarrassment when Penelope kissed his cheek. This did not lift Evelyn's spirits, however.

"Don't leave," she whispered, tears rolling down her cheeks in the gentle rain.

Using my able hand, I dried her eyes, holding back tears of my own. "I'll see you in a week, okay?"

She looked down wistfully, and the stablemaster called for us to get going.

Noah and I climbed onto the front of the caravan, each leaning against a bushel, and were on our way. We traveled up the dirt road through gloomy surroundings, the rain steadily increasing. I couldn't bear to look back; I knew she would be crying.

"Is Evelyn all right?" Noah asked, his eyes brimming with empathy.

"She's just a bit sad, but she'll be fine. Anyway"—I ruffled his hair—"congrats on that kiss. Penelope seems like a sweet girl." My face feigned happiness while my heart sank into depression, thinking about our secret conversation and the words I wasn't brave enough to say.

"Don't worry, Samuel," Noah assured. "It's only because she loves you."

"You really think so?" I gazed with optimism at the gifted twelve-year-old.

"Definitely. I see the way she looks at you."

"I think so too," I affirmed. "But what if we can never truly be together?"

"Then maybe you should give each other something to hold on to. I always see her wearing that locket around her neck. If she can let you borrow it, you'll have a piece of her always with you."

"I can't take that. It has her mother and father in it. It's very special to her."

"Then you can give her something of yours so she won't be so lonely."

I sighed. "That's a good idea, but I don't have anything."

"Well, you have your eyes. Evelyn thinks they're special."

"You're right!" I cupped my hand over an eye. "I'll just pop them out and hand them to her next time I see her!"

It was incredible how quickly Noah's laugh could heighten my mood, lending me hope that everything would be okay after all. This was despite the worsening weather and the tired horses struggling to pull the load up the muddy road. Meanwhile, what sounded like rats rustled stealthily in the back, helping themselves to a share of food.

Soon, the entrance to the Facility came into view. One of the vehicles arrived before us, and a soldier with more senior marks on his armor than the others stepped out to place his hand on the sensor. The huge metal gates creaked open.

The storehouse containing the surplus of crops taken from different villages wasn't far from the entrance. The stablemaster halted the caravan in front, fastened the horses to a post, and blessed us with a rare sentence. "You know the drill."

I hopped to the ground while Noah maneuvered to the rear. His job was to hand me the bushels, and I would carry them into the storehouse. I felt drained as I fixated on the approaching dark clouds, but we were being timed for efficiency. With a deep breath, we commenced unloading. I suspected that my partner was using a hidden degree of psychic ability to make up for his small stature.

~

Twenty minutes passed before my arms started weakening, and the rain did not help my grip. But I was more worried about Noah, who seemed to be rapidly exhausting his will; he began having trouble lifting the bushels and appeared quite pale. We were around halfway finished when I told him to go rest, feeling the soldiers watching us closely.

"I'm okay," he objected. "Let me help."

He undeniably wasn't, for he wobbled uneasily while lifting another bushel, then suddenly collapsed.

"Noah!" I rushed onto the caravan, kneeling beside him amid scattered corn. "Are you hurt?"

"No, just feeling a bit funny," he said, his eyes struggling to stay open. "I was fine, then it just . . . took hold of me. I'm sorry, Samuel."

"Please. Don't be." I placed my hand on his forehead to find him burning up. Back through the opening, the stablemaster was scowling.

"What are you doing? Pick up the corn!"

"He's sick," I pleaded. "Please, he needs medical attention. I can carry it from here."

He had no compassion, but his reaction was thwarted when the senior soldier stepped in, ordering the others, "Get the boy to his quarters and notify his handler. He's too precious an asset to lose."

I nodded in gratitude and gazed at Noah with the same empathy he always showed me.

"You'll make it through this," I whispered as two men came to take him away.

"You better work quickly," the stablemaster grumbled when they left. "My horses are getting wet out here."

I exhaled with irritation, gathering corn into the basket before carrying it to the storehouse. Working alone, I had to climb onto the caravan, drag a bushel to the rear, hop off, and hoist it from there. After a few more trips, my body begged for rest. The wound beneath my bandage was bleeding again, and I wasn't close to being finished.

Tired and angry, and with no one watching, I glared at the next bushel with quickening breath, deciding to try something, if only as an experiment.

"*Come to me,*" I uttered. I envisioned my palms as magnets, giving them energy. To my surprise, the basket budged and began moving toward me. But as my heart rate accelerated with the memory of the dead rabbit, a psychic spasm jerked the basket straight into my chest, knocking me down with a thud.

"Again?!" yelled the stablemaster, poking his head under the wagon cover to scold me once more. Oddly, I no longer heard what he was saying, as if his voice, as well as the world around me, were dialed to a different frequency. In its place, I heard a girl giggling. I thought I was simply imagining things until she emerged from the shadows behind the remaining bushels.

The girl was a few years younger than me, with black robes, a shaved head, and huge, luminous, mischievous eyes. The emblem of a dragon on her wrist caught my attention before a telepathic force sucked my focus back in. "*You'll learn to control your abilities with the right methods,*" she transmitted to my mind.

Disquiet sank into my gut as I glanced at the stablemaster, still muted to white noise. He didn't appear to notice the girl even as she stood right next to me.

"*Are you really here?*" I sent back through the telepathic channel.

"*For all who have eyes to see.*" She gestured to the stablemaster, hatred forming in her eyes. "*Look how they treat those with our gifts.*

It is all so backward. They should show more respect." With a lift of her hand, the man stopped yelling; his demeanor changed.

"Of course, sir." I heard him again—along with the world and the rain. Then he smiled for the first time I'd ever seen. "Take as long of a break as you need."

As he walked away, I sat up to stare at her, astonished. Although she was young, she was clearly formidable. "How is that possible?" I asked aloud. She smirked.

"I am part of a revolutionary collective that shines light on our true nature. You can do the same thing, Samuel, if you stop letting them stifle your abilities. You are also very powerful. You just don't realize it yet."

I crawled back warily. "Who are you, really? And how do you know my name?"

"Connect with me, and I will show you," she answered.

Advancing closer, she rubbed her hands methodically until steam emerged from between them. In a moment of clarity, I rose to my feet and started toward the opening but immediately tripped on an ear of corn.

I fell once again, and as soon as I turned, her hands were on my forehead like a hot iron, sending me on a journey through the depths of my mind. I saw Mabus's tantalized smile when I first arrived at the Facility; then years flew by in an instant. I saw Evelyn. Walter. Cyrus. Noah. Dr. Salazar injecting a dark substance into me. I felt powerless as the girl rummaged through an entire decade of memory as if trying to find something.

Finally, I was trapped in a single scene—it was of my interaction with the strange girl who had winked at me and spoken two words telepathically: *"They're coming."* This scene looped in my awareness several times until I opened my eyes to the bald girl grinning.

"We're here."

CHAPTER 4

I STARED DUMBFOUNDED as the girl in black pranced down the central path, toward the guarded gates. Not one soldier reacted as she passed. Perhaps, somehow, she had convinced them all she was invisible.

Either that or I was indeed delusional, hallucinating from a combination of exhaustion and lasting side effects of mind-altering substances. I gazed at my hands to ground myself in reality while remnants of memories lingered in my consciousness.

When I looked up again, the girl had vanished.

And the stablemaster was out of his trance. "Taking a break, are you? Get back to work and finish unloading!"

Scanning our surroundings for the invisible girl, I turned toward him with such intensity that he was startled.

"What's wrong with you, kid?" He marched to my side.

"Didn't you see her?"

"See who? Are you sick too?"

I felt my heartbeat down to my fingertips, a sense of foreboding filling my stomach. "I think it's best that you leave," I told him, to which he scoffed, looking to the nearest soldiers, who were simply standing quietly.

"Hey! Did you hear this kid? He just threatened an employee!"

Still no movement.

Flustered, he approached the one in command. "Aren't you gonna—"

The senior soldier took out his rifle, but not with the intent of using it. Shockingly, he started to disassemble it, emptying the bullets.

"Wha . . ." the stablemaster stuttered. "What is going on?"

"Orders" was the only response.

"*Orders*? Orders from who? Aren't you the captain around here?"

The soldier did not say more, merely disposing of his dismantled rifle.

Then, like a sickness spreading from mind to mind, each of the nearby soldiers did the same, until finally the one closest to the gates dropped his rifle and placed his hand on a sensor. The gates slowly parted again while several men—including the senior soldier—raised a finger to the cloudy sky in some silent salute to an unseen commander. Eerily, all of their helmeted heads were facing me.

I became increasingly convinced that I was in a dream.

Suddenly, the horses began squealing, tugging so violently on their restraints that they broke away from their post and galloped toward the open gates.

A look of horror spread across the stablemaster's face. "This is the work of demons!" he yelled, chasing after them, past the motionless soldiers and out of sight down the curving dirt road.

For a moment, there was stillness. I begged myself to wake up. But as I cautiously drew close to the senior soldier, I saw that not one detail on his suit of armor was out of place, from his boots to the helmet that revealed only solemn lips. I could never dream such detail.

"Show me your eyes," I asked of him, but he simply wouldn't budge. "Please, show them to me. Let me help you."

His body started squirming as if struggling to burst from invisible ropes. Finally, he was able to move his arm, though only enough to shift the direction of his finger from the sky to the open gates. That's when I realized that I could no longer afford to question my reality.

Terrible screams echoed in the distance, along with what sounded like crushing bones.

After a few long moments, two smirking teenagers—a male and a female—came into view, strolling through the entrance. They possessed the same black robes as the girl from the caravan, similarly shaved heads, and large eyes exuding an aura of death. The stablemaster's body trailed them by no physical means, seemingly trampled by his own horses. With a wave of his arm, the boy sent the lifeless corpse flying ahead with psychic force. It thumped to the ground in front of me.

"We've got a Code Saturn!" the senior soldier shouted through his radio, causing the others to snap out of it. But they were defenseless without their rifles. Two guards in close range charged at the boy, only to be cast backward. The girl, on the other hand, appeared satisfied to play mind games, laughing while soldiers began to wrestle with each other.

Alarms blared, and right as reinforcements came to the guards' aid, a signal between the teenagers prompted dozens of black-robed children to charge through the gates, shielding their leaders with superhuman powers. Some used telekinetic strength, blasting rocks into the heads of oncoming soldiers, while others stood back like the female leader, manipulating the soldiers through psychic will.

The girl from the caravan reappeared out of nowhere, standing beside the two leaders. She whispered something to the male and pointed at me, eliciting a smile as his eyes pierced mine. I read his intentions. Gruesome images popped into my mind.

I gasped in revulsion, for I knew where they were headed.

I turned to sprint down the path while soldiers flooded from the barracks. They passed me as if I were a ghost, their bullets soon blending with the deafening alarms, though I couldn't tell what they were hitting. Meanwhile, Facility children came out into the rain to witness what was occurring, unshaken by threats to get back in their chambers. I wasn't familiar with any of them, but I saw it in their eyes: most were frightened, though some beheld the psychic intruders with excitement.

I quickly reached the laboratory complex at the center of the Facility, where many scientists were scrambling to get inside— including one I recognized. I stopped to catch my breath while Alice opened a heavy door to a bunker-like structure, waving others in before her. As her eyes met mine, a memory sprang into my awareness of a woman kneeling beside me, asking if I was hurt; in the present moment, she mirrored that concern.

"Samuel, come!" she shouted through the commotion.

I shook my head decisively, set on whom I needed to protect. With a quiet nod, she closed the door behind her. Either from roaring bullets or malevolent psychic children, I accepted the possibility of dying at any moment. Still, I continued onward, adrenaline dissolving my previous exhaustion.

I was about to turn a corner of the complex when I collided with an invisible barrier so dense that I stumbled backward. After regaining my balance, I prepared for a fight, wondering if this would indeed be the end. I was shocked to see Noah approaching from behind me.

Although he still looked feverish, his spirit was unquestionably strong, evidenced by his glowing eyes. He raised a finger to his lips and gestured around the corner cautiously.

There I glimpsed a boy no older than nine, with a shaved head and darkness in his eyes, clothed in the white robes of the Facility. He was concentrating on something with malicious intent, raising his hand in a clench as if choking the wind. I angled my neck to peer further and found Dr. Salazar pressed up against the side of the building, his face turning blue, appearing close to death.

With only moments to spare, I glanced back at Noah—who nodded anxiously—and then charged at the boy, tackling him to the ground using my physical advantage.

I had not anticipated, however, the boy's mental advantage. He threw me aside using telekinesis, sending me tumbling in front of a panting Salazar. He then rose and stalked toward me with a spiteful glare, speaking clearly inside my mind through the alarms: *"It is unwise to sympathize with your captors."*

Just as he was about to unleash once more, Noah stepped forward and roared like I had never heard, letting out his remaining energy—but the boy shielded himself cleverly, and it was only enough to push him back a few feet. He grinned as he gathered himself, countering with a force that flung Noah to the wall.

Noah slammed against it, his body going limp.

A beast took hold of me.

I climbed to my knees and screamed with all my might, wanting to take the life out of the boy, to stop his young heart from beating. Soon after, my cruel wish was seemingly granted, but not by any action of my own.

Bullets flew into his shoulder from a semiautomatic weapon. The boy wailed in agony as he hit the ground. The lieutenant emerged with a troop of soldiers, aiming his rifle directly at me.

"No! He's not with them!"

Salazar crawled over to put his body between us, forcing the lieutenant to lower his weapon. His glare shifted to Noah, who thankfully was stirring, then down to the boy, whose blood rinsed away in the rain. Without a word, he led his soldiers past the bitter scene and back into battle with children just as young.

I glided to Noah, who was breathing heavily, but at least I saw the light in his gaze. "Don't worry," he insisted. "I'm gonna get through this, just like you told me."

"Of course you will," I consoled him before lifting him into my arms, using all of my strength. "But let's get you out of here, okay?"

I stumbled back to the shaved-headed boy, who was wheezing, fighting to stay alive. With his skin pale from the loss of blood, the black emblem on his wrist stood out ominously: a dragon. He must have been planted in the Facility to scope it out before the attack. I wondered how many others were here. And as I gazed into his dimming eyes, I recognized him from another repressed memory: he was behind a glass wall, telling me to escape.

"It's our fault." Dr. Salazar sounded pained. "All of it. We thought we were helping, but we lost our way. We failed, and for that I am sorry."

I exchanged a final glance with my handler, who appeared too weak to stand and resigned to his fate. Emotional fallout from ten years of experimentation clashed with appreciation for his potentially saving my life. "Be well," I told him. Nothing more could be said.

Noah directed me to his quarters, which were nearby, away from the battle. I set him gently on his bed; this prison cell felt like a haven from the outside bloodshed.

"Don't go anywhere," I urged my friend. "I'll come back for you as soon as I can."

"Where are you going?" he asked.

"To make sure somebody is safe."

"Evelyn. Penelope. Do you think they're okay?"

"They'll be fine down at the village. The black robes just want vengeance on the people at the Facility. We'll come for them afterward. I promise."

"We can run away together." He smiled, shutting his eyes in rest.

I shook my head at this twist of destiny. Just this morning, Evelyn had pleaded with me to find a way to escape. All this was too much to comprehend, and I did not have time to linger.

"Thank you, Noah." I patted him warmly.

"Thanks for being there for me, Samuel."

Mustering energy, I ran back outside as thunder erupted in the sky.

Then I bolted for the home of my tutor.

～

It was a godsend that Walter lived on the opposite end from the open gates. When I arrived, the gunshots were muted by distance. Even the alarms weren't nearly as blaring. I could only hope that he was aware of what was happening and was acting accordingly.

Bursting into the living room, I was relieved to find everything in its right place. His books and furniture were all as I last saw them. "Walter!" I called, expecting him to appear, yet there was no answer.

I did, however, hear familiar sounds coming from his office. It almost made me sick to my stomach, though I was not surprised: despite all the turmoil outside, Walter was listening to music.

I hurried down the corridor and opened the door.

He was sitting calmly behind his desk as the voice of Jimi Hendrix filled the air:

"There must be some kind of way out of here,
Said the joker to the thief . . ."

I was speechless for a moment but quickly snapped out of it.

"Walter! We need to leave, now!"

"Samuel," he said without a hint of emotion. "Why all the worry? Relax. Listen with me."

"You don't understand." I panted, bending over in exhaustion. "We have to get out of here! Or hide, at least. They're coming for everybody."

"Who's coming?"

"Dangerous children . . . wearing black robes. They're killing soldiers!"

It took too long for him to answer, engendering an eerie feeling the music couldn't veil. I beheld a disturbing grin on the face of the man I thought was my friend.

"I suppose it's a revolution, then."

My heart sank. But as I hesitantly stepped toward his desk, I realized that this wasn't the same Walter I knew and loved. His eyes were black voids, emptied of a brilliant spirit. Even then, something else was missing. My mind raced in a million different directions.

As if lending a sign, an object glinted on the floor amid a mess of albums.

A monocle. The same one he always wore. Smashed in two.

Dread filled me when I reached out to touch his hand; I passed right through him. With this awareness, what I thought was his body began to vanish. As the music hit a crescendo, the record player broke abruptly. In its place came devilish laughter.

I spun around in anger to find the female leader leaning against the wall.

"What have you done?!" I yelled and didn't wait for an answer, charging straight at her. She vanished as I was about to make contact, causing me to bump my head violently.

I staggered backward, nauseous and dizzy, and fought the urge to vomit. Blood dripped from a gash on my forehead, trickling into my eyes.

"Such a primitive form of travel," the girl transmitted. *"You could have arrived here sooner if you understood your true power."*

My vision calibrated to find her behind Walter's desk, flaunting the dragon on her wrist. I had never seen such an ability, and I couldn't help feeling that time was my enemy.

"Don't you dare hurt him," I said.

"Too late for that, brother."

Standing in the doorway was her male counterpart, similar in every sense except for a pyramidal amulet around his neck. Around my age if not older, he and his twin were the clear orchestrators of the attack. And the images I saw when I first connected with him unfortunately felt like precognition.

Drifting behind the boy as he strolled into the office was the Walter I had known for ten years, tied and gagged with physical rope, genuine emotion filling his eyes. He made muffled noises but was quickly silenced by the black-robed boy.

Darkness triggered inside me, but I realized I needed to be tactful.

After struggling to calm my racing heart, one shaky word emerged: "Why?"

The boy sighed, letting Walter drop to the floor. "For the life of me, I cannot understand why this man means so much to you that you would run to him like a lab rat toward the back of its cage, even with liberation in plain sight. It is truly a deplorable syndrome. But one I believe we can help you with."

"Just let him go," I demanded. "Leave Walter out of this."

"Not unless you behave first, perhaps showing a little *gratitude* to your saviors."

"Saviors? What about those children outside who are dying instead of you? You've brainwashed them to be killers!"

"No, Samuel. We have only taught them to be free."

The girl teleported to his side, staring into his eyes in silent communication. I clenched my fists and tried to calculate whether I was in range to land a hard punch, but a glance at the man restrained by their feet urged otherwise. Walter shook his head minimally. *Patience.* I breathed in as deeply as my lungs would allow, channeling what he'd taught me about controlling my emotions.

"What is it that you want?" I asked, glaring.

"We simply want the same for you," the boy responded.

"Then take another! I am not interested in what you label as freedom."

The boy smiled. "This was to be expected, was it not, sister?" She nodded while he paced back and forth. "My apologies if Tiana here comes across as introverted. She's a bit of a purist when it comes to methods of interaction. And I understand how this could all seem especially strange. We know so much about you, yet you don't even know my name. Please allow an introduction." Halting in front of me, he extended his hand. "My name is—"

"I don't give a damn about your name." I slapped his hand away. "Or what you think you know about who I am."

"Oh, Samuel Helen, we've been watching you for quite a while now. We've seen the way they treat you here. The drugs they give you. The pain they put you through. They do it under the guise of assistance, but it is all a lie! Believe me when I say that they wanted to enslave you the moment they beheld your eyes. God knows what you could accomplish if you did not have to toil beneath the light of the sun with others who do not share our same gifts."

Thoughts emerged of Evelyn and the orphans, but I blocked them out and averted my eyes. "How have you been watching me?" I questioned.

"The minds of the new breed need not be bound by space and time, unless they believe themselves to be so. I'm sorry to have to tell you this, Samuel, but you are the one who has been brainwashed, hypnotized, to be so much less than you are. And you had to endure it longer than anyone else in this prison. That is why you have been chosen to be the first to receive liberation, to at last realize your divine right in this world."

"And what is that right, exactly?"

He smirked. "It should be evident for all who have eyes to see. We are the next stage, brother. To hold us captive is to delay the inevitable—to deny the will of the earth. Because those with our DNA possess true dominion over her majesty." He brushed his fingers over his amulet, which bore the symbol of an eye; I remembered it from Walter's teachings about Egypt. "The revolution has been prophesied and is now coming to fruition. Yet it fails to be recognized by the unilluminated swine."

"I want no part in a revolution that encourages such violence," I contended.

"It is only right for what they have done. You have been shocked and tortured, have you not? By those useless hypocrites who call themselves scientists. And outside of these gates, we are being *hunted*. Rounded up for the same degradation. We are simply carrying out a karmic balance, a necessity of self-defense—a preservation of human evolution!"

"But not everyone here has a choice!" I gestured to the portrait of Mabus. "Most people here are just following orders. Even if what you're saying is true, they don't deserve to die like this."

"If your tutor taught you anything of value, you'd know that the greatest atrocities this world has ever seen were carried out by those sheeple who just follow orders, not bothering to question what is truly God's will."

"So your goal is to murder them?" I thought of Salazar suffocating.

"Our mission is to set you free." His gaze flared formidably. "We've been gathering strength for years in preparation for this moment, brother. All three of us were among the first born on this earth with the eyes of enlightenment, and hence it is destiny that we unite in our power." He extended his hand once more. "To join us is to actualize the coming of the new age."

I looked down at the emblem he shared with his sister. Then I glanced at Walter, who was not bothering to struggle. I remembered similar words from our last session together. I wondered if this encounter was indeed a consequence of destiny.

"Release him unharmed," I said to the boy, "then we can talk freedom. There is no need for any more violence."

He slowly withdrew the offer of his hand as Tiana giggled wickedly.

He replied, "Here's where you are mistaken, brother. You can never truly be free if you remain a slave to the old blood." Using only his mind, he slid Walter before me. "As part of initiation, you must destroy previous attachments."

"But Walter is innocent. He has helped me enormously!"

"And where has that gotten you? Living as an obedient minion with no control over his mind?" He snickered. "You have already pointed out where he gets his orders from. Do you think it is an accident that he has introduced you to all these archaic records, to keep you entertained? It is all to mold you into a docile slave, unable to realize your rightful royalty."

"No." I shook my head. "He went against the lesson plan. He taught me how to think for myself."

"He convinced you that there is a purpose to your enslavement. He is perfectly content with our kind being dragged into captivity, taken from their parents." He spit on him venomously. "To him, you are nothing more than a failed experiment. His mission was to kill time until his little pet was put to sleep. God knows they wouldn't let you turn twenty."

I stared into Walter's sympathetic eyes, frightened at what I might find. He wasn't trying to defend himself from what the boy was saying, but nothing would change what I felt with my entire being. "That's not true. You're wrong about him."

The boy grimaced. "As long as he remains alive, you will forever be blinded. You will always be connected to this prison."

"I'm not going to let you kill him," I growled.

"You're right, brother." He pulled a dagger from beneath his robes, which he tossed to the floor to stick in the wood beside Walter. "It has to be you."

I tried not to show weakness, but I trembled nonetheless, unable to process the horror of his request. I wished that I could rewind time, yet the seconds pressed on. The two of them seemed too powerful to fight. I had to make a choice.

The boy nodded while Tiana imparted a telepathic message: *"Do it, and you can have anything you desire."*

With sharpened breath, I bent down and grabbed the dagger. "Okay."

"It is the only way, Samuel," the boy maintained. "The path to true liberation. It is time to free yourself from the past. To release your inner demons. To unshackle yourself from the chains of your mind! And to free *him*." He frowned at Walter. "The poor thing must very much miss his family. That bloodline, unfortunately, can no longer survive in the coming world."

I locked eyes one last time with my sagacious tutor. They expressed serenity.

Meanwhile, a monster raged inside of me. With all the strength in my limbs, I lunged to stab the boy—but was stopped an inch from his chest, frozen by a dark energy. He easily plucked the dagger from my hands and cast it aside before forcibly seizing my mind.

"How morbid it is that you care for these pigs."

I was sent flying across the room, landing hard on Walter's desk and toppling over with it. I groaned in pain as the boy approached, seething. "I'm afraid he's too weak, Tia, corrupted by his programming. It is a sickness of the mind, viewing his saviors as the enemy!"

The shelves of records on either side came crashing down on top of me. As I crawled out from underneath, I saw the rainbow Buddha split into pieces, as well as the cracked photograph of Walter's wife and son, lost in an eternal moment. I became aware of a greater presence hovering above, watching . . . waiting.

But it wasn't time yet.

"You're not my savior," I baited the boy. "Deep down, you're just scared and lonely."

He stepped forward so that his shadow enveloped me, his animosity palpable. "It is a tragedy that your perception is so distorted. You have the eyes, and yet you cannot see. I could have given you power beyond imagination!"

"Yeah? And what makes you so special?"

He laughed. "I am the next step in evolution. The face of revolution. The embodiment of human potential." He spun me around using telekinesis, brandishing his cherished amulet. "I am—"

I kicked his legs so forcefully that he fell flat on the floor. I pounced. One punch was enough to temporarily blind him while I reached for a pointed shard of a record . . .

Tiana teleported in the nick of time, blocking my hand and lifting me effortlessly with her mind. Her eyes burned vehemently as she constricted every part of my body. Next thing I knew, I was against the wall, my arms grazing the portrait of Mabus, choking in the same manner as Salazar. I struggled for air while the boy got to his feet and grinned diabolically.

"You say you're against violence, brother." He wiped blood from his nose. "I guess we're not so different, you and me. But as my sister here can assure you, we choose to foster our gifts, not treat them like a disease!" Stomping toward Walter, he held out his hand, and the dagger shot into his grasp. "This is your fault."

Tiana relinquished her hold, and I dropped along with the portrait. "*No!*" I shouted, springing upright, but he was already behind Walter, lifting him to his knees and pressing the dagger to his throat.

Hope drained rapidly. There was nothing I could do but beg.

"Please. I'll join you. I'll do anything. Just don't kill him."

"You have already made your choice," said the boy.

"You don't have to do this. It's not *right.*"

"It is the will of the divine," he declared as his sister came to his side, "to let mediocrity—"

Walter finally attempted to speak again, which visibly pleased his captor. The boy cut the rope from Walter's mouth and nudged him with the dagger. "Come on, then. Beg for mercy! Tell Samuel yourself how you have deceived him for a decade. Exhibit your cowardice. Then *maybe* we can let you live."

In an act of rebellion, Walter beamed lovingly, but not at me; rather, he gazed above my head.

"Break the strings," he said.

These words appeared to perturb the boy. His eyes revealed a demonic presence. And he slashed Walter's throat without a second thought.

I screamed, releasing a wave of such profound energy that it seemed to sway the tides of the earth, though the boy vanished with his sister. I collapsed to my knees while the man who was a second father to me bled out before my eyes.

CHAPTER 5

I **DIDN'T KNOW** how I managed to resume standing, but I soon found myself running.

Away from Walter's home, down the Facility's roads.

The alarms had ceased. The buildings were burning. And the dwindling rain couldn't wash the blood from my robes.

I had no concept of how much time had passed, but I had been holding a dead body for what seemed like an eternity. Now I was numb to the death all around—to the bunkers broken into, the massacred scientists, the military helicopters flying overhead, evacuating surviving soldiers.

The children of the dragon had won. And they had spared no one.

Lining the roads with the soldiers were several of their own, slain by bullets. They were just children. My heart would have broken had it not already been torn apart. Nothing sparked a reaction; it was too painful to continue feeling. My single imperative was to get to the last person I loved. All other parts of my brain had shut off entirely.

I screamed for my legs to keep going, then screamed some more to repress the memory that would haunt me for the rest of my life. Through tears, blood, and unrelenting trauma, I carried on.

Children had gathered on the central path. Some gasped when they saw me, and others tried to talk, but none of it registered. Most were recovering from the battle—those in white robes as well as in black. Miraculously, no one stopped me as I passed the open gates. There were no invisible barriers, nor any sign of the two psychopathic teenagers who had murdered the man whose blood I bore.

An ominous feeling lurked in my gut, and just as I was wondering where they could have gone, I saw it: black smoke rising from the village in the distance.

No.

One final surge of energy sprang from a hidden source, and I sprinted down the road. But as the fire grew larger and larger, the world kept getting smaller and smaller. Soon, my fight wasn't so much against exhaustion as it was against hopelessness and the images in my mind of the girl I loved being burned alive—images that became increasingly vivid once I realized that most of the village was aflame.

I wasn't even close to reaching the smoke, but I choked up regardless. I did not want to be in this world any longer. I despised what it had done to me.

I had woken from a nightmare into a more terrible one.

Catching my breath, I stared at my bloody hands, one of them still bandaged loosely. Bit by bit, I undid the wrapping to reveal the self-inflicted wound underneath. The rain had passed, and on the side of the road was a nice patch of wet grass, untarnished by human depravity. The next moment, I was on my back, watching the rays of the sun break through the clouds, warm and healing.

I recalled the way my mother used to hold me, stroking my hair and singing softly. As the pain dissipated, I knew that I could never go back to the nightmare. I closed my eyes in a willful forgetting, wishing I could lie there forever.

Then, as I sank further, I heard the earth herself calling my name. I smiled, longing to be at one with her, as it was for all the animals and songbirds. "For you, there'll be no more crying," I sang in a whisper. "For you, the sun will be—"

There was a touch on my face, gentle, physical. My eyes opened to find Evelyn kneeling over me, gasping in surprise.

"Samuel, thank God you're alive! Are you okay? What happened to you?!" Her gaze was sad and worried, reddened by crying. Yet I could not understand what it was about.

"Evelyn, don't worry. Of course I'm alive! I was just napping." I laughed in an attempt to cheer her up, but for some reason, this only made things worse.

She trembled before speaking. "Samuel, you're covered in blood."

"Oh, it's not that bad." I showed her the palm of my hand. "I cut it in the cornfield, remember? You patched it up pretty good though, so I decided to take it off."

She shook her head slowly. "What *happened* to you?"

I sat up in an instant; after pausing with apprehension, I gazed down at my robes. Neurons fired through darkened avenues, and remnants of harrowing memory resurfaced. "It's not . . ." I could hardly get the words out, gagging on the thought alone. "It's not my blood."

I looked up to see the village burning—and three black-robed children approaching from down the road. Evelyn took my hand, helping me to my feet.

"We have to go!" She tugged, but I didn't budge.

"It's not my blood," I repeated, piecing together the events of the day.

"Please, Samuel, come with me!" she shouted. "Samuel?"

That name did not click. A program activated, and suddenly I was possessed, glaring at the children with tunnel vision. I waited for them, seething while neglecting the cries of the girl by my side. A confident darkness took hold of me with no resistance from my conscious mind, having not felt such power for quite a long time.

The black robes drew close to us, then halted all at once. They were young adolescents, two boys and one girl, but with shaved heads, dragon emblems, and huge, hateful eyes, they were all the same as their murderous leaders. I sensed their thoughts as they stared back and forth between me and Evelyn with arrogant smirks.

"You shouldn't be with her," one boy said.

"You must join the revolution," urged the other.

I didn't answer, intensifying my gaze until I felt their pulses escalate. I noticed that Evelyn's anxiety rose as well, but not because of them.

The girl sneered. "Don't try to intimidate us. We know you can never achieve true ability unless you align with the dragon. So, what's it going to be?"

I said, "You murder the closest thing I have to a father, you burn down her village, and you're asking me to join you?"

"We're not asking," she replied as fire flickered in her eyes. "Being with her is a violation of our code."

Evelyn stepped forward. "Leave us al—"

One of the boys tripped her with telekinesis. With a shriek of rage, I flung him fifteen feet backward to tumble through the grass.

The girl countered by levitating several stones and hurling them at me simultaneously; by some means, I stopped them all. Fury replaced thought, and it took a single rock shot back at her stomach to take the wind out of her.

The last kid tried to run away, but I grabbed him with my mind and pulled him toward me. After a lapse in consciousness, I became aware of myself choking him with my hands, my voice enraged. "Where are they?!"

His heart was pounding. I knew that I could stop it if I focused my anger, and I did not care to control the monster inside any longer.

"Where are your leaders?"

A caress on the cheek turned my head to the side. Evelyn clenched her locket, her clear blue eyes penetrating my soul and reminding me of home. "Remember who you are," she whispered, as if channeling a higher mind.

I turned back to the boy, surrendering the delusions that had possessed me. Although terror filled his gaze, beneath I recognized a greater essence. After a few long moments of wrestling with demons, I was finally able to let him go. He regrouped with the others, who were similarly afraid. I would have remained standing in a daze had Evelyn not taken my hand and pulled me away. This time, I listened.

We ran for the forest, and a dam within me finally released the overwhelming surge of emotion from all that had transpired.

The grief for Walter.

The hatred toward his killers—the shame at what it had made me become.

And the despair at realizing that I had left Noah in his quarters. I thought about turning back for him, but one broken promise was not enough motive to risk what remained. I held Evelyn's hand tight, knowing that she did not possess the eyes that would protect her.

We became immersed under the cover of pine trees. I had never traveled so far since arriving at the Facility, but there was no time to take it in. We ran a little further until Evelyn's gasps forced us to stop. She sat by a rock as she caught her breath. I watched with a tired heart.

"I knew you'd come," she said when she could speak. "The others ran here soon after they showed up, but I stayed behind to look for you. There was no way I was leaving without you, Samuel."

I wanted to reply but couldn't form words. Instead, I sat silently in front of her, baring the anguish in my eyes. Evelyn crawled into my arms, each of us unleashing our emotions.

"They murdered Walter," I cried.

"I'm so sorry, Samuel. I know how much you cared for him. They did the same to Maggie when she tried to stop them. They didn't even need to touch her."

"Those *monsters.* I'm going to kill them for what they've done."

"No. You're not." She took my shoulders. "Because you're not like them. Promise that you'll never show that side to me again."

Through much resistance, I released a heavy sigh. "I promise."

"I'm so glad I found you."

We embraced in the forest twilight, our wet faces pressed together. Meanwhile, a bluebird perched on a branch nearby, oblivious to the suffering and to the sadness of our strange human lives.

~

The next few hours were spent scouring the woods for the others in Evelyn's group. To our dismay, there was no trace of them. She called their names, but we were greeted only by the hooting of an owl, signaling the approaching dusk.

She didn't question me further about what happened at the Facility, and I was thankful to remain largely in silence, still unable to process what I had witnessed—much less contemplate how we would survive. But if only for Evelyn, I kept my legs moving, my mind planted firmly in reality, as difficult as it was. And in an act of desperation, I prayed for a sign.

A comment Evelyn had made about following the heart came to me; she'd said those words just that morning, though it seemed like a lifetime ago. Nonetheless, it was as if a part of her knew this would happen, that we would be put in a situation that forced us to trust our intuition. So, despite our exhaustion and fruitless search, I got the urge to walk a little bit farther, which I shared with Evelyn.

She appeared surprised but relieved that I was speaking again. "You sense it too, then? That someone or something is guiding us?"

"I just think we need to find water," I said, though secretly I wondered the same.

"How are you feeling, Samuel?"

"Tired. Thirsty."

"Yes, but besides that." She reached for my hand, her eyes wet in her own process of mourning. "It's been a day of such darkness— for both of us, really—but I can't understand what you must be going through. It doesn't have to be now, but you know that you can talk to me."

"Don't worry about me. All I care about is that you are okay."

"I'm alive." She sighed, her face growing wistful. "I just hope we can find the others."

"We'll find them." I curved my lips upward, trying to find hope. "Even if it's not today, we know at least they have each other."

Evelyn nodded, somewhat encouraged, giving my hand a gentle squeeze before we continued through the forest. If it was any consolation, she'd had not one coughing fit; her lungs seemed replenished by the surrounding trees, which appeared healthy and vibrant, without hazardous radiation. Previously, I had no idea that nature ran this deep. I would have been mesmerized had I not been so caught up in my mind, often while inhaling the stench of blood. Each time I wished to disconnect from the painful memory, the odor returned to remind me. I recalled Walter's last words.

Before I had the chance to ponder them, the breaking of a branch startled us.

Then another, but closer.

We scanned the twilight between the thick pines. "Is anyone there?" Evelyn called, no doubt hoping it was one of the orphans.

Leaves rustled while shadows danced on the ground. Something was surely moving toward us, but it didn't feel human. Evelyn took my hand again, and finally a figure revealed itself.

"Don't move," she whispered.

It was an animal I had only ever seen in books and heard about in old tunes, an animal I'd believed was largely extinct. Even with my limited understanding of the natural world, I knew this was an anomaly: a doe alone at sundown, exhibiting no fear of human beings.

And pulsating with magic.

The doe stepped forward slowly, with perky ears and gentle eyes, until, remarkably, she was within arm's reach. Evelyn glanced at me speechlessly before touching her on the snout. "She's beautiful. And so very friendly."

"Why is she doing this?" I asked.

"Well, why wouldn't she?" Evelyn petted her while they peered at each other fondly.

"Shouldn't she be afraid?"

"Nobody ever *has* to be afraid."

I was dumbfounded. I couldn't explain the animal's behavior; perhaps she was also simply following her heart. It wasn't long before I reached out to pet her myself, triggering a visceral reaction. Tears fell from my eyes, releasing a hoard of pent-up emotion, and I felt seeds take root within my heart.

The doe gazed at me lovingly, then turned the other direction. We followed without thinking, entranced by an otherworldly connection. We walked and walked as the sun continued to set, and the woods seemed to open up a bit.

Finally, as if fulfilling my wish, sounds of running water came to us. We couldn't help but dash ahead of the majestic creature, arriving at a tranquil stream flowing through the forest.

Evelyn knelt first, lifting a handful to her mouth. "It's clean!"

I drank after her, and it was so refreshing I almost felt guilty, gulping several mouthfuls and then splashing it over my face. By the time I glanced back, the doe was headed into the trees, not bothering to drink with us. I stood, but Evelyn stopped me.

"It's time to let her be. The current is moving that way."

We strolled along the stream by instinct until we came upon a gorgeous scene. The water coursed among the rocks, tumbled down a tiny waterfall, and pooled into a small, circular lake. Lining the lake were bushes brimming with clusters of berries.

"Look at these, Samuel," Evelyn marveled, approaching the nearest bush. "There's enough here to feed us for weeks."

"What are they?"

She plucked one out, inspected it in the faint light, then popped it into her mouth. "Blueberries!"

We momentarily forgot about the day's tragedies. Soon, we were stuffing our mouths, washing the berries down with water. The berries were ripe and sweet, and the lake shined with a higher energy. It felt like we had stumbled into an alternate reality.

Evelyn managed a melancholy smile. "That doe was a sign, Samuel. Someone is watching us, guiding us, and making sure we are okay. This place is a sanctuary. It's like a little Eden."

"Yeah, in the middle of the forest." I surveyed the pristine environment.

"As far as I'm concerned, this is the center of the world."

We then did something we had never done: we took off our sandals, stripped out of our robes, and bathed together in the cool water. Even though it was the first time seeing each other naked, embarrassment was the last thing on our minds, along with sexuality. Her slender figure, however, was undeniably beautiful. Like a blue-eyed angel, she cleaned the wounds on my face and body, then rinsed the blood from my robes to the best of her ability. The lake had an unmistakable healing quality, soothing our minds yet bringing everything to the surface.

Hence, as the pale full moon illumined the night sky, tears of remorse again formed in my eyes. "It wasn't supposed to be like this," I said.

"What do you mean?" Evelyn waded back after laying out my robes to dry. This section of the lake was barely shallow enough for us to stand.

"Well, just this morning you were talking about running away together, escaping from our old lives. And since then, so much has happened. You said that we could find a way, and here we are, alone in this strange place. Don't you find that odd?"

She pondered for a moment. "Yes, it is weird how things work sometimes. But we have to focus on the present. We are here together, right? No matter how it came to be. And this place has all we need to stay for a while."

"And live off blueberries?"

"Until we find another source of food, why not? I can't go back to working in the fields. And you can never go back to the Facility. We need to move forward from the way things were."

I took her hand and pulled her closer. "I've always wanted a chance to be with you. And it is quite a miracle that we were led here, thanks to that doe. But the way everything happened back there was all too much. Those kids weren't supposed to show up." My weary bones trembled. "He wasn't supposed to die."

"Believe me, Samuel, I'm upset too. About losing Maggie and not finding the others. But even though I've never met Walter, I know for a fact he wouldn't want you to spend too much time mourning his death. Didn't he always say that everything happens for a reason? That God works in mysterious—"

"Two psychopaths tied him up and slit his throat. That's the reason. And their gang of followers slaughtered everyone else who didn't have eyes like mine!"

I turned and trekked out of the water, settling on the shore between the blueberry bushes. Evelyn came after and sat by my side, kindly sharing her robes so we could dry off.

"Talk to me. Tell me what happened."

With a sigh, I started to unload. I told her about my encounter with the girl in the caravan and the incident with the spellbound soldiers; the attack of the black robes, my fight with the young boy, and how I unfortunately left Noah behind; the cruelty of the two leaders proclaiming a revolution, then murdering Walter when I refused to join them; and the wickedness of using children in their agenda of violence and their unwillingness to spare the unarmed scientists.

Tears flowed effortlessly when I finished; processing the events through words, as awful as it all was, took a weight off my shoulders.

"Evelyn?"

"Yes, Samuel?"

"Thank you for everything. I'm very sorry about Maggie. She was a good, kind woman who I know helped raise you for most of your life. It's okay if you need a release too."

Her eyes watered as she motioned to her locket. "One thing she would always tell me, after I lost them, is that death is far from the end. They just become your guardian angels. She would have wanted to pass protecting us, so there's really no reason to be sorry. I just know her soul is out there now, meeting with Walter's and guiding the children to a safe place."

"I hope that's true," I breathed. "We're both a bit numb to losing people close to us, aren't we?"

"As long as I have you here with me."

"I won't be going anywhere."

Time became a blur as we lay hand in hand. The night was warm enough to remain without our robes and dark enough to see the light from the stars above, which the lake reflected. Sounds of the wind teased us with secrets while the full moon conspired to hypnotize our minds.

As I listened to the gentle flow of the water, the present moment finally replaced the pain of yesterday. The seeds in my heart somehow sprouted an inch, and soon after, I felt something crawl onto my finger.

It was a caterpillar. Small and green and searching for its wings.

"Break the strings," I said, though I had no idea what it meant.

Suddenly, a vision of me and another boy from the Facility— Cyrus, whom I had not seen since before the attack—manifested in my mind's eye. It was of us going through a blue door and stumbling upon a projector showing both old memories and things to come. Sleepy and disoriented, I blocked it out, unsure if it was real.

I just knew that if we found him, we would be led to a new home, as well as true sanctuary for the girl I loved.

I was then able to rest, drifting asleep to the image of a doe while a female voice echoed in the background of my awareness, singing songs from my childhood.

~

"Do you hear me when you sleep?" was the line that opened my eyes, leaving me wondering if I truly had a guardian angel.

Amazingly, I had slept until morning. And in an occurrence previously unimaginable, I woke up in a place that was not the Facility, with sunlight winking through the trees. Moreover, Evelyn lay beside me, sleeping in her silver robes. Despite the memory of what led us here momentarily thickening the air, I willed myself to move forward into a new life together. Walter would have wanted that. I breathed in deeply. I sat up. And I remembered I was naked.

With returning self-consciousness, I retrieved my robes from the rock they were draped over. Not only was I feeling better physically—practically resurrected—but the lake had for the most part erased the bloodstains, strengthening my conviction that it possessed supernatural properties.

Before getting dressed, however, I stared at my reflection in the water. A young man with wavy hair and enormous eyes stared back—a man I loved and feared and was still in the process of knowing. My mind quieted, touched by sublimity, while the sun rose in accordance with the assembly of birds singing the chorus of dawn. The lake was flooded with rays to brighten its darkest shadows.

An orb of light flashed in the reflection.

"Twist your head around," whispered the voice from my dreams, taking the breath out of me.

I wasn't crazy. But I nearly fell over backward as I followed its request; there was no one to be found but Evelyn, still sleeping among the blueberries.

I put on my robes and sandals and scurried over. This was my first time seeing her sleep. With her red hair sprawled across the earth and a peaceful smile, she seemed so beautiful and unaware. I hated doing it, but I needed to wake her.

"Evelyn," I said, nudging her shoulder. "I think there's someone here with us."

She groaned. Rolled over. And gave a curious chuckle. "Ice cream . . . tastes like *snozzberries!*" she mumbled before drifting off again. I decided to let her be because one thing I knew for sure was that it was not her voice I had heard.

Sensing an energetic pull, I headed into the forest, searching behind every tree for the source that guided me while being careful not to stray too far from the lake. After failing to find any sign of angels, I suspected the delusions of a troubled mind. Dejected, I walked back to the Eden in which Evelyn slept.

My mouth dropped. *It can't be.*

Standing above the girl I loved was the majestic doe, gazing down at her protectively. The creature noticed me, and again I felt an inexplicable connection. It was an intuitive recognition—a soul-level memory, her essence at one with a certain human being.

A moment passed, and the doe took off, not letting me near her this time. Maybe she didn't recognize me. Or perhaps she was trying to lead me in another direction.

I chased her like a fool.

It took several minutes of racing through the woods to realize my insanity. The doe was fast, but she seemed to be playing a game with me, lingering at the outskirts of my perception until, finally, she vanished. "Wait!" I called in desperation, bending over with my hands on my knees. I was suddenly ashamed I had left Evelyn to run after an animal. Surely it was a delusion to believe she could talk telepathically or was in any way connected to those souls I had cherished.

I started back in the direction I had come, hoping my memory would guide me through the dense trees. I walked for some time and found no opening in the forest—no tranquil stream, no mystical lake, and no bushes packed with blueberries. Panic set in, and I began running again, but this only worsened my surroundings. Branches blocked out the sun, and the warmth of the earth was reduced to a chill. Even the songbirds weren't singing anymore. Just as I was about to cry, I closed my eyes and simply breathed.

"It's all right," I whispered. "I know it's right."

The wind picked up, and I felt a presence near me. I tuned into its familiar, comforting energy, then opened my eyes slowly. Through the woods, about twenty feet away, I caught the doe's compelling gaze. Tears of gratitude dripped down my face, for I knew unequivocally that she was sent to be our guide, to help us in our time of need. I stood mesmerized for a few long moments, praying not to lose her again.

Then, I carefully approached, raising my hand in a calming manner, attempting to transmit benevolent thoughts. *I heard you speak. Please don't run. You can show me who you really are.*

In return, I received nothing, save for the sense that she didn't want me near her again—at least, not without Evelyn. She ran, and I sighed in resignation. For some odd reason, she was now frightened of me.

A gunshot blasted through the forest.

Time slowed. My entire body froze. I didn't know whether to run or hide; all I could think about was Evelyn and the obligation to stay alive.

A second shot nearly shocked me off my feet, but I realized it wasn't aimed at me. Out of the cover of trees came two camouflaged men: beards overgrown, hunting rifles in hand, and fury in their eyes.

"You just cost us our game!" yelled the burlier one. "What in God's name were you—"

He abruptly fell silent. I could not speak, could hardly catch my breath. The hunters glanced at one another, then back at me as anger gave way to curiosity.

"What's your name, boy?" the skinny one asked.

"Samuel," I said.

"And what are you doing out here, Samuel?"

"Just trying to survive."

He smirked. "With anybody else?"

"No. Just me."

They whispered between themselves, inspecting my eyes menacingly. I should have run right then. Instead, I tried to reason.

"Listen," I began, "I'm sorry about the deer. I didn't realize you were there. And please, I don't mean any trouble, so I'll just be on my way now."

"Oh, we don't believe that you mean us trouble, Samuel," the skinny one replied, matching each of my steps backward. "We're just trying to figure out what brought a boy like you so far out into these woods. That's all."

"I told you. I'm just—"

"Look at us when you talk!"

I hesitantly met their threatening gazes. They were fascinated by me, and they didn't try to hide it. Although I was barely familiar with people, a terrifying thought kept pestering my mind: *Maybe Walter was right.*

"You see those things?" the burly one blurted out. "He's one of those kids with the funny eyes. Dangerous too." He glared me down. "Aren't you?"

I was off before they could raise their rifles. More shots echoed, and bullets whizzed by. To my horror, I was now the prey. Seconds turned into minutes, and minutes turned into what seemed like an eternity of toying with death. I sprinted through the pines, clinging to a life I would not be afraid to leave but for a single reason.

Fortunately, the forest shielded me faithfully. I couldn't help feeling that it had a consciousness of its own, an awareness of what I had been through and why it wasn't my time to die. Yet just as I dashed behind a trunk, thinking I had lost them, the crack of a gunshot sent me fleeing again.

"We just want to talk, Samuel! Stop running!"

I continued my escape, though I had no clue if I was escaping anything. The forest was my friend, but it was also playing games with me. For all I knew, I was running in circles. So, with gunshots resounding, I trusted my intuition, closing my eyes for a fleeting second, then feeling the urge to make a sudden turn.

As fate would have it, we collided. Together, we fell to the dirt. I prayed that time would stop for us, but it kept ticking away. I sat up simultaneously with Evelyn. Her eyes were wide with astonishment, and she opened her mouth to speak.

But the hunters closed in on us with guns.

"Don't move!" the burly one warned, though I was too lost in Evelyn's gaze to do so anyway, apologizing to her silently and questioning if it was the last thing I'd ever see.

The skinny one circled us. "Well, well, you got yourself a girl, don't you?"

"You have no right to do this!" Evelyn yelled.

He cocked his rifle. "We'll do as we please."

A hidden side of me clamored to come out, but I suppressed it.

"Just let us be," I pleaded. "There's no need for any more death. We've seen enough of it already."

The skinny one grinned. "Like I said, Samuel, we don't wanna kill you. 'Cause we heard the broadcast earlier about them funny-eyed children. Didn't we, Jim?"

"That's right, Raymond." Jim nodded. "The prize is sweeter if we take you alive." He snickered as he stroked Evelyn's hair. "And this one doesn't have funny eyes, but she sure is pretty."

I didn't care to control it at this point; I let my anger rise. I wished to kill both men in an instant.

"Samuel."

My attention turned to Evelyn's trembling lips as primordial emotion seemed to burst out from them.

"I love you."

I had a chance to reply but choked on my tongue. Jim laughed and struck the back of her head with the butt of his rifle. That was the last thing I saw before I, too, was whacked hard, sedating my rage and sending me to another reality.

CHAPTER 6

"*ILLUMINE THE SHADOWS of your mind, my darling. Can't you see me?*"

I wake to Mommy holding me in her arms. I feel confused for a second, but then I remember that we're on the sofa in the living room, near a window with the sun shining through. I love it when she holds me like this. She looks like an angel in her white dress. I feel so comfy and safe in my soft PJs, but also a little woozy. I must have been asleep for a while.

"Mommy," I whisper up to her. "I see you."

She smiles down and pokes my nose. "I see you too, sugar bear. And I especially love to see those eyes of yours."

I stretch and yawn. "Was I sleeping?"

"Yes, you were. Did you have nice dreams?"

"Not really." I think back to a fuzzy memory. "I had a bit of a nightmare, actually."

"Oh no. It must be the fever." She touches my forehead, a little worried. "That medicine didn't do anything, did it?"

I shrug. "I don't think so. But I know what will make me feel better."

"What's that, sweetie?"

"You know."

She laughs, and I feel so warm inside. "Which song do you want me to sing? The one about the birds or the butterflies?"

"Birds, please."

She runs her fingers through my hair, then starts singing.

"For you, there'll be no more crying,
For you, the sun will be shining . . ."

I love it when she sings. It makes me feel like I'm in heaven. A fire burns in the fireplace, and above the mantel are pictures of three angels—Michael, Gabriel, and Rafael. Michael is the warrior who protects from evil. Gabriel is the messenger who is sent by God. And Rafael is the one who heals. I've never met any of them, but that's okay, because I also have my own guardian angel who teaches me how to love. Mommy says to listen well because there are many people in the world who forget how to love. But I think they would all remember if they listened to her sing.

I look back up and relax to her voice. There are no more worries. Nobody tries to hurt me. There is no radiation. The world is beautiful again.

"And the songbirds keep singing, like they know the score,
And I love you, I love you, I love you, like never before . . ."

She finishes the song. Her smile brings me so much happiness. She looks like an angel, and she smells like red roses.

"Mommy. I missed you."

"I've missed you too, Samuel," she says, "but you've been in my arms this whole time."

"I know. It just didn't feel that way in the nightmare."

"They're only dreams, my love. There's no reason to be afraid of them."

Three knocks come from the front door.

"Oh, your father's home from the mines. He hasn't seen you in quite a long time. Why don't you go open the door for him?"

I feel my heart beating. I hold tight to Mommy. "Does Daddy forgive me?"

"For what, sweetie?"

I can't answer. My head feels dizzy.

"Samuel. Why would Daddy need to forgive you?"

"For what happened last time," I whisper. "He was *really* angry."

Knocks come again, but harder.

"Of course he forgives you." Mommy leans close to my face. I see the sparkle in her eyes. "It may not seem that way sometimes, but he really loves you. Now go say hi."

"Okay." I stand up and try to be brave. But when I get near the door, it slams open.

Daddy is there with his boots and orange jacket. His face is dark as coal, but underneath he looks like he's seen a ghost. He walks in clumsily, shuts the door, then wobbles back and forth. I don't like it when he's like this.

"Hi, Daddy," I say to him.

He stares at me. I can tell he's angry, even a little scared. I look back to Mommy, who rises and comes between us. "Your son just said hi to you. Aren't you going to give him a hug?"

He doesn't move. I don't know what to do. I say, "I love you, Daddy."

But he doesn't say it back. I don't think he forgives me.

He says, "Marilyn, we need to talk."

"Our son is ill. Whatever this is, it can—"

"We need to talk!" he says louder.

Mommy gets upset. "What's the problem, Luther?"

"You wanna know what the problem is?" He nods at me. "The problem is that you let him out of the house when he's a danger to society."

There is quiet for many seconds. I shiver, but Mommy holds me. Her voice grows shaky. "What are you talking about?"

He huffs angrily. "You know how he likes to go over to the Tompkins' and play with that golden retriever?"

Mommy doesn't answer. He walks in closer.

"Do you?!"

"Yes. I do."

"Well, the dog is dead! They found her lying in the yard. Bill told me earlier. Apparently, our *son* was there just this morning." He looks into my eyes. "Weren't you, Samuel?"

"Dogs die, Luther! They die! That's not the problem. You're scaring us both!"

"Five years old, Marilyn, and her heart just stopped. No signs of injury, but a little too young for a dog to die naturally. They couldn't figure out what happened. Well, I think I know the answer—and it ain't pretty!"

I begin to cry. I don't know why he's so angry. I run back to the sofa, but Daddy follows.

"Get out of our house!" Mommy yells.

"I just wanna speak with my son! Did you do it, Samuel? Did you do something to that dog?" I bury my face in the cushion and hope he goes away. "Hello? Is there anybody in there?"

"Stop it, you bastard! You're not helping anyone."

"This is for our own good! I just want an answer. You killed the dog, didn't you, Samuel? How did you do it? *Why* did you do it?"

I keep crying. I can't think, but I know I love dogs. I turn to look at him.

"I love dogs, Daddy. Especially Lucy."

Mommy steps in and puts her hand on his shoulder. "He loves that dog. He would never try to hurt her. Just listen to yourself for a moment, how ridiculous you sound."

"Don't you see, Marilyn? That's the problem! He loves dogs. He adores them, for goodness' sake." His eyes become teary. "Just like he adores you."

Mommy shakes her head. "You're crazy."

"You won't call me crazy when I save you from your living end!"

I get off the sofa and run to the stairs. Mommy calls after me, but I can't stay down there. "Now look at what you've done!" I hear her shout. "Your six-year-old son is absolutely terrified of you! You of all people should know that he needs to remain calm!"

I come to the second floor and dive into my safe place, shutting the door. I look up to see Teddy on a high shelf. I can't reach him, so I use my superpowers to get him down. He knows I'm sad and gives me a big hug. I like him and other animals because they never get angry when they're around me. I cozy up with him in a corner. It's dark and small and we cry together.

I then see a tiny bubble of light watching from above, and it makes me happier. But I still hear them arguing downstairs. They are coming closer.

"Just look at his eyes!" Daddy shouts. "It's like they're mutated or something. We already know what he's capable of."

"Oh, for Christ's sake. If you'd actually spent some time with him, you'd know he's incapable of hurting a fly."

"Even if it was an accident, we should still be worried."

"We should be proud that we have a son so gifted. The boy is an angel, Luther."

"Yeah? And what if he turns out to be a killer? We heard about those girls with the military—how dangerous they can be. They have the same mutation!"

Mommy groans. "Delve all you want into your drunken delusions. It's your fault you can't see that he might save the world someday."

Daddy laughs. "And you're saying I'm deluded? You may brush this off with that nonsense, but I'm taking him next door. He's gotta own up to what he's done!"

More yells, then I hear loud footsteps up the stairs. I hold tight to Teddy. He's coming to get me.

"He needs to rest. He has a fever!"

"He's probably hiding in that damn closet again!"

I'm shaking when the door opens. I feel dizzier than ever. Daddy calls my name, but I don't move. He grabs my arm and starts to drag me, but Mommy stops him.

"Get out of my way, Marilyn."

"Don't you dare lay a hand on him!"

"It needs to be done. He's a danger to us all!"

"The only danger is your failure to recognize the work of God."

Daddy becomes quiet. I get up with Teddy and stand behind Mommy. He says, "*Now* of all times you bring that up?! Have you looked outside lately? Just open the damn door. God is dead! Or if he's not, then he sure as hell doesn't care about any of us anymore. Look at what he's done to our planet." His eyes turn to me. "Look at what he's done to my only son."

He stomps forward. Mommy fights to stop him, but he wrestles her away. She falls on the floor, crying. He tries to grab my arm again.

"Come here!" he shouts.

"No." I pull back and shake my head.

"Come with your father. That's an order!"

"*No!*" I scream with all my might.

Daddy flies through the hallway and tumbles behind Mommy. The whole world is now quiet. When he opens his eyes, he looks confused but then becomes very angry. He doesn't like that I used my powers.

Mommy pants. Her lips don't move, but I hear what she's saying: "*Run, my love. Head out through the door. I'll meet you by the river.*"

I race past them. Daddy leans in with his arms, but I'm too quick, and I hurry down the stairs. There are shouts from behind. He's chasing after me.

"You're dead!" he yells when I make it to the first floor.

I run to the door as fast as I can and turn the handle. I begin to go through, but I stop with a gasp as Teddy falls over the edge. I have to grab the frame to keep from going with him.

I can't believe what I'm seeing: the house is high in the clouds.

On the earth below is a huge, green forest. The trees look tiny from where I stand. I glance back, but Daddy isn't chasing me anymore. The fire is out, and I'm all alone. I don't know what's going on. I stare at my little hands and cry.

The sky soon catches my attention. The sun is setting fast, and once it disappears under the horizon, the moon rises from the other end, bringing the night with it. The moon sails across the starlit sky, sets in the same place, and then the sun is born again. This cycle repeats over and over, spinning faster every time, until the sky looks like a giant wheel where dark and light blend together.

With every second, I grow a little taller. My legs become longer. My hands appear bigger. And PJs are replaced by flowing white robes. I realize that the world is beautiful, yet I can't stop crying. The only other sound is that of the wind.

Something . . . *shifts.*

~

My adult mind came back to me at once, and with it the years of loneliness and grief. I felt no longer in the present but burdened by past memory.

Hearing footsteps behind me, I twisted around. My father descended from the second floor, but he was not the least bit angry. Coal no longer stained his face; it was glowing with natural color, and he appeared heavenly in robes of light. He halted at the foot of the stairs to gaze at me with warmth and pride.

"Where is she?" I asked, tears falling from my eyes.

He smiled. "You will see her again."

"I'm so sorry." I let out a sigh.

He put his hand to his heart, and I felt an energy in mine. "Open your eyes, my son."

As remembrance trickled in, I yearned to go back in time—to stay in her arms when everything was right. But I knew that I had to return. Someone else needed me.

I looked to the sun, which rested in the sky, then back to my guardian angel. He nodded in encouragement while I reminisced of another old song my mother used to sing.

"Butterflies are free to fly," I whispered, closing my eyes.

I jumped.

~

"Samuel, open your eyes," a voice sang through my mind.

Dizziness. Pulsating. The feeling of drifting.

Voices reverberating from some far-off world.

I received the impression that I was beginning to awaken but was caught between two planes of reality. A moment passed, and I inhaled sharply. My eyes were wide open, yet I could hardly see a thing. A small sliver of light, however, was enough to detect a familiar face a few inches away. We were lying on our sides, staring at one another.

"Evelyn." I smiled. "I'm here. I'm with you."

I hoped that she would smile back, but there was only sadness.

"Open your eyes," she said.

With great remorse, I remembered: the doe, the hunters, and the blows that knocked us out cold. Right on cue, the back of my head throbbed painfully. I could barely move. We were crammed into a tight space, our hands and feet tied with rope.

"What happened?" I asked, scanning the darkness. "Where are we?"

She did not answer. She just gazed sorrowfully.

"Evelyn, are you hurt?"

Still no answer. Her breathing grew heavy. And I started to get very worried.

"Hang in there. I'm going to get us out of here!"

I positioned my legs above my chest and thrust them against the barrier. It didn't budge; it was made of metal. We seemed to be in the trunk of a vehicle.

I heard the hunters talking outside, their voices getting louder and louder.

"Come on!" I urged her. "We've got to do it together!"

She shook her head. Tears fell from her eyes.

"What's going on?" I asked. "You are hurt, aren't you?"

"Please wake up, Samuel. I really do love you!"

Doors slammed shut before the engine ignited. The acceleration of the vehicle slid us apart, but I wriggled my way back next to her, proclaiming, "I love you too! I love you with all my heart. I'm sorry I've never said it before, but I swear that it's true!"

Save for more tears falling, there was no reaction.

"Evelyn? Can't you hear me?"

She squirmed forward and somehow passed through my body. I rolled over, incredulous, seeing somebody else with us—a young man, comatose. She pressed her face against his and whispered, "Why won't you open your eyes?" It was dark and small, and she cried alone.

It was then I realized I had left my body. And my limbs were tied by nothing but my own mind.

With this epiphany, I discovered my inner light and drifted outside with zero resistance. I stared up at the sun in the sky, then down at the vehicle taking us to a place we did not belong.

Inside the trunk, I simultaneously felt Evelyn kissing me. I was in two places at once, though I experienced an immeasurable oneness—for only on the brink of death could we transcend ourselves in ways unimaginable. For some reason, I understood this now. There was no fear in this oneness, no doubt in my abilities. I willed the wheel to move ever so slightly, steering the vehicle off the dirt road and down a steep hill, headed for a tree.

I opened my eyes. And she smiled at seeing me.

Then came a thud, causing hers to close.

~

In the time that followed, there were no dreams, visions, or mystical states. I was simply in and out of consciousness, though with a clear sense of being dragged out into the light. I heard myself gasping for breath, fighting to stay awake, but my vision was blurred, and an invisible force kept bringing me down to darkness.

Eventually, there came a harsh prodding in the middle of my forehead. The ringing in my ears was supplanted by a voice of fear: "He's starting to wake up!"

As sight returned, I found myself staring down the barrel of a rifle held by the skinny hunter. Immediately, his fear became masked by rage. Insanity flickered in his eyes, blood dripping from a swollen face. And his rifle trembled.

"Don't you move, or I'll send a bullet through your skull!"

I didn't bother to try. I was confined within my body, my back against a rock. But it wasn't me I was worried about. My heart raced as I recalled the absurdity of what had happened. I darted my eyes from side to side, praying they would not find what I feared the most.

"He awake, Raymond?" yelled the burly hunter, Jim.

"For now he is."

"Well, this one isn't!"

"Bring her over here."

The breath left my lungs as I caught sight of the wreck nearby; their vehicle had sped downhill from the road and crashed into a thick tree. What hope I had left lay in unbearable limbo as Jim carried the girl I loved out from the trunk, visibly unconscious.

I couldn't help but shout her name, though this didn't cause her eyes to open.

Raymond nudged his rifle against my cheek. "Don't talk unless we tell you to, boy!"

As Evelyn was plopped down next to me, I was relieved to find that not only was she breathing, but there were no bruises in sight, nor blood. She was simply asleep—just as I was previously. It was as if we had taken each other's places, and I wondered if part of her was watching from another realm.

Jim aimed his rifle at her, appearing even more frightened than his partner. "Yeah, she's alive. But if you try to make a move, I won't think twice!"

"You did that, didn't you?" Raymond spat.

Evelyn's life was now in my hands, yet all I could do was cough up blood. "Did what?"

"You know what. You wrecked our truck! Because I sure as hell didn't turn the wheel that way. You know how rare those are these days?" His rifle shook more than ever. "I should pull this trigger right now."

Something told me not to be afraid. I pressed my head confidently against the barrel, growling, "Do it then. And see what happens."

"I told you, man," Jim said nervously. "These kids are like wizard demons or—"

"Shut up!" yelled Raymond, reinforcing his glare. "I don't care who you are or what you can do. All I know is that you should be begging for both of your lives right now."

"If you so much as touch her again, it is you who will be begging," I countered, my voice quivering.

"It ain't our fault the girl is unconscious now, is it?"

This broke the façade. Overwhelming guilt sank in. And as much as I played up my abilities, I had no idea what I was going to do or how we would stay alive. I looked to the side and prayed for Evelyn to open her eyes.

"That's right," Jim asserted. "We heard her speaking before that wheel turned. The rumors are true, then—*dangerous*, your kind."

I was forced to give in, my eyes watering as I spoke. "Please, she needs assistance. I'll do whatever you say as long as she receives it. What do you want from me?"

"That's more like it." Raymond grinned, relieved at my weakness. "Lucky for you, we're merciful men, and we can try one more thing before putting a bullet through your head. See, we've got connections, so Jim here is gonna head up to the cabin and send out . . ."

Although his lips continued to move, I heard less and less of what he was saying. The entire outside world was gradually drowned out by a bizarre static from the back of my brain, like an untuned radio. Just when I thought I was having a stroke, a live transmission leaked through:

"Do you believe in miracles?" asked the voice of a girl before the static cleared suddenly.

". . . if you're lucky, they'll agree to fly over here and take you off our hands. And if not, well, I hope you've said your last prayers. Understand?"

I was too puzzled to speak, trying to figure out what that message meant and where it came from.

Raymond jabbed me again with his rifle. "Don't make me change my mind. Do you—"

"Hello!"

At the disarmingly carefree voice, the hunters spun around, as bewildered as I was.

It was the same strange girl I had met by the stable, wearing white Facility robes and cheerfully waving while she approached. She had appeared from out of nowhere, passing by the wrecked vehicle yet curiously oblivious to the current situation. When catching sight of me and Evelyn, however, she stopped in her tracks and feigned a surprised gasp.

"I'm sorry to intrude. I didn't realize you were in such a pickle!"

The hunters glanced at each other with mouths wide open before clumsily pointing their guns. "Where in God's name did you come from?" shouted Raymond.

"The forest." The girl shrugged. "Anyways, I was just in the area, and me and my birdie friends heard a loud boom, so I came to check it out. It's probably none of my business, but I'm a pacifist, if I have to be honest. What did Gandhi say, exactly? An eye for an eye will leave us all—"

"Do you want to die as well?" Raymond snarled.

"Not particularly." She sighed. "At least not at this moment, because we all gotta kick the bucket eventually. Truthfully, I was hoping one of you two lovely gentlemen could spare me a cigarette. But if you're too busy with . . . whatever you're doing, that's fine!"

Raymond fumed while fixing his aim. "What kinda game are you trying to play, girl?"

"Oh, don't think it's any game. It's an addiction! Quite a nasty one, really."

"Are you out of your damn mind?"

"Just a little." She grinned, fearlessly taking one step closer. "But more than anything, I'm in dire need of a smoke!"

Jim joined in: "Well, we don't have any cigarettes. I haven't seen one of those in—"

"She ain't here for no cigarette, you dimwit," his partner intervened. "She's one of them. Just look at her eyes."

"Why thank you!" She beamed. "I know, I know—they are quite beautiful, if I must say so myself." Indeed, they glowed a magnificent green. She turned her gaze to pierce right through me; in that moment, we connected on a very deep level. I felt as if I had known her for much longer than I could consciously remember. Earrings shaped like golden spirals glinted between strands of black hair, correlating with the cuff on her wrist. She winked at me playfully before continuing to the hunters, "You two are not my type, I'm afraid."

Raymond snickered. "Well now, beautiful friend, I'm afraid, for you, this is the end."

As he was about to pull the trigger, she flung both of their guns twenty feet away with a mere wave of her hand. The hunters froze in shock, and the girl seemed thrilled. "Is that a Doors reference?" she exclaimed.

They raced for the rifles and hit an invisible barrier. Raymond stuttered while Jim looked like he was about to pass out. "Wizard . . . demons . . ."

"I'm sorry for the scare," she said, retrieving a box of matches from underneath her robes. "But a song of theirs has been stuck in my head all day. How does it go again?"

"Light," she began, striking a match. "*My . . .*" Her voice grew louder, stretching with the flame in front of her.

With a howl, Raymond brandished a hidden revolver. This time, he pulled the trigger.

It jammed.

The girl smirked ruthlessly, finishing the melody in her mind. "Fire!" she shrieked, spreading the flame forth to engulf the two men, who proceeded to burn alive before my bulging eyes. I watched in horror as they wailed, rolling in the grass until their skin was charred black. Finally, their bodies lay still in release.

Meanwhile, mine was shaking. Evelyn remained soundly asleep. And the strange girl strolled up, blissfully unaffected by the scene she had just caused and bending to untie our bonds. She gave one more mischievous wink, as if this were truly all one big game.

"Now do you believe?"

CHAPTER 7

THE GIRL KEPT humming her song while she worked on the rope, seemingly in her own little world where she could play with fire all she wanted and death was merely a joke. A shard of glass floated over from the crash, and she used it to saw at the ropes. She was unnerving in both attitude and ability. Only several feet away lay the men she had killed mercilessly.

"There we go," she said as she loosened my hands. "You're a free man! I don't know if you remember me, Sammy, but we met a couple days ago when you were napping on the grass, before that whole . . . fiasco. Anyway, in case you forgot"—she extended her hand—"my name is Luna."

I had no time for greetings. I was focused on Evelyn, untangling the knots around her feet and wrists. Once freed, I took her hand in mine, still trembling. I caressed her hair with the other, pleading softly, "You can open your eyes now, Evelyn. They're gone. I'm here for you."

They didn't budge, even as I continued whispering her name. I examined her head, but there was no wound to explain her comatose state. Luna attempted to join in before I slapped her hand away.

"Okay, I get it. You don't trust me," she said. "But that was quite rude after saving your lives."

"We don't know that you did," I replied.

"They were going to kill you."

"They were trying to turn us in."

"Oh yeah? To where? You were dead either way, sweetheart. I know these things. And yes, maybe I lied a little bit back there, but I promise I'm a pacifist like ninety-nine percent of the time. I made an exception because these guys were asking for it. I was just trying to help them burn some karma, if you know what I mean."

"By burning them alive?" I asked, terrified.

"Only their bodies. Their souls will thank me. The birds were really adamant that I needed to save you guys, even if it meant making a couple sacrifices in the process."

Clearly, this girl was out of her mind, though extremely psychically gifted, which made the situation all the more unsettling. I was compelled to stare into her extraordinary eyes, seeking to drill into them as they did mine—but it was of no use. Aside from the distinct feeling that we knew each other, I had no idea of her true intentions. She seemed purposefully closed off to any further connection.

"What's wrong with her?" I lamented, gazing sorrowfully upon Evelyn. I had no choice but to rely on this stranger.

"I'm no doctor, but I'd be happy to help, Sammy!" Luna ran her fingers over Evelyn's scalp. She cracked open her eyes, then analyzed her breath with curiosity. Finally, she nodded to the wreck. "According to my diagnosis, she blew her mind out in a car. Didn't notice that the light had changed, sadly."

I fumed. "Do you think this is funny?"

"On the contrary, I think it's rather morbid, but I'm trying to cheer you up, honey. Life is far too serious to be taken seriously. On the bright side, she still looks pretty—unlike you. Her breathing is normal. Her pulse is steady. And it's quite a miracle that she doesn't have any major physical injury." She placed a hand on Evelyn's forehead as if feeling into her mind. "Unfortunately, this seems to be something deeper—an issue on the spiritual level. And she doesn't appear to be waking up anytime soon."

"She has to!" I took Evelyn by the shoulders, shaking her gently. "You don't understand."

"I understand enough to know that shaking her probably isn't going to help."

"Then what will? Isn't there anything we can do?"

She sighed. "You really care about her, don't you? Evelyn is her name?"

I nodded. "Yes. I love her."

"Luckily for you, I know a place where we can take her. It's precisely where I was traveling to, believe it or not, before this little detour. And if you're not rude to me, I can let you join in on the adventure."

"What kind of place is it, exactly?"

"They call it Sanctuary. It's a safe haven for pacifists like us. Also, there's someone there who I know can help her. I'll explain more later. For now, let's get her out of this mess, shall we?" She gestured uphill. "These hillbillies have a cabin close by. We can stop there and see if it has anything useful."

I hesitated, glancing at the charred bodies, then reluctantly agreed. Although I should have been much weaker after the accident, a latent strength made the girl I loved as light as a feather. Cradling Evelyn in my arms, I followed Luna up the hill and away from the disturbing scene. I knew perfectly well that she could be lying. She was clearly dangerous and possibly insane. But with Evelyn in this state, I took a leap of faith.

From the road, the cabin came into view; presumably, this was where they took us while I was similarly unconscious. Nausea overcame me, but Luna remained untroubled. "Looks like we've found ourselves a new home, honey!"

I shook my head in disbelief, shifting direction toward a nearby oak tree. "I'm not going in there," I said as I rested Evelyn under the shade of the branches. "Killing those men and then looting their cabin just doesn't feel right."

She frowned. "Fine by me, mister morality. You can be the lookout. But I'm sensing there is something inside that can assist in our adventure."

"Did the birds tell you that?" I asked dryly.

"No, just my brain. We have a full day ahead, darling, and we need all the help we can get. Anyhow, I'm heading home now. Call me if you need me!"

Those words sparked a memory of our meeting by the stable, and my eyes went wide. She had been aware of the rabbit then, which meant she was in some way linked with the forgotten experiment. And she was aware of even more than that.

"You knew!" I shouted as she turned her back.

She spun around with a tolerant expression. "Knew what?"

"The attack of the black robes. You told me they were coming. And the next day, they came and slaughtered everyone." I glared at her impenetrable eyes, recalling the ease with which she'd burned the hunters alive. "You're with them, aren't you?"

"Oh, don't be like that, Sammy."

"It's Samuel. In fact, how do you even know my name? I've never mentioned it to you. And yet you magically show up at the Facility and tell me that right before the attack."

"Ugh. How boring. But okay, *Samuel*, let me ask you a question: do I look like I'm with those bald-headed psychos?" She put on a cheerful smile. "There's a reason why I was out here all alone. Why I refused to join them and was heading to Sanctuary. Plus, I quite like my hair."

"Then how did you know?"

"Because I'm a badass psychic, sweetie," she said telepathically. She continued aloud, "Same reason I know your name. But even if I saw them coming, I had no clue about the horrible things they would do. You may not believe me. All I'm asking is that you trust me."

"I don't." I sighed. "But I guess I have to."

"That's what I like to hear!" She beamed. "So, I'm gonna leave now, Sammy. I'll bring back the goods, but I don't know when. Then, if you're still by this tree—which you should be, if you trust me—I can tell you more about our little adventure. Just stay put and be patient, darling!"

She pranced off toward the cabin, leaving me struggling to make a decision. It was difficult to trust a girl so unusual, and I still couldn't help feeling she was connected to Walter's killers. Nonetheless, I had to do what was best for Evelyn, even if it meant taking a risk. As crazy as it all seemed, Luna offered a glimmer of hope.

"She did save our lives," I finally admitted to the unconscious Evelyn, only beginning to scratch the surface of the shock.

I sat in the shade next to her. She was sleeping surprisingly peacefully, though I fretted each breath might be her last. I held her hand. Then I positioned her heart-shaped locket above the one still beating. I didn't care that my face was bleeding. Using my thumb, I brushed the dirt from her cheeks. Afterward, my mind replayed every single action that led us here, from following the doe to moving the wheel while out of body.

One thing became clear: it was my fault that Evelyn was unconscious. This dread had no outlet and boiled up inside.

"I'm so sorry. She spoke to me—the doe. And I'm such an idiot for running after her." I wiped tears from my eyes. "She had the voice of my mother."

I had lost Walter, and now Evelyn's life hung by a thread. If God existed, then surely this was some sick joke. I sobbed quietly beneath the branches of the oak as the sun rose in the sky. The birds sang all the while.

I whispered to Evelyn, "I got you into this position, but I promise I'm going to get you out. Please, just keep breathing. I can't do this alone." I squeezed her hand, hoping at the very least that her mind was in a good place.

~

It took a while for Luna to return. But when she did, she was rolling a wheelbarrow.

"You didn't run away!" she exclaimed with glee as she approached. "Lucky for you, Christmas came early."

I stood and noticed that the wheelbarrow was filled with cloths and blankets, as well as two satchels with shoulder straps. "You found those in their cabin?"

"Of course I did. It's a reward from the universe for being so moral. And just look at all the goodies I packed!" She tossed me a satchel while going through the other; they each held several apples and an empty jar. Mine had a flimsy flashlight, while hers carried a pocketknife.

"Santa doesn't usually get me knives for Christmas," she said with a wink, "but I've been a *bad* girl this year."

"I get the knife," I demanded. "You can get the flashlight."

"You promise not to stab me with it?" she asked. I maintained my glare until she swapped. "Fine. But just remember, I still have my matches!"

"Where did you get the apples, anyway?"

"They had a tree out back. Can you believe it?" She pulled out a red one and took a large bite, grunting with satisfaction. She then released her grip, but instead of falling to gravity, the apple hovered toward my mouth. "You want a taste? They're so juicy!"

I gagged from the memory of my last session with Walter. "I'm not hungry."

"Oh, Sammy. I know you don't like stealing food from dead people, but it's the least they can do after trying to kill you." She grabbed the apple and nodded to the wheelbarrow. "Not to mention, we found a new home for Evelyn!"

"In there?" I asked, though she was already stacking blankets.

"How else do you expect to carry her on our adventure? Not with your skinny arms. And it's not like I can just levitate her the whole way. It's harder than it looks, you know."

I sighed, lifting Evelyn into the wheelbarrow and removing her sandals. "Just lead us to this Sanctuary place, please. She needs a healer."

"All we have to do is follow the river, and it will guide us straight there."

"Okay. So how do we get to the river?"

"I don't have the slightest idea." Luna smiled toward the woods. "But the birds do! You can find it if you listen to them closely. I was almost there before they told me to save you. Now, come on. We need to get off this road and go deep into the forest."

~

The world became absurd with Luna by my side as I navigated Evelyn between the pines. For hours I observed as the strange girl communicated with strange birds, mimicking strange noises in the process. I had so many questions for her, but I didn't know if I wanted the answers, and she was unlikely to provide a straight answer anyway. All that mattered was that our lives depended on this girl.

The forest appeared to go on forever. I tamed my thirst with the promise of fresh water, though a part of me felt unworthy of this comfort while Evelyn slept. With every bounce of the wheelbarrow, I prayed for her to open her eyes—to snap out of her reverie and tell me about an extraordinary dream. After some time, I recognized the futility. We continued until I was lightheaded, and Luna demanded to take over.

"Only I push her," I argued.

"You need a break," she maintained. "We should switch off every few hours. Don't worry, honey. I promise she won't die on me."

It didn't take much convincing; I was physically and mentally drained, while Luna remained energetic and lively. Though my patience was waning, I saw no other alternative.

"How much longer to the river?" I asked as Luna took the wheelbarrow. "I thought you said we were close."

We came to a large tree. Instead of answering normally, she made several high-pitched squawking noises. I would have given up right then had three little birds not landed on a low branch, chirping back at her. I wondered if they were truly conversing or if I was hallucinating.

"Such nice birdies," she said after they flew away. "A bit flirty, though, don't you think?"

I lost touch with reality. "What did they say?"

"They said that this forest is a high-energy vortex. It is one of the last preserved remnants of Mother Earth's beauty and therefore carries a very powerful frequency. The rules act a little looser around here. Time and space are malleable and changing. So we can't have any expectations regarding the river, but if we have faith, then we'll arrive sooner rather than later."

I stared blankly. "The birds said that?"

"In their own birdie way, yes. They're very in tune with this kind of stuff." More chirps came from above, causing Luna to laugh. "They also say that being so cynical won't help anything. Trust me, Sammy. Trust the birdies. Everything is gonna be all right."

We walked for a few more minutes. I then paused to regain my sanity.

"Luna?" I called after her.

She swung around, smiling. "Yes, Sammy?"

"All this talk about the river, the talking birds, and a sanctuary where Evelyn can be healed. It's . . . it's all real, right?"

She slapped her thigh sarcastically. "Oh, you caught me. It's an *imaginary* river filled with chocolate, and instead of fish, there are strawberries! And it will lead us straight to the chocolate factory, where we'll meet Willy Wonka and live off gumdrops for the rest of our lives. You happy?"

"Willy . . . Wonka?" I inquired, my brain as scattered as ever. "Is he the one who can heal Evelyn?"

She stared quietly for several moments. "Yes. Yes, he is. Now cheer up, Sammy. Walk free, come with me, and give yourself to nature's melody. Because birds don't talk—they sing, silly! And that language is universal."

Leading the way with Evelyn, Luna spoke more of her relationship with the earth and her telepathic connection with its creatures—especially the birds, whom she termed her spirit animals. Considering that she'd said the same of the rabbit, I didn't take that too seriously. And in spite of her eccentricity, I realized how wrong I was to judge. Before long, I found myself divulging our encounter with the doe and how it first led to a lake of higher energy.

"How did you feel when that happened?" she asked.

"Hope. Like someone was looking out for us."

"Emulate that state, and we will find more water. Except this time it will come as a guiding river."

"But following the doe ended up getting Evelyn into this position," I said, confessing my stupidity in having run straight into the hunters.

"Well, maybe, just maybe, this is exactly where you need to be. Right here, with me, and with your lover soundly asleep. Just have faith, Sammy. Faith is often far more farsighted than we are led to believe."

Though I had difficulty accepting her words, at that precise moment, a radiant blue feather spiraled down from above. Together we watched as it rocked gracefully in the wind, settling miraculously on Evelyn's chest, right beside her heart-shaped locket. I felt Walter's presence near me, urging us to pay attention to signs and synchronicity. I recalled what Evelyn said about trusting the heart. And for a cherished second, I rose above my fear and doubt.

"Feathers fall around you," sang Luna, a hand above her own heart, "and show you the way to go." She had a beautiful voice, much like Evelyn, adding dissonance to the notion that she had just killed two men. She picked up the feather and handed it to me. I continued to clutch it for the rest of the day's journey.

I refused to eat, and a frenzy took over from lack of water. But even as I grew tired and dizzy, I walked with purpose through the twilit forest, leading with my heart and listening to Evelyn breathe steadily.

Finally, when the sun hung low in the sky, the songbirds started singing louder and louder. Luna laughed and tapped me on the shoulder. "They're excited," she said.

"Excited for what?"

"For us to find what we've been looking for."

Sure enough, as the woods parted, sounds of saving grace surfaced below the singing. But even when I saw it, I wasn't certain it was real—a gorgeous river about fifty feet across, flowing between the trees as far as the eyes could see. We stopped beside it, and Luna beamed as I let out a tremendous sigh of relief.

Then Evelyn's breath began to quicken.

~

The river was fresh. Its water was healing. I hoped it would be healing enough.

Luna lifted Evelyn's head while I gently poured gulp after gulp down her throat; surprisingly, she swallowed it fine. *Let this water open your eyes,* I repeated in my mind, trying to connect on a spiritual level, clinging to the blue feather. It took three full jars for her breath to settle. We waited anxiously, but she remained snug in her wheelbarrow, stuck in a dream.

Luna smiled softly. "She was probably just thirsty. She must have sensed the water."

"And yet she won't wake up," I said with remorse.

"I told you that this is some deep stuff, sweetheart. Far more than just an afternoon nap. Luckily, until we get to Sanctuary, I can whip up some of my famous applesauce and feed her like our own little baby—perhaps put on a diaper while we're at it."

I glared at her. "Please don't tell me you still think this is funny. We cannot take each of her breaths for granted."

"*Okay*, Sammy. The healer is down the river."

"Then let's go!" I shouted emphatically.

Swinging the satchel over my shoulders, I pushed the wheelbarrow along the grassy riverbank, powered by pure will. I was still very thirsty, having had just enough water to inspect its quality; but it felt better to deny the satisfaction. Luna urged me to rest more, but I didn't care. I left my heart, went back into my mind, and chose to stay there.

I didn't make it another hour, however, before collapsing. I struggled to rise, but my body wouldn't let me. I wanted to cry, but no tears formed in my eyes. As a hellish migraine arrested my psyche, all I could do was lie on my back and stare up at the darkening sky.

Luna bent down with a jarful of water, lifting my head as she had with Evelyn.

"Drink," she said. "There is no purpose in torturing yourself." And so I gave in, guzzling the water in a matter of seconds. She refilled it in the river and brought it back, but right as I reached for it again, she splashed it all over me. "Wash your face too, for goodness' sake!"

I sat up and wiped the water from my eyes, annoyed yet somewhat replenished. "How long until we get there?" I asked.

"Could be several hours, or it could be several days." She shrugged. "Time cannot be trusted, and the birds can only take us so far. We must put faith in the river."

"Luna?"

"Yes?"

I knew the answer before I asked it. "You've never actually been to Sanctuary, have you?"

She seemed offended for a moment before stopping to think. "Well, technically not physically, but I've seen it through psychic visions." I looked down in disappointment, but with a telekinetic force, she helped me to my feet. "I was right about the river, wasn't I? So please continue to trust me. I'm keeping my promise that I won't let her die."

I barely slept that night, lying on blankets by the water. The trauma I'd been suppressing crept up on me, not only regarding events of recent days but also from memories of my life before the Facility. Dreams were fleeting—akin to nightmarish delusions—and I awakened violently to listen for breathing, praying that I wouldn't lose the love I had left. The feather had already disappeared from my grasp, blown away in the wind.

It was then I noticed a faceless figure, composed purely of shadow, staring down at me. I tried to fight it off, yet it wouldn't let us be, prowling menacingly until dawn.

~

For three days we persisted on our journey, pushing Evelyn along a river winding through the forest but ultimately leading nowhere. Hope diminished quickly during this time. The shadow continued to torment me.

For three days I remained agonizingly awake to the world, increasingly far away from the girl lost in a dream.

On the first day, all my worries seemed acutely amplified. I subsisted on adrenaline, eating scarcely enough to survive. My concern lay in how to get Evelyn a basic amount of nutrition; I was thankful to the river in this regard, which provided lush vegetation near its bank. And I was surprised at Luna's apparent expertise in a natural world so foreign to me.

She harvested wild berries to supplement the apples. "These look like elderberries," she said of several purplish clusters growing amid the green. "They're incredibly nutritious. Plus, they taste so tangy they just might wake her up."

"Or kill her," I contended. "Are you sure they aren't poisonous?"

"Don't worry. I'm almost ninety percent positive." She grabbed a handful and popped them all in her mouth at once, swallowing uneasily, then smiling with colored teeth. "Yep, these definitely aren't the deadly kind."

We filled a jar to the brim with ripe berries and used the knife to mash them. Although the gooey mixture did not go down as easily as the water, it was encouraging to know that Evelyn could receive nourishment while comatose. A diaper thus turned out to be necessary, in the form of cloths wrapped around her groin, which we would later wash in the river.

"She's *peeing*!" Luna exclaimed when it first happened. "Her bodily functions are working normally."

I was left nodding vacantly, unconvinced that my lover pissing herself in a wheelbarrow was anything to get excited about.

My guilt grew larger with every hour she remained in that state. I was taking her to a place I wasn't sure even existed, depending on the visions of a girl I couldn't fully trust.

"Have faith," Luna repeated for the tenth time.

As much as I tried to feel it again, it became more difficult when the day went by with nothing in sight. There was no sign of civilization on this eerily preserved section of the planet. It would have been beautiful in any other situation; instead, it was just depressing.

I sensed the shadow lurking in the forest, waiting to greet me once more. The sun set into darkness that night, undeterred by my will to remain in the light.

On the second day, my mind became numb to the world. It was a fight against exhaustion and apathy as I took my turn wheeling

Evelyn downstream, feeling powerless to change anything. As I watched her sleep, my life seemed a tragic comedy. I wallowed in the fact that everyone I loved had passed because of me.

Luna must have noticed something was wrong, because she did her best to distract with random monologues about trees and animals.

"Do you think unicorns still exist?" she questioned at one point. "Because they say all the unicorns are dead, but I think there might be a few left out there! You know, sometimes I think I was born a unicorn, only trapped in a human's—"

"Please!" I couldn't stop myself from yelling. "Please, Luna, just stop talking."

I expected a sarcastic response; rather, she gazed down silently. From that point forward, the shadow became more daring, coming out from the forest to dance along the corners of my eyes, even in broad daylight. I slapped myself to stay awake and keep from going insane.

We took a break soon after. While Luna foraged for berries, I carried Evelyn into the river. A few steps put me waist-deep in the cool water, and Evelyn floated on the surface, her hair pulling toward the current. "Sail on, sweet girl," I sang, though I was never good at singing. I didn't even know what I was doing, relying on old religious tales of being cleansed through water.

Nothing changed as I moved her back and forth. We were just soaked. Yet it was uncanny how comfortable she seemed, as if she were happy to remain in a timeless dream. I felt a little mournful over the thought that she was not fighting to see me, but this was selfish. In waking life, she often struggled to breathe.

Luna looked on with quiet concern, her jovial personality absent for the time being. She still didn't speak as I carried Evelyn from the river and laid her among the blankets in the wheelbarrow.

"Maybe she's trying to show you something," she said finally.

I stared at her dubiously. "Show me what, exactly?"

"That life is only a dream. You decide how you want it to be."

I shook my head and strapped on my sandals, dispelling the idea that her coma had a deeper meaning. It was clearly a result of the accident. And the accident was because of me. We endured until nightfall with the birds silent and the shadow following constantly.

On the third day, the outside world collapsed inward on itself, choosing to mirror my darkness. Clouds blotted out the sun, and the breath of the earth grew dense and chilly. We trudged along an endless river that likely led to oblivion.

No matter what we did, my love would not awaken. Meanwhile, I was so deprived of restful sleep that my brain couldn't filter reality. Gone was the distinction of truth from illusion; within from without; this life from a dream. So maybe Luna was right.

I knew that she walked with me, helping to guide and care for Evelyn, but her voice was muffled by a menacing wind. With this wind, the shadow spoke in hisses, taunting me for hours, further draining my energy. *"She will die because of you,"* it whispered repeatedly. *"And you will die soon after."* Every so often, I turned my head and looked at it directly—a figure void of inner light, of love, of empathy. It spoke of evil things and had soulless vacuums where its eyes should have been. And soon, I started to believe it.

Too tired to fight any longer, I sensed this demon gradually taking over. It was late afternoon when, out of the blue, I lost it completely. My vision sharpened. My heart rate quickened. Hyperventilation kicked in, yet I felt like I couldn't breathe.

I stopped pushing Evelyn immediately. As I hunched over, growling in defiance, tree branches seemed to bend around me. I squeezed my eyes shut and backed away, afraid of what had been potentially unchained.

"Samuel. You need to relax."

It was Luna, her arm raised delicately, approaching calmly and steadily.

"I can't," I said with shaky breath. "I think I'm having a panic attack."

"Take charge of your thoughts. Discipline your emotions."

"You don't understand. It's not that easy!" My hands trembled with an energy too overwhelming to hold back. "I could never control this part of who I am." A rock by my feet shot off at speed, narrowly missing Luna and clanging against the wheelbarrow. For once, she appeared stunned. But I knew what had to be done.

"I cannot risk hurting another."

I ran into the river and swam to its deepest point. Then I closed my eyes, letting my body sink slowly. Although I felt the shadow follow after me, it was repelled by the water, cleansed by its higher frequency. A moment passed, and I was lost in a chain of memories, evoking the serenity of my mother's womb, listening to her gentle heartbeat. I remembered her smiling down on a sofa, comforting me while I was ill, and my father growing enraged during an altercation but ultimately appearing to forgive me. I gazed upon the earth from a house high in the clouds, diving into my astral form before the decisive accident.

Despite not knowing what was real and what was a dream, I knew it all had a significant meaning. I was aware then of a greater plan. And in the silence of the river, I thought I heard Evelyn whisper: *"You are not to blame,"* she told me.

I opened my eyes with newfound recognition. Something gold glinted on the outskirts of my vision. But before I could look, an invisible force pulled me up to breathe. The air tasted sweet as Luna assisted me to shore.

As soon as we made it, she put her hand on my forehead with a touch like fire.

I collapsed in her arms.

~

For a second I rested in darkness before waking to the universe. Although the sun was again setting, the sound of the river was everlasting.

I sat up on the grass with an unusual sense of peace. The shadow had vanished, so I was fully present at last. Evelyn lay in the wheelbarrow close by, breathing perfectly fine, and in front of me crouched Luna, assembling a firepit out of stones and branches.

"Welcome back," she greeted with a wink.

"How did I get here?" I asked calmly.

"You went a bit bonkers and almost drowned in the river, so I pulled you out and soothed your mind by emitting a frequency that you ended up matching. Are you feeling better now?"

"I am, actually." I nodded. "How long was I unconscious?"

"Thirty-four minutes," she answered with odd precision. "Sorry about that, but you were kind of a loose cannon."

I couldn't be angry, for I knew she was right. I stayed quiet for some time while, with the branches in the middle, she arranged the stones in a circle using only her mind. I watched as if I were a visitor on this planet, coming down to study the habits of human beings— except Luna wasn't all that human.

When finished, she stood and stared with sharp intensity. "You must know, Samuel, that killing yourself won't do any good for your soul."

"I wasn't trying to kill myself," I replied honestly.

"You were underwater for a pretty long time."

"I just wanted to reconnect with who I truly am."

"Is that so?" She smirked. "And how'd that work out for you?"

"The shadow people are gone."

"Oh, how wonderful. And here I was thinking that *I'm* the crazy one."

Miraculously, I laughed.

"Truthfully, I don't blame you," she continued, combing through her satchel. "The energy of the forest will force everything to the surface. It can be a struggle to integrate, but either that or you go insane. It is crucial to make peace with your karma and allow the river to wash it away." Locating her matches, she took one out and struck it against the box. "Hell, burn it if you have to."

The flame grew in her fingers, just as it had during our encounter with the hunters. Her eyes likewise ignited as fire sprang toward the branches; within moments, it became huge yet evenly contained, lending warmth to a cold day thankfully soon to end.

"I can't create fire out of nothing, but I sure can control it," Luna proudly remarked, marching to the river. "Now it's time for dinner."

I got up and stood by Evelyn as Luna halted in the shallow end.

"What are you doing?" I asked. I received only the sarcastic assurance that she wasn't going to drown. Minutes passed with her staring into the water. Suddenly, a glistening fish leaped out, landing on the bank to die instantly. She picked it up and brought it over, amused by my look of incredulity.

"No need for fishing poles when you have telekinesis!"

Luna used her masterful powers to rotate the fish above the fire. Meanwhile, I took care of Evelyn, quenching her thirst and washing her hands and feet. I desperately wanted to say something—to tell her how strong my love was and how it would never leave. But I simply cherished the feeling, hoping that what I'd heard in the river was more than just a product of insanity. Light flickered on her heavenly face as the moon reflected the last of the sun's rays.

Luna floated the fish to me once it was properly cooked. "Dinner's ready, sweetie!"

I stared at it uneasily; with glossy scales and bulging eyes, it hovered about like a restless spirit. "You can have some first," I replied.

"I appreciate the offer, Sammy, but it's not something I can eat."

"Let me guess: fish are your spirit animal?" I chuckled.

"Don't be ridiculous. Actually, I'm a strict vegan. It comes with the pacifism."

"But you killed the fish." I didn't even mention the hunters.

"Do you honestly think I let him transition without asking permission first? I can see that you haven't been sleeping, and you're hardly eating your apples. You need protein! And this brave rainbowfish offered himself telepathically, if only because he saw firsthand how crazy you were earlier." She sighed. "Such a selfless little guy, but sometimes individuals must make sacrifices in order to serve a higher purpose." The fish poked against my cheek. "I demand that you eat! Or would you prefer to die before Evelyn wakes up?"

She had a point. I very well might have been closer to death than the girl who could not open her eyes. But perhaps these trials were meticulously designed to help me appreciate the beauty of life, guiding me to where I needed to be. I grabbed the fish and settled by the fire, scouring for meat to pick off its bones.

I said, "Maybe there is a higher purpose. Maybe there must be sacrifices. But it's hard to have faith in something greater than yourself when destiny always seems so unfair. Throughout my life, everyone I cared for has died right in front of me. Either that, or I lost them through other means." I shook my head, thinking of Noah. "All I know is that I can't let Evelyn suffer the same fate."

Luna gazed from her cross-legged position across the flames; even in comparison, her eyes were dazzling. They were not quite as beautiful as Evelyn's, but they were certainly more striking. These eyes signified she could do great things. And though it was difficult to talk about my past, I sensed that she was reading me, her light colliding valiantly with my shadows. I suspected that she was already aware of everyone I had lost and all I had been through.

"Samuel, do you know how I first heard about Sanctuary?"

"Yeah, I get it. You're super psychic. You saw it in your mind."

"I won't deny the first part." She grinned. "But technically, it wasn't my mind I saw it in."

I froze with a handful of fish at my mouth. "What are you talking about?"

"I saw it through the mind of my sister during a shared, lucid dream. She heads Sanctuary. We've been able to enter each other's dreams ever since we were little, but then we . . . we lost touch for a while." Her eyes became watery for the first time. "She came back to me, Samuel, right when I arrived at the Facility. She didn't only tell me about Sanctuary. She warned me about the attack of the black-robed children. That's how I knew."

I was unsure of how to handle this new revelation. "You didn't mention anything about your sister, Luna. Why didn't you tell me this earlier?"

"Let's just say you're not the only one who's had a rough past with family, losing those you've held dear. There's a reason why I know how to survive in these woods. And why I was almost grateful when the military took me in. But Johanna is forgiving—she always has been. Plus, the children she's raising are absolutely amazing. According to recent dreams, they're already prepping for our arrival. All we have to do is follow the river."

"How old is she?" I asked with curiosity.

"Older than you and me. One of the first new youths."

"Until a few days ago, I didn't realize there might be anyone older. And what about the healer?"

"She didn't tell me much except that there is one child in particular who can cure any malady, be it a burning fever or unending sleep." She gestured to Evelyn. "My point is, Samuel, that you are always in touch with those you love, even if it isn't on a conscious level. You may see them in dreams every night and simply not remember. We all have this ability. Johanna and I are just able to do it lucidly. Once you are awake to the rules of your reality, you gain powers unimaginable."

An apple from her satchel flew into Luna's hand. She bit into the fruit while I ate the fish, which tasted delicious after days of self-starvation. While I chewed on its meat, I processed what she was saying. I barely knew anything about her, but I felt in my heart she was telling the truth.

"Evelyn did mention how our loved ones never leave," I recalled, gazing tenderly at the sleeping beauty. "You know, while I was in the river, I thought I heard her speak."

Luna's eyes lit up. "She was obviously trying to reach out to you! She's still very much aware. Her consciousness is just existing at a different frequency. If you want to reach back, then allow yourself to rest deeply. She cannot get through if you refuse to forgive yourself and truly let go of all that fear."

I stared peculiarly at Luna. It felt like she was channeling Walter, displaying wisdom and maturity beyond what I believed her capable of. With this epiphany, my mind drifted through parallel realities in which she'd never shown up: if not murdered, we would have been sold back to Mabus and the military; or perhaps I would have turned into a monster, adorned with my own black robes, defeated by the shadow of guilt and anger. Instead, there was hope that Evelyn would open her eyes, as well as the promise of sanctuary from a war between the two sides.

"Luna, thank you for saving our lives. Multiple times." I sighed, my eyes on the fish. "I don't know where we'd be without you."

She smiled, her cuff and earrings both gleaming in the fire. "I've been secretly waiting to hear those words. But you know, you still haven't answered my question."

"What question?"

Through telepathy, a memory surfaced of being threatened by a rifle and hearing a girl emerge through static to ask about miracles. It took a few seconds to readjust to the present.

I said, "I guess it's to be determined. If Evelyn wakes up, then I'd certainly believe."

"That's where you are misled, Samuel. You say you're afraid that Evelyn will suffer a terrible fate, but at some level, we are the writers and conductors of this symphony called life. Don't let it be decided by an external power. *Choose* to be part of the miracles you see in every moment. The same flame of creation that burns fate into the stars also rages within you."

I pondered this carefully. "What does that mean, exactly?"

"It means that worrying obsessively will only reap dead weeds. Manifest the miracle you ask for—of her awakening and recovery—by taking that marvelous energy of yours and turning it toward the light."

Just as an image began forming in her eyes, she looked away, urging me to continue eating. But even with an aching hunger, I felt more fulfilled by her words, the words of a girl whose brilliance seemed balanced by eccentricity. Something told me she knew a lot more than she was letting on.

I finished the fish in silent gratitude while she fed Evelyn her blend of berries. Afterward, I drank clear, clean water and, as implored by Luna, used a bristly twig to clean my teeth. My beard had grown, my ribs were showing, and my eyes felt heavy, surely weighted by dark circles. If I wanted to keep my promise and manifest a miracle, I had to start taking care of myself.

Near the river was a crop of wild lilies. I plucked one and placed it behind Evelyn's ear. "I'm sorry I almost abandoned you," I whispered. "I will be by your side until you awaken. I will stay strong, and I will stay sane. And never will I become so severed from love again."

I took her firmly in my arms, lifting her from the wheelbarrow to rest her on a blanket by the fire. I lay next to her and stared at a starlit sky suddenly free of clouds. There was a constellation I identified as Orion's Belt, from what Walter taught me, but what my mother used to call the Three Sisters. I perceived the stars as holes of light in a galactic tapestry, all ultimately shining from a single flame. I wondered if they wrote our destiny or if it was possible to rearrange their order.

Either way, I was thankful that my heart felt open once more, with space to grow and bloom. It yearned to heal all the suffering in this world and to help the caterpillars hatch from their cocoons.

The shadow visited later that night, but I was ready to recognize it as a part of me—that monster in my mind I had feared for so long. It crouched over us as it called out in need. I hugged it until I went to sleep, crying tears of release.

CHAPTER 8

ON ONE END of the earth, snow-covered hills lined the distant horizon.

On the other end were fantastic pyramids built upon desert sand.

I stood at the balance point, forming a trinity, inexplicably naked in a meadow of flowers. Directly in front of me was a small, circular lake shining with higher energy. This lake looked familiar, though in a different setting than I remembered. There were no birds, no trees, and no gentle stream. The only sound was that of the wind.

I stretched my arms and breathed it in, glad to be alive. Strangely, however, I couldn't recall what I was doing here. I would have pondered this further had I not been distracted by the sky: it was brilliantly blue yet granted no sun, leaving me to wonder where all the light was coming from.

I walked to the edge of the lake, the stillness of the water providing a perfect mirror. In it I saw my image: my face was clean, my body lean and wiry, my eyes glowing with inexhaustible energy.

That there, I thought with a smile, *that is me.*

The lake did not merely reflect the sky; a hidden design emerged. Shimmering swirls of gold and violet materialized in the background, the swirls themselves composed of geometry beyond words, branching into smaller yet similar patterns. As I leaned into the stillness, I thought I could sense the whole of existence.

Crystal-blue eyes flashed in front of mine. I stared, on the verge of a greater realization, until a ripple in the water shattered my reflection, and everything was forgotten.

I traced the ripple to the center of the lake, where more of them spread in concentric rings all the way to shore. There rose a woman who was not fully human; with sparkling white skin and feathery wings, she could only be described as an angel. She didn't seem to notice me as she turned onto her back, floating gracefully on the surface of the water.

I did not care to think or analyze. Already, I was mesmerized. There was a hole in my heart that I couldn't explain. And I desperately wanted to meet her.

As luck would have it, a rowboat rested nearby, halfway in the lake with oars on each side. Moments later, I was on my way to the angel, steering the boat smoothly despite having no prior experience. I felt secretly aided by a mystical power and imagined that I was rowing to heaven.

Only when I drew closer did I see that this was no ordinary angel. Her overall complexion was unnaturally pale, and she had snake-like features and silky hair. Moreover, her extremities were webbed like those of some reptiles. Nevertheless, she was beautiful, with outstretched wings evidencing her divinity. I now found it odd that they were feathered. It only added to the intrigue of this being, who appeared to be sleeping.

I anchored the boat and called out, "Hello there." I received no answer. "Wake up," I pressed. Still she slept. With slits for ears, perhaps she couldn't hear.

A whisper of logic told me to stop, but it was overtaken by curiosity. I grabbed an oar and poked her wing, prompting a burnished feather to break free and drift in the wind. It fell right into my cupped hands, and I grinned at the astounding serendipity. Then I looked back toward the angel, who had twisted her head to glare directly at me.

Her eyes were large—even larger than mine—yet deprived of any apparent light. There was a force to them that pulled me in before I broke the connection, determined to row back to shore. That's when I realized that two other angels had latched on to my oars.

The boat shook. I heard myself scream. And I was dragged underwater by these devilish beings.

I kicked and fought, but they were strong, bringing me down into a seemingly bottomless lake. The third one circled menacingly, her wings flapping. We soon halted, and she swam within a few feet. Already feeling weak from lack of breath, I couldn't help but surrender to her huge black eyes. Like spheres of infinite gravity, they were quick to suck me in completely.

Somehow, there existed a universe inside, with holes of light burning through an unfathomable darkness. I recognized them as stars in our galaxy. And in a spellbound trance, I saw myself as a wave of energy, zipping from star to star through a web of electricity. As this occurred, each star flashed its light to encompass the planets around it. Although somewhat scary, it felt necessary, for life not only survived but also became altered by it.

With one last jolt, I shot through a wormhole and arrived at our planet, watching from a place outside of time. I was shown terrible scenes of war and destruction: Earth's landmasses being blasted by radiation; enormous forests swept away, depriving her of oxygen. But then something peculiar happened—a subtle transformation quickening her aura and setting off the light of the sun.

This became too much for me to handle. I snapped out of the trance and let out a shriek, prompting an uncanny discovery that I could, by some means, breathe underwater.

Acting as a fish, I escaped the grips of the submarine angels, swimming in one direction faster than I thought possible. I didn't know how I could do all this, but regardless, I was no match for the three entities. With their extraordinary wings, they toyed with me, zooming past and trapping me in a vortex. With their infinite eyes, they sucked all the light from the watery surroundings until their pale bodies were all I could see. Suddenly, I was floating again in the vacuum of space, wandering aimlessly.

Circling me, they closed in.

I lowered my sight in defeat, wishing they would just let me be.

Only then did I perceive that everything I thought was me—my torso, limbs, even my head—had vanished into the vacuum. Incredibly, I no longer felt my body, though my awareness was pristine. I was wistfully reminded of a far-off dream with a beloved tutor teaching me the philosophy of a man named Descartes. Even beyond the realm of thought, there was a greater magnificence to who I truly was.

A golden energy erupted where my heart should have been, freezing the entities in place. I looked up to find that the surface of the lake perfectly reflected our image below. We formed a triangle with an inexhaustible light at the center; that light was me. Burning crystal blue for a fleeting moment, I finally gained a sense of clarity.

I rose toward my reflection at an unmatched speed. While I ascended, my physical frame projected out of the golden energy. With little time before the entities caught up, I stretched my arm above the surface of the lake.

"Evelyn," I whispered.

Lightning burst out of the cloudless sky and struck my fingers. Miraculously, I was not injured. Rather, my body served as a prism, funneling the electricity into my arm and out through my heart, filling the lake with a spectrum of color all the way down to its bottomless depths. Startled, the entities scurried away. And a great wave emanated from the lake's center, carrying me graciously out to shore.

All I could do was laugh as I glided into the meadow, breathing the air once more.

I stood and shook my head in amazement. While the preceding experience was exceedingly strange, the clarity about it swiftly faded.

I then noticed that one of the entities had ridden the wave with me. The same one I'd seen floating on the lake initially now lay by my side. Obtaining another feather that had separated from her wing, I offered it to her, trying to make peace.

Instead, she grabbed my ankles and yanked them out from under me. Fear intensified as I was dragged back into the water. I raised my arm again to the sky, praying to God for more lightning. This time, a hand grasped mine. Then another, tender yet determined. The balance shifted, and I was pulled out from the lake, free from the hold of the black-eyed creature. Seemingly outmatched, she averted her gaze and finally flew down and away.

I turned to my saviors. They were two hooded figures, a man and a woman, wearing flowing robes of light. Their eyes were veiled, yet their auras were undeniable, exuding a warmth so palpable that I was dry within seconds. Although they weren't quite God, they were certainly divine. It soon became clear that these were the true angels.

I rose to my feet with awe and admiration, albeit a bit embarrassed to be naked. "Thank you," I said earnestly.

They smiled from beneath their hoods. *"Twist your head around,"* replied the woman telepathically.

I did as she advised, and what I saw only added to the chain of miracles. A bridge began forming out of nothing from where I stood, a wooden path and golden railing arching over the water. Assembling itself rapidly with no explanation but magic, its quality was otherworldly. It reached its apex at the center, then curved down to the opposite shore.

I looked back, and the hooded figures were gone. In their place were my robes and sandals, resting among the wildflowers. I dressed in a daze, then stepped onto the bridge, not daring to stop and analyze. Even as the entities leaped out and clashed against the railing, I was no longer afraid. I walked across a bridge supported by no physical means, knowing that I was protected. Plus, the wings of the entities would not work above water, however hard they tried. I sensed the workings of a transcendent mind governing the rules of our reality.

I hit the verge of lucidity at the bridge's zenith; I saw who stood at the other end.

Evelyn!

Overcome by passion, I shut down any part of my brain that made me question or feel pain. The only thing that mattered was that she was here with me, watching from the shade of a single cherry blossom tree. I sprinted the rest of the way, calling her name.

I was breathless when I arrived. Looking into her eyes created a moment that stopped time. With her heart-shaped locket and silver robes, she was the girl I had always known, yet her soul glowed within those blue windows. I immediately came to recognize that she, too, was unquestionably divine.

"Samuel, you came." She had a knowing expression.

I nearly cried. "You listened."

"I've always been listening." Her face grew a tad melancholy yet still radiated affection. "How was your swim with the angels?"

"They're not angels, Evelyn. Those things are more like demons!"

"They're black-eyed angels," she replied. "They show you what you need to see and make you experience what you need to experience."

I told her about my vision of space and my incredible escape—culminating with being saved by two beings of light—while Evelyn clutched her locket emotionally.

"They're here with me, Samuel. They've been keeping me company so I am not so lonely. And they are telling me of what is to come."

"I'm here with you now, so you don't have to be lonely." I took her hand from her locket and placed it on my chest. "See?"

She surveyed my eyes solemnly. "You don't remember, do you?"

A hint of dread crept from within. "What don't I remember?"

She pulled back her hand and softly wept while cherry blossoms flurried around her. It pained me to see her suddenly unhappy. I forgot how to talk, so I started to sing:

"Do you realize,
That you have the most beautiful face . . ."

But it had no effect, and I was not nearly as good of a singer as Evelyn. She continued to cry as rain fell unexpectedly, dripping from the branches and mingling with her tears. On impulse, I leaned in for a kiss, only to be denied.

"Not the time, Samuel."

I became extremely remorseful, though I couldn't say why.

"I did something stupid, didn't I, Evelyn?" I tried in vain to push through the blockage of memory. "I don't know exactly what I did, but whatever it is, I just want to say that I'm sorry."

She gazed with glossy eyes. "For what you are speaking of, you are forgiven. You simply need to remember and focus on your mission. That is of far greater importance. The events have been set in motion, but there are dark forces that wish to put an end to it." She shook her head and sighed. "You cannot stay, Samuel. As much as I want you to."

Something didn't feel right. My vision blurred for several seconds. I already knew the answer, but I didn't want it to be true. "Why can't I stay with you?"

"Because I am in danger."

"Danger?" I questioned. "What kind of danger?"

"They wish for me to be enlightened so that I will never sleep again." A terrible scar flashed across the middle of her forehead. "It is time for you to wake up."

The wind accelerated to hurricane force as thunder roared and rain poured down. I was thrust back instantly from the eye of the storm—until realizing the eye was Evelyn herself. I desperately resisted, and yet I was no match for her. I had no idea she held such power.

"Please!" I begged. "I don't understand!"

I thought she would give in, but the storm didn't wane. She paced forward unwaveringly with her soul ablaze and masses of flower petals spiraling around her body. With each slow step, I helplessly slid back, becoming filled with panic when reminded of where I was headed.

There was one more miracle as I glanced over my shoulder: the lake had been replaced by an undulating opening, a portal to another dimension—a dimension that held our physical existence and the endless river of time, whose flow was pointless to resist. I stared with revelation into Evelyn's eyes, knowing it might be my last chance to see them, before letting the astral wind carry me away.

When stumbling over the edge, I cried out her name, extending my hand up in prayer.

She grasped me just as her angels had, with a strength belied by her slender frame. And so I found myself in an impossible limbo, hanging between two realities.

"What should I do?" I asked, tears falling. "I feel so lost without you."

She transmitted her thoughts through the wind and the rain: *"Follow the river and trust it will take us to our true home. Look to your heart for all the answers. You have the spark of the creator within you."* Our grip slipped until we were holding on by fingertips. Then came a shared understanding that our bond was everlasting. "God, I've missed those eyes of yours. Be brave, my love."

I dropped into the portal and out through the night sky, tumbling down to the earth, toward a young man dreaming.

∼

I came awake with my entire body pulsating as if it had been struck by lightning. The fire was out, so I sat up in darkness, panting heavily, struggling to adjust to the present reality. I had slept for hours, yet the sun still lingered over more grim parts of the world. Even the moon was nowhere to be found, its comforting radiance smothered by dark clouds.

My dreams had been moving and uncanny, but I could not say for certain that they were more than fantasy. As I ran my hands over my tingling scalp, the images were already slipping through the pores of memory. Nevertheless, I held tight to cherished fragments—her eyes, her smile, the presence of true angels—refusing to let them fade into nothingness.

After my panting settled, I listened closely for more breathing beside me, from the Evelyn I knew genuinely existed. All I heard was the unending river.

I reached to where she should have been but touched only dirt. *No. Where is she?*

Even the blanket she had lain on had vanished. I combed around in a frenzy and found only my satchel, which unfortunately was of no use; Luna's held the flashlight. I forced in a breath, attempting to calm my racing heart with a rational explanation.

"Luna!" I shouted. "Luna, wake up!"

I waited anxiously but received no answer. And there was not a speck of starlight to help me see.

I climbed to my feet and immediately felt dizzy. The girl I had finally started to trust, who claimed she was trying to help us: had she done all of it for a nefarious purpose? Had she waited for me to finally fall asleep? Had she . . .

"I am in danger," Evelyn had said in my dream.

I nearly vomited, but it was no time to panic. I had to be brave for Evelyn, even as tears trickled down my cheeks. Despair turned into anger as I wandered barefoot through the void.

"Luna! Do you think this is a game?! Do you think this is—" A bird of the night wailed overhead, sending a shiver up my spine and out through my breath. "This isn't funny."

I gasped as I subsequently stepped on a stone, slightly puncturing the skin of my sole. As I brushed it with my toes, I realized with horror that it wasn't what I thought it was.

My heart plummeted as I bent down to pick up Evelyn's locket—the locket that immortalized her parents, the one she had treasured for as long as I'd known her. It was just lying there.

I shook and sobbed, wishing this were a nightmare.

"What have I done?" I asked no one.

And then it came—the sound of a girl giggling.

I was ready to explode with rage when it dawned on me that the laugh wasn't Luna's. It sounded too pure, like that of a girl who had not spoken for quite some time, charmed by her own voice.

"Who's there?" I called out hesitantly.

"It's me, Samuel," Evelyn answered in my mind.

Astonished, I scanned my surroundings, finally making out the shape of the wheelbarrow.

I approached it hesitantly and spotted movement.

Tears continued falling, but this time in wonderment. Thought escaped me altogether as I halted over a resting body. She was lying on her side with her back toward me, buried under the blanket. I placed my hand on her shoulder and carefully turned her over, whispering her name.

I was captivated by open eyes, yet they were not crystal blue; they were large and sinister, the ones from the day of the massacre.

She laughed a wicked laugh while I stood stupefied.

"We found you, we found you," said the voice over and over, gradually distorting into demonic tones.

I was grabbed from behind and tossed onto my back. My body ached to fight, but I was paralyzed; all I could move was my neck.

The fire suddenly ignited again, revealing two teenagers in thick black robes approaching with menacing grins.

"I told you, Tia," said the boy who killed Walter. "He is fooled by cheap tricks. He prefers to be a victim of his pitiful attachments."

Their horde of followers rushed in from the shadows, forming a circle around us with fiery gazes and vicious smiles. The only one showing remorse was a gentle-looking boy, who despite his shaved head was still recognizable by the light in his eyes, forever bright, yet utterly terrified.

"I'm sorry," Noah whispered as Tiana took Evelyn's locket out of my trembling hand.

CHAPTER 9

I STRUGGLED.

I screamed.

Nothing alleviated the crushing psychic weight. I gazed around in anguish, hoping to gain some sympathy. Most of these children were young. Several I could identify from the Facility. But Noah was the only one I could call a friend, feeling my pain as I felt his. And it was my fault he was with them. It broke my heart.

Tiana giggled again, Evelyn's locket now around her neck, while the boy flaunted his pyramidal amulet.

"How amusing it is that you try," he taunted, his eyes mirroring the scorching flame.

"You monster!" I roared. "Where is Evelyn?"

"Perhaps you can tell us that," he coldly replied. "We found her in quite a morbid condition. She appears to be sleeping but barely alive."

"I swear, if you hurt her, you die!"

He scoffed at me while his followers laughed on cue. "You care so much for a child of the old breed. Your audacity is charming, and yet you *both* are at our mercy. So might I suggest choosing your next words wisely."

My body shook like an animal in chains. I craved for lightning to come from above and strike him where he stood.

"I think it's time for a proper introduction," he continued, crouching over me before grasping my hand. "My name is Matteo."

My consciousness was abruptly hijacked by the dragon on his wrist, as if it were a separate entity. A deathly energy flowed from it, bringing me gruesome memories. I saw a woman suffocating on a bedroom wall and an arm stretched toward her, marked with a matching dragon. Next, a girl, her head speckled with the regrowth of hair, being shoved from behind, made to dig her own grave. Then finally—and most disturbingly—Walter's throat being slit open from the perspective of his killer. I peered into my own terror-filled eyes and jumped back into the present, tears streaming as Matteo finished with scorn, "Though haven't we met before, brother, under brighter skies above?"

"You're a murderer," I whispered. "You killed him. You killed everyone. You and your brainwashed followers."

He laughed, leaning closer. "How deluded you are. You assume that we don't know anything about you. Yet you know as well as I do that you're capable of the same."

A beast within me shrieked with rage. I jerked my head forward and butted him on the nose, drawing blood. He reeled back. Tiana glided over, but Matteo motioned her to stay.

"It's all right, sister. Let him bathe in his resentment, believing he is somehow different."

"I am nothing like you," I growled with conviction.

"You really think so?" He stomped on my gut violently and watched with a bloody grin as I wheezed in agony. "Show me then, Samuel! Show me what you can do!"

I wanted to kill him right then, and something told me I could. But Evelyn's influence superseded my shadow, urging me to rise above.

Matteo snickered and addressed his followers: "He knows nothing about himself or his place in this world. We offered him freedom, yet he lives in a cage, rejecting his divinity in favor of shame. He fails to comprehend that those he suffers over have no purpose on the new earth anyway." He strolled forth to stare into the fire. "He doesn't even know the origins of the girl he puts his trust in."

My chest heaved with animosity. "Luna did this, didn't she? She betrayed us and told you where to find us."

"Luna?" he repeated mockingly. Several of the older kids chuckled. "How misled you are, brother."

He gestured to his sister, who disappeared into thin air. It took only seconds for her to return, dragging the girl I suspected was a traitor. Except much like Walter before he was murdered, Luna's body and mouth were tied by rope. Moreover, there was no struggle as she was thrust before me. The look in her eyes—sorrowful and afraid—said everything, sparking the realization that she couldn't have been part of this.

"Aleister!" Matteo called into the crowd, which parted to make room for a young boy with a wounded shoulder who gave me a vengeful glare. This was the boy I'd caught choking Salazar the day of the massacre, who I thought had been killed by Lieutenant Hernandez.

He too carried behind him a hostage—though not by physical means. All eyes were on Evelyn as she hovered in the wind, stiff as a board, facing the sky.

I leaped to my feet. My first instinct was to charge at the boy, until I recognized the damage that action would cause. Matteo smirked as he stood next to him, the hostages positioned at each side. "Don't worry, he's quite gifted—prodigious, actually. The trick is to nurture it from a young age, an opportunity you've unfortunately chosen to waste." He gazed smugly at Evelyn. "Besides, we thought the wheelbarrow was rather depressing. Maybe now she'll have dreams of flying!"

"Just let her go," I heard myself say, feeling numb and powerless to change what was quickly developing into the same situation as with Walter. "She doesn't deserve this. Neither of them deserves this."

"It's a pity that you hold to such foolish beliefs. Luckily, I can see things more clearly." He pulled out the dagger that had shed Walter's blood. "Let's play a game, shall we? It's called who should live and who should die—the unevolved Evelyn or the backstabbing Madeleine?"

"No!" I cried out, hardly registering the unfamiliar name.

Children cheered as I lunged toward him, only to be quickly thwarted, choking on my own tongue. "Thank you, Tia. Some people like to spoil all the fun." Matteo smiled at his sister, who, with eyes ignited, clenched me in her psychic grip. "Yet we shouldn't be rude. Why don't you give Samuel a more comfortable view?"

Something struck me from behind. I was swept into the wheelbarrow, which rolled on its own toward the other side of the fire. By a miracle of black magic, its wooden handles bent inward like rubber, compressing my neck until hardening again. *"Behold our true power,"* Tiana transmitted, happy to keep me fighting for breath as her brother stood above the one I called Luna.

"Oh, dear Madeleine, what should we do with you?" he snarled, brandishing his dagger. "Now, in spite of what Samuel here thinks, only we are aware of the misery she deserves. She plays games with the mind, sucking others into her web of deception while she plans their demise. It's no surprise that she refuses to even give her real name." He sighed while Luna gazed down tearfully. "She is truly an exception to those of us blessed with the eyes of evolution. Hence it would be a joy to watch her bleed, especially given her . . . family history. But then again, we've killed her before, haven't we? Regardless of how she survived, what devilish contracts she was forced to sign, it might not be as enjoyable the second time around."

He approached Evelyn, who floated innocently with her silver robes hanging. I let out a suppressed howl, frantically trying to pry apart the handles, but Tiana tightened her hold.

"As if it's not obvious which he prefers." Matteo laughed as I gasped, helpless and dizzy. "Although personally I'm not a fan of bestiality, I can't completely blame you, brother. Ten years in that place where they taught you to be a slave, treated you like a lab mouse—it's easy to fall for a lesser being when you think so low of yourself."

He continued his heartless lecture while I entered a delirious state. Right as my vision started to dim into unconsciousness, my eyes fell to Tiana's neck and Evelyn's locket. Inexplicably, I sensed it speaking to me, pleading to be returned to its rightful owner. Hopelessness became fury as angels slowly loosened my throat.

". . . I have to admit that she is quite pretty—a *diamond* among the old breed, I dare say," Matteo said. "Sadly, the poor thing is half-dead anyway. And how's that old saying go, again? What good is a jewel that ain't still—"

With a scream, I erupted like a flaring sun, sending out a shock wave of energy from my heart. Startled children were shoved back; many fell down, including Aleister. Evelyn remained completely unaffected, protected by the unseen.

I hopped out of the wheelbarrow, breathing smoke. A swarm of followers were ready to counter until Matteo signaled a halt. "Let it be just him and me." He grinned, aiming his dagger at the hovering beauty. "Now we know how to get it out, don't we?"

I swiped my arm and flung him away from her. The crowd gasped as he slammed against the ground, dropping his dagger. He rose gleefully with madness in his eyes, quick to dismiss his concerned-looking sister. "Not yet, Tia. You'll disturb the symphony. Let his hatred grow. Let his anger rise!"

"You murdered Walter!" I cried savagely.

"And I'd happily do it many more times."

I shook hands with my demons and let them take over. Soon after, the wheelbarrow went flying at him. He dodged it confidently while those behind him dove out of the way.

"*Very good, brother,*" he said telepathically. "*Now it's my turn.*"

I stepped back warily, the fire between us growing threefold in an instant, then watched in shock as it developed a face and arms. It soared for an embrace and set my robes aflame, sending me stumbling to the ground in panic. I howled and writhed and remembered the hunters while my skin blistered hellishly. I wondered in disbelief if this was truly my time to die.

"All I wanted was a little appreciation!" Matteo shouted as he stalked toward me. "For saving you from that prison, giving you a chance at self-liberation! If you had any sense, you would be bowing at my feet rather than picking a fight you cannot win. The only reason you're still living is because we recognize the mark of divinity!"

He snapped his fingers, and everything vanished. There was no more pain; my robes had never been aflame. There were bizarre burn marks on my palms, but otherwise I was fine.

"All I wanted was for you to realize the power of your mind," he finished, sneering. "How tragic that you cloud it with so much illusion."

I sat up and stared into his unsympathetic eyes, something greater coming through me after feeling like I had died. "I don't know who or what made you this way, but you're not the person you think you are, no matter how hard you try. Many of your followers might be fooled by the mask. But all I see is a frightened little boy." He frowned uneasily. "It's never too late to choose the right path."

A fist struck my cheek; he pounced on me, enraged, holding me down with one hand around my neck and the other on the amulet engraved with the Egyptian eye. "I am *enlightened*," he hissed, and I swore that his pupils became vertical slits.

All I could whisper back was one word: "Why?"

He stood angrily and marched toward the hostages. "Tia, it's time."

A sharp pain arose in the middle of my head, as if my own brain were being compressed. I clawed at my skull, groaning in distress, overwhelmed by an uncanny sense of dread.

"Neat trick, isn't it?" said Matteo while I stumbled to my feet to meet his sister's glare. "Psychokinetic manipulation of the organs, directed at the third eye, rendering you essentially powerless. For now, you really are no better than a slave!"

I charged at them but bumped against a psychic barrier, then again and again, each attempt more pathetic than the last. The children were laughing. My vision was blurring. And the pain stubbornly persisted. I focused in and saw Matteo retrieve his dagger through telekinetic means, then pace between Luna and Evelyn. Forcing a scream, I struggled to bring out that murderous side of me—yet those demons were suddenly sound asleep.

"What a shame it is, sister. So much potential, squandered on filth. He's never had a sibling that shares his gifts, so instead he resorts to befriending animals." He halted beside Evelyn and put the dagger to her throat. "Any child born within the last twenty years without our eyes stems from a bloodline that is tainted and impure. You may enjoy the scent of her, but deep down you know this to be true. We are the new breed, brother. Her DNA is of no use."

On the verge of surrender, I closed my eyes, praying to any higher power. Every memory I had with Evelyn played in my mind over the course of seconds. I saw her when she was seven, holding my hand and smiling with those blue eyes. Then a decade flew by, and she was leading me to the forest with the village burning. I must have kissed her a thousand times. But now it was all over. And I'd never even told her how much I loved her.

"No."

It was little Noah, stepping forward with quivering legs to the jeers of several others. Matteo glowered at him.

"*What* did you say to me?"

"Please, master. Please not her."

After an excruciating few seconds, Matteo lowered his dagger. Just as I managed a breath, he pivoted unexpectedly and threw it at Noah, freezing it in the air inches ahead of my friend's astonished face. "You dare question your savior in favor of the one who abandoned you? Have I made an error in letting you live?"

"Matteo." Appearing by Noah was a girl a few years my junior who had previously seemed invisible. I recognized the telepath I had met on the caravan right before the attack. She was clearly held in higher esteem, for Matteo contorted his mouth slyly while they carried out a silent exchange.

Then he proclaimed, "Selena here has made me reconsider. It is time once again, my marvelous friends, to free the soul of Madeleine."

"Because if anyone is going to kill my sister," Selena muttered as she grabbed the dagger, "it's going to be me."

My jaw dropped open, and Luna responded with tormented whimpers as Selena approached. I wanted to do something, but the barrier was strong, and the horror of it all left me frozen. No other child risked getting in their way. Some looked as sickened as I felt.

I braced for the worst as Selena raised her weapon. Luna's eyes widened, and I heard a muffled cry. Here was another who would die while I watched, paralyzed, only hours after speaking of purpose and sacrifice.

But Selena drove the dagger into the earth in front of her. "Come on, Maddie, did you really think I would kill you?" she snarled, to a few nervous chuckles. "What's the need when you're already dead to me?"

Luna sobbed uncontrollably. Her younger sister appeared eerily unconcerned as she returned to the group, catching my stare and whispering three words: "Don't trust her."

"This display of weakness has been entertaining," announced Matteo. "Be grateful, Samuel, that I have chosen to be merciful.

Now take the imposter and your filthy lover and go starve yourselves to death with Johanna's commune of hippies, because we know that's where you're headed. But while you're hiding away, we'll be at the capital, finishing what we started. Believe me when I say we're in the midst of a war. It's kill or be killed, and they'll be begging for breath. You'll be sorry you missed your chance to join the revolution."

He retrieved his dagger and motioned to Aleister, who roughly dropped Evelyn on the grass.

"Though it would be improper for me to leave without a parting gift."

"What are you doing?" I shouted as Tiana reasserted her hold on my brain.

"Just helping the poor thing to awaken." He crouched and abruptly carved the blade into Evelyn's forehead. I yelled and fought with everything I had left, but my energy was utterly spent. She moaned with anguish as he penetrated her skin, blood seeping across her face in a sight too terrible to bear. When he'd finally finished, the fire illuminated a pattern underneath, mirroring the symbol on his pyramidal amulet. "Now she'll always have one eye open." He grinned maniacally. Tiana came to his side.

Their defenses dissipated, and I dove at them, deranged. Right as we were about to collide, they vanished without a trace. Their followers scattered back into the shadows, leaving our trio stunned and broken on the brink of dawn.

$\sim$

For a moment I seethed, letting the hatred pass through me. I wished this were the dream, that I could awaken to a healthy Evelyn smiling from beneath the cherry blossom tree. But there she lay, gasping in pain, her eyelids fluttering. Raindrops peppered her face but did not alleviate the bleeding.

I hurried to grab a cloth that had fallen out of the wheelbarrow and pressed it against the wound, my mind bursting with a million emotions. I cursed. I prayed. I promised violent revenge, then professed my love through tortured tears, struggling to cease my focus on darkness. Her skin was as pale as I'd ever seen.

I hardly noticed when the girl I called Luna squirmed over to us. She reached for Evelyn with her arms still tied, and I swiftly caught her by the wrist, staring into her eyes.

"You *lied* to me," I said bitterly before piercing through to her soul as deeply as she would allow.

In it, I saw shadows like mine. Traumatized as a child. Disowned by family. The energy was so profound that I broke away, overwhelmed. She then stretched her hands toward the suffering Evelyn, humming a vibration while emanating golden light.

This light was healing, enveloping the wound and soon stopping the bleeding so that I was able to wipe it clean. Evelyn's face relaxed as she settled into steady breathing. All that was left was a terrible scar formed in the shape of an eye.

I exhaled hard, thankful we'd made it out alive. But I wondered if Evelyn felt her locket missing, and I made a quiet vow to retrieve it by any means.

It took some time to untie Luna's bonds, and it reminded me of what she'd done for us after our capture by the hunters. Once freed, she didn't immediately speak. Instead she slid the golden cuff from her wrist, revealing a black dragon underneath.

"I'm so sorry," she said, crying softly.

We sat in silence for the next several minutes as the rain rinsed Evelyn's blood from the palms of her hands.

～

Luna continued to weep as we gathered our belongings. Meanwhile, I fought an internal battle between anger and empathy.

The sight of the river swayed me toward the latter. I briefly allowed it to take my pain. On its edge, the wheelbarrow bobbed like a rowboat, but the current refused to carry it away. Other than handles bent by sorcery, it was miraculously intact.

We quietly packed it with blankets and lifted Evelyn from the wet grass. Despite the noticeable absence on her chest, her heart kept on beating. And though the huge scar was admittedly upsetting, a blade could never harm her spirit.

The rain was fleeting; in place of the clouds came the sun of the morning. Luna sat below Evelyn to watch the dwindling fire. I settled beside her, waiting for her to say something.

She fiddled with her cuff before clearing her throat.

"I'm obviously not proud of it. We knew each other since we were kids. I didn't know they would turn out to be—"

"Murderers," I finished for her.

"Yes," she sighed, "but it's more than that. There was comfort in the fact that there were others like us. A brother and a sister whose parents had abandoned them, of the same age, with the same eyes. Same supernormal abilities of the mind. We were shunned by what was left of our shattered society and met each other at the perfect time. At first, I thought it was fated. Soon, I felt I was falling in love."

"With Matteo?" I asked.

"With Tiana," she replied. "She was never much of a talker. But there was this aura about her that was spellbinding."

"So, what happened?"

"It started as a game: discovering our nature, honing our abilities. But as we grew older, they became obsessed with the idea of dominion. They perceive it as destiny that most of the population perished before we were born and see it as their divine right to rule over the ones who survived—at least, anybody without their eyes. Johanna saw through them quickly and tried to stop me from getting involved further. But I was brainwashed by their lies." She choked with remorse. "We performed strange blood rituals. Contacted negative entities. Anything to gain more power. We were still only children, going down such a dark path."

"It's okay, Luna."

"No, it's not! I abandoned my mother, Samuel. And both of my sisters, when Selena was very young, just like our father did before me. Our mother fell ill; she wasn't right in the head. And I left them to deal with it."

Sparks flew from an aggravated flame. I didn't know what to think or say. "The important thing is that you came to your senses."

She nodded. "We had our disagreements when they found more children with our eyes and did whatever it took to lure them from their parents—even if it meant sacrificing innocents. It was a harsh realization that I should've listened to Johanna."

"And they also lured Selena?" I questioned somberly.

She responded with a heartbroken gaze, "Let's just say that Tiana had long wanted our baby sister. Hence, we had a rather . . . violent breakup. In fact, I tried to kill her to protect Selena, but she was too powerful. Out of spite, Matteo slaughtered our mother like he was putting down a sick animal."

I gasped, reliving the gruesome vision of the woman suffocating on a bedroom wall.

Luna wiped away tears before she resumed. "Meanwhile, Tiana used her trickery, implanting horrible ideas in Selena's mind that it was my fault she died and they were her saviors. Once corrupted by darkness, she was easy to snag from Johanna. She's exceptionally gifted but still too young to see the deception."

I then remembered how perfectly Tiana had mimicked Evelyn's voice, as well as the eerie hologram of Walter smiling in his office chair.

"And what did they do to you?" I asked, transfixed.

"They . . ." She choked up again and continued in something close to song: "Their love died three years ago. By spoken words, I cannot show."

Her hands glowed as they had when healing Evelyn. I nodded, giving her permission to place them on my head.

It burned; and suddenly, gone was the present moment. Initially I went back recently in time, digging holes by the stable with Noah by my side. He pointed out a girl sitting in the grass, seemingly carefree, and our eyes met like magnets.

I entered another scene. While the full moon replaced the sun in the sky, I stared down breathlessly at my female body. Still holding a shovel, I was thrust from behind, forced to dig what looked like a grave.

"They buried you alive," I said in a trance.

"Either I went through with it or my sisters would die."

Next, I lay in a wooden coffin as it was lowered into the ground. I felt the onset of despair and misery. I saw myself struggle. I heard myself scream.

"I fought for so many hours," Luna narrated. "I thought I could cheat death when all I was doing was wasting more air. Eventually, I prayed to anything that would hear me. Because after everything I had learned, my powers were useless against the weight of the earth." With gravity, she said, "I know what it's like to be dead, Samuel. I know what it is to be truly hopeless."

"How did you survive?" I questioned, motionless and lightheaded.

"Technically, I didn't. The old me died that night. And only when I accepted this fate could something greater walk into my body." I sensed the coming of a transcendent energy as Luna emotionally described, "In that life, I did terrible things. If there was a reality beyond, I was sure that I would be cruelly judged. Yet in that moment, my whole soul seemed to melt under the power of unconditional love."

The energy flooded into my crown, benevolent and divine, and I became blinded by an otherworldly light. I reached for it in wonderment and entered a state of bliss, ascending through the earth and toward the sky until Luna broke the vision.

She spoke with sincerity. "I may not have told you about my dark past or about having more than one sister, but I was not lying about my name. Madeleine is the girl who was buried alive. Luna was resurrected."

"But why?" I asked, mesmerized, vibrating.

"Because I have a mission to fulfill."

"To seek revenge?"

"To save my sister."

Evelyn's breath accelerated again, promptly ending my daze. As I went to fill the jar in the river, I grappled with my sense of identity. Even while gazing down at a familiar reflection, I experienced another's thoughts and memories.

I posed the question as we stood over Evelyn, gently giving her water. "Luna, you didn't show up at the Facility just because you had nowhere else to go, did you?"

Before she answered, her silence said everything. "Johanna came in a dream, after years of me living alone with no friends but the birds and no home but the trees. I didn't think she would ever want to speak to me, but like I've told you, she is forgiving, and that's how I knew about the attack and Sanctuary. As you've probably already guessed, only after our meeting did I turn myself in willingly. And it was not to try to warn anybody."

"You wanted to convince Selena to come to Sanctuary."

"Yes. And to have the three sisters united again." She shook her head with regret. "I obviously failed miserably. She still despises me, and although much of that is deserved, she has also been misguided by fear and lies. They did to her what they did to the old me and what they are attempting to do to your little friend. The worst part is that they think they're enlightened."

"They tried to recruit me as well," I said, describing my first encounter with Matteo and Tiana and how they'd murdered my second father. Beneath my words existed a psychic connection, confirming my suspicion that Luna had already been aware of this.

"I'm sorry, Samuel."

"I'm sorry, too. But hey, you didn't fail completely. If things turned out differently, you wouldn't have rescued us. And we wouldn't be following the river."

Luna regarded Evelyn fondly, lifting her chin to help her finish the water.

"I appreciate you saying that, but this is far from over. If there's one thing Matteo was right about, it's the war that has now begun. The military will want to hunt down everyone like us, regardless of robe color. We need to get to Sanctuary to heal her spiritually, but also for safety. The whole area is psychically protected."

"Do you really think she'll pull through?" I asked anxiously.

"It's about trusting, Samuel. Know that at some level, *we* decide."

Near the edges of my vision, lights flashed in the sky, though upon looking I saw nothing but the rising sun. Apparently, my mind was still playing tricks.

"What about your father, Luna? Why did he abandon you?"

"Isn't it obvious? His wife gave birth to three girls with freaky powers and mutant eyes. He left when Selena was only a toddler. I guess he didn't know how to handle us."

"I'm sure that deep down he still loves you and he's sorry," I said instinctively. It was great to see her smile again, albeit tearfully.

As Evelyn sank into a more peaceful sleep, my anger toward Luna all but evaporated. Despite whatever happened in the past, one thing was clear: we shared a common enemy.

She touched the bent handles of the wheelbarrow and closed her eyes as if communicating with the inner intelligence of the wood itself. When I asked her what she was doing, she calmly replied, "I did become powerful while following the dragon. I learned about the occult, alchemy, and black magic—but it isn't worth losing your soul in the process. During my time in nature, I've learned a much better way."

"What is the way?" I inquired hopefully.

"Through love, you can transmute." She channeled a limitless energy, and the wood seemed to restructure its molecular composition, both handles straightening within a matter of seconds.

With trust, I told her, "I want you to teach me."

CHAPTER 10

THE ENSUING DAY was devoted to rest and recovery, so not much progress was made along the river. The universe showed us sympathy: our sun shined brightly while the songbirds sang an especially soothing melody.

Luna quietly processed the encounter, preferring to spend several hours in the forest. The apples were almost gone, so she searched for edible plants to vary our diet. Meanwhile, I washed Evelyn with a wet cloth, conversing with her as if she could hear me, gently reassuring her and wondering what she would say about our mystifying partner. Despite Luna's ties with the black-robed children, I felt closer to her, and the spiritual connection from the vision lingered.

I reiterated my request to learn that afternoon, and Luna instructed me to sit and watch the trees.

"Trees are the best teachers," she said. "They are rooted in stillness, extending into the earth as much as they grow toward the sky, their branches separating yet forever remaining connected. See how they dance with the wind, always in balance with nature."

Indeed, the rhythm of the earth was fine therapy. I could finally appreciate its incredible beauty rather than being trapped within artificial walls. I wished Evelyn could watch with me; I wished I had run away with her a long time ago. Because the more I saw of our untouched planet, the more it validated something she believed:

that fear was the only force imprisoning us, not deadly radiation. The only trouble we faced was from misguided human beings.

When I'd had enough of staring at trees, I positioned my palms above Evelyn's scar, recalling the bliss of a mystical light and fruitlessly attempting to radiate it to her. I caught Luna smiling.

"Don't worry. She's in a good place."

"I know," I replied, conjuring up scattered memories of a shared lucid dream. I knew that even without the locket that honored them, her angels would never leave her side. Plus, after surviving such a dark night, I was struck by true faith that Evelyn would keep on breathing, along with confirmation that Sanctuary was real, no matter how long we had to follow the river. Then, she could meet the universal healer.

The next day, well rested, we traveled for many hours without seeing a hint of human settlement. But the animals of the forest—squirrels, foxes, even a rabbit—came out to greet us, which immensely lifted Luna's spirits. Claiming good fortune, she explained their symbolic meanings while I nodded attentively, secretly hoping that a doe would join too. Regardless, I was happy that she was distracted by trivial matters. Anything to forget that her younger sister had recently threatened to kill her.

Later, I fed Evelyn fresh berries while Luna cooked up some unusual mushrooms. Although they did not taste the greatest, she was adamant about their nutritional value, and so I ate in gratitude. After the meal, I brought up my request, yet she deferred once more, this time telling me to watch the river.

"The river is the best teacher," she said. "Observe it like you do the mind, letting your thoughts flow as effortlessly as water. See how it glides through any obstacle, never using force, yet always finding a way."

Though initially frustrated, I soon understood, observing how the water curved around boulders. With enough watching, I lost track of time, and then of my body, becoming as formless as that which I perceived, in harmony with the dance of nature. My problems dissolved, and I forgot about the world. I even forgot that Evelyn was not beside me, but this realization shook me out of my uncanny stupor.

I rushed to the wheelbarrow to hold her hand, promising not to forget about her again.

By the third day after our encounter, Luna seemed back to her jovial self: singing with the birds, skipping like a child, exuding a unique blend of sarcasm and wisdom. It was as if nothing had happened. A part of me wondered if she was putting on an act, trying to veil those shadows. Yet stronger was the inspiration I felt at her ability to laugh so freely while carrying such a dark past. Luna lived in a world of her own. If anything, I wanted to join her there.

We walked throughout the morning. When the sun reached its peak, she sat me down on the riverbank. "Staring at rocks this time?" I asked jokingly.

"Don't be silly. Rocks are quite rigid when it comes to their privacy. Today, I'm simply asking you to look within."

"Luna, when I asked you to teach me, I wanted to learn how to defend myself, not how to become a yogi."

She grinned, kneeling in front of me. "In order to defend yourself, you must first *know* thyself. Or are you afraid you might not like what you see?"

I held her gaze for several seconds before sighing in defeat. "To be honest, sometimes I think there's a monster inside me."

"Well, let's find out, shall we?" Crawling forward, she used her thumbs to lift my eyelids and inspect me like a manic scientist. "Yep, you've got the freak gene, alright! It's in there pretty good, though, hiding from the light."

"Like you've seen, it only really comes out when I'm in pain or very angry. Normally, I can't control it."

She sat back inquisitively. "Why do you think that is?"

A little boy screaming sprang into my awareness. I averted my eyes, concealing those shadows I still didn't want her to find.

She then said calmly, "I think you have long realized that your powers are wired to states of trauma and rage. This has caused compartmentalization in your brain rather than integration."

"It didn't help that I was treated like a monstrosity my whole life," I responded, lost in memory. "All because of having bigger eyes."

"We don't just have bigger eyes, Sammy." She pointed to the middle of her forehead. "We also have a bigger third eye. Have you ever heard of the pineal gland?"

"Yes, actually. When Walter taught me philosophy. Descartes called it the seat of the soul." I thought back further to ancient texts corresponding with Matteo's amulet. I glanced at Evelyn in the wheelbarrow nearby and almost felt sick saying, "You don't believe that we're some kind of new breed, do you?"

"Although size does matter"—she winked awkwardly—"the greatest secret they fail to realize is that any normal-eyed human can possess extraordinary abilities. We're just born with that door already open, if you know what I mean. Yet all of your life, they've tried to lock it back up and throw away the key, denying you access to that godlike consciousness."

"My handlers always claimed they just wanted to help me," I affirmed, remembering Salazar's last words.

"With pain? Drugs? Dead rabbits?" She raised a disbelieving eyebrow.

"Are you saying their research was all in vain?"

"I'm saying that the people they worked for must have been afraid of how powerful you really are without those pills and injections. *You* just have to believe it. Know it. Remember it, by dissolving that egoic fear and improving your relationship with your subconscious. Then you will see that the monster inside you is not such a meanie after all."

"Okay," I breathed. "Where do we begin?"

"Well, what do you think we've been doing for the past two days? I want you to practice becoming one with your perceptions. Practice understanding that space and time flow through you and not the other way around. For they do so as naturally as the wind and the water."

"What do you mean?"

"I mean that consciousness takes priority." She stretched her hand toward the forest, and a pine cone shot into it without warning. "The same creative mind is behind everything in this reality. Behind all that you touch and all that you see. Even behind you and me." As her eyes flared, the pine cone hovered in the air, proceeding to revolve around Evelyn. "Awaken to this mind by embodying pure awareness. Only once you become nothing will you find yourself in everything. This is a lesson in transcending your identity." After a full revolution, she caught the pine cone again, then set it on the ground before me. "Now you try. *Be* the pine cone."

I gazed at it peculiarly. However impressed I was by Luna's demonstration, my perspective remained stubbornly rational. It was a pine cone. I was a human.

"It's a pine cone," I said.

"That may be, but beyond words and labels, what are you really seeing? Come on, Sammy. Strive for lucidity!"

Recalling the clarity of recent dreams, I stared at my palms— every callus, every crease. Then I looked at the pine cone again, invoking philosophers such as Hegel and scientists like Wheeler. "What I perceive in itself is just an idea, a field of information decoded by my senses. It cannot exist independently of observation."

She nodded, pleased. "It is but a projection of consciousness, as is everything you see. Our minds act as prisms in filtering our reality."

"So, how does this help me to control my abilities?"

"By clearing your prism of limiting beliefs. When you view an object as an extension of yourself, you allow for a reality in which you can manipulate it easily."

"Fine." I gave in. "I'll *be* the pine cone."

"Now, that's the spirit I was looking for!"

With sudden determination, I focused my eyes, trying to connect with a transcendent mind. I reached out and touched the object's uneven texture, then slowly retracted my fingers, imagining that it was still a part of me. As the river flowed on one side, the branches danced playfully on the other. This created a dissolving effect, and there came a point where I no longer had to try.

"Fly," I requested. It lifted into the air, floating miraculously with the direction of my hand—though this only lasted seconds before it started wobbling. As thought intervened, the pine cone was quickly stolen by gravity.

Nevertheless, Luna was happy. "That was amazing! I'm proud of you, Sammy. And you didn't even have to burst a blood vessel with anger."

"No." I smiled. "I just had to surrender. Still, I can't control it nearly as well as you can."

"It will take time to master, as with any musical instrument. But you're one step closer to playing a marvelous melody."

I regarded her curiously. "You know, it's incredible how much you sound like Walter. He loved music. He was quite brilliant. And he also believed in a sort of oversoul, or a unity consciousness." I was reminded of his fondness for a man named Emerson. "He called that God."

"It doesn't matter what you call it. What matters is that you can tap into it, attuning to the strings of a cosmic symphony. Once that happens, reality turns into a dream. And nothing is outside the realm of possibility."

"Walter also taught me about string theory," I said with fascination. "How there were huge advances in quantum physics right before the bombings. He thought there was a link between those scientific theories and some of our abilities."

"That's nice and all, but do you really think science could explain why Martha Halford had three daughters who could read her mind and in their free time played telekinetic catch with the kitten?" We sat for a second in silence. "Certain things you just can't solve using equations. You have to experience them from within. And this brings us to our main lesson. Now get into lotus position!"

With Luna's guidance, I placed each foot on the opposite thigh and rested my hands on my knees. "More meditation?" I asked with slightly less sarcasm than before.

"How else are you going to befriend your higher self? You've come a long way since I caught you digging holes, but you still have some distortion to smooth out. Your brain is a bit like Sonic Youth. We want to get it to a state of total harmony, like, say, the Beach Boys!"

I cocked my head suspiciously. "Luna, how do you know the music of the old world?"

"I can give you an answer," she sighed, "but does it really matter?"

"I guess it doesn't."

"Stop with all the analyzing. That's part of the problem. The path toward knowing thyself manifests with knowing that you know nothing. Forget the past, for you will not find yourself there, and do not fear the future. Understand instead that everything in existence, what was and ever will be, emanates from a single moment." She snapped her fingers. "Lean into it, Samuel, by recognizing your full awareness. Close your eyes. Be still. And *breathe.*"

The result was hypnotizing; my lungs expanded beyond capacity, and my eyelids became tired and heavy.

Luna continued serenely, "With each breath in, you receive more healing light, and with each breath out, you release anything obscuring your being: fear, judgment, traumatic memory. Observe it without attachment, for it is a phantom of the mind, and though it may have served you at one point in your life, now it is time to let go and love without condition. As layers disintegrate and you tune into the silence, your true self is revealed as the handsome composer of the cosmic symphony. And you play it as masterfully as Ludwig van Beethoven, risen from the dead and given back sight."

I cracked open one eye. "Beethoven was deaf, not blind, Luna."

She scowled. "Really, Samuel? What musician would you prefer, then?"

With a wistful smile, I recalled the last song Walter ever heard. "I've always liked the way Jimi Hendrix played the guitar."

"Okay, fine then. You're psychic, freaky-eyed Jimi, hatching out of your psychedelic cocoon, growing your little butterfly wings, and learning to fly. As you ride with the wind and soar through the trees, you realize there is music all around that you couldn't hear previously. You are struck by the epiphany that your nature is divine and you may orchestrate the melody! So you grab your little butterfly electric guitar and—"

I burst out laughing. Luna rolled her eyes.

"What's so funny?"

"I just find this hard to take seriously."

"So let the laughter fill your heart with good vibrations, then reconnect with stillness and operate from there." Placing both hands over her chest, she added softly, "Beyond the thinking mind, escaping its never-ending labyrinth of illusion, there exists a force infinitely more intelligent. Now, obviously, I should stop talking so much. Simply focus on your breath. Plunge into your subconscious's shadowy depths. And let the energy flow from your root to your crown."

I nodded, closing my eyes once more. For a while, I just breathed deeper and deeper, until my breath synchronized with the sounds of wind and water. Though traumas of the past inevitably resurfaced, I observed them neutrally instead of reacting, forgiving those demons to the best of my ability and gently letting them pass. Finally, I felt able to put it all behind me—for thoughts could only ever briefly mask the truth of who I was.

Doors locked since my youth suddenly creaked open, awakening a hidden vitality. What started as a tingling at the top of my head turned into a cord of golden light beaming down from the sky, spiraling through each node of my spine before anchoring into the earth. Neural pathways rewired as my energy transmuted.

Eventually, Luna whispered, "As you utterly relax and float downstream, you spread your glorious monarch wings. And may the branches of the trees forever hang lower."

My consciousness expanded even further. Space and time were no longer factors. Emptiness inside gave way to sovereignty. I became blissfully whole, content with everything. Then I sensed a connection to a higher reality where separation was a delusion, as all things danced in perfect unison. And despite what I normally perceived, there truly existed only one being. My eyes gradually began to see . . . though not quite physically.

Flickers of light transformed into complex geometry, which gorgeously coalesced into an image of three angels flying above a heavenly flame. Yet I also noticed a fourth presence at my side, stroking my hair, faintly singing a familiar lullaby. My inner child smiled while my adult mind wept, for it was almost as if—

"Boo!"

In shock, I sent Luna tumbling through the grass to land on her back about twenty feet away.

Then I hit the ground myself, for I had been sitting on nothing but the wind. I jumped to my feet and ran toward her, frantically apologizing, but she was laughing.

"Look what you did!" she exclaimed joyfully.

"Yeah, because you scared me!" I settled down next to her and shook my head. "It's not funny, Luna. I could've—"

"Killed me?" She sat up, grinning. "You know I can't help myself. The important thing is that you felt it, didn't you? All that divine potential within you? You were levitating with ease! Then you basically shot me with a laser beam of consciousness. It'll take some practice to master your instrument, to truly become psychic Jimi, but God only knows the pure magnificence of what you could accomplish."

"I *did* feel things," I said with emotion. "Indescribable sensations I've never felt before. And I know it sounds crazy, but when I listened very closely, I thought I heard singing."

"You're not crazy, Samuel. You're just more aware of what has always been there." She put her hand on my shoulder, and the songbirds shifted their tunes. "You see now why I love music too. There's no barrier between you and the experience. It's the form of expression . . ."

". . . that is closest to the soul."

She smiled. "Took the words from my mouth."

As I looked Luna over, I could not deny that she was an attractive girl. The aura about her was enchanting, her golden spiral earrings glinting in the sunlight. I was drawn to her eyes and found myself strangely spellbound. The meditation had obviously aroused other parts of my brain.

"Samuel."

"Yes?"

"You're a live wire right now. I can tell what you're thinking."

Luna leaned in for a kiss, and for a moment I didn't resist. Only when her lips touched mine did I truly comprehend what was happening.

~

The next few hours were a dreadful blur. I walked with nausea and an ache in my chest, unable to escape the feeling that I had stabbed Evelyn in the back. My happiness had been sabotaged by well-deserved shame, and I tearfully questioned how I could have let that occur. All those epiphanies gained during the meditation— experiences of self-love and higher realization—were extinguished with one simple action.

As I pushed Evelyn along the river, I was tortured by the thought that she was already aware of my infidelity, judging me as harshly as I judged myself. And no amount of apologizing could erase the image in my mind of her staring, red eyed, from the center of a hurricane. She had always been faithful and now lay helpless and ill. And this was how I repaid her. This was what I did.

Meanwhile, Luna viewed it as a comical situation, chuckling, teasing, and visibly amused at my sudden humiliation. I wasn't surprised. To her, the kiss was insignificant. And she futilely tried to convince me to see it the same way.

"Oh, come on, Sammy! It was just a little peck!" she insisted. I glared and shook my head, continuing my trek onward.

She may have been wise in other areas but clearly did not understand the seriousness of my relationship with Evelyn. The worst part, however, was not that I couldn't trust her but that I could no longer trust myself. In my heart I knew I loved Evelyn; still, I endured a tough lesson of what could happen when I stopped listening to it for even a second.

Later, Luna cooked clusters of clovers and dandelions, though I could hardly eat anything. Rather, I fed Evelyn her mixture of berries, thinking about how miserable life would be if she ever left.

"Please forgive me," I whispered in her ear as Luna stood watching by the fire.

"So, we're just not going to talk about it?" she asked.

"There's nothing to talk about," I asserted. "It was a mistake, Luna. One that will never happen again."

She groaned in resignation, spreading blankets on the grass. We had traveled almost until dusk, so naturally we would rest for the night. But as I tuned into my tired heart, I was told to walk just a little bit farther, if only to not sit still with my feelings of guilt. I remembered the last time I'd had this feeling—before we encountered the doe and she led us to a stream. I strapped on my satchel and urged Luna to do so as well.

We journeyed through dwindling twilight for nearly another hour before we saw it: like a fish out of water, a large wooden structure between the woods and the river.

For a moment, everything was forgotten. I thanked my intuition, then gazed at Luna with rekindling optimism. "Is it Sanctuary?"

She laughed. "No, silly, look at the top!"

Squinting at its triangular roof, I recognized a symbol from my youth. "It's a cross."

"Exactly. Unless Johanna became a born-again Christian, I don't think this is the place."

Although disappointed, I was intrigued. I rolled Evelyn forward with restless uncertainty. We arrived at the building's doors right as the sun set completely.

"There's something written up there," I observed, pointing above the entrance.

Luna pulled out the flashlight. "I knew this would come in handy!" Then she revealed the name of the structure:

THE CHURCH OF NATURE'S RIVER

"Well, what do you know?" she quipped, reaching for a door handle. "The river we've been following *is* religious after all!"

"Wait, Luna. Shouldn't we find out if there's more civilization?"

She shined the light lazily through the adjacent forest. "Nope. Doesn't look like it."

"So we'll just spend the night in a random church that appeared out of nowhere with nothing else around?"

"Yes, precisely. What's so weird about that?" She held the door open for me and Evelyn. "I know you've been all pissy at me lately, but we have to continue to trust the river and whatever synchronicity it may bring."

Surrendering, I pushed the wheelbarrow inside. But in the doorway I was attacked by a chilling memory that froze me in my tracks.

"Samuel? Are you coming?"

"Yeah," I grunted, shaking off the past. "Yeah, I am."

As the door shut behind us, we called out and were greeted with silence. The flashlight illuminated a blue carpet at our feet that showed the likeness of the river and stretched between several rows of long wooden benches, all the way up to an altar at the opposite end. A nearby table held dozens of candles.

"This place was expecting us," Luna remarked, replacing the flashlight with a burning match. Using her mind, she spread the flame to each candle simultaneously before distributing them evenly throughout the interior, filling the space with a soft, dancing glow.

Furnished simply, the church was relatively clean except for dust on the seats. Its scarce decoration included beautiful stained-glass windows and a striking sculpture now revealed above the altar, portraying the one called Christ.

I couldn't say why, but something came over me. I lifted Evelyn out of the wheelbarrow and walked steadily along the carpet, laying her on the altar, which barely fit her body. Kissing her lips as I caressed her hair, I half expected her to open her eyes. But I wasn't even sure if she would want to see me at this point. A tear rolled down my cheek from the awful feeling that I'd lost my love before I had the chance to save her.

Approaching, Luna put her hand on my shoulder. "Samuel, about our little smooch. I can tell you're beating yourself up about it, but I think you just need to—"

"You know that I love her!" I erupted, candles flaring as I swiped her arm away in anger.

Luna remained frustratingly lighthearted. "See, you've never really elaborated on what that meant. Love can mean a lot of things. Friends can love each other in a platonic sort of way, for example. It's not my fault you never told me that you two were exclusive."

"And you never told me that you even liked men!"

"Any way the wind blows, baby." She winked playfully, making a kissing face. "Come on, Sammy. Land one on me, honeybun!"

"It's *not* funny."

"It's quite hysterical, actually. I just want to see you blush again."

"That was because you seduced me," I accused her bitterly.

"You sure that was me and not something else?" she muttered, gesturing downward.

I stared at her speechlessly, annoyed yet embarrassed.

She said, "Yes, we're a bit *weirder* than most teenagers, but we still got those same dang hormones running through our bodies. So relax a little, sweetie, and let yourself laugh like you did this morning. There's no need for such piety. Embrace your humanity!"

"Just cut it out, Luna. We're in a church."

"They may call it horny," she purred seductively, "but it's only devilish if you make it out to be."

I turned toward Jesus, taking long, deep breaths. Luna was truly an anomaly; I couldn't believe that a girl with so much wisdom was now tempting me to cheat. It was as if her sage self were competing with an alternate personality.

I then noted something curious about the sculpture. Although I didn't know much about religion, Walter having only taught me the shared teachings at their core, from what I recalled, Christ usually took on a more mournful visage—suffering, bleeding, nailed to a cross. This one was different. He was smiling, with one hand over his heart and the other raised to all living beings, spreading his love, totally at peace.

"Well, isn't this a sweet relic?" Luna commented, changing her tone.

"I thought religion was destroyed after the bombings," I confessed. "That most people believed God was dead."

"Systems can collapse. Love never dies," she said.

"Like you mentioned, Luna, love can mean a lot of things."

"I mean the type of love that means everything. The kind that holds together the atoms in matter and makes our hearts beat." Her eyes shined as they rested on me. "In any case, have you ever been inside one of these?"

"Only once," I responded, continuing my controlled breathing.

"You must have been very young."

"I don't want to talk about it." I dropped my head.

"Somebody's still moody." She turned back down the aisle. "Anyway, honey, I'm going away for a while. Talk to me once you tame those hormones!"

"Where are you going?" I asked.

She grinned, settling into lotus position in the middle of the church. "I'll be on the astral plane. Maybe there I can seduce some wandering spirits."

As Luna performed her meditation, I was left alone with Christ and Evelyn. Unfortunately, just one of them had eyes I could see. Even though he was not physically alive, they seemed to penetrate my soul, and I would've assumed he was judging me; but I remembered he wasn't into that kind of thing.

I sighed with the thought that maybe Luna was right. Despite my careless mistake, the judgment came solely from me. Only time could say if Evelyn would feel the same. Until then, I needed to forgive myself and love unconditionally.

A gust of wind blew in from an open window, carrying an object that drifted toward us—an object I thought I had lost several days earlier: the brilliant-blue feather. In sheer astonishment, I almost believed I was dreaming.

I had no proof, but I knew it was the same one that had fallen on Evelyn the day of the accident, when I was in desperate need of faith. It was as if it had followed us all this way to lend a sign of protection and guidance when needed.

I was about to catch the feather when a second gust sent it gliding to a dark corner. And I was so distracted by chasing it that

I bumped into a shelf on the wall I didn't realize was there. I fell to the floor simultaneously with a single book I had knocked off. The feather landed nearby. Surprisingly, Luna didn't react to the noise; she must have been deep in her subconscious.

I grabbed a couple of candles and sat with the book, which was encased in a cover that bore no name. I skimmed through it, finding handwritten musings about a variety of life's questions: the soul's purpose, free will and destiny, the presence of God, and the nature of reality. It was also brimming with Bible verses. I reckoned Walter would have enjoyed this manuscript. It amounted to hours of philosophical sermons never intended for anyone to hear.

However, the book was only halfway written, ending with an uplifting proclamation:

We look forward to the resurrection of the dead.
And the life of the world to come.

Although I didn't know the meaning behind those words, they filled me with a sense of encouragement, as well as the spiritual empowerment to create a true miracle. All in all, whoever wrote this was no ordinary priest. I became inspired to use the feather to finish the second half, but I had no ink.

I returned to the altar and got down on my knees, picturing all of the mothers and fathers, sons and daughters, and every child affected by the planet's ongoing sickness, whether or not they had eyes like mine. Then, with conviction that someone was listening, I asked for their safety and healing.

Lastly, I focused my intention on Evelyn's well-being, praying for a resurrection while hoping that all would be forgiven.

CHAPTER 11

MY EYES OPENED before the crack of dawn, and I was tempted to close them again. But a gentle wind arrived to whisper in my ear, kindly requesting me to rise from my slumber.

I sat up sluggishly on the frontmost seat, still in a stupor. Evelyn rested peacefully between blankets on the altar with the feather placed beneath her palm, the mixture of candlelight and glass-stained moonbeams making for a mystical air. The miracle I strived toward had not yet manifested, as my hazy sleep yielded no dreams.

Smiling above her was the sculpture of Christ, one hand over his heart and the other raised, something gleaming in his grasp. I did a double take to be certain of what I was seeing; it was as if he were offering a hidden gift uncovered by the morning twilight.

My body felt inexplicably light, and so I almost hovered to the altar. There I could discern precisely what he was holding: a golden key, shining to garner my attention. I was far too short to reach it.

Memories surfaced from when I was young, of using my abilities to fly toys off shelves. I would play this way to the delight of my mother, but only when my father wasn't watching.

It was time to connect with my child self again, putting Luna's lessons to good use. I breathed with an understanding that I was perfect and complete, fundamentally at one with all I perceived. The key budged, then lifted from Jesus's hand, floating into my outstretched fingers without faltering. I grasped it tightly and thought about how proud my mother would be. It was easy to change things with enough confidence and belief, even if it meant embracing the childlike notion of a magical world.

Although I did not know its function, the key carried a magnificent energy. The lingering moonbeams from the windows appeared to brighten. A sense of true spirituality permeated the church. The universe was listening closely. And if I posed the right questions, I had faith that someone would answer.

"What is this for?" I asked initially, presenting the key above Evelyn.

Though I wasn't given any words, I felt a tingling on the crown of my head and heard a faint ringing. An undeniable presence emerged by my side, and the sensation was so overwhelming that my eyes watered.

"The loved ones I've lost," I whispered softly, "are they still watching me?"

My hand burned like fire, and I dropped the key to the blue carpet. But as I bent to pick it up, I noticed letters materializing in the gold: Sum Du In Spirit.

My emotion triggered an accelerated wind. The veil between realities was swiftly unraveling. By the time I stood again, the section of the wall where Christ had been situated had become a mirror. Through it, I gazed upon a seven-year-old me clutching his teddy bear in a closet and gazing back tearfully.

The wind blew him away before I had the chance to say anything.

"Samuel," murmured a heart-stopping voice.

It was Evelyn, staring from the altar in a distressing scene. Her scar was bleeding. Instead of the feather, she was holding a dagger. And yet, there was something even more disturbing.

"Evelyn. Your eyes."

They were Luna's, twice the size and glowing green. A harsh whistle sounded outside, and I became petrified in the midst of a strengthening hurricane that shattered the windows while the church walls collapsed.

"Now do you love me?" she asked telepathically, pulling me in as I started to scream.

~

The hand across my cheek was a rude awakening.

"Sometimes he needs a good ol' slap!" I heard Luna say, and I was about to lash out when someone else laughed.

I sat up frantically on the front wooden bench, reliving the experience of my bewildering sleep. Thankfully, the church was intact, and the rays of the sun streaming through stained glass indicated it was morning.

Luna stood over me, grinning. Behind her was an elderly man dressed in simple brown garments, a gentle smile gracing his wizened face.

"Hello, Sammy. I apologize for the scare, but it is so wonderful to meet you." He approached me to extend his hand. "My name is Leon."

I froze for a second, locking eyes with the first adult outsider we'd seen since the hunters. Yet in them I recognized a genuine kindness without any mist to disguise it, sparking a remembrance of a soul to whom I felt connected.

"It's Samuel, actually." I shook his hand and caught Luna chuckling. "But it is nice to meet you too."

"I wanted to let you catch up on some sleep," said Luna, "but I couldn't talk to this nice old man with you whimpering like a newborn baby."

"Guess I had a nightmare," I replied somberly, overcoming hesitation to turn toward Evelyn. She lay peacefully on the altar with the feather beneath her palm, her body bathed in colored light. Still reeling from the inner realm I had entered, created from my mind as a perfect mirror, I couldn't be sure that I wasn't still dreaming.

"Dreams can reveal many unprocessed feelings," Leon affirmed, reading my expression. "Fears and insecurities which may have been repressed, as well as hidden messages that can inspire important growth. Your friend here was explaining the horror of what you've been through, and for that I am deeply sorry, for you are far too young to be dealing with such matters."

I rose heavily and trudged to the altar, hoping that my vision came purely from my subconscious. "She's been like this for a week now," I informed Leon, who accompanied me.

"From our limited perspective, it is a frightening predicament. Yet from the moment I saw her, I could sense her tenacious spirit, as well as a heart that carries too much love to abandon this world so early. Know that God is taking care of her; the love she holds is sorely needed."

"You really think so?" I asked, affected.

He nodded. "Trust that these trials are for a reason and her scars will be cleansed in time. She is going deep within herself only to ascend from this transformative sleep as a further perfected being."

I was taken aback by the familiar stranger, obviously a spiritual man, who in spite of his age and modest appearance exhibited a striking sharpness in his wisdom.

"Tell me, Leon, is this your church?"

"My wife and I built it many years ago, but truly it belongs to the river. Still, I like to visit when the opportunity arrives, and it fills me with joy to find new faces making use of its shelter." He let out a sigh. "Since she passed away, I've been quite lonely."

"We can be your friends as long as you don't mind our big, spooky eyes," Luna jested.

He laughed. "All the better. Perhaps I can borrow them, as I'm going blind."

As we conversed with our newfound friend, I realized that the knowledge imparted from his experience alone could rival that of any holy text. He was old enough to remember what the world was like before the bombings; in a time of great suffering, he clung to his faith, found true love, and managed to survive. Afterward he lived in harmony with nature, learning from the mishaps of humanity's past. For this reason, he acted as a bridge between realities.

Overcome with curiosity, I fetched the unnamed book I had stored in my satchel. "This came to me by accident. You wrote it, didn't you?"

He took it and squinted at the first page. "Oh, perhaps I did, though once one ponders the source of their thoughts, it might be inappropriate to give me credit." He handed it back with a youthful wink. "Did you find anything interesting, Samuel, from this so-called accident?"

"It was all very interesting, but the final words especially stood out to me—something about a resurrection of the dead and a world to come. It's eloquently written, but what exactly does it mean?"

"Well, I know for sure that did not come from me, as it is an old religious saying. My wife and I always felt there was some deeper truth to it. After witnessing so much destruction, we dreamt of a world of peace, beauty, and lasting unity, born from the ashes of the earth. Furthermore, souls who have died to their corporeal selves will be risen in the new world within new bodies. From my humble perspective, this is what that saying means."

"That's beautiful," I said, wondering if Evelyn was listening. "I'm sorry about your wife."

"It's quite all right. She simply left before me. I'd like to think that she is there already, patiently waiting, for she has always been an overachieving soul. It is a world we may also come to know if we follow the right path."

"What is the path?" Luna asked, captivated.

He said, "The path of which I speak is one of love and selfless service, seeing the Kingdom of God within all others as you recognize it within yourself. This implies respecting each person you meet as the divine beings they are, even if they forget it themselves. This is the path of the sacred light."

"But in order to know the light, we must first know darkness," I responded, reminded of the vision of Luna being buried alive. "One cannot exist without the other, can it?"

"Very astute of you," he commended, before pausing in reflection. "I suppose from God's point of view, light is all that truly exists. But he designed a system of balance and polarity for his children to experience. It is comparable to the properties of electricity, where charges exist both positive and negative, yet either can generate a powerful force."

"So, there is a separate path of negativity?" I asked. Matteo smirked in my mind's eye.

He nodded. "This is the path of fear and dominance, chosen by those whose sole endeavor is to manipulate others as a means to serve themselves. Indeed, this path also breeds power, though the lack of trust between the individuals consumed by it will eventually lead to great disharmony."

"You don't have to tell *me* that," Luna retorted.

Leon continued, "In a previous life, too many people in positions of authority were in alignment with this second path. Motivated only by power and greed, they wanted nothing more than to rule over others, manipulating society behind a mask while committing horrible deeds in the shadows. They gained the world and lost their souls in the process, for there came a point when there was no regard for human life nor for the earth herself. And how they treated her, she gave back in return."

He sighed, looking toward the sculpture of Christ.

"During these times, people were afraid and losing their faith, questioning how a loving God would allow such evil. And yet most were so caught up awaiting the coming of a savior that they forgot to look within. This is why the world is the way it is."

"Because of those on the negative path," I said.

"No," he replied. "Because of the failure of the majority to counterbalance the actions of evil men, who were much fewer in number. This is the third and most fruitless path, generating no electricity. It is the path of indifference."

"What happens to people on that path?" I asked.

"They will find themselves placed in the same positions, repeating both personal and collective cycles of experience until they gain the courage to act. As it was, so shall it be again; thus we are forced to learn our lessons."

"I call that karma," Luna remarked. "You're saying that if we want to clear it, we have to kick the bad guys in the butt!"

"That is one way of putting it." Leon chuckled. "You must be cautious not to become further entangled, however, for in my experience, violent action begets a violent world. Rather, my friends, there is a spiritual battle going on, one raged in consciousness itself. And I am telling you as someone who has seen the darkness in the hearts of men, my own included, that the best course of action to transcend this madness is that of forgiveness."

Luna frowned. "Just when I thought things were getting exciting. That isn't very fun."

"Indeed, it isn't," he responded, "and thus we have nearly destroyed our species. In order to heal our planet, we must act on love rather than fear and forgive without exception. This isn't to say not to defend ourselves when necessary, or that those responsible should not be held accountable for their terrible actions, free from natural consequences. But know that they are only confused, for they have forgotten the universal love of God that is infinitely present within them as it is within others. Hence, we may choose compassion over hatred, recognizing ourselves in their eyes and being an example of the sacred light. This is a process of transmutation."

"Easier said than done," I muttered, gesturing to the eye etched into Evelyn's forehead. "Some people are stuck in their ways and will never change; the world would be better off without them. Forgiveness can come only after the battle is won."

"You may be correct," Leon confessed. "Please understand, my wise young friend, that God is so unconditionally loving he would never take free will from any of his children, no matter what they do. So he does the next best thing: he uses them for a purpose."

"What purpose could people like that possibly serve?" I demanded.

His expression was serene. "We wouldn't grow very much without obstacles to overcome, would we? They provide tremendous opportunities for our spiritual evolution. In fact, adversity forms the catalyst for any brilliant work of art, soulful piece of music, or fascinating story of a hero's journey." He strolled to stand directly within the path of the sun's rays. "As you have said yourself, Samuel, without darkness, it wouldn't be possible to appreciate the light."

"I guess you're right," I said, acknowledging the value of my own painful shadows and the perspective they had given me. Then I imagined Evelyn wrapped in a chrysalis, evolving from the struggle slowly yet surely; I wondered if a metamorphosis would be worth all the suffering.

Leon resumed, "All experience, whether positive or negative, contains pertinent wisdom we may glean. Nothing is wasted, and nothing is judged, even those follies for which you have judged yourselves harshly."

Luna rubbed my shoulder with surprising sincerity while Leon rejoined us by the altar, adding tenderly, "As for others who have wronged you and those you care for, it is only natural to feel anger. Never lose hope that they can be healed, for I believe that ultimately, in the grand design, both sides will be unified—the two becoming one—as all paths invariably lead back to love. Some simply take much longer than others."

I thought of all the people who had hurt me and Evelyn, as well as those I had hurt. Then I asked, "Leon, sir, which path do you think we're on?"

"That is for you to decide," he answered. "The important thing is that you do decide. Because the very nature of that choice will determine whether you are driven by demons or guided by angels." He gave a warm laugh. "Although I must admit that finding this church along this river hints that you are on the right one."

I smiled. "Do you really think that the river has mystical properties?"

"Tell me, Samuel, have you looked outside lately? Open your eyes to all the untouched beauty, startlingly free from the folly of man. One might find that exceptionally strange, unless we concede that, at least in our reality, we are already well on the way."

I recalled Luna's teaching that we were one with all we perceived. Of course, she seemed to know what I was thinking, winking at me before saying to Leon, "We should be close to Sanctuary by now, filled with children who also follow the path of the hippie. It's headed by my older sister and is supposed to be somewhere along the river. You haven't heard anything about it, have you?"

He shook his head. "I wish I knew what you were looking for, dear girl. But not far downstream is a village of kind people who might know more than I do. Yet please be careful, my wise and loving, large-eyed friends, for even after the earth's initial reckoning, there are those in command who have not learned their lessons. Reports are emerging of power-hungry men taking what does not belong to them while looking for children who fit your description. Still, until you find your sanctuary, maybe someone there can help."

"Thank you." My heart pulsated with gratitude. "We'll keep that in mind. There is a child at Sanctuary who should be able to heal Evelyn, but as silly as it sounds, I almost thought she would open her eyes on the altar. I used to hear stories about miraculous healing." I nodded toward the sculpture of Christ before grasping the hand of my love above the blue feather. "And I thought I was seeing signs."

Leon joined in with his own wrinkled hand, then gazed straight into my soul. "It is telling, Samuel, that even in the Bible, Jesus assures his followers they will do even greater things than he."

"Anyone can perform miraculous healing?" I questioned with growing emotion.

"Of the self, one does nothing; through Him, there is no limitation. God gave us all the tools we need to create along with him and the freedom to do it within every possible moment. All you have to do is remember the true magnificence of who you really are, thus accepting the responsibility for the circumstances of your creation. That, my friends, is how Evelyn will be resurrected—and how together we can cocreate the world to come."

My eyes watered while Luna said cheerfully, "To be honest, Leon, I was always uneasy about religion and the whole Jesus thing, but I have to admit you're pretty cool for a Christian."

Beaming, he replied, "The secret key to Christianity is that Christ was teaching us to be like him. Once you have that, it becomes so easy." He turned toward a window that was aglow with the rising sun. "In any case, it looks like the day is coming on, and you travelers must be very hungry. I will pick some fresh strawberries out back, which should energize you for your journey ahead."

"Strawberries?" Luna gasped. "Do you need help?"

"Fear not, my friends, for despite my age, I am more than able. You three deserve some rest, which I would hate to interrupt again." He ambled down the blue carpet and glanced back fondly. "I would at least suggest turning inward for the time being, following the wise lead of Evelyn. Now please excuse me, as the fields are ripe and ready to harvest."

～

Evelyn remained asleep on the altar as I nourished her with berries and water, helping her to swallow with an unusual amount of difficulty. I wondered if she was as tired of Luna's nature diet as I was and was secretly reminiscing of her agricultural life with Maggie, as well as the other orphans we could only hope had found a way to survive. Then I wondered if she missed my eyes as much as I missed hers, despite their shadowy imperfections.

Regardless, I simply hoped that when she woke from her coma, she would remember the true magnificence of who she was, knowing without question just how much she was loved. Until that day, I would feed and bathe her, doing whatever it took for her to remember. I was patient as she finished the berries, then gently wiped the stains from her face.

"Strawberries are your favorite," I whispered encouragingly, waiting with anticipation for Leon to return. "I promise they'll taste better than these other ones."

Meanwhile, Luna lay quietly on a wooden bench, apparently taking Leon's guidance to heart. I was glad that she seemed equally moved by the spiritual teachings of our elderly friend. And though I couldn't escape the guilt about our little kiss, I chose to forgive her as I forgave myself, knowing it was best to let it go.

"How are you feeling, Luna?" I asked, storing the jars in my satchel.

"I'm doing fine. Just contemplating." She smiled but clearly wanted to be left alone.

I picked up the unnamed book and considered whether to skim through it again; instead, I placed it on the shelf where I had found it, acknowledging that it belonged to the church itself. Then I sat against the altar, restless from waiting.

"He told us he would just be out back," I mentioned. "Should we go check on him?"

"You heard what he said, Samuel." Luna sighed. "He wants to go out on his own. He can handle picking strawberries."

Sensing irritation, I refrained from further questioning. With nothing else to do, I decided to do nothing.

Lotus position already felt natural to me; almost as soon as I closed my eyes, I experienced a rush of soothing energy. After plunging into a state of relaxation, I discerned the presence of another consciousness. It was not Evelyn breathing above me, nor was it Luna on the wooden bench. Rather, it was transcendent, as if a higher spirit or soul of the universe were personally looking out for us, watching events unfold from outside of time and affording the solace that everything was going to be fine.

Incredibly, I heard an unmistakable melody, beginning as a soft humming and quickly developing. My excitement fizzled as I recognized the voice—this time, it was Luna. She sang while stretching her legs on the seat. I listened silently.

"Well I wonder,
Do you hear me when you sleep?
I hoarsely cry . . ."

She stopped at my look of fascination.

"I thought you only sang birdsong," I joked.

"Whatever I feel in my heart," she replied, solemnly.

I paused, concerned by her demeanor. "So why do you feel like crying?"

Her eyes turned red as she stared at me. Then her body started quivering.

"Luna?" I stood and stepped toward her. "Luna, what's wrong?"

The church doors opened, and Leon walked in. Immediately, I sensed it: an aura of dread. He didn't try to hide his troubled expression. Still, he carried a basket of strawberries, ripe and red and freshly picked.

We joined him in the aisle.

"Somebody found us," Luna said.

He nodded. "About a dozen soldiers. Somehow, they know that you stayed the night. I tried to deny it, but they claim to have the church closely monitored. Either I did what they told me, or they'd blow it to pieces."

Luna and I exchanged worried glances. "And what did they tell you?" I asked, my pulse racing.

"These strawberries are laced with a substance that should put you to sleep." He held up the basket, showing remnants of a strange powder. "Even though they're all armed, they still don't want to face you with your eyes open. I'm so sorry, dear friends. We only built one entrance, and they have it covered."

I glanced back at Evelyn and steadied myself before marching toward the doors, following the urging of my heart.

"Samuel, what are you doing?" Luna called after me.

"Taking action," I responded.

"But they'll kill you," she said.

"No. They won't."

Seconds later, the doors were kicked open. Charging in formation was a squad of white soldiers, decked in their usual helmets and armor, all aiming their guns directly at me. Finally, in came the only one with an eye exposed: Lieutenant Hernandez, scowling vengefully. Burn scars now swept across half of his face, a patch covering the afflicted eye, yet his lips curved upward as he met my gaze, proudly exhibiting that he was still alive.

"Samuel Helen." He strolled forward with his hands behind his back. "Under orders from General Mabus, you are arrested for crimes against the Union."

Leon was quick to rush to my side. "How misguided you are to bring weapons into this church. There is no such Union if you're coercing its children with threats of violence."

The lieutenant laughed, glancing at the strawberries. "We knew you wouldn't go through with it. We're not stupid, old man. We have eyes to see."

"Then you should know that we had nothing to do with the attack on the Facility," I countered, recalling the time I last saw him and Salazar's defense of me.

"This is now a bigger issue: a threat to our species. Just look at what your kind did to me!" His hand shook with anger as he pointed to his injured eye. "Never mind the slaughter of our innocent scientists. You should be grateful that the general prefers you alive, but I doubt he'll be too bothered if we are forced to kill you."

"You'll have to go through me," said Leon.

"And me." Luna arrived next to us with a formidable glare. "Or did your *eye* not see that I was here too?"

The lieutenant fumed. "You've got some nerve, girl, but don't think we'll hesitate to do the same to you." He approached Leon. "As for the old man, he's already broken our deal. Isn't that supposed to be a sin?"

"I do not fear death," Leon answered. "And yet I will never compromise the integrity of my soul by willfully participating in the harm of children. That, I'm afraid, is far more dangerous."

The lieutenant snickered. "You really are a religious fool." He dragged Leon toward him by the neck, putting a pistol to his head. "This is in case you try anything."

The basket of strawberries fell to the ground.

The previous version of me would've acted on fury. This time, I controlled my emotions and chose my words carefully.

"Release him, please. We will cooperate if he isn't harmed."

Leon responded by shaking his head, showing no signs of distress, merely disappointment with foolish men.

"That is smart of you, boy," snarled the lieutenant. "But I suggest that you look around. *I* will decide how this plays out." As the soldiers adjusted their weapons, he briefly loosened his hold to retrieve two strips of black cloth from a pouch on his belt, which he tossed in front of us. "Begin by tying these tightly around your eyes. No wrong moves, and nobody dies."

"Okay," I complied, slowly bending to pick up the blindfolds while my heart beat out of my chest. I gave one to Luna and caught her tense stare, wondering if she had any sort of plan, waiting in desperation for some telepathic message.

"No, my friends. Do not deliberately blind yourselves!" Leon shouted in rebellion. "Please, not for me."

The lieutenant pressed the gun against his cheek. "Are you crazy, old man? I'm giving you a chance to live."

"And I'm giving you all a chance to leave these children and be healed of your affliction. May the light of God shine into your hearts, allowing no room for darkness."

The soldiers' helmeted heads turned toward one another while the lieutenant sneered. "You hear that, men? Lay down your weapons! God is protecting them." This sparked a few laughs, though most stayed quiet.

"For heaven's sake," Leon wheezed, "you cannot take these children! The girl needs the two of them. She's comatose!"

I held my breath as all the attention shifted to Evelyn. With the approval of the lieutenant, a soldier stowed his gun and went to examine her. He did not need more than twenty seconds to return with a judgment. "She's not one of them, sir."

"Then she's not our concern," Lieutenant Hernandez decided. "We've already wasted enough time fussing about those damn eyes. Cuff them both and—"

He was interrupted by Leon, who used all the strength in his feeble frame to break free of his hold and reach for the pistol. As he wrestled against the imposing lieutenant, there could be no doubt, even to him, who was going to win.

"I'm sorry" were his final words before a shot resounded, the bullet entering his skull and killing him instantly.

"God can't save anyone," the lieutenant said callously as the priest's limp body dropped to the blue carpet. The shock was so devastating that even the soldiers seemed frozen. "Well, what are you waiting for? Take them!"

Luna was able to disarm many, but she was not quick enough. More shots rang out, and I watched in horror as she clutched her bloody leg. What followed was a nauseating blur of being tackled to the ground while the lieutenant yelled, "Hold your fire!"

As much as my mind and body yearned to fight, my heart felt connected to a spirit that could see things clearer, promising me that even in the most hopeless of moments, sometimes the best option was to simply surrender. So as Leon's killer glared into my eyes, I made a silent plea to be guided toward a higher understanding, illuminating the path I needed to take in order to rescue us from this situation.

A heavy fist struck my head and sent me out of my body.

~

It was a transcendent experience to be conscious in another realm, standing on astral limbs, staring out of ethereal eyes. The feeling was one of sublimity yet also strange familiarity, as full memories during similar experiences were suddenly accessible, including the lucid dream from earlier that morning.

This experience, however, was especially uncanny. Not only could I perceive all happenings on the physical plane, but time was elapsing at a snail's pace. I saw soldiers crowding in slow motion around my body, working to apply the blindfold after the lieutenant punched my head. I saw several more pointing their guns at Luna, who lay in agony from her wounded leg. Then I saw Leon lying dead, his kind eyes empty, his blood staining the carpet.

I heard nothing but silence as the entire scene shimmered in celestial light. Worry seemed an impossible emotion; everything was exactly as it needed to be. The moment I acknowledged this, a glowing white orb shot out of Leon's chest.

Pulsating with intelligence, it zipped around the church before whizzing right past me, clearly trying to catch my attention. It then stopped by the altar where Evelyn slept, and out of it manifested a bodily projection.

Leon! Clad in luminous robes, his astral form peacefully observed Evelyn. I looked down and noticed that I was also a sort of hologram, projected from a heart-based source. As pure awareness, I hovered to the altar to greet my newly deceased friend, who gazed at me with starlike eyes overflowing with love and light.

"Samuel," he said, moving his lips even though it all felt telepathic. "How nice of you to join us."

I paused to take it all in: Evelyn was caught in a single breath while the material world turned ever so slowly. As I examined the fabric of our reality, not a freckle on her face was out of place. A surge of astonishment set in.

"The lieutenant killed you," I said to him.

"That he did." He smiled in acceptance. "Again, I apologize for causing such a mess. I was struck by an understanding that I could be of much more assistance once freed from that body."

I glanced back at the chaotic scene. "Am I dead too?" I asked hesitantly.

"Your body is fine. And from what I'm seeing, your friend will survive. You pop out very easily, don't you?"

I nodded. "Especially when my life is in danger. I guess it's a hidden ability."

"Then your soul is certainly trying to teach you something."

I replayed the experience of being tied up by the hunters before rising out of my body and willing the truck wheel to veer off that path. Although things seemed similarly hopeless then, from a higher perspective I was aware of a cosmic order, of epiphanies that I could barely remember consciously and even now couldn't quite reach.

Thankfully, the soldiers had barely moved, and together we left the altar to float toward our bodies: Leon's was vacant, mine was blinded—despite seeing so clearly—and Luna's was in pain. I felt bad that her consciousness was not with us, but that might have been a good thing.

"Why does death happen?" I asked the wise spirit. "Is it simply an accident we have no choice in, or is it all part of a larger orchestration?"

"I suppose that depends, doesn't it?" he replied. "In my case, I had lived a long life and recognized that my purpose was satisfied. All decisions in time and space led up to this moment. So yes, this was orchestrated. In a way, it was preordained."

"Then our lives and deaths are dictated by fate?" I questioned, recalling my last conversation with Walter.

"What we call fate is simply free will from the level of the soul. Mine desired to return home, and so this nice gentleman helped me find a way." He gestured to Lieutenant Hernandez. "He even sent a blow to the exact part of your brain that would recalibrate the pineal gland, allowing for your current state while prolonging the flow of time. Therefore, he has served us both by setting the stage for this extraordinary meeting, and his waking mind isn't even aware of it. There are no accidents in the perfection of the grand design. Nor are there any real victims—or villains."

I stared into the spiteful eyes of Leon's killer and had a hard time believing those words. "Then why are some people so angry?"

"Because we're all actors carrying out a script," he answered. "We are but dream characters in the mind of God, striving for Self-realization, though only a select few may consciously remember this. Most identify entirely with their egos, and this generates great inner conflict. In the case of my kind liberator, he has forgotten who he is and thus chooses to experience what he is not. In turn, he obstructs the understanding of the child deep within, and of his infinite soul. If only he could see it as clearly as we can."

After focusing my intent, a radiant sphere of energy appeared above the lieutenant. It extended down into everyone present, each of us becoming the ray of a central sun or branches of a single tree.

I saw shadows lurking over his shoulder, distorting that loving purity by whispering falsehoods into his ear.

"He's just confused," I marveled, acknowledging others who had given in to the same deception.

"Yes." He nodded. "But regardless of his motives, the opposition he generates can only assist in our evolution if used as an opportunity. This is why you must love your enemies. For even the demons may turn into angels when seen in the right light."

The soldiers had progressed in restraining our bodies, ensuring we were cuffed and blinded, while Luna's leg continued to bleed. Although I still wasn't worried, it became difficult to imagine how we might escape or how the situation could be utilized positively.

"I don't want to die," I professed to the spirit. "It's not that I'm afraid—not after this. But I promised my love that I would see her eyes open." I reminisced of the lucid dream with otherworldly creatures, mysterious angels, and a storm-inducing Evelyn. "She told me that she missed me. And that I have a mission."

Leon beamed and grazed my astral body with his fingers, bestowing the same serenity that he was experiencing. "As I have told you, Samuel, God gave us all the tools we need to create along with him. The only question is whether we will surrender to His will, allowing Him to work his miraculous solutions. Between you, Him, and all of them, there truly exists no separation. Recognize this, and you may rewrite the script whenever you wish."

"I will do my best," I said with appreciation before glancing back at Evelyn. There I noticed something gleaming beneath her hand, where the blue feather should have been.

"She carries a gift," Leon commented. We rejoined her at the altar to discern what it was: a golden key, shining uncommonly, the same one Christ had previously carried in my dream.

"What does it mean?" I asked in wonderment.

"I'm not sure, exactly." He laughed. "What I can tell you is that following my physical death, so many memories are coming back to me, as if I am awakening from a most convincing dream. And I shall declare with certainty that even in life, we always hold the key to the Kingdom of Heaven—not by way of judgment from something outside of ourselves . . ."

"But through lifting the veil of misunderstanding that we ever left in the first place," I finished for him.

With this statement, Evelyn's hand lifted on its own, and the key gravitated toward me. It halted in the air before me, offering its abilities. I stared at it speechlessly.

"She wants you to have it," Leon encouraged. "If only to give you permission to unlock more of your true self."

I nodded and extended my hand. With the simplest touch, the key transformed into a pure light that funneled through my being. I felt utter bliss while my heart ignited with an energy that brightened the entire dimension. Even Christ's eyes seemed enlivened.

"Thank you, Evelyn," I whispered, kissing her with my astral lips, knowing that with our combined spirit, we could accomplish anything.

"And my deepest gratitude for making such remarkable friends," Leon added warmly. "I hope you don't mind that I have another appointment. Come now. It's about that time."

Following his lead, I floated through the church wall and arrived by the river, which glittered with the same brilliance as the grass and the trees. Drifting downstream toward us was a little rowboat I recognized from a lucid dream.

"Leon?"

"Yes, Samuel?"

"How do I know if this is real?" I surveyed the mystical setting.

He replied, "One can spend their whole life analyzing, judging their experience against a definition of reality, but the experience itself is what matters. Because that's what life is all about, isn't it? Death too. Even if it is all just a stubborn illusion."

The rowboat grounded on the riverbank, waiting for him to hop in.

"You may forget most of this anyway, but if you had to remember one thing, know that those you've watched die, myself included, are still very much alive, as the greater part of our essence is always in spirit. And it is all in accordance with the grand design, one in which we have the free will to create, to live, and to die. You are not to blame for any of our choices to leave."

As he glided toward the boat, I felt loving presences emerge beside me; invisible, they observed from just outside our present frequency. A giant weight lifted, and I began to cry with emotions as real as I'd ever experienced.

"I know time acts funny on these planes," Leon said as he boarded, emitting a joyful glow, "but I have a meeting with somebody I haven't seen for quite some time. Be well, dear friend. Until we meet again."

"Goodbye, Leon." I watched the boat take him further downstream before ascending into a bright light that seemingly led to infinity. I then looked to the sky and noticed its beauty, brimming as it was with swirls of gold and violet.

"I'm ready to go back now," I said to no one in particular.

To my surprise, a voice answered: *"As you wish."*

Suddenly, I was thrust back into my body, with my hands cuffed behind my back, my eyes blind behind the cloth. Space and time sped up again as soldiers attempted to carry me, and silence was replaced by Luna's screams. Regardless, I channeled the serenity of a higher realm, knowing that nothing could restrain me but my own mind. I shook off the soldiers and crossed my legs into a lotus position, deciding it was time to finish my meditation.

Almost immediately, a force exploded from my core and drove the soldiers back, stabilizing around me like a psychic shield. As I concentrated, it continued to expand, sparking cries of confusion from those who could not break through.

"What should we do, sir?" a soldier shouted to the lieutenant.

"Kill him," I heard him reply. Yet I had no fear, for although I could not see physically, I felt everything: their conflicted emotions, their hearts racing, the bullets loaded in their rifles. I chose to respond with unconditional love, for in the grand design, everything was perfect; even the strawberries scattered on the ground were instilled with hidden purpose. And with a single breath, I became one with all of it.

Each time a trigger was pulled, the weapon jammed and backfired violently. Though the soldiers tried over and over, it seemed as if they were shooting themselves. One by one, they ran in panic, ignoring Lieutenant Hernandez's furious commands. The shield dropped, for it was no longer necessary, and my bodily restraints fell away. I opened my eyes to find myself levitating and gazed compassionately at the man who wanted me dead.

"Don't run, you cowards! Where are you going?" he yelled to no avail before approaching with the same pistol that ended Leon's life. "I'll just have to do this myself."

It refused to work, for I had connected with his light. He aimed it right at my head and was driven back several steps with a look of disbelief. Finally, he pulled out a knife.

Luna intervened. "Don't you *dare*." With her handcuffs broken and a fiery glare burning holes through the blindfold, she flung the lieutenant all the way back against the entrance wall, then left him there, hanging. She seethed as she limped toward him through obvious suffering, trailing blood on the carpet.

The weaponless lieutenant could only struggle and wheeze.

"Luna," I said, climbing to my feet. She paid me no mind as he stretched out his arms in desperation.

"You poor thing," she taunted. "Have you confused your power with mine?"

I passed Leon's body and watched as she gradually choked his killer, waiting for her to let up. He stared at me with terror in his eye, baring scars buried deeper than the burns, which sadly had never properly healed. Then, as his breath waned, he gazed in incredulity toward the opposite end of the church, as if witnessing something unseen.

"Luna!" I demanded. "Let him go."

With a profound exhale, she reluctantly conceded. The lieutenant fell to the floor, gasping in shock before scurrying through the adjacent doors. Immediately afterward, Luna collapsed.

I dashed to her side and dropped to my knees, troubled as she lay dangerously pale, her breathing strained. Lifting her bloodstained robes, I found the nasty bullet wound on her hip. Rather than trying to heal herself, she had exhausted her remaining energy defending me and Evelyn.

Even in her dire condition, she managed a smile.

"It's not so bad, really," she said through the pain. "I've died in worse ways."

Gesturing over my shoulder, I replied, "It was his time, Luna. But it's definitely not yours."

Suddenly, an energy blossomed from within my heart, yearning to express itself in our reality. I let it flow through my arms and into my palms and fingers until they were gifted with golden light.

"You have it too," Luna uttered in amazement.

I calmly placed them above the wound in the same manner as she had for Evelyn, spontaneously affirming, "Only the light may be here. All else must leave!" Like magic, the bullet exited the wound before the hole closed up completely, critically ceasing any further bleeding. Luna breathed with relief, but something behind me caught her attention.

"Samuel, look!"

The rays of the sun had focused on Leon's body, which emanated rainbow-colored geometry not of this plane. Simultaneously, the body shrank in size, the awful head wound miraculously vanishing as if healed in harmony with Luna's injury. Beautiful violins played along a soft breeze, hinting that his essence flowed eternally with the cosmic symphony, merely shifting to a higher octave.

In the background was the altar on which Evelyn dreamed, guarded by a sculpture that observed without judgment. For a brief moment, we saw through the illusion and knew we were protected by something greater than ourselves—though never truly separate.

CHAPTER 12

I COULDN'T TELL how much time we spent sitting there. My mind was still a step out of time, gradually adjusting from a larger reality. As I stared at the altar, I did not want to leave. Even the sight of Leon's body did not cause grief, despite my former attitudes about death. Rather, I caught myself smiling, holding on to the memory of his soul's final advice to me before sailing into an infinite light.

All the while, Luna rested with her head on my shoulder; it would have been heartless to push her away. Only the distant noise of a helicopter snapped us out of our stupor, though fortunately it passed quickly.

"Don't worry," I assured her. "They're not coming back."

"They'd be absolute fools," she said, the light in her eyes returning, though her voice sounded dry and weak. An astonished glimpse of her blood on my hands reminded me that she too had nearly left and that everything we'd experienced had truly happened. When I finally stood to check on Evelyn, the blue feather had mysteriously vanished.

The ensuing hours were devoted to cleaning the church with cloths I wet in the river and supplying Luna with enough jarfuls of water for her to continue to recover. I rolled up the bloodstained carpet all the way from the entrance to the altar, then disposed of it in the forest along with the lieutenant's weapons. Lastly, I lifted

Leon's inexplicably shrunken body into the wheelbarrow and rolled it out the doors and toward the back of the church, feeling led by some power.

Gorgeous green bushes of ripe strawberries graced the fertile land, planted in rows around a central area on which the high sun focused its shine. I stationed the wheelbarrow at the perimeter and walked into the field, arriving at a rose-covered mound with a golden plaque reading, IN LOVING MEMORY OF ELEANOR McKENZIE. Following were words of inspiring poetry:

WE ARE THE MUSIC MAKERS
AND WE ARE THE DREAMERS OF DREAMS
WANDERING BY LONE SEA-BREAKERS
AND SITTING BY DESOLATE STREAMS
EVEN IN THE AGES LYING
IN THE BURIED PAST OF THE EARTH
FOR EACH AGE IS A DREAM THAT IS DYING
OR ONE THAT IS COMING TO BIRTH

I recognized it as a variation on a centuries-old piece Walter once showed me, written by a man named Arthur. While I pondered, the birds sang a joyous new melody. It gave me hope that all good souls would be reborn into a better world.

Near the mound, a shovel lay in the dirt next to a portion of land allocated ahead of time to be the neighboring grave. "Okay," I consented to the clear blue sky once it became obvious what was being asked of me.

"Who are you talking to?" Luna called, passing Leon's body to enter the strawberry field with his empty basket.

"You shouldn't be here," I said. "You've been shot."

"And I've been healed," she replied. She crouched over a vibrant bush to inspect its harvest. "Mind over body. Spirit over mind. Plus, I think these strawberries are exactly what my spirit needs."

She plopped one into her mouth and groaned with satisfaction, gathering several more into the basket. "You have to try these!"

She came by to offer them. I hesitantly took one and bit it off the leaf, then another and another, their heavenly flavor bursting in my mouth. After such a gruesome morning, the sweetness felt shamefully comforting, cleansing my lingering pain. But before I could thank her, Luna had dropped to her knees, her eyes filling with tears as she read the plaque, then gazed back toward the wheelbarrow.

"He's in a better place, isn't he?"

"He is." I nodded with full knowing, grasping her hand to help her up. "Take care of Evelyn, please. Give her water if you can. I'll make sure he gets the burial he deserves."

The bulk of the remaining daylight was spent digging, only stopping for water and strawberries, running off energies that stemmed from an unseen plane. My body ached, my mind was dazed, and my skin oozed under the unrelenting sun, conjuring memories of my duties at the Facility. The difference, however, was the conscious realization that my true identity existed in none of those things, and so I dug tirelessly until I found myself eye level with the top of the grave.

Climbing out, I saw that Luna had managed to bring Evelyn by the grassy riverbank. She washed my love's face while humming softly, in between feeding her from a jar of mashed strawberries. I sat on the edge of the grave and watched in a dreamlike state before asking for assistance.

Together, we carried Leon's body to the place of burial; I hopped down as she passed him to me, and I laid him down gently, wondering if he was watching from above, smiling.

"I know you're with your wife again," I whispered affectionately. "I'll see you in the world to come."

Tears flooded out in cathartic release, not only for Leon but for my beloved tutor, who could never be granted a proper funeral. I used this as an opportunity to say goodbye to both enlightened men: one who became my second father and one whom I was made to meet for a single morning so that he could impart wisdom that would last a lifetime.

"Rest easy, sweet friend," Luna said as I climbed up next to her. She plucked a pink rose from Eleanor's grave and dropped it onto his body. After a few minutes of silent processing, I retrieved the shovel and started to fill in the huge pile of dirt, but Luna intervened. "Allow me."

She quickly covered the body through several rhythmic sweeping motions. The only work that remained was to pat down the grave.

Bestowed with an extra layer of appreciation for the life we still shared, however implausible the odds seemed, we joined Evelyn at the riverbank.

"How do you think they found us?" I asked Luna finally as I sat in contemplation.

She sighed and settled next to Evelyn. "I've been wondering that since this morning, and the only explanation is that they have new youth working for them. They used them to view our location remotely and arrived while we slept."

"But who would help them capture us?"

"I'm not sure." She shrugged. "But they are probably not willing."

"Well, so much for this place being secret and hidden."

"How would Leon see the situation?" she responded with encouragement. "Trust that the river brought them for a reason, even if it was to bring out something special in you. It goes without saying, Samuel, but that was really incredible, what you did back there."

"Thank you." I turned toward the trees. "But I can't even tell if it was me who did it. I used your meditation to attune to a higher energy, and that certain energy is what protected us. I was just a vessel for it."

"Don't be so modest. I've never seen anybody with the power to stop guns from shooting. I'm honestly so proud of you, darling. It may have been Leon's time, but the love you tapped into saved our lives."

"We saved each other's," I affirmed, proceeding to tell her the pieces I remembered from my out-of-body experience: my otherworldly exchange with Leon's luminous spirit and being entrusted a key from Evelyn.

"So that's where you received it," said Luna, her eyes glistening.

"Yes." I nodded, struck by an idea. With a hint of excitement, I placed my hands over Evelyn. However, as much as I tried to connect with my heart, I felt no healing energy and saw no golden light.

Luna chuckled. "You can't force it to come through. But know it will be there when you need it. I guess you can say it's a gift of the divine."

"When did it first come for you?" I asked.

"After the old me died by losing all fear of death. It's surely a sign, my star apprentice, that you're going through your own little metamorphosis." She winked with welcomed happiness, then glanced down. "I could really hatch out of these old bloody robes. Leon said something about a nearby village, didn't he? Maybe I can get new clothes there."

"Tomorrow," I said, as tired as the setting sun. "Tonight, we stay and rest."

That evening, we slept in the strawberry field, blanketed by the soft moonlight and unbothered by a passing rain.

The following morning, a dazzling rainbow arced over the church, and roses had sprouted on Leon's grave, spreading from his wife's. A monarch butterfly flew from flower to flower, showcasing its glorious wings.

∼

With reinvigorated confidence, we resumed our journey, distilling the wisdom of our experiences while letting go of a past that lay out of our control, as tough as it was to say goodbye to Leon's gentle soul. I similarly couldn't say where the future would lead and when we would find our safe haven, but faith brewed within me as I pushed Evelyn downstream. I left these decisions to a greater part of ourselves, allowing my conscious mind to flow with the river.

Meanwhile, Luna seemed rejuvenated after the previous morning's miracles, her leg's magical recovery, and a good night's sleep. I wasn't even bothered as she performed her bizarre bird calls, simply heartened to see her true self on display only a day after dodging death yet again.

"Any intel from your sources?" I joked.

Cheerfully, she tuned in to a melody along the trees. "They say to keep on walking, and we'll come across a comforting friend before the day's end."

"What does that mean?"

"Beats me. But when the songbirds sing like this, we better listen carefully."

"Like they know the score," I quoted, revisiting some of my happiest memories.

"Always," she replied.

This triggered my inner child to surface, if only for a short time. My mind became blissfully empty. Meanwhile, the world all around us flaunted sheer beauty, each blade of grass and tree branch perfectly placed on the blueprint of creation. Colors appeared to intensify, and I felt life within everything, giving myself permission to fall in love with it after witnessing firsthand the illusion of death. During this time, I wept intermittently, having nearly forgotten these truths that were once obvious.

My attention inevitably returned to my exhausted and hungry body. Even Luna was panting. We settled in the shade at the forest's edge, where we snacked on the strawberries we had stuffed in our satchels.

I urged her to rest. "Don't overexert yourself. We aren't in any hurry."

"Okay," she yawned, "but just a quick nap."

Within minutes, she was snoring, and it was oddly contagious. After I finished feeding the mashed jam to Evelyn, I decided to lie next to her, too tired to fight the tranquilizing effects of our surroundings. In the state between sleep and wakefulness, my mind turned its focus to my childhood once more—with some less pleasant memories.

My mother lay ill on a sofa by a window, an unsightly blotch growing on her skin. She smiled nonetheless as soon as she saw me.

"I love you, sugar bear." She extended her hand. "And that love never dies. Never forget that."

"I love you too, Mommy," I told her through tears, placing my tiny hand in hers, praying that her suffering would go away.

The scene shifted suddenly, and my father came in. He was drunk and angry, screaming and toppling chairs. With a spiteful glare, he turned his rage toward me. I scurried up to the second floor, seeking refuge within a half-empty closet . . .

A shriek snapped me back to reality, but I could not tell if it came from the dream.

"Luna—"

She hushed me. I sat up to see her staring wide eyed with a finger to her lips, nodding to something over my shoulder. Turning, I was met by the growl of a hulking black bear emerging from the forest in close range.

"Don't . . . move," she whispered as I shook off my decade-old memories.

It was the first of its kind I'd ever encountered, but I felt strangely unafraid. For a while, we stayed frozen as it inspected us. Then, noticing my satchel within arm's reach, I opened it slowly and pulled out several strawberries; I tossed them to the bear, and it ate them up gladly.

"Good call, Sammy." Luna rose to her feet. "I've got this from here."

In an unusual spectacle, she commenced a stare-down with the bear, fixating on its eyes. They grunted back and forth as if holding a friendly conversation. This lasted for over a minute, Luna erupting into laughter at one point while gesturing toward me. Finally, the bear gazed at Evelyn with surprising affection for such an intimidating creature and continued on its way.

"What was that?" I asked in bewilderment, not entirely convinced I wasn't still in a dream.

"Oh, we were just talking," Luna recounted with rosy cheeks. "He's really a charming bear. Funny too. He is a guardian of this forest and was making sure that our souls meet a certain standard of purity."

"Birds were fine." I stood to face her. "But you can speak bear now?"

"A little, but most of the speaking part was us messing around. When using animal telepathy, you communicate with pictures and feelings. Just like you would with little babies!" An image of a pine cone popped into my mind. "See?"

"Fair enough," I conceded, remembering the doe and reserving judgment on what could be considered crazy. "What were you two 'talking' about?"

"Well, first of all, I told him that bears are my spirit animal, which definitely helped to calm him a bit. Then I asked him about a village, and he said we would find one right through these trees. All we have to do is go toward the fire." She led me back to get a broader perspective and pointed out smoke rising a few miles in the distance. "It might be somewhat of a trek. But it should be the one that Leon said could help us."

"Wow," I said, genuinely impressed. "Did the bear tell you anything else?"

"Yeah, that you're extremely lucky to be hanging out in the forest with two gorgeous girls." She winked. "All in picture form, of course."

My face grew warm, though I immediately composed myself.

Judging by the sun, it was late afternoon, so we had to travel quickly. But if there was any opportunity to find assistance for

Evelyn, we needed to take it, even if it wasn't the final destination. We filled up on water before I grabbed hold of the wheelbarrow and ventured into the forest.

Thankfully, we had more to rely on than faith in our hearts, for the trail of smoke remained as a beacon, visible between the branches, gradually getting closer. Journeying unwaveringly with the encouragement of the songbirds, we came to an opening in just over an hour.

"Finally, civilization," I uttered.

Indeed, there resided a village in the middle of the woods, seemingly enclosed in its own bubble of reality. I didn't notice any roads leading to it, though its outskirts teemed with golden fields of wheat. Between these fields was the source that guided us: a giant bonfire.

"Never doubt a telepathic bear," Luna affirmed. I tucked away that nugget of wisdom.

We watched from afar as a dozen people labored in the oncoming twilight. It took some time to figure out that they were plucking weeds from the fields of wheat, gathering them in bundles, and throwing them into the fire to burn.

"How should we go about this?" I asked apprehensively.

"Don't be shy, Sammy." Luna patted my shoulder before stepping from the shadows. "Leon said it's a village of kind people. Come on. I'll do the talking."

She strode toward them confidently while I trailed behind with Evelyn, unsure what to think. One noticed us. He alerted the others, halting their work. All young men and women, they stared anxiously out of ordinary eyes.

"Hi!" Luna waved without a care in the world. "We're so happy that we found you guys!"

Unfortunately, this seemed to unnerve them; they bolted in the opposite direction, leaving the fire to burn unattended.

"Was it something I said?" She pouted in disappointment.

"I don't know." I let out a sigh. "But something tells me we should've kept the blindfolds."

We traversed the fields to enter the central part of the village, where wooden buildings and houses lined a deserted lane. Sounds of closing doors and quiet murmurs made for an eerie setting. Clearly, we were being observed. I glimpsed a face through a window before the blinds were hastily shut. After waiting in vain for any sort of greeting, Luna and I stopped to gaze at one another.

"They're afraid of us," I said, receiving flashbacks from my youth.

"I guess not everyone here thinks we're so gorgeous," she teased, grabbing my cheek. "But don't worry, Sammy. I still think you're adorable."

I glanced at Evelyn with a newfound appreciation for how she had always accepted me for who I was—and I loved her for that. Yet a part of me wondered how she would have reacted had her village not been right down the road from the Facility. Here, obviously, they were wary of outsiders and had probably never encountered humans like us.

Just as we turned to leave, the creak of a door opening seized our attention, coming from a nearby two-story home. Out walked a middle-aged woman with dark, curly hair, wearing a stoic expression and an apron.

Luna and I hesitantly stepped forward to greet her. Thankfully, she remained unperturbed, even as she met our stares. She seemed to be the only one in the village willing to talk to us.

She spoke with a gruff voice. "My nieces came running about strangers with the big eyes. But I do not judge until I see what is inside." She surveyed the windows of our souls, then grimaced at our stained robes. "What is your business here, children?"

"Well, we're kind of on this secret adventure," Luna answered. "I saved his life, and ever since then, we've been following the river . . . though we almost died a couple more times. Luckily, this afternoon we met a friendly bear and—"

"There's been an accident," I loudly interjected, moving aside to show the woman the wheelbarrow.

"Oh dear." The woman's serious demeanor turned sympathetic as she approached Evelyn to examine her, frowning at the sight of her scar.

"We are heading to a sanctuary," I explained, "where there are children like us who can help wake her. But a kind priest told us about this village, and we thought it would be best to stop here first. My name is Samuel, by the way. This is Luna. And her name is Evelyn."

"You can call me Artemis," she said, motioning toward her home. "Come, before anyone sees."

Luna contorted her face. "Why is everyone here so afraid?"

"Because you're not the first large-eyed outsiders who have stumbled upon us in recent days. There was a group of strangely dressed children. Most of their souls were corrupted, however. And their leader was carrying an amulet quite similar to the scar on your friend's forehead."

~

Artemis's home was cozy and old fashioned. The first floor was divided into a sitting area near the entrance and a kitchen the next room over, from which pleasant aromas drifted. Leaving the wheelbarrow outside, I laid Evelyn on a sofa by the staircase while the rest of us gathered around a large table. There, we told Artemis more about our journey and, with the exception of some personal details, described our encounters with the black robes. Then she explained how Matteo and his gang had discovered her village two days prior.

"They came during the night and woke us up yelling," she said. "Once they got our attention, they showed off their abilities like parlor tricks and threatened to burn down our entire village if they didn't get exactly what they wanted."

"What did they want?" I asked bitterly.

"Food, mostly." She dropped her head. "They stole a good portion of our spring harvest, which is the reason we like to keep hidden from that grubby general and his minions. These teenagers claimed to have found us through some kind of remote perception. And they boasted of their divine supremacy; they plan to establish a global new order with them as the rulers."

"Sounds familiar," I sighed. "I'm so sorry that happened, but I promise you that we are not with them. Most of us"—I glanced at Luna, who was quietly rubbing her golden cuff—"are not like that at all. And I'm sure neither are many of their followers."

"Believe me, children, if I suspected bad intentions, I wouldn't have invited you into my home. All things considered, we came away relatively unscathed, even if we have been living in fear. Normally, we are a lot more welcoming. And that reminds me." She stood and called to the second floor, "Girls! You can come down now!"

Three young women with olive skin and long brown hair appeared on the staircase, wearing the same farming attire as the group we'd seen by the bonfire. Unlike earlier, now we had time to see each other's eyes.

"These are my nieces." Artemis introduced them with a smile. Eirene, the eldest, looked at least twenty; Elizabeth, the middle child, seemed around our age; and Alexandra couldn't have been older than thirteen. "This is Samuel, Luna, and Evelyn, who has been in a coma for over a week."

"I'm sorry. We had no idea." Eirene led her sisters to the sofa, compassion filling their gazes. "We should never have run away."

"It's okay," replied Luna. "We're used to people calling us wizard demons and pointing guns at our faces. Anything other than that is definitely an improvement."

"Eirene, please inform Dr. Robert about the situation," Artemis requested. "As for you two, set the table and make our guests comfortable. They will be staying for supper."

"That would be much appreciated," I said, delighted that we had found yet another kind stranger to help us along our way and possibly bring Evelyn some real medical attention.

While Eirene went to the doctor, her aunt cooked in the kitchen, and her younger sisters arranged plates and silverware between obvious stares of fascination. Elizabeth complimented Luna's spiral earrings, and Alexandra blushed as she handed us glasses of water.

It didn't take long for the eldest to return.

"Dr. Robert is busy with Angela," she informed Artemis before turning to me. "But he promises to stop by first thing in the morning, if that's all right with you."

"That's fine," I said with a hint of disappointment, not wanting to question further. "Thank you for doing this."

"I guess they have no choice but to spend the night," Artemis announced from the kitchen.

"Shall we prepare their quarters?" inquired Elizabeth.

"Yes, my dear." From the kitchen, Artemis carried out a big bowl of spaghetti, a food I'd only seen in history lessons. "But first, we eat."

The pasta was embellished with tomato sauce and eggplant. A loaf of soft bread and a jug of red wine were set beside it, adding to an already irresistible meal. As her nieces sat on the other side of the table, Artemis served food onto our plates.

She explained, "This cuisine originates from countries now largely buried beneath the sea. But we try to keep our ancestors' traditions. Would either of you like a glass of wine?"

I paused before politely declining, never having tasted alcohol yet knowing what it could do to a person.

"I'll have some!" Luna blurted out excitedly, nudging me with her elbow. "You gotta have some fun in life, Sammy."

The two older sisters were also poured glasses, and we all toasted to Evelyn's health.

"I wish she could eat with us," Elizabeth sympathized.

"She's currently on my exquisite berry mush diet," Luna clarified, slurping her red wine. "Seems to be loving the strawberries. Hasn't thrown them up yet, at least."

Artemis smiled from the head of the table. "I'll make sure to serve her a nice steaming plate as soon as she awakens."

The food was unlike anything I'd tasted in my ten years at the Facility and clearly made with affection. I made sure to savor each mouthful. But while the girls taught me how to properly twirl spaghetti, Luna had already devoured her first serving and was reaching for seconds with tomato sauce staining her face.

"Wait." She looked at Artemis with sudden hesitation. "This pasta is vegan, right?"

"Why, yes, it should be."

"Good." She grabbed more and gobbled it down. "If I have any dairy, I'll lose my abilities."

The sisters watched Luna with quiet intrigue, unsure whether to take her seriously.

"Anyway, what brings you all here?" Eirene asked finally.

I could only chuckle. "Well, that's a long story."

Doing most of the talking, I described the extraordinary events of our quest for Sanctuary, culminating with our close call with the military soon after making an unforgettable friend. Thankfully, they refrained from asking us certain questions, just as we did for them. I was content to see the glimmer of wonder in the eyes of Alexandra, who finished her plate to revel in our story.

"So, you really have special powers, like those mean kids?" she inquired.

"We all have special powers, including you," I told her. "But it's up to us to choose how we use them."

"I'd like to use them to get even with my sisters!" She pretended to shoot energy from her fingers while the rest of us laughed and Luna guzzled more wine.

"You know, I *also* have two sisters," she said with a drunken slur. "We're gonna go see my big one, Johanna, at her hippie gathering down the river!"

"Oh, how nice," Artemis responded. "What about the other one?"

"Selena? Uh, we don't really have the healthiest relationship. The last time I saw her she threatened me with a—"

"Luna," I butted in. "You seem quite sleepy. Maybe you should rest?"

"Nonsense, Sammy. I'm feeling *good* all of a sudden! Now, stop being a party pooper and dance with me!" She got up and swayed to a silent melody, proceeding to hop clumsily around the table. "I've always thought about how fun it would be to live life as a bunny."

"That's enough wine for you," Artemis insisted, taking her glass. "Eirene, how about you help our guest hop on upstairs? And get her a fresh change of clothes while you're at it."

"Sounds like a slumber party!" Luna happily went along, slinging her arm around the eldest niece and staggering her way to the second floor. Meanwhile, I felt satisfied after the excellent meal, thanking our hosts from the bottom of my heart as I brought my plate to the kitchen.

"It is truly our pleasure," Artemis responded warmly. "All we want is for you to feel at home after the hell you've been through. Tonight you may sleep in Elizabeth's room. Evelyn, of course, is welcome there too."

"That is so generous," I said, relishing the thought of a comfortable bed. "I know that Luna is grateful as well, even if her way of showing it is strange sometimes."

She laughed. "It's perfectly fine. I'm glad that somebody enjoyed the wine. Personally, I prefer tea at this hour, and I'm going to make some using mint from my garden. Would you like to join me?"

I smiled. "Yes, please."

"I'll call you once it's ready."

The sisters had headed upstairs, so while Artemis heated water on the stove, I took Evelyn in my arms and carried her up. The distinct sounds of Luna's snores echoed from the nearest room. I entered to find her sprawled ungraciously across a two-person bed as Eirene stood over her in bemusement.

"So much for a change of clothes," I said, causing the eldest to chuckle.

"She doesn't drink very much, does she?"

I shook my head. "I think that's clear." Suddenly, I heard a voice floating from a room down the hall, and I followed as if hypnotized. The door was cracked open just enough to see Elizabeth arranging new sheets, singing splendidly in front of a balcony, backed by a waning moon.

"When the rain falls to the sea,
They'll be waiting for you and for me,
And the sky reflects our image,
Trying to sleep right through our lives . . ."

She gasped when she noticed me.

"I'm sorry!" I stepped into the well-kept bedroom. "I didn't mean to scare you, but you have a beautiful voice."

"Thank you." Her cheeks turned red. "Usually I don't sing so openly; maybe it's the wine. But I honestly don't know where it comes from sometimes. Songs that I can't even put a name to just pop into my head."

"I love music too," I said, "but I'm not so great at singing."

"Well, I bet she likes it when you sing to her." She gestured to the girl asleep in my arms. "You love her, don't you?"

I nodded, surprised.

"I can see it in your eyes. They are not like the others. There is a great kindness to them. I should have given you more of a chance before I ran."

"I don't blame you." I sighed. "I've been running from myself my entire life."

"And why have you been running?"

"Because I was scared of who I am. I denied my true abilities."

Her eyes sparkled with a hint of magic. "Can you show me?"

In agreement, I rested Evelyn on the bed before scanning the room for a suitable object, deciding on a small, round clock atop a nightstand several feet away. I tuned into the tranquility of the soft breeze.

With every breath in, I gathered more energy, and with every breath out, I released any doubt. Gone was the past and the lies I told myself, the limitations I bought into at the Facility, for I knew after these recent days that we were entering an age of miracles. While the ticking clock synced with my heartbeat, it lifted elegantly and floated into Elizabeth's hand.

"He *does* have superpowers!" Alexandra shouted from the doorway, staring in amazement.

Calls from Artemis indicated that the tea was ready. Alexandra turned to go downstairs, and I was about to follow when Elizabeth grabbed my arm.

"Samuel, I need to tell you something I haven't told anyone." Her face became serious, so I listened attentively. "Months ago, I wandered to the river all on my own. I know that I shouldn't have, but I felt an indescribable pull. There, I came across two teenage boys, tall and handsome with your gentle eyes and their bodies painted unusually. They gave me a warning about dark forces lurking. And they told me of their home not far down the river, where any of our children are allowed to seek refuge."

My heart enlivened. "What did you say to them?"

"I said nothing. I didn't know what to say at the time." Her voice swelled with emotion, and she wiped her eyes before continuing, "The point is, Samuel, whatever you're looking for might be closer than you think."

"You don't know how much this means to me." Without thinking, I embraced her, though fortunately she didn't seem fazed by it. I then glanced at the clock she was carrying and was puzzled to see it read 12:35, as if we'd experienced a slippage through time.

"I guess you broke it," she commented, enchantment refilling her gaze. "Surely it can't be long past eight."

I thanked Elizabeth for the message as well as for inspiring confidence in my abilities. Before I headed downstairs, I kissed Evelyn on the forehead, knowing that she was in safe hands.

Artemis sat at the table with Alexandra beaming by her side, in the midst of describing what she'd witnessed before being hushed by her aunt.

"There you are, Samuel. I didn't want yours to get cold." Artemis nodded to a mug across from her filled with hot tea, green from the mint leaves. "I hope that my nieces didn't bug you up there."

"Not at all." I sat down and smirked at Alexandra. "They are quite wonderful, actually."

Artemis chuckled, then sipped her tea thoughtfully. "Events happen in your life that you neither expect nor understand. I had never planned for them to live with me. Only once you look back are you able to see how love changes everything." She gave her youngest niece a tender hug. "With enough of it, something transformational can happen."

I basked in the moment while I drank from my cup, hit by a wave of pure serenity. We watched in soothing silence as water turned into steam, freed from the limits of its former state.

CHAPTER 13

MUCH OF THE night was spent staring at the ceiling, listening to Evelyn's breath at my side, and faithfully envisioning her coming awake.

By dawn, I was ripe with restless energy. I used the washroom to freshen up before carrying Evelyn downstairs, where I laid her on the sofa and nourished her with river water.

"Did you sleep well?" asked Artemis, emerging from the kitchen with a basket of bread.

"Well enough," I said with gratitude. "The bed was very comfortable. I'm just excited for what today might bring."

"Dr. Robert should be here soon."

The sisters came down to bid us good morning. They had replaced their farming outfits with comfortable gowns, taking the day to rest. Alexandra yawned as she grabbed a slice of bread and covered it with a delicious-looking almond spread. Elizabeth sat near me and smiled, undoubtedly still thinking of our exchange the night before. A feeling of anticipation was in the air, even nervousness.

"There goes today's shift," noted Eirene.

Through the window we watched a group of farmers heading to the fields to preserve the autonomy of their impressive village. Meanwhile, the girls explained how every person contributed, whether as an electrician, plumber, or wise old storyteller. Moreover, they worked as a community, driven by compassion and cooperation rather than greed and materialism. I wondered how much everyone knew of the world outside their bubble.

The creaking of footsteps down the stairs reminded me of who was missing.

"Why, aren't you early birds?" Luna quipped, showing off a violet dress borrowed from Eirene with a spin and a wink. "How do you like it? Do I look sexy?"

"It fits perfectly!" complimented Elizabeth. Her sisters agreed.

"How are you feeling?" Artemis inquired.

"Oh, only slightly less wonderful than usual," she responded, sitting at the table. "It was fun while it lasted, but I think my drinking days are done."

A knock sounded from the doorway. I stood in apprehension while Artemis went to welcome her visitor. "Robert, thank you for doing this." She made way for the doctor to enter. "These are our guests: Samuel, Luna, and Evelyn."

A man in his sixties carried in a small bag. He wore modest clothing and looked nothing like the scientists at the Facility. Pausing to study each of us with tired eyes, he nodded somberly, then approached the sofa with no further greeting.

"How long has she been comatose?" he asked, pulling up a chair.

"Nine days," I answered. His eyebrows lifted in surprise.

"And do you know the root cause?"

"Yes." I exchanged glances with Luna. "It happened after we were kidnapped."

Again, I described the encounter with the hunters, which seemed like a lifetime ago, ending with the crash that left Evelyn in a coma. Then we explained how we had taken care of her ever since, giving her water and nutrients while using cloths for diapers.

"I applaud you for trying," the doctor replied, "but usually nourishment to unconscious patients would require more specialized equipment, such as a feeding tube and catheter. Especially if there's any sort of brain damage."

"She swallows my special berry mix just fine," Luna said, showing him the jar of purplish goo. "And I must say, she pees a good amount for a girl who sleeps all day."

He seemed perplexed as he looked at her forehead. "And this is from the accident?"

"The scar is unrelated, actually." I sighed. "It came after she was already unconscious."

As he probed her scalp, his confusion only intensified. "With what you are describing, there should be noticeable trauma to the head. But strangely enough, I cannot feel anything." From his bag he grabbed a stethoscope and placed it to her chest.

"When she was awake, she had a lung problem," I mentioned as he listened closely.

"Everything seems fine, thankfully—her heart, her breathing. There are no signs of injury. She's simply not here. It's uncanny." With his fingers, he opened her eyes and shined a flashlight into them, making me uneasy, before they shut again automatically. At a loss, the doctor turned to me. "Did you give her two-week sleeping pills or something?"

The door burst open with no warning. Barging in was a woman not much older than Eirene, sleepless eyes filled with anguish.

"Angela," Artemis breathed, rising from her chair.

The woman brushed her off. "You know why I'm here, Artemis."

A tense moment elapsed. The air was thick and the silence deafening. She set her gaze on me and Luna, then started sobbing.

The doctor stepped forward, clearing his throat. "Angela, is the medication—"

"No, Robert, it isn't helping!" She wiped away tears, yet her eyes didn't budge. "Only *they* can fix what happened to me!"

"I'm sorry," Luna countered, "but what is this about?"

Angela glared around with rising frustration. "You didn't tell them? None of you told them?"

There was no answer. Eirene lowered her head. Artemis went to comfort Alexandra, and Elizabeth teared up.

"Tell us what?" I asked finally.

"How they took my only son!"

My heart dropped in my chest as she wept, my bewilderment giving way to a wave of sympathy toward the grieving young mother.

Carefully, I approached her. "He has eyes like us, doesn't he?" I glanced at Luna, who had tears of her own, and I was reminded of the reason she'd left the black robes. I looked back toward Angela. "I'm truly sorry."

She grabbed me by the shoulders and shouted, "You have abilities, don't you? Just like them. You know where he is! You know where they took him!"

Artemis intervened. "There's no need for that, Angela."

I remained composed and opted to settle things.

"I do have abilities, but I cannot say where your son is. Fortunately, we will soon be with others who might have a clearer picture. We can band together and fight back." My heartbeat quickened. "We can stand up to them and bring home the children."

"And how do I know I can trust you?" she questioned.

"I was taken too when I was a child. I was experimented on as property of the Union." I cleared my throat. "As for the black robes, they have my young friend. They stole Evelyn's locket"—I gestured to the sofa—"and carved that into her forehead."

"They also killed my mother, if you really want to know," Luna professed from behind me, triggering a stunned silence. "They did it after I tried to leave. And then they took my little sister."

Angela's wet gaze was suffused with empathy. "Do you promise to also rescue my Justin? He's such a sensitive boy, and he's barely three."

The answer seemed to come from an unfathomable level of my being: "I promise."

She embraced me tearfully, then did the same to Luna, wishing us well on our quest to save the children and restore Evelyn's health. Afterward, she was led from the house by Dr. Robert, who told us with humble sincerity, "I am sorry if I wasted your time, but whatever this is goes beyond my capabilities. I doubt that any conventional treatment would accomplish anything. Keep doing what you're doing—because it's keeping her alive."

I nodded in acceptance and thanked him. As soon as the door closed behind him, Artemis addressed the unsaid.

"Three years ago, an unusual child was born in our village. It was more than just his large, bright eyes; he was extraordinary in ways we could never have imagined. Small, strange miracles would happen around him. We thought we were safely sheltered from the outside, protected from the reach of any government facility, though ultimately we realized we were naive." She shook her head. "It goes without saying, but when those kids came, they took more than just crops. They want to round up the rest from their alleged bloodline, even if that means taking them right out of their mothers' arms."

"Why didn't you tell us?" Luna asked. "It's something we can help with—and not an issue we haven't already been exposed to."

"I didn't want you to become swept further into a war I thought you had no business being involved in. Clearly, I was mistaken."

I glanced at Evelyn, then said with conviction, "It is our war whether we like it or not. Between Mabus's soldiers and Matteo's black robes, we're caught right in the middle. And we can't stand by while both factions steal innocent children."

As her nieces came to her side, a twinkle emerged in Artemis's eyes. "You must promise us to find yourselves a home first, filled with others of like mind, where together you'll be powerful. Just as Evelyn cannot awaken through conventional medicine, this war will not be won through conventional means. If you choose to fight, fight the right way. That is how the light will triumph in the end."

~

It was tough to say goodbye to our kind hosts. As a final parting gift, Artemis gave us jars filled with vegetables from her garden—carrots, radishes, and delicious eggplant—while her nieces packed fresh blankets into the wheelbarrow for Evelyn. We hugged all of them, thankful for the hospitality.

"Will we see each other again?" Elizabeth questioned.

"I'm sure we will," I said. "Maybe then you can properly meet Evelyn."

"And you can teach us about your powers!" Alexandra added.

"I would like nothing better," Luna responded.

Eirene smiled with her sisters. "Good luck on your journey."

I smiled back as we departed. "If you ever want to visit, we'll be right down the river."

We trekked along the central road and through the fields of wheat, where the fire still burned strongly. Farmers watched us pass, and to my relief, they nodded cordially. Perhaps word had spread quickly that we were not the enemy. Or perhaps they simply felt for the girl in the wheelbarrow, intuitively understanding our situation.

We returned to the forest and gazed once more upon the village. "It may have been a bit of a detour, but it was definitely worth it," Luna said, enamored with her new dress.

I echoed the words of an enlightened priest. "Nothing is wasted. There is wisdom to be gained from every experience."

Indeed, despite the sadness of our encounter with the young mother, we left the village with a clearer sense of purpose, as well as an appreciation for the small pleasures of living, whether it be a plate of spaghetti or a cup of hot tea. We hiked through the woods feeling renewed vitality, and with the help of our twittering friends among the trees, we found the river again before the sun reached its peak.

Luna observed the endless current. "It's beautiful, isn't it?"

"Almost feels like home," I said fondly.

"Almost." She winked. "We better get going."

I shook my head in amusement as she pranced through the grass. What Elizabeth had told me about the boys she'd met at the river confirmed the inner knowing we already possessed. We were close. The river seemed an inevitable path leading us to Sanctuary. There we would meet the universal healer and figure out how to win our war.

I visualized Evelyn opening her eyes. "Just a little longer," I whispered to her, feeling destiny within reach.

We traveled for hours as I held to this feeling, though there was nothing in sight but the untouched earth. I reveled in every sensation, from the flowing of the water to the rustling of distant leaves. All of nature appeared as one interconnected being, the air it breathed pure and life affirming, so I relaxed in the moment.

We waited until midafternoon to rest and eat some of Artemis's vegetables. She had not only sliced and seasoned them but also given us each a pair of utensils. We happily stuffed ourselves beneath the shade of the pines, soothed by a tranquil breeze. Subsequently, I retrieved the blend of strawberries and stood over the wheelbarrow to spoon-feed Evelyn.

She swallowed several mouthfuls without difficulty, and while wiping the residue, I swore that the edges of her lips curved upward into a smile. "Living is easy with eyes closed, isn't it?" I whispered.

The branches shifted unexpectedly, and the sun's rays reflected off the metal spoon, sparking a heightened state. I meditated on the object until I felt myself becoming the spoon, merging my awareness with every atom as well as the space in between. After gradually releasing my physical grasp, the spoon remained hovering, dispelling its need to bow down to gravity.

"*Very good, Sammy,*" Luna transmitted, ten feet to my side. "*But it's my spoon now.*"

She pulled it toward her with glowing eyes, but I pulled back, refusing to let it settle into her outstretched hand. "Not so fast!" I shouted with a grin before sharpening my focus, thus commencing a telekinetic tug-of-war with the spoon swaying back and forth in the center. It soon became obvious she was toying with me, however, for I had to expend nearly all my energy while she flaunted the luxury of twirling and dancing. Though my abilities had drastically improved, she was simply more powerful.

"You may be able to stop a bullet or two," she teased. "But remember that at the end of the day, I'm the big spoon, you're the little spoon, and it is futile to fight with me!"

The spoon was then seized by a force so robust that it bent in midair and glided to her fingertips. But right as she was about to win, another level of consciousness stepped in.

"No," I said.

The spoon came to a halt and reversed direction, appearing to surprise even Luna. At that point she realized she had to get serious. I sensed my aura doubling in size, and the spoon had no choice but to gravitate toward me. This state was effortless in that I did not have to think—but I couldn't shake the feeling that Evelyn was somehow assisting.

A woodland creature moved in the distance, abruptly breaking my psychic connection. Released, the spoon zoomed toward Luna at an unchecked speed, missing her hand and striking her chest, sending her to the ground.

"Are you okay?!" I rushed to her side and got down on my knees. To my annoyance and relief, she was laughing.

"That was amazing," she wheezed, the lethal utensil resting close by. "It hit me right in the heart."

"It's not a joke, Luna. You could have died."

"I know!" She continued laughing. "That's what makes it so damn funny."

As we caught each other's eyes, it was undeniable that we had a connection; just like her, I felt myself being reborn into a completely different person. Yet while our position was strangely similar to the day she taught me how to meditate, I could not even think about making the same mistake.

I glanced around to see what had distracted me, and my heart jumped with excitement: what I'd thought was an animal was, without a doubt, another human being. Alerting Luna, we watched intently as the stranger meandered along a riverbend in the distance before disappearing behind the trees.

"Let's find out who it is," I said. She enthusiastically agreed.

We packed up quickly and hastened down the river, trying to catch up to the mysterious wanderer, who we could only hope would be a friend. The river itself reflected a restless optimism, flowing faster with each passing minute. Even Evelyn's breathing elevated as we finally made it around the bend.

My jaw dropped in disbelief.

"What is this?" Luna demanded, equally alarmed.

A giant concrete dam dominated the landscape, obstructing the flow of the river. The current crashed against it and went no further. Although there was no hint of other people, that swiftly became the least of our worries, for as we turned our attention to the edges of the structure and beyond, we caught sight of something more disturbing.

Luna gasped while I uttered with incredulity, "It can't be."

In silence we approached a chain-link fence attached on either side of the dam that separated the earth into two polarities. Before it was the beautiful forest and river. Beyond it, however, existed an entirely different world: the water was blocked, and the trees stopped growing almost immediately. For miles on end, there was nothing but shockingly desolate wasteland. A nearby signpost warned of toxic radiation ahead.

I was struck by all my worst fears, unready to deal with the painful realization that the people at the Facility had been right—that the outside world was largely unsafe and the promise of Sanctuary was a pipe dream. It seemed that we came all this way just to end in dismay and, most terrible of all, a broken vow to Evelyn.

"I'm sorry, Samuel." Luna faced me tearfully. "I don't know what to say. Johanna told me that it was along this river."

I gazed back quietly and breathed in the air, which, as far as my body could tell, was pristine. Then I turned to the girl sleeping in the wheelbarrow and noticed something interesting. Her breathing was indeed quicker than usual, but she did not appear worried; rather, a smile was now unmistakable.

As I listened very carefully to the world around us, a paradox became glaring. The panic in my mind was misaligned with what my heart was telling me.

"Samuel?" Luna asked hesitantly.

"It's here." I became imbued with confidence as the faces of everyone we'd met along our journey flashed through my awareness. "It has to be."

Following my instinct, I dropped down into the lotus position and closed my eyes, feeling the warmth of the dirt below me, breathing until I became still and empty. With the clarity of effortless thought, I asked my higher self for an answer.

Without a moment's pause, I received an image of Walter, followed by a sudden immersion into a memory of one of our earliest meetings. He was reclining behind his desk, eating an apple and observing me closely through his silly monocle while the first Beatles record I'd ever heard played in the background. At the time, I was living beneath a shell of trauma, but by virtue of the miracles of music—along with the help of an orphan girl I'd met—I was slowly getting better. And Walter knew it.

After the song finished, he rose from his chair to flip the record over, though not before giving me a look of affection. "This next one is a bit different. It was written by George Harrison about those who hide behind a wall of illusion. There are people in this world, Samuel, who will pressure you into hiding with them and try to convince you that *you* are the crazy one for imagining a larger existence. But people like you and me cannot be swayed by illusion." He took a bite from his apple and winked. "We are here to see through it."

The memory faded to the sounds of a unique instrument, causing my eyes to open back within the present. As I calmly scanned the scene in front of me—the fence, the dam, and the boundless wasteland—uncanny cracks started appearing, like glitches in a hologram. I was struck by the epiphany that this was only a test.

"Are you okay, Samuel?" Luna stared, puzzled, as I rose with a grin.

"Do you remember what you told me, Luna? About our reality and everything we see?"

"What do you mean?"

"It is but a projection."

I moved to the fence and placed my hand against the metal. Although it seemed unusually malleable, the habits of my mind wouldn't quite let me push through. That's when I decided to abandon any judgments or limiting beliefs, stripping away layers of the old version of me.

I undressed right then and there to stand completely naked, dropping my robes, sandals, and satchel next to Evelyn in the wheelbarrow.

"What in God's name are you doing?" Luna regarded me like I'd gone absolutely crazy.

"Trusting the river," I told her excitedly.

"You've really lost your marbles this time, haven't you, Samuel?"

"Perhaps," I said, thinking it might be true. "Wait here. I'll come back for you."

I plunged into the river. The embrace of the cool water was instantly invigorating, and it gave me encouragement that I was doing the right thing. I swam to the center and rolled onto my back, letting the current take hold of me. More strange music echoed into my consciousness, poetically repeating a single affirmation to turn off my mind, relax, and float downstream.

I felt myself move increasingly faster and tried to remain thoughtless, though fears and doubts slyly crept to the surface. They were remnants of shadows I had not yet illuminated, attempting to persuade me that the world was cruel, my heart was a liar, my newfound friends were not to be trusted, and my love and I were soon going to die. I didn't buy into any of it, however, and so without my belief, they held no power.

"There is no wall," I whispered. "There are no barriers. It is all within me."

For a moment, there was stillness and transcendent silence.

Then I picked up on the reverberations of shouting. The voice was not Luna's; it was that of a young man.

I came to my senses amid a frenzy, for instead of stopping against the dam, I was swept along at a pace accelerating to the level of rapids. Elation was quickly overtaken by the need to swim against the heavy current, dodging boulders. Flailing in the water and gasping for air, I called out for assistance and discerned a psychic presence pulling me to shore.

"Take this!" the voice urged as I neared the bank.

I stretched my arm to grasp it instinctively—a sturdy branch, stabilizing me enough to get to my feet and finally out of the water.

"Samuel," my helper said, suddenly sounding familiar.

It took a second for my sight to clear. When it did, my heart skipped a beat. His eyes were not tormented like they were when I saw him last; rather, they brimmed with a sense of happiness and liberation.

"Cyrus," I uttered to my bushy-haired friend, his dazzling golden robes swaying in the wind.

He responded to my astonishment with a wide grin, not questioning the odd state he found me in. And although we had grown up together as two of the eldest at the Facility, we hugged each other for the first time in our lives.

"You made it!" he exclaimed with joy. He sounded like he had been waiting.

Tears dripped from my eyes, which I let shine without fear, recalling a vision I once had of him by the blueberry plants with Evelyn. "Yeah, I guess we did."

"Guys!" he called to others nearby, who were emerging from meditation. "It's okay. He's my friend!"

They were two boys our age, tall and handsome, their mostly bare bodies painted with brilliant patterns—just as Elizabeth had described them. Instead of introducing themselves, they signaled for me to turn in the other direction.

The illusion had vanished, and I recognized with certainty that we were living on a beautiful earth indeed. Luna beamed as she rolled the wheelbarrow toward us, triggering my unbounded gratitude for her and the guiding river, both of whom I knew would never lie. And Evelyn still smiled as she slept, as if aware that everything would come together at just the right time.

~

Sidney was lean and muscular, with long blond hair and skin covered in spirals of orange and gold. Ezra had a darker complexion and a beard like my own and had decorated his body with blue and violet. Both had kind eyes and radiant auras transcending their physical frames.

It was fascinating to meet more new youths from the original wave who—despite their visible eccentricities—managed to evade the clutches of the Facility. Strangely, I sensed on a subconscious level that I already knew them. And as I put on my robes to introduce them to Evelyn, I realized that they knew us, too.

"Johanna has been saying for weeks to expect you," Ezra said warmly.

"That there was an accident, and a girl needs healing," added Sidney. He gazed toward the wheelbarrow. "We are glad you have found us, and that we finally get to meet the beautiful Evelyn."

An enormous burden I didn't know I was holding was released from my shoulders. This came along with the uncanny epiphany that someone else was aware of our story, watching us remotely, just waiting for us to arrive. Luna seemed amused by my realization that she had been right about everything.

"At first Sammy here thought I was crazy for talking about entering dreams and all. I've gotta hand it to him, though. I thought he went a bit cuckoo himself back there."

I had to laugh at her comment before turning to the boys. "We've traveled for many days and have been through a lot just to bring Evelyn to Sanctuary. I have to ask, if you knew we were coming, why did you put up that veil?"

"Forgive us, my friend," Sidney said. "Usually we get a clear sense of anyone approaching. But today our viewers were overwhelmed by an extremely strong, unknown energy. We do our best to shield the children from any influence of the Order of the Dragon, among others who would like to know our location." He patted my arm amiably. "Don't take it personally. It is a normal rite of passage for anyone to join, because those with pure hearts and positive intentions will always make it through, even if at first they cannot distinguish illusion from reality."

What came next made me step back in stupefaction. Strolling forth from the shadows behind him was a perfect mirror of the girl I loved, down to each strand of rose-red hair, wearing the same silver robes, moving toward me with astounding fluidity. As I stared into her blue eyes, I detected no soul—only a false light. And I was gloomily reminded of falling for a similar trick before Walter's death.

Stopping right in front of me, she reached out to place her hand on my chest before vanishing into the ether. Sidney smiled in her place with a fiery gaze.

"I would trade all of my powers for that ability," proclaimed Luna, undoubtedly thinking of all the mischievous possibilities.

"It can definitely be useful, but there are some things in this world you just can't emulate," Ezra said. He was standing next to the real Evelyn, holding his palms above her. "There is a heavenly quality emanating from this one, almost like that of angels. However, there is also a certain darkness." After shifting his attention to the scar on her forehead, his eyes went wide. "You had a run-in with Matteo?"

"Unfortunately," I said. "As well as the Union military. Like I said, we've been through a lot to get here. We've also met several amazing friends—and one died to help us."

"Maybe that's what we were perceiving," Ezra replied. "I'm sorry for your rough journey, but you will be safe where we're going. We have psychic protection that can't be broken easily. And I must add, Luna, that I'm glad you're on our side. You look just like your sister."

She blushed before Cyrus chimed in.

"Yes, it's wonderful to meet you." He approached her clumsily. "I'm not sure if Samuel told you, but we were together for years at the Facility."

"I know who you are, sweetie. I was there too, for a little bit. You just didn't see me."

"In any case, Cyrus"—I stared at him curiously—"how are you here?"

He softly reminisced, "It's a long story. I had help from a couple of friends. But you didn't come all this way for my story. Shall we get going?"

Agreeing, I took the wheelbarrow and trailed the painted boys as they led us down the final stretch of our roller coaster of a journey. Meanwhile, Cyrus described his escape from the Facility with two other children I was familiar with: Maya, who possessed a gift of precognition, and Lila, who specialized in remote viewing. According to him, Maya knew of the attack weeks in advance, seeing visions of the black robes and sensing impending death. The three of them hoarded food in preparation while attempting to pinpoint the exact time of the invasion.

He said, "Once it began, we were already hiding near the gates, waiting for the chance to make a run for it. We had to fight through a few bald-headed kids, but they weren't an issue. After that, Lila was able to locate the coordinates of Sanctuary."

"We transmit a psychic signal daily," Sidney clarified, "amplifying the one sent by the river itself. Whether or not they are conscious of it, any child seeking refuge will be led here like a beacon. No wonder she picked up on it."

Cyrus nodded. "We were fortunate to have a smooth journey, and we arrived a few days ago." He glanced at me and at Evelyn in her wheelbarrow, and I sensed the remorse in his eyes. "I'm really sorry, Samuel. You know how closely monitored we were during experiments. But the girls and I had duties together, so we could talk more openly. If it were up to me, I would've warned everybody at the Facility. But no one—not even Maya—could foresee the extent of the massacre."

Luna joined the conversation. "You didn't have to warn him. He had me."

I recalled the obscure message she'd relayed while I was with Noah a day before the attack and only hours before my last lesson with Walter. Things could've been different if she had been more specific—though the flash of resentment swiftly dissipated when acknowledging the multiple times she'd saved my life, guiding me and Evelyn to the present moment. I wanted to bring up the final experiment, where I had a faint memory of both Luna and Cyrus connected in some capacity, but something told me to let it be.

"And we also had the songbirds," I remarked. My spirits lifted while listening to their chirps.

"We always have them," Luna insisted, proceeding to stride up to the painted boys. "Anyway, I happened to notice as we were walking that you handsome men are very colorful. Is everyone at Sanctuary like the two of you?"

"No." Sidney laughed. "Just us, really."

"And why is that?" she asked.

"To make life more interesting," Ezra replied.

"Well, luckily, we're matching," she said flirtatiously, showing off her golden cuff and earrings, as well as her violet dress. She glanced back with a grin as if to cause jealousy, all while trying to squeeze between them. I chuckled at her startled expression when they cut her off to hold hands with each other.

"We're almost there," mentioned Sidney, causing my heart to leap.

The river's current rushed with excitement, eager for us to reach our destination. Cyrus smiled by my side, gesturing down to Evelyn. And I trusted that she was on the cusp of awakening.

Finally, the boys pointed something out in the distance, but it wasn't what we were expecting: we had seemingly reached the end of the earth, where the river dropped off suddenly.

The sound of a waterfall soon reached us.

"Last one there is a rotten egg!" Luna shouted, dashing downstream.

Ezra and Sidney exchanged glances before chasing after her playfully.

"No hard feelings." Cyrus joined them in running, leaving me and Evelyn to follow at our own pace.

"That's not fair!" I yelled, laughing.

The race to the waterfall ended with Luna boasting of her victory. I positioned the wheelbarrow next to her, gazing out over a breathtaking scene as Ezra spread his arms and announced, "We welcome you to Sanctuary."

The water cascaded thirty feet, pooling into a small lake. Surrounding the lake was an ample clearing with bountiful gardens on which the sun shined splendidly, though sections were shaded by gorgeous willow trees. Dozens of children tended these gardens, all dressed in gold, but several more were running around and playing. One of them noticed us, and the focus shifted rapidly, until we were being stared at by a sea of luminous eyes and greeted with many waving hands.

The energy was magnificent and the sight beautiful to behold. Joy swept over me, for it felt like I was coming home—or perhaps simply remembering that the divine spark that had begun to ignite was within me all along.

Luna glowed with jubilation. "This must be the place."

I nodded as the roiling emotions within me released.

The river did not truly end here; it merely rested in the lake before continuing again in the distance, flowing forevermore. There was a route around the cliff by which we could join those below, but as I was about to go ahead, Ezra stopped me.

"There is one more rite of passage we like to do—only if you want to, of course."

"Okay."

His golden companion put his arms around me and Luna, then gestured down the cliff. "Jump," he said.

"Are you crazy?" I laughed. *Right when I thought we were safe.*

"You passed through a concrete damn, didn't you?" Ezra encouraged. "Think of it as a final leap of faith, and a much easier one, at that."

"Don't worry; I did it just the other day," said Cyrus. "It's not at all dangerous . . . if you know how to swim, that is."

Luna smirked. "I've been there when Samuel tries to drown himself. As for the jumping part, I'm totally down."

"What about Evelyn?" I rested a hand on the wheelbarrow, wishing she could experience it with me.

"We'll roll her downhill," assured Sidney. "Again, no pressure, it's just something that we—"

"I'll do it," I affirmed as I tuned into my heart, sensing its growing anticipation.

"That's the spirit, Sammy!" Luna celebrated. "We're jumping buddies! But unlike you earlier, I'm having some decency, as much as you would *love* for me to get naked." She winked. "There are children watching. And I'm not seeing my sister for the first time in years with bare nipples."

I let out a chuckle, then went to kiss Evelyn's cheek. "We made it," I whispered with unrestrained happiness before following Luna in removing our sandals and stepping to the edge. Children cheered when they realized what we were doing.

"You ready?" she asked above the gushing of the water.

"There's no backing out now," I responded, acknowledging all the kids wanting a show.

I peered down the thirty-foot drop. Though this might have been intimidating once, after cheating death it felt like nothing. One deep breath dissolved any fear, allowing the presence of those who had passed to come into my awareness, hailing our arrival. I saw Leon in his little rowboat, Walter at his office desk—and my biological father in a flashback of a dream, asking me to open my eyes.

A monarch butterfly landed on my hand before taking off in front of me. I imagined that I had grown wings to fly into the sunlight.

I was soon submerged in the lake. Its water was purifying, cleansing my mind and body. I beheld a memory of my mother taking me to the sea, telling me about the dolphins, teaching me how to swim.

I wanted to stay. Away from all the insanity of the world that was presented as reality, I was embraced by a silence so comforting that I could almost hear the pulse of the earth. This was a place where I could simply *listen*.

The silence was broken when Luna jumped in after me, and I opened my eyes to the glint of her golden earrings. As I swam to the surface, she grabbed my ankle and jokingly tugged me down before ascending with me toward the sun.

We emerged to more cheering, but Luna was suddenly lost in her head.

"She's underneath," she said, pointing to the waterfall. And I realized she was guided by spirits of her own.

Indeed, the cliff was hollowed out. A pathway curved behind the pouring water, connecting both sides of the lake. Moving with purpose, we returned to land and entered a true hidden wonder of nature.

The cave mirrored the river above, winding through the earth with no end in sight, and although we were sheltered from sunlight, dazzling quartz crystals lining the walls bestowed the space with an ethereal glow. At that instant, a girl who looked very much like Luna appeared from around the corner—except that she was slightly older with braided black hair. She gasped when she saw us, and they locked eyes. Luna stepped toward her sister.

"Hanna," she said, her dress dripping wet.

Johanna stared at her like she was a ghost. "Maddie."

There was a long pause until Luna cleared her throat. "It's Luna now, remember? Listen, I'm sorry that I haven't been the best sister. I know I've made a lot of mistakes. And I'm sorry I couldn't convince her to come with me." Her voice cracked, and she continued tearfully, "But we'll get her back, I promise, even if I have to—"

The leader of Sanctuary ran to embrace her little sister, who cried on her shoulder. Meanwhile, a crowd of golden children assembled in the cave. They were mostly younger, and some teared up themselves as they watched the intimate scene. Maya and Lila came to greet me with quiet delight. Surprisingly, not all the other children possessed the eyes of the new youth.

And then it hit me.

I recognized several as Maggie's orphans, who we'd thought were long lost. My heart rejoiced that they had found their way.

"It's her!" one of Maggie's girls exclaimed as the painted boys arrived through the entrance with the wheelbarrow.

Cyrus beamed as he joined us. "I forgot to mention that we managed to bring a few more along our journey."

I hugged each one of them while the sisters whispered together below the sounds of the waterfall. Their eyes were filled with love and forgiveness, knowing that everything had led to this moment. And beneath the river, in a crystal cave, the children of Sanctuary gathered around Evelyn.

CHAPTER 14

"TODAY IS A special day," Johanna announced inside the cave. "Through our shared dreams, my sister, Luna, has returned to me, though not without the help of two new friends to whom I am indebted. Samuel Helen, who comes from the same testing facility as a few of our other newcomers, and Evelyn Agartha, who also returns to her brothers and sisters, albeit in a deep sleep. From this day forth, however, they are all our brothers and sisters. In unbounded love and gratitude, we welcome them."

The sisters embraced again while applause erupted from a crowd of what must have been a hundred children. The cave's crystals seemed to brighten. Johanna approached us, radiating compassion, and touched Evelyn's arm.

She continued, "It goes without saying that Evelyn needs our assistance. Together we must set our intentions toward her healing and awakening, through all of our prayers and meditations. She will be aided to the best of our ability." She smiled at me. "In the meantime, we must do anything we can to help our new siblings adjust to their new home."

"We can get Samuel out of those wet old robes," Cyrus joked.

"Or get them something to eat," Lila said. "The food here is much better than at the Facility!"

"Best of all, we are finally free," added little Maya, who, like her purple-haired best friend, had only known a life of government experimentation.

Cyrus rubbed my shoulder. "We're just glad that you're here instead of with those dragon worshippers, buddy."

There was a moment of silence as I gazed at all of them and into the crowd of children, basking in their welcoming energy. Luna seemed lost in contemplation, so everyone was waiting for me to speak.

"Thank you all," I said finally. "The promise of this sanctuary has kept us alive at points when we should have died. But as grateful as I am to be here at last, this journey was not about me." I took Evelyn's hand. "I was told that you have a universal healer—one who can cure even sickness of the soul. Please, if you're listening, reveal yourself."

I scanned the crowd, but no one came forward. I then looked at Johanna, but she had nothing to say.

"He means Sangeetha," declared a sonorous voice near the entrance of the cave. The children whispered as they parted for the speaker: he was a man who—although still young—appeared older than any new youth I had seen, perhaps in his twenties, his dark skin contrasting with striking blue eyes. Carrying a distinguished aura, he was also one of the few not wearing gold, instead donning robes in a beautiful shade of indigo.

He greeted Luna before extending his hand toward me. "Welcome, Samuel," he said with calming serenity. "My name is Felix. Johanna and I were the first to find this sanctuary."

I shook his hand as the children watched quietly.

"It is wonderful to meet you," I told him, yet as was the case with several others, I sensed that we'd already met.

He turned his attention downward. "This must be Evelyn. Stuck in a dream, is she?"

"For many days." I nodded solemnly. "So, this Sangeetha, is she a great healer?"

"She is," he said.

"Where can I find her?"

He locked eyes with Johanna, likely in a telepathic exchange. Then he answered, "She is deep within the cave. I will take you to her. She does not often like to be disturbed, but this is a matter of high importance."

"Thank you," I breathed, feeling invigorated. After bending down to strap on my sandals, I rose to the sight of a hundred children forming the same stance—each with one hand over their heart and the other stretched toward Evelyn, sending a healing light.

The exception was Luna, who to my surprise came over and kissed her on the forehead. "Open your eyes, for there is a better world for you to see," she said, smiling softly. "There must be."

I caught her gaze, and for a moment we communicated through the unspoken language of the universe. I nodded with appreciation toward her and all the children before taking the wheelbarrow and following Felix down into the mystical cave.

The crystals lit the way as I rolled Evelyn across the jagged ground. With the waterfall behind us, we soon entered a silence that seemed to drown out even the rattle of the wheels. The structure of the cave was uncannily symmetrical, its walls forming a perfect semicircle that guided us along a predetermined path. I was in awe at nature's impeccable creation and wondered about its ultimate origin.

Felix glanced at me with amusement. "Are you enjoying your new home?"

"It's beautiful," I told him. "How deep does it go?"

"This cave is as infinite as the river that flows above. Through the years we have been here, we have never found an end."

The lighting grew dimmer and the silence more encompassing as we continued on. I was startled when I spotted a young boy but then realized that he was in meditation. We passed more children who were simply sitting quietly, seemingly off in another reality, for they did not react to the sounds of our travel. At one point, I could barely see ahead of me, so I rummaged through my satchel in search of the flashlight. Felix stopped me.

"No artificial light," he whispered. "It will disturb those who journey through the void."

"But it's so dark," I whispered back.

"Not to them." In his eyes, he showcased a flame of intense blue before resuming the journey. "We don't need it, anyway. The crystals reflect our own energy, if we allow them."

With a wave of his hand, the quartz lit up in our immediate vicinity, proceeding to follow us with every step. I gawked in wonderment; it was as if the cave had a consciousness.

"This is an extraordinary place, isn't it?" I asked.

"That is a good word to describe it. But you'd be amazed at what becomes ordinary."

I thought back to my days at the Facility. "It wasn't too long ago that I didn't believe beauty like this still existed."

"Believe me, Samuel, there was a time when I thought the same."

"Until you and Johanna found Sanctuary?"

"Yes." He nodded. "Or perhaps I should say that it found us. We met each other at a stage when both of our worlds were falling apart, and our love became the only thing holding us together. Sanctuary called to us when we needed it the most, sending visions of a place we weren't even sure was real. But now it is like we are living in a different world, one more aligned with what is truly real, and what we thought was reality before was only shadows."

Walter grinned within my mind's eye, reminding me of an allegory created by a man named Plato. "You awakened to a higher purpose?" I inquired.

He seemed gratified by my words as we passed a few more children. "Spirit gave us seeds to create a blueprint for the new earth but is only attracting those of a proper resonance, those who choose to be part of the cure. At first, it was just us. You three make one hundred and forty-four."

"Wow." My gaze fell upon Evelyn in shock at how many children simply needed a home. "Who was the first to join you? Ezra? Sidney?"

"That would be the one I'm taking you to. She joined us when developing in the womb."

I halted, staring. "Sangeetha is your—"

He laughed. "Yes, Samuel, she is our daughter. Johanna gave birth shortly after we arrived here. I believe that the visions we received—this gift of Sanctuary—were in response to our prayers to provide her a better life, where she would not have to grow up in a culture of fear nor worry about people judging her many abilities." He sighed as we resumed walking. "Thankfully, this is the only reality she knows. But do not be fooled by appearance. Her soul is way older than any of us, and she was born unencumbered by the veil of forgetting."

My eyes went wide as we turned a corner. "And I would assume that her light shines brighter."

A straight and narrow passageway stretched before us as far as the eye could see, illuminated by a commanding light that fluctuated between all colors of the rainbow. The source was not in the main cavity; rather, it seemed to come from an opening about half a mile in the distance. After a period of darkness, it was like seeing the sun for the first time.

I turned to Felix, and he was smiling. "It appears that she is expecting us."

Drawn in an almost spellbound state, I rolled Evelyn onward with a sense of hope and magic, each flash immersing me deeper into this new reality not far divorced from a dream. It took several minutes to reach the opening, and one look inside had me utterly hypnotized.

The spherical chamber of light shined so radiantly that it was nearly blinding. Magnificent crystals jutted out from all sides. Not only were they a hundredfold brighter than the ones in the main cavity, but colors flowed through them as gracefully as water. At the center of it all was the source of the energy: a girl only a few years of age—practically a toddler—with dark skin like her father, eyes closed in meditation, legs crossed, levitating.

"Sangeetha." Felix beamed. "My beautiful daughter."

She remained meditating, though a peculiar phenomenon took place in the crystals behind her. Out of the chaos, order began to form, with the once scattered colors coalescing and taking shape. Orange mist, black lines, and specks of white came together to paint ghostly wings on either side of her floating body.

"A monarch butterfly," I whispered. Perhaps she had sensed my encounter with one earlier. The symbol seemed to be following me, and I remembered Walter teaching the writings of Jung and Pauli, emphasizing the idea of synchronicity.

Sangeetha opened her eyes, and they exuded as much light as I'd ever witnessed. Maybe it was a consequence of evolution as a second-generation new youth. Or maybe, as Felix claimed, she simply remembered her true spiritual essence.

Slowly, the girl descended. As the crystals dimmed to a more manageable level, the monarch wings dissolved into pure white light. I noticed that her petite robes were of a dark violet, matching Luna's dress. Her aura likewise glowed with this color.

Felix walked us into the chamber, appearing equally reverential of his gifted daughter. "Sangeetha, I would like you to meet Samuel and Evelyn. They are our new friends here. But Evelyn is asleep—and in great need of healing."

She scanned my eyes and seemed to instantly know everything about me, illuminating even those darkest shadows. Then she stood on her toes to see Evelyn in the wheelbarrow, staring at the scar on her forehead.

"I am very thankful to meet you," I said softly. "Evelyn got hurt many days ago, before the scar. I was told that you can do something to help her?"

I waited apprehensively for the child to speak; instead, she quietly extended her tiny hand. I smiled at the gesture, bending down to shake it—but as soon as I touched her fingers, I was stunned by electricity.

"*Show me,*" she requested telepathically as she clung to my hand and reignited her eyes.

I was thrown out of my body while she connected with my mind.

Suddenly I became lost in memory, though I felt Sangeetha with me, rummaging through my consciousness like she was tuning a radio, trying to find the proper channel. Quickly, the shadows intervened. I went all the way back to my days at the Facility, suffering in experiments, receiving shock therapy. I skipped forward in time to the attack of the black robes, where Matteo urged me to kill a tied-up Walter. Then, I went ten years into the past—and my father was in a rage, chasing me, screaming. He dragged me out from an upstairs closet before I blocked the memory out completely.

"*Silence yourself,*" I heard Sangeetha's kind voice say. "*They are only thoughts. There is no reason to be afraid.*"

Heeding her advice, I relaxed into the process. I shifted my focus to Evelyn's crystal-blue eyes, sparking an elevated awareness of all that we had been through, our timeline together happening simultaneously in my mind's eye. I saw our first meeting, when she found the younger me curled up on the grass and offered to become friends, slowly helping me to smile again. There we were, laughing together while tending the land, and our first kiss in the cornfield when no one was watching. As we moved closer to the present, I saw her bandaging my hand after I cut it with a knife, followed by me comforting her when she had trouble breathing.

At last, we located the relevant chain of events: escaping into the forest; being guided by a doe to a place we thought was safe; and the next morning being captured by the hunters. The final memory was of me turning the wheel of their truck to steer it down a steep hill, slamming into a tree.

I broke the connection when I jerked my hand back sharply. "There was an accident." I trembled with emotion.

"There are no accidents," she sent into my mind, projecting an image of stars in the night sky. She stretched to touch Evelyn's hand and frowned in apparent confusion. A moon-shaped crystal floated into her grasp, after which she looked toward her father.

"She needs her to lie on the ground," he said.

I grimaced at the coarse surface. "Okay. We just have to make it more comfortable." While I gathered blankets to use as a cushion, Sangeetha was already addressing my concern. She waved her palms across an area, and the rock alchemized into matter that was smooth and malleable, forming a natural bed.

"That's incredible," I said. She flashed a sly grin that reminded me of her aunt.

I laid my love atop the soft space, which conformed to the shape of her body. Sangeetha wasted no time working on her energy, rubbing the crystal over her third eye. And though Evelyn's breath quickened, I was not worried. I had faith that this would lead to her awakening.

"We should go," Felix insisted. "She will take good care of her."

I gazed at Evelyn, recalling our shared memories, and could not yet bring myself to leave. "I'm going to stay for a bit. If that's all right with her."

Sangeetha was already nodding.

"Okay." Felix patted my shoulder. "But you've been through enough. The children would love to have you for supper." He turned to depart yet stopped before exiting the chamber. "And Samuel?"

"Yes?"

"Thank you for bringing at least one of Johanna's sisters back to her. It means more than you know."

He headed up the passageway, each footstep echoing in the vast silence. As I stared at the beauty of the crystals around me, I realized that our journey was of a much greater magnitude than I could have imagined.

~

I watched in a state of childlike wonder as Sangeetha performed her rituals.

She hummed, she danced, she hit crystal bowls to produce soothing frequencies, and she even came close to singing, all while telekinetically revolving an array of unique crystals above each of Evelyn's energy centers—or chakras, from what Walter taught me of Indian philosophy. She did this several times, moving from the base of my love's spine all the way up to the crown of her head, and the light in the chamber harmonized accordingly by ascending through the color spectrum.

She performed strange movements afterward, of which I had little understanding. Nevertheless, I sat captivated without daring to interrupt, because the only thing that mattered was that the young healer knew exactly what she was doing, and so I had full confidence in her abilities.

As I turned inward, my heart rested happily, for it suddenly became easy to anticipate a miracle; rather than waiting, though, I couldn't help feeling that we would create one together.

I wasn't aware of how much time had passed when Sangeetha stopped and stared into my eyes, communicating not with words but with mental images: I saw a scene of the sun setting in the sky and a feast being arranged by the Sanctuary children on a long wooden table within a garden of roses.

Clearly, she wanted me to go eat with them.

"But I want to be here when she awakens," I said.

"You will know when she does," she answered telepathically.

I sighed as I projected the image of our accident. "You know well I'm the reason she's like this."

"You are not to blame," she reassured me as she transmuted the image to a far-off dream of Evelyn smiling in the shade of a cherry blossom tree.

"What about you? Aren't you going to eat?"

Her eyes flared with white light, mirrored in the surrounding crystals. And I got the sense that she subsisted on an unlimited source of energy.

"Thank you." I nodded. "I will return soon."

I slung my satchel over my shoulders, leaving a jar of water and what was left of the mashed strawberries on the ground next to Evelyn's sandals. Then I ventured back through the cave, the crystals lighting the way. Those I passed in meditation were now levitating with ease, experiencing transcendence.

When I emerged through the waterfall, it was almost twilight. Just as I had been shown in my mind's eye, most of the children were assembled on one side of the lake, preparing for a feast. I headed over to join them.

"Sammy!" Luna waved from the distance, where she stood by Felix and Johanna. "I saved you a seat!"

A plethora of vegetables lined the path along the water, as well as various fruit trees—a beautiful one with almonds standing out particularly. Children were collecting the last of the day's harvest. All eyes turned to me as I arrived at the crowded area encircled by a bed of pink roses. Johanna approached with her sister.

"How is she?" she asked.

"Making progress," I said, wanting to believe. "Your daughter is very gifted, Johanna. And, Luna, you didn't tell me that you had a niece."

"Life is better when you don't spoil the surprises."

"Don't you want to meet her?" I asked.

Smiling, she poked her head with her finger. "I already have."

Johanna escorted us to the long table, and I was amazed to see it held nearly every crop imaginable: sweet potatoes, an assortment of greens, peppers and beans; figs, grapes, peaches, and of course various delicious berries. There was also a huge bowl of what I recognized as pine nuts, along with a pile of cooked fish. Not only was the food incredibly enticing, but by some miracle there was more than enough for every child.

I decided to add the rest of Artemis's vegetables to a spare plate; it was a small contribution, relatively speaking, but one I thought she'd approve of.

Meanwhile, Luna beamed by my side. "Isn't it gorgeous? A vegan's paradise." She glanced at the fish. "Well, mostly."

"Better than wild elderberries," I said. She stuck her tongue out playfully.

Preparations soon ceased. Johanna separated herself from the crowd of children, who all turned their attention toward her.

"My dearest brothers and sisters," she announced with affection. "I stand before you humbled by gratitude. Not only for the obvious fruits that we see but for the land that bestowed it, the river that brings fertility, and for the sun that generously shares its warmth. I am grateful for Mother Earth herself, her grass and her trees, as well as for the air we breathe. I am grateful for our healthy bodies and our perfect souls, and for the spirits that guide us when we think we're alone. Finally, I am grateful for every one of you, as in each of your eyes I recognize the eternal light of the Creator, which resides within the hearts and minds of every living being."

Joyous cheers came from the crowd. "She was always the eloquent one in the family," Luna whispered before her sister resumed.

"I ask, however, that we commence a prayer for one of our beautiful newcomers, Evelyn. She is currently in the crystal cave under the care of my daughter, striving to awaken. And I know there are many here close to her who would do anything to see that happen." She gazed fondly toward me, then to Maggie's orphans. "So I encourage you to utilize that divine creativity to help her now, picturing her surrounded by golden light and bathing her in the vibration of health and perfection."

In a scene that nearly moved me to tears, the children held hands one by one, closing their eyes in prayer for the girl I loved.

Luna took my left hand with a heartfelt smile, and Felix came up and took my right. *"Know that it is already done,"* he communicated. *"See it written in destiny that her eyes have opened."*

As I joined them in silence, I did just that: I visualized the healing light triggering an awakening, with Evelyn emerging from a chrysalis with butterfly wings. I sensed a hundred souls with me in collective bliss, transmitting our love across unseen strings—and it didn't even matter that we weren't there physically, for truly there was no distance between consciousness.

Johanna's gentle voice brought us back to our bodies. "We pray for the health of Evelyn just as we pray for that of the earth as she goes through her own metamorphosis, recovering from an illness she has braved for millennia. We ask that all be given the opportunity to be reborn with her, and as for those of her children still lost, allow them the understanding to connect with their soul, and let true love guide them to Sanctuary."

More cheers came, and many began to embrace. I received a hug from Luna, then Felix and Cyrus, then from smaller children I didn't even know; yet with a full and open heart, I hugged them back tenderly.

As the attention of the crowd returned to the feast, Johanna concluded enthusiastically, "Now we eat!"

A progression of children was called to the table to take a wooden plate from a stack. The very oldest went first, including Ezra and Sidney, who filled their plates with the best-looking crops and the ripest berries. But instead of sitting to eat, they gave them to the very youngest in the crowd, whose eyes lit up with appreciation. It was heartwarming to see that there was no competition for the food, only a sense of harmony.

"Don't make us serve you plates too!" teased Sidney, directing us to the table.

"This is your home, so have as much as you like," Ezra added amiably. "Trust me, you both deserve it."

"Don't mind if I do." Luna delightedly grabbed a plate and beelined for some peculiar-looking mushrooms. I filled mine with an assortment of fruits and vegetables, several of which I had never tasted. We sat on the grass, next to the bed of roses, and were accompanied by others from the Facility.

"This place is awesome," Cyrus remarked, munching on pine nuts.

Maya grinned as she bit into an apple. "The food tastes better when you help grow it yourself."

Indeed, it was delicious, seemingly imbued with a higher frequency. We were soon joined by Felix and Johanna, who chuckled at our satisfied expressions. I enjoyed every bite, though in the back of my mind, I wondered about Evelyn.

We stayed there for an hour, eating and conversing yet barely bringing up the past. We didn't speak of our childhoods or our days at the Facility—not even of our journeys, even though we were in a space where we could've talked freely. Rather, we kept our awareness firmly in the present, admiring the elegance of the willow trees and watching the gorgeous sunset. Luna played a game of furtively floating roses to unsuspecting recipients, particularly Ezra and Sidney, at which everyone laughed. A part of me was grateful to stray from serious matters and amazed by how quickly old memories attempted to slip away once we shifted into another reality.

Afterward, children took turns introducing themselves, with many simultaneously displaying their abilities. There was Ariel, a girl who could raise her vibration to the point where she turned invisible; Antheia, who could bring flowers to full bloom straight from the seed—which undoubtedly helped with the gardening; and Jeremy, a boy who could generate electricity. He demonstrated this ability by sending currents through a crystal he was holding, which proceeded to shine with the same boundless energy I'd witnessed in the cave, lighting up the vicinity.

Dozens of others had their own special powers, all of different ages and skin colors, but one thing remained universal—they all had love in their eyes, plain to see.

Finally, a group of children introduced themselves as the Welders of Light. "We made this for you," one of them said as she presented beautiful golden robes fit just for me.

"Thank you." I received them with gratitude, not questioning how they had been made so quickly. Judging by their luminosity, I supposed they were manifested out of the ether.

I was ready to leave my old self behind and adorn robes of a more exalted vibration. The same were offered to Luna, yet while she took them gladly, I could tell she preferred her violet dress.

It wasn't until I wandered away from the crowd that Maggie's orphans approached me. There were twelve of them in total, and I didn't know any too well, for they were always shy, and none had been at Maggie's farm since the beginning of my time at the Facility. But they came to me like they were greeting a close friend, hope suffusing their eyes, along with a bit of worry.

An innocent-looking little boy was the first to speak, asking softly, "Will Evelyn be okay?"

"She will." I smiled, telepathically sending him my earlier vision.

Then a young girl stepped forward, her kind features recognizable in the dimming twilight. "Samuel, do you remember me?"

My mind shot back to the day of the attack. "Of course I do, Penelope."

She asked with a resigned expression, "Noah isn't coming here, is he?"

"No. He isn't." I chose to be honest but added with optimism, "But we can still rescue him."

I looked toward Johanna, laughing with her sister, and recalled the anguish of the mother in the village. As precious as the moment seemed, I knew that we had to do something for those less fortunate.

~

The night sky was a comforting sight—an experience I was deprived of during my time at the Facility. Even after our escape, I seldom stopped to appreciate the beauty.

Now at Sanctuary, the stars were out and as clear as ever, sparking a remembrance of what my mother had taught me about astronomy. There were the Three Sisters; the cluster of the Pleiades—the Seven Sisters; Sirius, the brightest star in the sky; and Arcturus not far behind.

As a child I had felt an inexplicable connection to these distant giants, and only now did the wonder return to me. I sensed a pulling upward, a beckoning from the stars, while their light appeared to amplify. I knew intuitively that someone was watching. Still, there was loneliness; something was missing.

I returned to earth to the sounds of laughter: Maya and Lila were playing hide-and-seek with a group that included Maggie's orphans. Others prepared for the night by setting up hammocks among the willow trees, aided by beacons of the energized crystals that illuminated areas throughout Sanctuary. Meanwhile, I sat alone by the lake, clutching my golden robes in my hands, not yet wanting to change. I had planned to visit Evelyn, but a small voice told me to sit there and wait.

I gazed up at the stars once more, whispering, "If anyone is listening, please show me the way."

I waited several minutes and received nothing except a gust of wind. The night grew darker, and the children were finishing their game. I sighed, about to head toward the cave. Then I noticed ripples in the water.

They emanated from near the center of the lake, where I recognized auras shining through the darkness. Ezra and Sidney swam gracefully beneath the sliver of moonlight. I watched for a while as they danced and embraced, enamored of their obvious devotion. They seemed to be soulmates of a timeless nature, and I wondered if I was the same for Evelyn.

Eventually, they noticed me—and I turned away in embarrassment. But when I turned back, Sidney was whispering to Ezra, who swam over to me.

"Gorgeous night, isn't it, Samuel?" The blue boy smiled as he emerged from the lake with a wet piece of fabric wrapped around his waist.

"It is." I nodded as he settled beside me.

"So, what are you doing here all alone, my friend?" He nudged me with his elbow.

"Maybe you can tell me."

"My telepathy may not be as refined as some others, but I can tell that something is on your mind. It's okay if you want to be left alone; just know that you can talk to me."

I caught his kind, nonjudging eyes and relaxed in his presence. "I'm happy to be here, believe me. This place is beautiful, and the children are wonderful—never mind the great food," I said with sincerity. "But outside of Sanctuary, there are others being taken. I have friends who are stuck in a bad situation, and many are caught up in the middle of a war. A part of me is thankful to be away from it all. But I feel that I should be doing more."

"You want to help too many people. It is an admirable trait. But you can't save the world all by yourself, Samuel. The best thing you can do right now is focus on the positive. And look at all that has happened the past few days alone. We gave a home to all those orphans. We've reunited lost sisters—thanks to your efforts. And now Evelyn is under the care of our greatest healer."

"That's true," I acknowledged. "But it's hard for me to focus on anything as long as she's still asleep."

He chuckled. "You really love her, don't you?"

"Yes, I do. And I have faith that she'll awaken. But that's the other thing." I glanced anxiously toward the cave. "When she does,

I don't know if she'll love me the same way I love her. I don't know if she'll forgive my mistakes."

His empathy was palpable, and though his eyes weren't as piercing as Sangeetha's, I could tell that he was reading my energy. "It is clear that she loves you. That is helping her to stay alive and pull through. But first and foremost, you must love yourself and do so unconditionally—not based on whatever happened in the past but on who you *choose* to be in the present. You don't need anyone else's acceptance. Love them just the same, whether or not they are open to it."

"Do you love Sidney?" I asked, gesturing to the boy unwinding in the lake.

"Of course I love him." He laughed. "You saw us, didn't you? But I love you too, Samuel, as well as everyone here. It is a universal force that binds us, and life is much more fulfilling when you make the choice to open to the joys of loving without fear."

"What about people like Matteo?" I grimaced as I said it.

"I've had unpleasant encounters with him too. But what's holding on to hate going to do? It's like willfully drinking poison. It's not that I condone their actions, but forgiveness, in a weird way, allows us to be free. You learn to honor the darkness for what it is and be an example of love to help those trapped within it."

I was struck by a fleeting memory of communicating with Leon right after his death and recognizing the shadows that plagued Lieutenant Hernandez. "I've been trying to do that—to be the best person I can and forgive no matter what. But I don't think I'm quite there yet."

"And that's okay. We're human, aren't we? But that doesn't mean we can't strive to connect with something greater." From his hands came a glistening hologram of a butterfly, and I realized my prayer had been received. "There is a certain irony that through working with illusions, you begin developing an appreciation for what's real."

"It is within us," I said, feeling the love in my heart.

"Yes. But look around, Samuel. It is also all around you."

I did as he requested and took in the beauty: the flowers and gardens and branches of the trees; the waterfall peacefully burbling; the children laughing and crickets chirping; and a spiral shell I found at my feet, mirroring our greater galaxy. The universe existed in perfect harmony, for there was one life shining behind everyone and everything. I gazed back at the friend I had been guided to meet with perfect timing, and his eyes radiated unconditional love. In that moment, all was full of it.

"Ezra?"

"Yes?"

"Do you believe in God?"

He sat back in contemplation. "We didn't come from nothing, did we? All this miraculous order to things. Something tells me that our being, our consciousness, is intimately linked with whatever God is."

"Beyond the illusion," I affirmed.

He nodded. "Beyond time itself. Yet you may glimpse it from time to time. He gives us signs in the form of small things we're normally too busy to appreciate."

"Like the very fact that we're conscious and alive."

"Beneath the light of a thousand stars."

I quieted. "A man I was close to would always say how at the tiniest level, everything is made of vibrating strings. So even our bodies are just part of this larger symphony of frequency and geometry."

He smiled. "You can look for God in science or philosophy, but in reality it is so simple, and that's where we get confused. In my opinion, those who wish to learn the secrets of the universe need only listen to the wind."

CHAPTER 15

A BELL ECHOED throughout Sanctuary, waking me.

I lay on a hammock I had set up in the branches of a willow, swaying gently by the lake. The sun watched our world from just over the horizon, to the songbirds' greeting. I paused to process this new reality; it was the first time I hadn't slept by Evelyn's side since her coma-inducing injury.

"Let her be for the night," I'd heard Sangeetha whisper soon after my conversation with Ezra; our telepathic connection lingered. Trusting the young healer, I chose to listen.

"Way better than waking up in those cots at the Facility," said a familiar voice.

I sat up to find Cyrus breezily stretching his arms. He and others who had slept in a slew of hammocks throughout the surrounding branches were hopping to the ground to begin the morning.

"That was the best sleep I've had in some time," I agreed with a yawn.

"Great to hear! So, you must be ready then."

I climbed down to put on my sandals. "Ready for what?"

"You'll see," he said as those around him chuckled.

I followed them to an open field where the chiming had originated. There, children congregated from all corners of Sanctuary, and many came to greet me warmly. There was no sign of little Sangeetha.

"Samuel!" Johanna beamed when she saw me. "How was your first night? I hope you slept well."

"I did." I smiled. "But what is this all about?"

"It is perhaps the oldest tradition we have at Sanctuary. We begin every morning by doing nothing."

Luna approached with a wide grin and put her arm around me. "Isn't this place marvelous?" She was still in her violet dress, while I had on my golden robes like most of the others.

"We're meditating?" I asked.

"That's right," Felix interjected. "I hear that you've been practicing."

"Here and there. It has helped with my abilities."

"Always playing modest," Luna teased. "The day after I taught him, he basically stopped bullets. That's the benefit of having a good teacher, I guess."

Felix laughed. "Sounds impressive. But just wait until you experience it as a collective."

With nearly all of the children present, through Johanna's guidance, we arranged into concentric circles on the green grass. Some sat cross-legged; others preferred to lie on their backs. Cyrus and Luna sat at my sides, and Ezra positioned himself behind me; I turned and met his eyes fondly, thinking of what he'd told me the night before. Then I got into the lotus position and listened to the tranquil cascade of the waterfall as the meditation commenced.

Johanna spoke serenely. "Close your eyes and breathe, my brothers and sisters. Breathe so that you may find true peace. Breathe until all the layers are stripped away and your soul is revealed underneath."

Her words triggered something instantly. I went deep. So did everyone around me, for I felt each a note resonating in a symphony to uplift the whole to an elevated frequency. My sense of self dissipated, and we began operating as one consciousness—perhaps simply evoking the awareness of what had always been, beyond the illusion.

A sensation began at the base of my spine, traveling in spirals up through my heart and attempting to push open the crown of my head. The pressure built until a crack formed, allowing an enormous energy to emerge. Time released its stubborn grip as I transcended physicality. I seemed to tune into another body and unveil my inner eyes.

Staring back vividly from the void of my mind was a dog I used to play with as a child. She was a beautiful golden retriever, loyal and friendly. And though she was happy to see me, I could tell she needed help with something important. She ran in the other direction and glanced back anxiously, beckoning me to follow.

"I'm coming," I said, stretching out my astral legs. I proceeded to chase her through the shadows of my subconscious while fleeting memories passed us by, ghostly whispers echoing from the darkness. A voice in distress soon became apparent over the rest: the voice of a little boy, screaming for assistance.

My guide barked as we came upon the chilling scene.

Lying before us was what looked like a mummy, with layers of bandages forming a cast around a small body. Within that cast was the little boy, barely able to move, struggling desperately.

"Hang in there!" I shouted as I rushed toward him, and out of pure will I manifested a dagger. I hurriedly cut him loose, feeling a strange release with each layer I tore through. Finally, he broke out of his cocoon, clutching a familiar teddy bear and wearing red pajamas.

It was me as a young child, before all the trauma.

He approached the dog first and petted her kindly. "Thank you, Lucy. You can go tell her that I'm okay now."

Lucy licked his cheek before disappearing. The whispers faded into a comforting silence.

He then stared at me, and through his eyes I recognized my soul.

"Are you my angel?" he asked with innocence.

My heart burst with loving energy. "I am," I replied.

We hugged each other tightly, our fractured spirit merging back into one. I beheld the cast that had entrapped my child self. In it I saw the grief for my mother as I watched her die helplessly; the torment I endured at the hands of my father, and the guilt as I screamed, dropping him to his knees; the suffering I went through in the cruel experiments at the Facility, getting shocked and drugged to bring out a monstrous side of me; and the fear that I would again be abandoned, unworthy of experiencing love's warm embrace. I continued to hug the little boy, deciding to leave that all behind.

Once the process finished and the child was gone, a cleansing rain fell from above. I stared at my hands with a greater sense of detachment from everything I once was. I breathed into the moment, taking charge of my destiny, and that's when I heard fingers snap behind me. Yet there wasn't anyone there—at least, not that I could perceive. There was only a wooden door standing in the void, inviting me to see what waited on the other side.

I stepped toward it, but before walking through, I looked back once more upon my egoic cocoon, evaporating in the pouring rain. This time, however, I observed it with gratitude. Although it did not represent who I was, it had prepared me for all I was going to become.

A bolt of lightning ignited the darkness as I turned the handle and was sucked into a portal, launching my consciousness through space and time.

~

It seemed as if every cell in my body were being split apart by needles before coming together suddenly at my destination—one that I was shocked to recognize.

Walter's office looked just as I remembered, with shelves of records on either far corner, many of them scattered across the floor. I gazed at it from a higher perspective, close to the ceiling, and remained floating there. Before I had the chance to question what was happening, Walter entered through the door.

He stood right below me, adjusting his monocle beneath a mess of frizzy hair, and I had the eerie realization that I was witnessing something real. Audible in the distance were the Facility alarms, signaling an attack by an outside enemy.

I expected him to be more concerned, but instead he just strolled about, perusing the records on the floor. "Walter!" I called out. I willed my way down next to him, but he passed right through me. As hard as it was to accept, some things weren't meant to be changed. I let an invisible force pull me back to the ceiling.

By then, Walter had settled on the record he would hear before his death, picking it up and spinning it on the player. Subsequently— giving me a surprising sense of peace—he smiled and bobbed to the groovy rhythm.

"Rainy day, dream away," he sang along to Jimi Hendrix, one of his favorite musicians.

His heart let loose, and I watched with amusement as he danced around his office to a couple of psychedelic tunes that drowned out the alarms. Afterward, the music turned unusually cryptic; a track came on without any lyrics, only a whooshing sound that reminded me of the wind. Nevertheless, Walter listened intently.

When the track finished, he flipped the record to its other side. Then, they arrived.

He barely had time to glance up from the player before Matteo seized him with telekinesis and yanked him to the floor, breaking his monocle. It was difficult to watch Matteo and his sister tie him up, but I was able to observe calmly instead of reacting emotionally, allowing me to continue floating.

As Walter futilely struggled, his captors gazed at each other with mischievous eyes, telepathically conversing. "He will come," Matteo declared aloud over the sounds of bluesy guitars, leaving the room with Walter while Tiana stayed behind.

Little did they know that I was already with them, watching from above. Neither did my former self, who came in right on cue with the opening lines of the album's most famous song. It was uncanny to watch him—for he truly seemed a separate entity from who I now was—plead with an illusory Walter, who from this perspective was clearly all in my mind. The record player broke. Tiana laughed. And he charged at her, bumping his head, before Matteo dragged Walter back in.

The rest was like a movie played in fast-forward, and I already knew the gruesome end: Matteo giving his pompous speech, bragging of their divine superiority; relinquishing his dagger, urging me to kill; throwing me across the room after my rebellion.

Yet I watched it all with loving detachment.

Only when the shelves of records crashed down on my former self did I notice another presence floating beside me: a gorgeous woman clad in garments of light, holding hands with a young boy who had the same eyes as his father. They smiled warmly at me before turning their attention to the scene, waiting for a passing that seemed written in destiny.

Soon my former self was up against the wall, choking beside the portrait of Mabus as Matteo stomped toward Walter and put the dagger to his throat. I saw shadows swarm around the boy, whispering in his ear, swaying him with deception.

My former self pleaded, and Walter attempted to speak, letting Matteo believe that he would beg for mercy.

Rather, he beamed at me as I stared from the ceiling.

"Break the strings." He connected to my astral eyes, and I finally understood what I was meant to hear at this moment in time. Then he left to join his wife and child before his body hit the ground.

At that instant, the scene was broken, and everything vanished. I felt my consciousness rise in density, now bestowed a body with golden robes, and I floated to the floor of an office that had also shifted correspondingly. Everything was in its right place again. Gone was the past with its violent memory. The previously scattered records were now organized on the shelves, shimmering ethereally.

I went to those on the left corner first, underneath the portrait of Dylan, and pulled one out to look at its sleeve; I found myself peering through a window to my past. It showed me sleeping in the grass outside the Facility while I was supposed to be digging holes with Noah.

"What does this mean?" I asked out loud, filing the record to examine some others.

There was me and Evelyn wandering the forest, coming across the majestic doe; being tied up in a trunk after getting captured by the hunters; and my mother holding me when I was very young, singing a silent melody.

I would have cried if I could, but I remained in a state of sublimity. I skipped a few records and saw us in the church. The village. Sanctuary. Every experience of the past two weeks, even those in my dreams, seemed to be recorded, albeit from a higher perspective—as if to let me know that a guardian was tagging along with my story, aware of my every move.

I started toward the shelves on the right corner, beneath Hendrix, but was promptly halted by an invisible barrier. Again I pushed forward, but I couldn't break through; clearly, these were records I wasn't meant to see. They sparkled with an aureate quality. That's when I noticed, smirking at my side, the portrait of Mabus, from which the barrier projected.

I shook my head with a chuckle. "So what now?" I questioned.

Like a magnet, my attention was pulled to the area beneath Walter's desk, where I recognized something hiding in the shadows.

It was a lone unfiled record, just waiting to be discovered. Retrieving it with my mind, I held it in the light to inspect a bright-red cover displaying a sketch of a humanoid creature weeping into its hands while seemingly random dots and lines connected around him. I knew that record, and I knew its music was strange, but as hard as I tried, I couldn't remember its name.

Suddenly, it started sparkling like those on the shelves, transforming into a holographic window. Revealing themselves for a moment were three winged, black-eyed entities I'd once encountered in a dream. The album then reverted to its normal appearance, but I knew what had to be done.

I slid it from its cover and dropped it onto the player.

As soon as it began spinning, the setting disintegrated atom by atom, like sands blown away by the wind. This transpired to the point where nothing was left but a speck of awareness. Still, there was a longing for light.

OOOOOMMMMMMMM.

Emanating from the silence was a low vibration; then came an explosion. Manifesting in its place through the flame of creation was a world of surreal beauty, arranging by way of higher intelligence until I stood in a meadow of flowers near a radiant, circular lake. Snow-covered hills lined one end of the horizon, fantastic pyramids the other.

I lit up with joy, for I knew where I was, remembering the fullness of the previous dream. This time, however, I arrived with lucidity and thus couldn't help but marvel at its sheer reality.

I stared down at my hands, examining every little crease, then up at a sky teeming with otherworldly geometry. The environment swayed harmoniously in a conscious dance; everything was vibrant and filled with life. I breathed in as the wind caressed my ear, carrying with it a gentle whisper.

"Samuel."

Twisting around, I caught bright-blue eyes. There stood my love, smiling from beneath a cherry blossom tree nearby.

"Evelyn."

I approached her in a trance. Nothing could describe the elation at seeing her alive and awake. She was as stunning as she had always been, with silver robes flowing in the wind, shining with a heavenly presence. Tenderness suffused her gaze as I stopped within a few feet of her. A tear dripped down my cheek, and I paused to feel it between my fingers, praying for it all to be real.

"I've missed you," I told her from the core of my being.

"I've missed you too." She took a step toward me. "Though you should know by now that I'll never leave."

We swiftly embraced, then stared into each other's eyes. Her soul was unmistakable. Her face was unscarred. And her heart-shaped locket was snug around her neck, carrying her parents' memory.

I still needed to ask. "Is it really you, or are you simply a part of me?"

"It is really me, Samuel." She laughed with emotion. "But why can't both be true?" She took my hand to place it on her chest, and as pink blossoms swirled around us, I sensed our hearts beating in loving unison. "Thank you for taking care of me," she added affectionately, as I was abruptly reminded of our physical reality.

"We're at Sanctuary, Evelyn," I said with excitement. "It's okay to wake up now. Sangeetha has been healing you."

"Is that so?" She wiped her wet eyes.

"Yes. Do you feel it working?"

"Perhaps. But the only thing that really matters is that you're here now with me." She passed me to head toward the lake, then glanced back. "Are you coming?"

"I am," I said confidently.

Together we strolled through a garden of sunflowers on our way to the glittering water.

"Look!" She pointed to ripples near the center.

Arising out of the stillness were the three mysterious entities stretching their wings to glide along the surface. Slowly they circled in a synchronized manner, remaining at a distance, observing us indifferently.

"The black-eyed angels," I uttered.

Evelyn seemed surprised. "You remember."

"I do." We continued walking. "What are they, anyway?"

"They're technically my creation, but truly they're within everybody. They are the good and the bad. The dark and the light. They are the choices we each have in creating our reality."

"Last time I was here, they attacked me," I said.

"If you react with fear, that's what you might manifest."

I recalled the fright when I first saw their eyes and the struggle of being dragged underwater. Only once I had surrendered was I given a vision—of the evolution of the earth, of transmutation by light. I turned to Evelyn and felt something different in her. She exuded an inner knowing, a divine creativity expressed through her dreams.

"This realm is extraordinary," I said as we arrived at the shore. "But all I want is to be with you again physically. In our waking reality."

"Is this not real enough for you?" she asked amusedly, stroking her hand against my cheek.

"It is as real as any dream can be." I perused her soft smile, each freckle placed perfectly. "But God only knows what I'd be if when I wake up, you can't be there with me."

A gust of wind crossed the landscape, disturbing the stillness of the circular lake. Sensing doubt, the entities started toward us, propelled through the water by their enormous wings.

"They're coming," I told Evelyn, drifting out of clear lucidity.

"When fear has cast us into the dark," she sang as impressively as ever, without any struggle, "love will bridge our hearts."

Struck by her voice, our dream world stabilized.

The black-eyed angels halted their charge.

And a bridge began forming from the melody she sang, with a spiraling, golden railing comprised of pure consciousness. It started at our feet and arced high over the lake, sustained solely by the mind, connecting to the other side.

Meanwhile, the fire of life flowed from Evelyn's eyes. "I used to not know what to think when you'd tell me Walter's theories. But he was right, Samuel. Music forms the fabric of our reality."

"And we are the music makers," I said automatically.

She nodded, offering her hand. "Shall we?"

I gave thanks to my old tutor—grateful to know he was now with family—before stepping onto the bridge, hand in hand with Evelyn. We ascended with the encouragement of a gentle, caressing wind, carrying with it faint sounds of violins. Guided by intuition rather than the mind, I felt thought subside with each step we took—as did the experience of linear time. When we made it to the bridge's apex, I could barely remember anything about my usual personality. But shining underneath was a deeper recollection, a timeless awareness, a state of pure being.

In that moment, I was staring into her blue eyes.

"You are awake," I told her. "You are here now with me."

"Always," she replied, seeing transcendently.

In the water below, as I peered over the railing, were the three entities, surrounded by beautiful lotus flowers and lilies. In their eyes I saw both positive and negative, darkness and light; a dog digging holes and a bird taking flight; the stars, the planets, and the void in between; a girl being born and an elderly man dying. Everything was as it should be. There was a balance to the world that bound all things in unity. And as I turned back to Evelyn, I saw only one essential reality.

"I love you," I said, and my heart's shackles were released.

"I love you too," she replied, a tear rolling down her cheek and an image forming in her eyes. We kissed, and for a moment time ceased to exist.

The next thing we heard was a high-pitched ringing. It came from underneath; I stared with Evelyn toward the black-eyed entities. What we saw was a transformation, a sudden quickening, with the three of them dissipating into orbs of white light. We watched in wonder as they rose, dancing around us as if in celebration. Then, ethereal forms materialized, ones I recognized from when I was a child and my mother would tell me stories of angels.

There was Gabriel, the messenger with a trumpet in hand; Rafael, the healer holding a mystical staff; and Michael, the warrior wielding a flaming blue sword.

With outstretched wings, they formed a circle around us, observing with penetrating eyes. Each shined with a celestial presence unlike anything of the earth we knew. I felt an acute surge in energy as we were bathed in a higher frequency.

"What's happening?" I asked, my entire body vibrating.

"We've made our choice." Evelyn smiled, and I knew then that she had been listening the whole time. As flutes and horns sounded in the background, the archangels began speaking:

"The time of earth's awakening has begun," proclaimed Gabriel.

"The songs of the ascension have been sung," declared Raphael.

"And with love in thy hearts, the two shall become one," finished Michael, planting his sword firmly at his feet.

This sparked a sudden opening. From my heart arose an extraordinary power. I let it flow through my arms and into my palms until they were once again gifted with golden light, shining numinously. No words needed to be said as I gazed toward Evelyn. I placed my hand on her chest to fill her own heart with this power, spreading it to her lungs, her blood, then each cell of her etheric body. There was a profound transmutation as she rejoiced in healing light.

Finally, it was time for her to awaken.

"Thank you," she whispered as the process concluded. The angels vanished, their purpose fulfilled.

Beside us was a gap in the bridge's railing, revealing the lake whose stillness mirrored the sky above. I stepped to the edge with Evelyn to observe the beauty and noticed previously unseen stars amid the geometry. It simply took an intention for these stars to rearrange. They moved into concentric circles and started flickering.

"This is more than just a dream, isn't it?" I said, with the faith that we could manifest miracles.

Indeed, directly below us a portal formed—down to earth, down to Sanctuary. I looked to the shore and spotted two hooded figures watching us from a distance.

Then I gazed once more into Evelyn's eyes, recognizing the image of a monarch butterfly. By way of this symbol, the veil was lifted, and I knew that this moment was the point of all creation. I saw the universe inside her as I saw my own being. And I remembered that we were angels ourselves having this experience, sharing the same story as if in a dream, yet writing our own intertwined destinies.

With her hand in mine, we jumped together.

~

A majestic doe was all I could see as I floated in space and drifted in time, existing in a realm between dreams and reality.

From there I was shown some of my last waking memories:

Waking up by the water, among clusters of blueberries.

Heading into the forest to search for my love.

Running toward gunshots, after which we collided.

And crying while captive in a small dark trunk, begging him to open his eyes.

Yet somehow I was observing from above simultaneously, like two points of awareness of a single mind. *"There are no accidents in the eyes of the universe,"* said a woman's voice, almost apologetically. *"Even the greatest tragedies are but strings in a larger tapestry."* The doe led me back to my body. With another set of memories intermingling with mine, I awoke to a single question: *Who am I?*

There came a deep breath—deeper than I could ever remember taking.

And with a shock of electricity, I opened my eyes.

I was met with a light that was initially blinding, and I couldn't move my arms. My body was paralyzed. I felt a wave washing over me, my heart pounding, and my breath accelerating. I tried to call out, but I couldn't speak. Remembrance of the realm I came from became replaced by anxiety. I had no idea where I was. So, I began to pray silently.

I reached out my consciousness. *God, if you're listening, lend me strength. And give me clarity!*

A sense of comfort immediately arrived; my breathing slowed, and my eyes adjusted as the light softened. I found myself staring at the ceiling of a cave filled with glowing crystals. Something within me recognized this place. But my mind scrambled to make sense of a reality it had not seen for quite some time.

I was lying on an area nested in the rock yet soft and cushiony.

I began by wiggling my toes, then stretching my feet.

Slowly, I touched my hand to my torso, my muscles weak. My ribs protruded beneath my robes. I felt frail and skinny. And there was a cloth wrapped around my waist and between my legs, placed there by the ones who had cared for me.

A sudden pain drew attention to my forehead; hesitantly, I touched it with fingers trembling, discerning the shape of a scar.

Finally, I felt the skin around my neck. It took a few moments to comprehend what was missing.

"Don't let it bring you down," I sang in a whisper, wiping tears from my eyes and summoning the strength to sit up and look around.

I was in a small chamber with an opening that led into a perpendicular passageway. On the ground nearby, crystals arranged in some sort of grid fluctuated between an array of colors. For a second I was breathless, overwhelmed by the beauty. Then I noticed what sat by the opening: a worn wheelbarrow packed with blankets. In its shadow sat a pair of sandals next to two jars—one filled with water, the other with red mush.

There was a fluttering in my stomach, and I suddenly felt nauseous.

"Come on," I urged myself. "Get up now. You can do this." After using all my willpower to stand on my feet, my legs gave in to a violent tremor, and I collapsed with a thud, feeling helpless.

Tears formed, and I considered screaming for assistance. But as I tuned into the silence, I was reminded of the power I had known in my dreams, along with the awareness that I was always being guided. At that moment, an inner voice told me there was no need to cry.

I gazed at my hands as I questioned reality, marveling at how small they were and how slender my fingers. Memories surfaced of swirling cherry blossoms, angelic entities, and gorgeous bridges sung into existence, and my palms seemed to glow with traces of gold. Intense love arose not only for those close to me but for the universe itself and all of its beings. That's when I noticed the makings of an image on the wall beside me, the same one I saw reflected before jumping from another realm.

A butterfly.

The crystals brightened as I came to this understanding, erasing the shadows and illuminating its wings.

"You're here, aren't you?" I whispered excitedly. "You really are with me. You're seeing through my eyes."

A joy in my heart confirmed this epiphany, and I was struck by a glimpse of something greater than ourselves. Only then did I let tears stream down. Simultaneously, energy ran up my spine, blossoming at my crown. I rose again with renewed strength, fully awake, feeling resurrected.

I tiptoed around the grid—which shined with violet light, creating a pattern on the ground like a lotus flower—before strapping on my sandals and finishing the water. Each gulp filled me with life. But I sensed I needed to hurry. I discarded the cloth around my groin and stepped through the opening, thanking the wheelbarrow before leaving it behind.

The adjoining passage was straight and narrow, tunneling far in either direction. Even though it was also filled with crystals, the lighting was dimmer than in the chamber, with more of a bluish-green hue on one side and a yellowish-orange on the other. I saw nothing to point me which way to go, nor any person to assist.

"Hello?" My voice echoed. "Is anybody out there?"

I waited, yet no one answered, and I wondered what had happened to my crystal-loving caretaker. On a whim, I headed toward the yellow, but my heart sped up unnaturally, forcing me to pause and feel within.

"It's not this way, is it?" I asked. My heart relaxed, beating in agreement.

Then, as I listened closely, I detected a low, rhythmic vibration, like humming, audible above the silence. And it seemed to come from the path behind me.

"Thank you," I whispered with a hand on my chest, turning the other direction.

I walked with a limp, my body still weak, but the strength of spirit willed me onward into the soft turquoise glow. The vibration grew louder with each passing minute, and though I had no idea where I was headed, I had no fear, for I knew that he was with me. Even when my surroundings grew dark, I clung to this knowing and asked again for clarity; the crystals around me lit up, following me with every step, acting as a guiding light.

My limp turned into a jog as I gained more confidence. I kept waiting to experience some shortness of breath, to be hampered by my lungs and to cough and wheeze, but despite all my muscles aching, I was breathing perfectly fine.

Finally, I arrived at a bend in the passageway, the vibration feeling closer than ever. I stopped for a moment and listened curiously, making out distinct voices that seemed to compose it. But nothing prepared me for what I saw when I turned the corner.

The path opened up into a wider cave. Lining the way were a dozen golden-robed children deep in meditation, levitating three feet in the air.

"OOOOOMMMMMMMM," they chanted as one. The crystals around them twinkled with white light.

I stared in amazement while they repeated this harmonious tone as if united by a collective awareness. Meanwhile, I felt the vibration in every cell of my body. Behind my scar, a pressure was forming, like a dormant energy vying to awaken. And though the eyes of the children were closed, I got the impression that they saw me.

"Welcome home," a young girl said in my mind, validating my suspicions and filling me with such gratitude that I wanted to cry.

They seemed to smile as I proceeded, and I felt infused by their gift of vitality.

"Keep going!" encouraged another as the mantra reverberated.

The last child I passed had dark skin and violet robes, clearly unique among the others. An inner part of me recognized her soul. She looked to be the youngest at only a few years old yet spoke like a sage when connecting telepathically: *"Step out of the darkness and awaken to your destiny. Your twin flame awaits the light of your gaze."* As she finished, the crystals flashed with such brilliance that I wondered if the sun had enveloped the whole planet.

Touched by higher energy, I ran the rest of the way, through the twists and turns of the cave until the sound of a waterfall emerged; light streamed from the other side.

Soon, I stepped out into the sun's healing rays, experiencing its warmth as if for the very first time. I was hypnotized by the setting: the glistening lake surrounded by willow trees and gardens. Then my attention shifted to a field nearby, where there appeared to be over a hundred children huddled together, focused on something. Many of them were crying, and I found myself reliving memories that weren't mine.

A little boy pointing set off gasps from the crowd, and the focus gradually turned toward me.

Their expressions switched from sadness to disbelief. I approached them as they started to disassemble, revealing their kind faces and large, radiant eyes. To my astonishment, some had normal eyes—though still brimming with so much light. I knew these children as my brothers and sisters. Elation set in that they had found their way to a safe place. And at least for the moment, they were happy to see me.

They gestured to the center of the crowd, which parted to show a disturbing scene.

How can this be? I wondered, my eyes wide with worry.

Lying on the ground was the man I loved, suffering dreadful convulsions, struggling to breathe with his eyes wide open and unseeing. Kneeling beside him was a girl of eccentric beauty, with long black hair and golden spiral earrings—a girl who I knew had helped us immensely. But through tears of distress, she seemed at a loss, shaking his face and calling out his name. Despite murmurs from the crowd, she still had not noticed me.

With a gift of insight, I reached into her mind.

"Luna," I whispered, *"give me his eyes."*

There was a moment in which she looked at me dumbfounded, clueless as to what was happening. Then something clicked, and she twisted his head to gaze right through me.

Those were the eyes of the man I loved, brilliant and virtuous, and from the entwining of our light sprang a greater understanding: that this love, this consciousness, was our sole identity. Yet in our delusion, we had become lost in our roles, forgetting that life was only a play, convinced of the dream of separation.

Through our love, I was able to recognize him *as* me. And I remembered that the name being called was my own.

"Samuel."

~

My breath vibrated across unseen strings, carrying my spirit through the physical plane until it reanimated its natural body.

My heart filled with life, and I inhaled, feeling like I was back from the dead. I found myself mesmerized by the shining sun, breathing freely beside friends who cried out in relief. Then there was Luna, who promptly slapped me on the cheek.

"Next time you decide to go on an out-of-body rescue mission"— she wiped tears from her eyes—"at least drop me a message or something so I know you're not dying!"

"I'll keep that in mind," I said with a smile as I sat up to a rejoicing crowd.

Felix and Johanna beamed in the background while the children of Sanctuary hugged and patted me. I saw Maya, Lila, Cyrus, Sidney, Ezra, and Maggie's orphans, a couple of whom then helped me to my feet. Standing further in the distance were two hooded figures wearing robes of light. They nodded with gratitude before vanishing abruptly.

"Evelyn," I whispered as the crowd parted and the murmurs faded into reverent silence. I saw her just as a light rain began to fall, hailing from a passing cloud.

The girl I loved, ascended from the ashes of unconsciousness, limped forward with an unwavering will and crystal-blue eyes reddened from crying. I stepped toward her with tears of my own, reliving every trial faced and decision made that led us, alive, to this moment. Meanwhile, the songbirds sang a comforting melody, as if they knew all along everything would be just fine, happening in perfect timing.

We stopped a few feet apart and gazed into each other's eyes. The feeling was overwhelming, for never had I been so connected to anyone or seen their soul so transparently. The entire essence of the earth seemed to radiate from her eyes, expressing a spirit more profound than I could possibly imagine. Still, I felt our hearts beating as one, our souls melded by unconditional love.

She grinned with affection. "Is it really you, or are you simply a part of me?"

"It is really me, Evelyn," I responded. "Yet I am a part of you as you are a part of me, just as the universe needs eyes to see."

As we smiled at one another in spiritual remembrance, she stretched her hand toward me, and I stretched mine just far enough to graze her slender fingers. Internally, we communicated in a language unspoken. The only sound was the gentle wind.

She then collapsed in my arms, overcome by the exhaustion of holding two souls in one body.

CHAPTER 16

A **RAINBOW ARCED** above the horizon as the sun broke through the clouds, shining down on a better world.

Evelyn swayed gently in a hammock below the willow tree. In the hours since first awakening, she'd drifted in and out of consciousness while dozens of children came to visit us during breaks from their responsibilities. Some brought flowers to celebrate her recovery; others offered fruits picked fresh from the gardens, which she ate happily whenever she was awake. The Welders of Light gifted new robes sewn out of the energy of the universe. Ezra and Sidney gleefully entertained us with holograms of hummingbirds flitting around her face.

All the while, she couldn't quite return to a fully conscious state, saying sparse words and smiling airily as if she could not tell what was dream or reality. I was grateful to see her eyes when they met mine, and she would broaden her smile before falling back asleep. At times, they widened at something over my shoulder, even though there was no one I could see. I felt the grace of God as I watched her breathe comfortably, knowing it wasn't yet her time to leave.

Likewise, I felt dazed by memories of a higher plane and the experience of unity before I separated from her body. I caught myself staring at the ripples forming whenever there was a disturbance in the lake.

"You should rest too, Samuel." Penelope, standing patiently with her orphan siblings, noted my disorientation. "We can watch her in the meantime."

I gazed at them in appreciation. Out of all the other children, they were the most attentive of Evelyn, rarely leaving her side. Her eyes brightened whenever she saw them, and she whispered their names in states nearing lucidity. I remembered how shy they'd seemed previously, perhaps because I looked different from them. But in Sanctuary we knew no such division. My heart filled with warmth, for we were also now family.

"I'm okay," I said, "don't worry about me."

"Are you sure about that, buddy?" Cyrus came to my side. Like Maya and Lila, he'd grown close to Maggie's group during their journey. "I know we went through worse at the Facility, but I would be lying if I said you didn't give me a scare back there."

I looked into his large, caring eyes, and an image of a blue door appeared in my mind, but I brushed it off with a smile. "Well, I'm here now, aren't I?" I turned to the orphans. "And I thank you all for being here too. I know we're all devastated by what happened to Maggie and your village, but Evelyn wouldn't have had the same strength to pull through if something had also happened to you."

"Anything for Evelyn," responded a little boy—the same one who'd asked me about her the night before and whom I now knew as Xavier.

"I may not have known her as long as most of us here," added Penelope, "but she quickly became an older sister to me, as well as a friend, just like she was for everyone she met. It wasn't easy for us either, but I'm glad she had you. And that you're okay, too."

Another image appeared, of Noah trembling with fear, but I observed it until it dissolved. "She *always* has me," I affirmed. "The same is true for all of you." The children hugged me, and Evelyn slept with growing serenity.

After a while, most went back to tending the gardens and preparing the harvest for a feast. Sounds of laughter erupted throughout Sanctuary; a collective weight had been released.

It wasn't until I was alone with Evelyn that Luna dropped in through the willow branches.

"How's our baby girl doing?" she asked with a playful nudge.

I chuckled, then quieted, somewhat concerned for my love's sanity. "She's been resting since this morning," I said, proceeding to tell her about the daze Evelyn was in even when her eyes were open, which I too experienced to a lesser degree.

"Well, after that soul-level craziness that happened, it should be expected. Let me see." She came to the hammock while munching on a handful of pine nuts, which she offered to me, but I declined. As she inspected Evelyn, I noticed in her eyes a dampening of their usual shine, a sheen of melancholy replacing the glow—though I didn't ask why. She placed a hand on Evelyn's forehead for a few tense seconds, then said reassuringly, "The experience this morning took a lot out of her, plus she definitely needs time to adjust to our reality, but she'll be just fine. Let her rest for the time being."

"Thank you, Luna," I exhaled in relief.

"My pleasure, Sammy. Just try and make sure she doesn't fall into a two-week sleep again!"

I laughed. "Seriously, thank you for everything." Immense gratitude welled up as I sifted through surreal memories. "We wouldn't be here without you. Remember the question you put into my mind right after the accident, when we were tied up, held at gunpoint?"

"How could I forget?" She popped a pine nut into her mouth. "It was quite a *miracle* that I found you guys."

"Well, after all that's happened, it's more than just a belief in miracles. It feels now that it's the natural order of things, like we're all living in one big miracle, one big dream, where the universe is alive and everything is linked."

The wind picked up as she gave a perceptive wink. "I'm glad that I can assist in your awakening so you may see the signs and know their meaning." To my embarrassment, she kissed me on the cheek. "We are the dreamers, after all, aren't we?"

Her earring grazed me as she turned away.

"But how do we know their meaning?" I asked before she could leave.

"By simply remembering that there are no accidents—just the universe speaking. Besides that, I cannot say what is true. Coincidence makes sense only to you." She almost sang these last sentences. "By the way, sorry I couldn't come earlier. I was hanging out on the other side of the lake, having a nice telepathic chat with my niece."

"Sangeetha?" My heart raced. "She's out of her cave?"

"Well, yeah, Samuel. She has to eat too, you know."

I peered through the drooping branches, and sure enough, a little girl in violet robes stood across the water next to a small gathering, staring in our direction. With Evelyn still smiling in her sleep, I thanked Luna again before heading around the lake.

"Sangeetha!" I called as I saw her strolling toward a peach tree.

She glanced at me with glowing eyes, then used her mind to pick a ripe-looking fruit from the branches, floating it to me while I approached.

"No thanks," I said. "But that's really kind of you."

She shrugged and brought it back to her, taking a bite. It was my first time seeing her out in the daylight, but her aura shined just as bright. Children sat in rows in the gathering close by, participating in a class led by her mother. I looked at Sangeetha and connected to her eyes.

"She's healing," she told me.

"Yes," I transmitted, together with an image of Evelyn in the hammock. *"I just wanted to thank you for what you did."*

The girl chuckled like she had played a joke on me, then, to my surprise, used her voice to speak. "I did nothing. It was your love."

She nodded toward my hands, which glinted with golden energy, before ambling past me toward the cave. And I realized that a universal healer was within every one of us, existing in the love we shared—the harmony of the universe.

Before she'd ventured far, she turned to catch my eyes once more. *"Please protect her. Something very special grows inside of her."* I was sent an image of our planet made beautiful.

"What does that mean?" I returned.

She grinned but didn't answer, taking another bite of the peach. Then something behind me caught her attention.

"Samuel." I turned to see Johanna approaching. "How is Evelyn holding up?"

"Doing well. Still resting." She and Felix had visited earlier, but attempts at talking with Evelyn hadn't registered.

"Good to hear. She'll come back fully with time." She exchanged looks with her daughter, conversing on another frequency of the mind, before they smiled and Sangeetha waved goodbye. Johanna turned back to me. "Is this a good time to speak?"

"Yes," I said. "But aren't you teaching?"

"They're in the middle of an exercise. I'll let them be."

Indeed, the children were practicing telekinesis by levitating blue stones in front of their faces. Some maintained it quite effortlessly; others with different psychic specialties—such as Maya and Lila— were struggling a bit more, though still getting it off the ground. I imagined Johanna taught her students like her sister taught me, instructing them to dissolve dualistic barriers between themselves and their surroundings.

"What is it you wanted to talk about?" I asked.

She stared into my soul with gorgeous green eyes, intertwining our shadows as well as the light underneath. "I haven't had the chance to thank you privately for bringing Mad—I mean, *Luna*—back to me. You don't know how much it means to be able to hug her physically again, and to see her bond with my daughter. It's an indescribable feeling."

"I'm so happy I could help." My heart swelled in my chest. "But it was your sister who saved me and Evelyn and brought us to Sanctuary. Along the way she taught me to hone my abilities. So, as much as she loves to tease sometimes, I know she's filled with compassion and wisdom."

"She must see something very special in you, Samuel, because that's another thing—just how much she's changed. It's like she's a different person altogether from the sister I tried to raise. I'm sure she told you about her past." She sighed. "I'm sure she told you about our father."

"Yes. He was very cruel for abandoning you."

"It was a horrible situation, and it definitely affected her. She started giving in to bad influences. She became very disturbed. And at one point I thought I had lost both of my sisters." Her eyes watered, and I saw her strive to hold it together. "Anyway, all we have is the here and now. The rest is only a memory. There is still one more I need to snag from the darkness, but I'm very grateful to have Luna in the light."

I paused before replying, "I saw Selena when we encountered Matteo and his gang. But she likely helped stop further harm to Evelyn." I described how she had stepped in at a crucial time, potentially saving Evelyn's life. Johanna's eyes filled with optimism. I went on to tell her how they had also taken Noah, whom they were controlling through fear, as well as the story of the mother in the village, grieving her toddler son abducted from her arms.

"That's truly terrible to hear." She shook her head with empathy. "Their tactics haven't changed. They manipulate children and feed off their fear. They take them from their parents at a young age."

"There must be some plan to rescue them?" I inquired hopefully. "Either from the black robes or from factions of the military."

"Why do you think Felix and I were guided here in the first place? We wanted a sanctuary for those who wished to get away from all the turmoil—and create a new world together." She gestured to the gardens filled with laughing children, then patted my shoulder. "You're only seventeen, Samuel. You're still so young, and your love is now awakening. Do not concern yourself with others' negativity. Enjoy the life they took from you at that godforsaken facility."

"You're probably right." I gazed at the willow tree across the lake, recalling what Sangeetha had told me. "But we still have to do something."

"We are doing something. Even a single child uplifts the entire planet when emitting love and positivity, like a candle flame lighting up the darkness. You will understand this once you realize how everything is connected. But more important than doing, we are first cultivating a state of being. True change starts by going within and making peace with yourself. All else is simply a reflection."

"So that we don't repeat the same cycles of conflict," I said, invoking Leon's wisdom.

"Exactly." She bestowed a beatific smile. "A new world must be born out of a new level of consciousness. And with enough of us raising our vibration, it can create a chain reaction, spreading from child to child until it sparks a quantum leap."

"It's like boiling a pot of tea," I said, fondly remembering our stay with Artemis.

"Yes! Or like going up a key on a musical scale. A few high frequencies can shift the state of the whole to the point of transfiguration. We have some especially gifted children who spend most of their days meditating with this purpose, lighting the way for the people of the earth to reach into new dimensions of consciousness. At the same time, they send a psychic beacon for any child in need, with guidance to Sanctuary. But it has to be of their own volition. We must honor the free will of those who choose the darkness, even if they are family."

"I understand what you're saying, but some don't have a choice. What about Noah? What about those little kids they're stealing? I made a promise to that mother."

"There is always a choice on some level," she said, and I thought back to my last lesson with Walter. "I'm sorry, Samuel, if this comes as a disappointment, but we live by a code, and that code includes nonaggression unless in self-defense. Yet trust me when I say there's a time for everything, whether for rest or for more pressing action. Sometimes instead of forcing things, it is better to wait until the big picture comes together and the timing is right. So have patience. There is a divine plan, but it may not always be made conscious."

The songbirds sang as I regarded her with admiration. "I know I speak for every child here when I say we're lucky to have a big sister so wise," I told her. A tear fell from her eye. "Still, I can't help thinking about when Evelyn snaps out of it and realizes that there's a huge scar on her forehead—and that her most prized possession, the locket holding the images of her parents, is missing from her neck." I fumed when I pictured Tiana wearing it. "I just can't help but get angry."

"Then your challenge is to not give in to vengeance, because that will only strengthen old paradigms. Recognize instead that the same divine consciousness lives through every single one of us, even if some try to deny it."

The light was made manifest through her soul's vast windows, expressing the true essence of everyone we had met—and not just those possessing wisdom and benevolence, like Walter, Leon, Artemis, and her nieces, but also the malicious hunters, the scientists who were murdered, the gang of black robes, and the militaristic leaders, though their essences were distorted.

"This is where unconditional love comes in," she finished. "This is where we birth the new world."

We smiled at each other as a warm, heavenly energy bridged our hearts, then that of every child of Sanctuary, turning worry into stillness, anger into forgiveness, and mind-based thinking into heart-centered presence. In that moment I sensed the whole of the earth being uplifted by means of the same intelligence that grew the flowers, the trees, and the fruit they held. And despite the conflict in the world, we laughed at a realization greater than ourselves.

From there, our attention turned back to the class she was teaching, where the children seemed to have entered another state of consciousness, and nearly all of them had the blue stone levitating.

The exception was little Xavier, whom I was surprised to see among the group of children with obviously different eyes. He was the only one with the stone still on the ground, but that didn't stop him from concentrating with all his might.

I glanced at Johanna. "It's admirable that he tries."

She watched him proudly. "The greatest gift these children possess is that they have not been conditioned by the ridiculous lie that they need big eyes to do something extraordinary."

As I looked closer, I saw his stone vibrating.

~

The rest of the afternoon was spent helping in the gardens, gathering armful after armful from the day's fruitful harvest and setting it on the table within the circle of roses.

Meanwhile, the children displayed a friendliness I had rarely seen, going out of their way to make sure I was okay and asking about Evelyn.

"She's doing just fine," I would answer encouragingly. "She only needs to build back her energy."

Yet as much as I tried to remain in the presence I had glimpsed, my mind stubbornly resisted, pestering me with fears that she would delve into another deep sleep. Every few minutes, I glanced across the lake to where she rested, checking for movement between the low branches.

As the sun began setting, the situation didn't change, so we assembled for the feast without her attendance. Johanna led a prayer of gratitude for everything we had, as well as the experience of that morning, and asked for Evelyn's further healing. She also made sure to request that the universe safeguard any children lost or suffering. Afterward, we each filled our plates, though I could barely eat a couple of mouthfuls of berries before feeling unexpectedly nauseous. The children smiled and laughed, but something else was bothering me.

"Samuel!" Luna walked up with a group of young kids. "I was just telling them some of our funniest adventure stories. Like that time you nearly drowned yourself in the river. Or when I scared you after I taught you how to meditate and your freaky powers almost killed me!"

"Yeah," I grunted, peering again at the willow. "Yeah, that was quite something."

Luna stared in disappointment, reading my expression, then murmured, "Just let her be, Samuel. She's not going to disappear."

I glared back in frustration, then looked apologetically toward the children.

"I'm sorry," I told them and left with my plate of food—though not before adding a piece of fish to it, recalling how it had helped me at a time when I thought I'd lost my sanity.

Evelyn's eyes were closed when I arrived at the hammock, her new golden robes yet to be worn, draped on a branch beside her. Intuitively, I filled a bowl with clean water, blessed it with positive energy, and helped her to drink just like I did while she was in the wheelbarrow. Still, she lay in her post-awakened daze, and my worries escalated.

"Why is this happening?" I asked the sky, sensing that someone was listening.

I sat on a large rock I had moved by her side and prayed again for her clarity of mind. Then I took her sweet hand in mine, attempting to feel into the situation from a higher perspective and discover the lessons it was trying to teach. Only then were my most deeply buried shadows illumined by enough light to arise; suddenly, I was transported to another space and time.

Lying on a sofa in front of me, with pained yet loving eyes, was my mother, no longer able to hide her suffering. The cancer had spread from her skin to her lungs, and I couldn't do anything as she struggled for each breath, her vitality slowly fading. Still, she had the strength to grasp my tiny hand and smile between fits of coughing, telling me about the angels that would always protect me, singing to me softly about the birds and the butterflies. I cried as I gazed at the window above her, the rays of light shining through, and despite my innocence and terrible sadness, I knew that it was best to just let go.

The scene shifted, and my father was in a rage, yelling at me at the top of his lungs, looking for someone or something to blame. Frightened, I scurried to the upstairs closet, but he knew where I was hiding. He dragged me out and held me against the wall, ripping my teddy bear away. His hands went around my little neck.

An unfathomable power soon came to my defense; his face turned blue, and he dropped to his knees, perishing along with his anger and grief.

His heart just stopped. Because I willed it to.

I found myself in an abandoned church, numb to the world, traumatized and lonely. I sat and stared at a man nailed to a cross until I felt my soul detach from my body. That's when they came to take me—somehow knowing what had happened. I was led to a general who had a ruthless grin, aiming to make me into a weapon.

Through the initial rounds of experimentation and shock therapy, my heart remained empty. It took a little girl approaching me while I lay curled up on the grass—unafraid to smile and offer her hand—to help me remember what it was to love.

"I thought I would never feel it again," I whispered tearfully, coming back to the present.

I experienced a release as I reviewed these memories and each of the characters, including my inner child. It was the first time I had been able to observe these particular memories without reacting, because I forgave them, and they forgave me. Only in retrospect could I see that all that suffering served a sacred purpose, forging who I was and leading to the beauty of this infinite moment, watching Evelyn breathe in peace. It was all part of a greater plan. And from the acceptance of the darkness came a boundless light shining from within and then reflecting in the sky.

There materialized a six-pointed star—or two counterrotating pyramids—flashing different colors throughout the spectrum. As I felt a corresponding surge in energy, I rose to my feet and stepped toward the lake, tears flooding my cheeks with the absolute knowing that someone was watching.

Then, a voice came.

"Do you realize,
That you have the most beautiful face . . ."

I stared back in awe at Evelyn singing—as effortlessly as I'd ever witnessed.

"Do you realize,
We're floating in space . . ."

She laughed like a newborn child. "That was quite an amazing dream."

I soared toward the hammock, my heart bursting.

"Evelyn!" I hugged her. "You're here with me!"

"Of course, silly. Where else would I be?" She faced me as I sat on the rock, brushing my wet cheeks. "Why were you crying, Samuel?"

"Oh, just going through some memories. And then I saw something." I looked toward the same spot in the sky, but the light had vanished, for the message had been received. Then I gazed into her crystal-blue eyes and was struck by a soul that was pure and bright. "Evelyn, do you know where we are?"

She peered through the branches at the waterfall, gardens, and golden-robed children gathered in the distance. "I suppose it's the Garden of Eden."

"We call it Sanctuary," I said, enamored. "Do you remember what happened?"

"Yes." She grimaced as she touched the back of her head. "We were tied up in that trunk before I went to sleep. How long has it been, exactly?"

"Around ten days."

She sighed. "I barely had a sense of it. Time wasn't the same. But all that matters is that we're here now together, right?" Her eyes went wide. "The orphans, too . . ."

I nodded with a smile. "They arrived here before us with the guidance of some friends. They're eating now, but they were by your side for hours."

"That's wonderful!" She beamed, then glanced at the lake suspiciously. "But how do you know that we're not still dreaming?"

"That's a good question." I chuckled, staring at my palms as I questioned reality. "I can't say for sure that we're not in a dream, but I reckon you could at least taste a difference in the food quality." I picked up the plate filled mainly with fish and vegetables. "You ate some fruit this morning, but I think you'd like something a little hardier."

She reached out, but rather than taking the food, she placed her hand on my chest, feeling my heartbeat. "You remember it too, don't you? Being there with me?"

Our eyes connected, and we were sent back into the dream, with cherry blossoms whirling around us and mighty archangels watching from above, guiding and protecting. The following moment, we snapped back into our reality, hearing the spilling of the waterfall. "Of course I do." I caressed her hand and helped her to sit up. "Now please eat."

After a quick blessing, she dug into the fish with her fingers and took a tentative bite. Her eyes lit up, and she went on to scarf down her plate without talking for the next few minutes, in between sips of water. I gave silent thanks as she finished it to the bone, grateful to the creatures of the river for providing her nourishment.

"You must have liked it," I said.

"Definitely better than mashed elderberries." She raised a teasing eyebrow before looking down at the hammock. "And so much more comfortable than a wheelbarrow."

"You really remember everything," I uttered, astonished.

"Well, not everything." She combed through her mind. "Only fragments at this point. But once I became awake in the dream, it was like I began existing in two dimensions at the same time. I was able to see all that we went through, but from a higher perspective. I felt like one of your guardian angels."

A shiver ran up my spine. "Even through the darkest parts of our journey?"

She nodded. "I heard Luna's cries when those dragon kids attacked. I was there with you in the church—when you desperately needed a key. I felt it when you were sad and lonely and listened to every word while you sang to me." She clasped my hand as tears streamed from her eyes. "I never wanted you to think you were to blame for anything."

"I know," I said, and as a light drizzle fell from the sky, I also started to cry. "Because I heard you sing too, when I went into the river." I glanced at her forehead. "Tell me, did you feel everything?"

"Yes." She touched her scar and flashed a bittersweet smile. "But *they* were there to comfort me. Along with the other angels." I received a vision in my mind's eye of the two hooded figures while Evelyn's hand hovered to her neck instinctively.

"Don't worry. I'll get it back from those bastards."

She shook her head. "Do you remember what you promised me after they first attacked and we escaped into the forest?" I recalled the rage I had unleashed on that group of children and my vow to never show it again. "It's okay, Samuel. Whether or not I have a picture of them, they're always there for me. I learned that in my dreams. Because while you and Luna were keeping me safe out here, they were doing the same in there, telling me of things to come, teaching me how to manipulate energy. They always said I would awaken when I was ready."

"I'm so glad you were able to be with them, Evelyn," I said earnestly. "But you really don't mind about the locket?"

"All I care about is that you're here with me. The love I received is what kept me alive." She drew in a long breath. "And it healed me too."

Gratitude washed over me. "You can breathe."

"Yes, perfectly. It's like God used my coma as an opportunity to heal my lungs. And now I wake up next to you in this beautiful sanctuary, away from all that suffering; this answers my prayers more thoroughly than I thought possible. It wasn't a tragedy, and it wasn't an accident. My body was going through a metamorphosis. And all of this turned out to be a blessing."

I nodded, recalling our time in the church. "Every experience contains a hidden purpose, no matter how dark it may seem at first."

"Oh, Samuel, you sound so wise," she laughed with light in her eyes. As we watched the sun dip below the horizon, I appreciated every being in the universe, including those hunters who kidnapped us; each of them played an important role in the grand design, whether they knew it or not. I met Evelyn's loving gaze, and she leaned her head toward me. As hard as it was, I turned my cheek. One more secret needed to be revealed.

I groaned. "Listen, Evelyn. Something happened while you were asleep. Something between me and—"

"You mean that little kiss?" she interjected.

I gawked at her. "You knew all this time?"

"Yes. In fact, I already forgave you for it. Don't you remember? Underneath the cherry blossom tree?"

A flashback of trying to kiss Evelyn and being denied in the same fashion came to me. I apologized for something I thought I had done, and she forgave me, asking me to remember. Then it hit me. "That was before it even happened!"

"But a part of you still remembered." She cocked her head. "Time is a funny thing. You know, when I was in the dream, I felt so aware and so powerful—at least, when I was lucid. I could create my reality through thought and emotion, and it was as real as anything. While I can't build bridges out of music just yet, I learned that this, too, is also a dream, just a different type of dream, one we share together." She quieted in reflection. "Does that sound crazy?"

"After all we've been through, that is the least crazy thing I've heard. Plus, you're not the only one who learned about energy. Luna taught me how to meditate and control my abilities."

I stood with the faith that I could do anything and focused on the rose garden across the lake, where many children were now playing. With each breath, I tuned more into the stillness, emptying my mind, until I found a point within from which I felt all life emanate. It was part of the same timeless consciousness that birthed galaxies and universes, but even in our tiny corner of the earth, it breathed a higher intelligence into every blade of grass. From there I communicated with a single pink rose, which graciously agreed to float in our direction, swaying above the water until it wove through the branches and into Evelyn's hands. As she stared at it in wonder, I sat again and clasped the rose with her.

"Never think that you're crazy. Walter always told me that the world used to believe these things were only possible in a dream."

"Samuel, that was extraordinary." Her eyes shined with affection, then turned toward the sky. "Can you also move the moon for me?"

I observed the crescent just visible in the twilight. "That remains to be seen. But I know I could at least rearrange the stars."

She connected through my eyes, remembering the words of angels. "Well, if this is a dream, I guess we're now awakening." Then, she seemed lost within another memory. "In the crystal cave, there was a little girl levitating with this incredible energy, and she was telling us to awaken to our destiny. That was Sangeetha, wasn't it?"

"How did you know?"

"You told me in the dream that she was healing me."

"That's right, I did." I chuckled in remembrance. "She's actually Luna's niece, and as soon as we arrived, I brought you to her. She works with crystals and healing frequencies. But when I went to thank her, she told me she did nothing—and that you have something special growing inside you."

She paused, contemplating. "What exactly does that mean?"

"I'm not sure. I asked the same thing, and she didn't answer. But I get the sense that she knows more than she's saying, like she's tapped into something greater." The rose wavered in a sudden gust of wind. "God is speaking to us constantly, and he seems to be orchestrating every little thing."

Her face filled with intrigue. "Samuel, since when do you speak so freely about God?"

"Since I realized how much I love you," I said, caressing her cheek. "Do you mind if I always do?"

She beamed. "Until I die. And after that, too."

We kissed while our hearts beat in harmony. This felt as good as any dream.

"It really is so simple, isn't it?" I whispered in a state of sublimity.

The branches beside us rustled, and our heads turned as Maya and Lila wandered in.

"We thought we would catch you guys at the right time." Maya grinned, presumably foreseeing the whole thing in her mind.

She signaled behind her, and all of Evelyn's orphan siblings entered, clearly overjoyed to see the soul behind her eyes. Evelyn clutched the pink rose as she climbed to her feet, tears of happiness forming.

"You all really made it." The love in her gaze was palpable. "I knew the angels would guide you always."

She opened her arms to hug each one tenderly, listening to the stories of their own special journey and thanking Maya and Lila for helping them along the way. It was heartwarming to witness.

Xavier didn't waste time in mentioning his telekinesis.

"I have powers now, Evelyn! I moved a stone with my mind today."

She laughed warmly. "Is that so?"

"I did! Samuel can tell you."

She glanced at me peculiarly, and I nodded with encouragement, knowing that the same boundless light shined from the core of every human.

Soon, more children gathered beneath the tree, including those older leaders of Sanctuary. Ezra and Sidney gave Evelyn a lively greeting with holograms of butterflies bursting from their cocoons. Cyrus was elated to meet her in a proper manner, telling her about all the experiments we overcame together. Then Felix and Johanna drifted in, their eyes radiating acceptance and compassion.

"Welcome home." Felix bowed with a hand over his heart. "We are so pleased that you have awakened at last."

"If there's anything you need, don't hesitate to ask," Johanna added. "Know that all of us here are now your family."

"Thank you," replied Evelyn. "That means so much to me."

To everyone's surprise, Sangeetha followed behind her parents. She quietly approached me and Evelyn, showing little expression. After staring at us with eyes of immense gravity, she offered both hands. *"I want to show you something,"* she told us telepathically. Evelyn looked at me before I took her hand in mine, and we touched Sangeetha's simultaneously.

With a spasm of electricity, we were transported to the chamber of light where Evelyn had first awakened. Within dazzling crystals glowed the compelling image of a monarch butterfly. But on the ground nearby, the moon-shaped crystal Sangeetha had used on Evelyn lay shattered. A high-pitched ringing disturbed the silence, and we sensed a darkness encroaching from outside.

"What are you trying to tell us?" I asked Sangeetha, my brain aching.

"Focus," she urged me, gesturing to the area of my heart.

The chakra began pulsating with an overwhelming energy; Evelyn gasped as hers did the same. While we clasped hands tightly, a glistening cord formed a bridge between our hearts, connecting to Sangeetha's and then launching from each of us to the monarch. Suddenly, we were encapsulated within an impenetrable pyramid of light. Even as the darkness came and the ringing intensified, nothing of the heart could be threatened. I glanced up to see our image reflected above, like three stars burning gloriously.

Sangeetha broke the connection, and we were sent back to our bodies beneath the willow tree.

"Wow," I breathed, my limbs shaking. "That was . . . astonishing."

"Yes, it was," Evelyn agreed. "Thank you for that, Sangeetha. I know that it will bring further wisdom and healing."

Sangeetha smiled in response, nodded slowly, then hugged her parents before walking away. The vision had been mysterious, frightening yet moving; but I knew better than to ask for its meaning.

Afterward, Johanna studied us curiously. "She doesn't usually put those kinds of gifts on display. Whatever you experienced should stay between the two of you, but I would advise to keep it firmly in mind."

"It would be hard to forget." I exchanged glances with Evelyn, traces of the butterfly still visible in her eyes. Then, I peered around at the captivated crowd, noticing a glaring absence. "Where's Luna, by the way?"

Johanna frowned. "That's a good question. I last saw her at the feast."

"Allow me." Lila took a deep breath and closed her eyes, tapping into her abilities. "She's in the woods. Looks like she's meditating. Do you want me to tell her we're here?"

"No, we'd better not disturb her. But thank you, Lila." Johanna addressed the others: "I'm sure that Evelyn needs time to process everything, and we should give her some privacy. Yet we will always remember this extraordinary day as we celebrate this miraculous awakening."

Cheers erupted. Although there were obvious differences in some of the children's appearances, a special bond existed through which all our hearts were linked. With watery eyes, Evelyn thanked everyone and gave more hugs before the crowd began departing. Maya, Lila, and the orphans were the last remaining.

"Do you want to join us?" asked Penelope. "We're playing hide-and-seek."

"You all go ahead," Evelyn replied fondly. "Maybe later we'll sneak up on you guys."

They giggled as they went to play, leaving us alone once more as dusk swept over the land.

"Perhaps you'd like to go somewhere with me?" I asked spontaneously. "There's a place where we can look out over all of Sanctuary."

She deliberated for a moment. "I was hoping we could find Luna, actually. I know she came by earlier to see me, but I didn't get the chance to thank her."

I took her hand and sank into her eyes, arousing in her a loving smile. "Let's just be together for tonight, if that's all right with you."

"Okay, Samuel." She glanced down at her old robes. "But first I need to get out of these clothes."

She grabbed the robes hanging nearby and undressed in front of me, exchanging silver for gold. Still carrying the pink rose, she followed me through the branches and into a new world, passing gardens, fruit trees, and crystal beacons of boundless energy before we ascended the cliff with barely any struggle. Soon we arrived at the same place where I had jumped into the lake, the waterfall cascading into an illuminated Sanctuary bustling with bright-eyed children at play. I led her back along the river, going over memories prior to her awakening, which no longer seemed of this reality.

"Were you scared?" she asked me. "At those times when we were trapped and any of us could have died?"

"Of course I was scared," I told her honestly. "But I'd gladly face death a thousand times to be with you and see your eyes."

My heart fluttered in my chest as we kissed. The next thing I knew, we were in the grass and in each other's arms, hearing the endless river flowing beside us as her soft lips pressed against mine.

A cracking noise sounded in the distance, and for a second I peered warily into the forest; I thought I saw the silhouette of a doe. All care vanished when Evelyn kissed me passionately. She shot me a sly expression, and together we undressed.

We spent the night alone with each other, under the stars and a watchful moon.

~

The next three days at Sanctuary provided a chance to bond with our greater family, offering a glimpse of what the world could be if we came together in unity and understanding.

In the mornings, Evelyn and I would join the group meditation, stretching our consciousnesses to realms unseen. Afterward, we helped tend the gardens and harvest fruit from the trees. At night we gathered for the feast. All the while, we were totally free, overjoyed to be able to communicate openly without fear of being monitored. We served the community out of our own hearts' desire rather than being forced into compliance.

We also took breaks to play with the children. It was truly a privilege to connect with them, for every child there was special indeed. I didn't know much about their backgrounds or their biological families, but I could tell they looked up to us as older members of Sanctuary. Their eyes lit up when we admired their marvelous abilities. We joined them and many non-new youths in the psychic classes, including telekinesis, telepathy, remote viewing, and energetic healing.

"It is more than just the eyes," Johanna said. "Silence the mind, and there is nothing we cannot attain."

Sanctuary was a joyous place, bestowing a sweet taste of an enlightened world. But even as I embraced this more peaceful reality, a perplexing issue turned the taste bitter, for it had been ongoing since the night of Evelyn's awakening—and it grew more and more glaring.

Luna was avoiding us.

At first, I thought it was simply bad timing; she wasn't present for the morning meditations, and for some reason she was always on the other side of the lake. Soon, however, I realized that it was deliberate. Whenever Evelyn and I approached her, she took off somewhere else. This happened even when she had her back to us.

She was also hardly interacting with anyone else and began eating meals by herself, often in the forest.

"What's the matter?" Evelyn asked me after an attempt to approach Luna by the lake. "Is everything okay?"

"I'm not sure."

"Is it something I did?" It was heartbreaking to see her eyes dim with sadness.

"No," I asserted. "You've done nothing wrong."

My heart beat erratically as we headed back to the gardens. I was upset that Luna was doing this to Evelyn. The dark-haired girl wasn't the same fun-loving sprite who had led us along our miraculous journey, telepathically conversing with birds and bears. I wondered how well I really knew her. Still, I did not want to lose her friendship or start a scene, so I did my best to hide my frustration.

Nonetheless, Johanna could see what was happening. All it took was one glance into her expressive eyes after Luna left the feast one night to communicate our shared worry. She took off after her sister to talk with her privately.

After three days of being avoided by someone I thought was my close friend and who had been my only lifeline during one of the darkest times of my life, I was at a loss. Although I suspected the reasons for Luna's behavior, I didn't want to admit that they could be a reality. Evelyn and I simply tried to be present for the children, hoping that the issue would resolve itself. But help came from an outside source.

"*Come*" was the psychic whisper I received while relaxing with Evelyn one evening under the willow tree. The whisper was accompanied by the image of the brilliant monarch.

Evelyn was already staring at me when I glanced down at her. "You got it too?"

I nodded, smiling. "We better get going, then."

As if recognizing our combined energy, the helpful crystals lit the way through the cave, guiding us toward Sangeetha's chamber.

We didn't expect to run into anyone, but we turned a corner, and there they were: Luna and her sister.

The faint sounds of the waterfall shrouded an awkward silence as Luna narrowed her gaze from twenty feet away. Finally, she had the decency to speak my name.

"Samuel," she acknowledged.

"Luna," I answered.

The stare-down persisted for a few tense seconds until Evelyn interjected in a friendly manner, "Hello, Luna."

Luna nodded toward her, though she offered no reply. I began to boil with anger before Johanna stepped in as the mediator.

"Whatever is going on between you guys, it needs to be settled. Here and now."

"I don't know about anything going on, Hanna," Luna retorted. "Why don't you ask Samuel?"

"Me?" I countered. "You're the one who's been acting so strange the past few days."

"That's what you think about me, don't you?" She scowled. "That I'm just strange?"

"Well, you *have* been avoiding us ever since I left the feast that night. I just want to know why."

"I think you already know the answer, Samuel. Deep inside."

Johanna thankfully intervened. "Look at me, sister. I know that you still have anger inside you from all that we went through, but I think it is misplaced. We should be so grateful that we are safe here together, and even if the situation is not perfect, it is so much better than back in the day. Please realize there is no reason to act like this. Samuel and Evelyn just want the best for you."

I was convinced Johanna's wisdom would help Luna come around, yet Luna merely snickered. "That's not how I see things, unfortunately." She glared at me. "I'm just acting the way that Samuel perceives me."

"And how do you think I perceive you?" I asked, concerned.

"Like I'm a disposable tool," she responded. "Because even after I saved you, poured my heart out to you, led you here, and taught you everything, it seems like you just used me, for her. And now I am worthless to you."

"That's not true!" I vehemently argued. "I am grateful for everything, Luna, because you are a valuable friend, and I still want you to be. You can read me, can't you? Look into my eyes and see the truth!"

I stepped toward her, putting my soul on full display. While the crystals around us flickered with color, I thought of all the times she'd helped us, from pulling me out of the river at my lowest point to crawling over to heal Evelyn after Matteo scarred her. Yet as I drew close, I felt my memory being redirected to a single moment—one I couldn't forget.

Her eyes watered as I halted in front of her. "I don't know, Samuel, you seem quite happy without me. And I can't blame you. She is quite pretty." She let out a sigh. "But a kiss also means something, you know?"

My heart dropped as my suspicions were confirmed. "I thought we were way past this." I shook my head. "You seemed perfectly fine until the other night—then something shifted. So just say it, will you? What's the trouble?"

"The trouble is, Samuel, that you're in love with someone else." A fire burned in her eyes as she cried, "It should be me!" Her voice echoed with an energy that toppled me backward, and for a moment I lay paralyzed while Luna stormed past me, the quartz on the ceiling glowing red.

Evelyn rushed to my side, helping me up as a tear trickled from her eye. Johanna sorrowfully apologized. "Please forgive her," she said. "She's just going through an episode." Then she chased after her troubled sister, who was on her way out of the cave.

We remained speechless until Evelyn turned to me with a wet gaze. "Are you okay?"

"I think so," I replied. Truthfully, I was bewildered. At times on our journey, Luna had seemed so spiritually enlightened and unaffected. For her to suddenly act with such pettiness and jealousy made me question how much she'd changed since her younger days.

Before we left, I peered back down into the depths of the cave and saw Sangeetha standing there, her aura unmistakable. We locked eyes from a distance, and she nodded slowly before walking away.

That same night, Luna went into the forest.

The following morning, she was gone without a trace.

CHAPTER 17

THERE WAS NO meditation the morning after Luna's disappearance.

Rather, after we fell asleep in the hammock together, Evelyn and I awoke to Johanna sidling through the branches of the willow, carrying an aura of unease.

"Sorry to disturb you," she said as we sat up and beheld her luminous yet tired eyes. "I just wanted to know if she was with you."

In the middle of a yawn, I was struck by the night's memories.

"Luna?" I asked anxiously.

She nodded, proceeding to tell us how others had seen her go into the forest soon after our confrontation, and she still had not returned.

I glanced at Evelyn, who sighed with worry.

"She'll return soon," I assured Johanna. "She would never leave like this. Not after everything."

"Yes. Of course." She put on a smile, but in her eyes I saw a terrible wound being reopened, one that had been present since she and her sisters were children.

For the next few hours, we tended the gardens, but I could barely focus. We caught Johanna wandering about Sanctuary, searching for her sister and trying hard to keep it together. The children could tell that something was wrong; they were not laughing and playing like usual. A heaviness permeated the air. Even the songbirds were silent.

All the while, I waited for Luna to emerge from the forest and say she was sorry—that her behavior was silly and she wanted to remain friends. I would accept her with open arms, forgiving everything in shared understanding. But with each passing hour, our worries grew, until Johanna finally called a Sanctuary-wide meeting.

As over a hundred children gathered under the midday sun, Johanna stood before us with a soul-baring gaze. We settled on the grass quietly, and Felix comforted her as she pleaded with us, "Help me find my sister."

First, we tried with psychic abilities, through which we expected to easily connect. Things soon became eerie. For all our combined efforts, no one could get a reading on Luna. We turned to the most gifted children to no avail.

Lila, the best remote viewer, spent several minutes in a meditative state yet came out flustered. "Something is blocking me. I'm really sorry. This has never happened."

"You didn't see anything?" Johanna questioned, concerned.

"A butterfly, for some reason," Lila answered. "But I think it was fake, like a sort of cover. When I tried to push through, I just heard this ringing and got a headache."

"I got that too," said Maya, who likewise had no visions of a probable future.

In desperation, Johanna called on her exceptional daughter. Even Sangeetha shook her head when asked if she could determine Luna's whereabouts.

Our abilities thwarted, we were forced to do things like the humans of old. The activities of the entire community were put on hold as we formed into a giant search party.

For the rest of the afternoon, dozens of volunteers scoured the forest up and down the river, looking behind every rock and tree until we'd covered everything within a several-mile radius. Evelyn and I stayed together, assigned to a large section of the forest along with Maya, Lila, Cyrus, and Maggie's orphans. But we found no hint of where Luna had gone. I even sat down against a tree and tried to communicate with it telepathically, along with the birds it hosted, sending requests for assistance. All I received was a gust of wind; either they knew nothing, I was simply crazy, or they were keeping a secret for their friend.

"Luna!" I called once more as I stood. "Luna, I'm sorry!" I half expected her to come out from behind a tree, laughing at her prank. I couldn't believe this was happening. I began thinking about what she had said, hoping it was a lie.

"Samuel." Evelyn approached me and placed her hand on my cheek. "You are not to blame, my love. There is no need to apologize."

I caught her empathetic eyes, nodded, and sighed. But the more I ran it through my mind, the more I questioned if I had given Luna the wrong impression and caused her to run away. Regardless, whatever made her feel like doing so certainly came down to more than a stupid little kiss.

As the sun began to set, we made our way back to Sanctuary, but not before meeting up with the other Facility kids and the orphans. They appeared similarly defeated.

"I still got nothing," Lila told us, shaking her head. "And we can't find any sign of her."

"Does that mean we won't see her again?" Xavier asked, upset.

"No, that's nonsense," assured Penelope. "I may not have psychic powers like most of us here, but I could tell when I met her. She's not the type of person that would just disappear."

"Yeah," I uttered. "I didn't think so either." I dared not speak about our argument.

Cyrus put his hand on my shoulder. "You knew her since our time at the Facility, Samuel. And I think we would agree that she can seem a bit . . . *spontaneous* sometimes. But did you ever suspect that she would have a reason for doing this?"

"Not to the point that she would abandon us," I affirmed. Vague, fragmented memories arose, consisting of dead rabbits and holographic projections. "But you saw her there, too, didn't you? You were there with her briefly. During an experiment?"

He stared at me peculiarly, but before he could reply, we heard a heartbreaking cry in the distance: "Maddie! Please come back to me!"

We followed it through the woods and found Johanna all alone, still searching for her sister. Tears dripped from her eyes, but she tried to compose herself when she saw us approaching.

"Sorry if my yelling startled you all," she said, running a hand across her face.

"We are all here for you, Johanna," Evelyn responded. "And you don't ever have to be sorry for expressing your feelings."

"Come with us." Xavier took her hand sweetly. "We'll get you something to eat."

We walked with her through the twilit forest until we heard the familiar waterfall. Once out into the clearing, dozens of children came our way, and though I sensed their disappointment that Luna wasn't with us, they were clearly relieved to see us all return safely. Felix ran to Johanna and embraced her, letting her sob gently on his shoulder.

"Have faith that we will get through this," he whispered as he nodded at us with appreciation.

Sangeetha was the next to join us, hugging her mother with compassion. While this happened, her potent gaze turned toward me, filled with knowing despite her age. There was no judgment in it and no clear telepathy, but I got the feeling that I had a greater responsibility.

Once most of the children had assembled, Johanna addressed the solemn crowd.

"Thank you so much for your help today, everyone. Often we face challenges we don't expect. The best we can do is accept and learn from them. Obviously, this is a tough situation." Her voice cracked as she said this, and we could tell she was devastated.

"Continue reaching out and let me know if you get anything, but I don't want anyone to worry. I will try tonight in my dreams."

We were all quiet for a moment. Then, one by one, the children went to her and wrapped their arms around her. This transpired until many dozens were huddled in solidarity, Evelyn and I joining at the periphery. The energy in our hearts pulsed as one and lit up the encroaching dusk. Only then did Johanna cry, comfortable enough to show her vulnerability. After everything she had given to the children in need, it was her time to open up and receive. No matter what, she would always have family.

Still, I felt a yearning to do something more.

It wasn't until later that night—cocooned in the hammock with Evelyn, when I gave up trying to sleep—that an idea popped into my head. Had I listened to logic, I would've brushed it off as crazy. Luckily, I had the wisdom to tune into my heart, which urged me to act on this intuition. But I had to do it alone.

Once Evelyn was fast asleep, I crawled out of the hammock and out through the branches. The night was so dark I could barely see, for the moon had all but vanished from the sky. I further relied on my heart to guide me confidently through the sleeping Sanctuary.

I soon found myself at the top of the waterfall, the stars the only light fending off the darkness. *What the hell am I doing?* I suddenly wondered. Yet I observed my trepidation until it passed, released the fears of my mind, and thought about what the Luna I knew would say.

So I suspended all thought and took a leap of faith.

My feet broke the surface, and I sank into the cool lake. Feeling no need to do anything, I simply remained in a state of pure being. There, I was able to drown out everything. And in the silence of the water, a message came:

"For my sister, tell her I am fine," her voice sang. *"To what I did, there is a design."*

Something glinted in the darkness, seeming to emit its own light. Swimming down to where it rested at the bottom of the lake,

I felt its smooth, metallic surface and grasped it in my hand before swimming up to breathe.

I emerged from the water with my robes dripping wet and held the object under a beacon shining nearby—where my thoughts were unfortunately verified. I did not know what to think.

It was Luna's golden cuff, which had concealed the black dragon.

~

After making my way back to the willow, I hung my robes to dry and climbed into a hammock of my own so as not to disturb Evelyn. Then I lay there perplexed, Luna's cuff in my hand, hardly sleeping for the rest of the night.

It was not so much the message that puzzled me. *Why did she take off her cuff to use as a sign?* I thought she wanted nothing to do with her past affiliation; I saw with my own eyes how Matteo had nearly killed her, years after leaving her to be buried alive. Yet now she was out there with their emblem unhidden. And despite her recent behavior, I was supposed to trust that her actions would ultimately be for the good of us all.

I got up before sunrise as the songbirds began singing. Stowing the cuff in my satchel, I went to look for Johanna.

I found her also awake, meditating under a tree. She opened her eyes suddenly as I approached, as if her soul had just returned to her body.

"Samuel," she said. "Do you have something to tell me?"

"Yes." Trying to sound optimistic, I recounted my jump into the lake, along with the entrusted message. A dark energy evaporated from Johanna's aura. She rose with a rejuvenated spirit, letting out a sigh of relief just as dawn swept over Sanctuary.

"Thank you, Samuel. I knew she would reach out to you. I've tried connecting, but it's been much more difficult than usual. I think any messages were obstructed by grief." She chuckled with watery eyes. "Can you please help gather everyone for the group meditation? They'd be happy to hear about your communication."

"Of course." I nodded kindly. But there was one more thing I had to ask before leaving. "Do you have any idea what she meant, though, by there being a design?"

She pondered a moment. "That's a good question. But she gave the message to you, didn't she? You might know more than I do. I know it sounds strange because she's my sister, but over the past few days, I've felt like I was getting to know her for the very first time." She shrugged. "In any case, it sounds like a good sign. I think she just needs some space."

"Yes, definitely," I replied and held off on mentioning my discovery of Luna's bracelet. "I'll go get the others."

I returned to our cherished willow tree, which was surrounded by a group of awakening friends: Maya, Lila, Cyrus, Ezra, Sidney, and, of course, Evelyn's siblings. Xavier pointed, and they all turned to me, a light flicking on in Evelyn's eyes.

"There you are, Samuel. You had me worried."

"You look tired," added Ezra. "You get any sleep?"

I yawned as I joined them. "Not much, honestly. I was just telling Johanna about a message I received." I shared with them what I had told the leader of Sanctuary.

"That's great news!" exclaimed Penelope. "See? There was no way she would leave us in the dark."

"She can reach us, but we can't reach her?" Lila asked suspiciously.

"I guess she got us beat." Cyrus laughed. "Though she could have let us know sooner before leading us on a wild goose chase."

"Yeah, but where could she be?" Sidney asked, his tawny skin glinting in the morning light. "We still have no idea, guys. And what is she talking about with this design, exactly?"

"I was wondering the same question," I confessed as a bell chimed in the distance. "Anyway, we'd better get going. Johanna wants us to meet for meditation."

We walked together to the open field to join the others. Although Luna wasn't with us, her message spread quickly, and a simmering hope proliferated throughout the crowd. It seemed that the entire Sanctuary—the remaining one hundred and forty-three—were gathering as a sign of unity, including Sangeetha and others rarely seen. We sat in concentric circles at the direction of Johanna, who seemed incredibly pleased.

Meanwhile, the cuff stayed hidden in my satchel. I wondered if it was selfish of me to keep it to myself, but I sensed this part of the message was meant only for me, and I didn't know what might happen if I let it be seen.

After we were settled, Johanna announced, "We have indeed received word that my sister is fine. And I feel that she will soon be coming home. But in the meantime, we all have a job to do—to maintain that high frequency—and it's very important to not let anything get in the way. Let us be done with the distractions of yesterday and turn our focus back toward the light!"

From there, we were led into group meditation. But even with the enormity of our collective energy, something kept blocking me from going too deep. Just when I thought I had released my worries, glimpsing the infinite void of my mind, images of Luna's cuff flashed vividly, as if to imply that there was something I was missing. Strangely, I then heard a ringing, and an ache spread from the center of my brain. Although it only lasted a second, it was enough to snap me out of my trance, leaving me startled and uneasy.

It wasn't until afterward, while talking with children in the gardens, that I realized I was not alone in this experience. Many of our best psychics and clairvoyants were still feeling blocked, and they had gotten ringing headaches when they tried to push past it. There were no premonitions or far-off visions; our minds were eerily confined within space and time. I previously assumed this was caused by Luna shielding herself psychically, and though that was probably at least partially the case, it seemed as if our abilities were suddenly deteriorating.

A heavy energy descended onto Sanctuary. Despite Luna's message and Johanna's encouragement, there was hardly any playing. Meanwhile, I couldn't focus on gardening as my mind kept returning to the cuff. I couldn't understand what I was missing, but I knew it was linked to this unusual dark cloud.

We were harvesting almonds from their beautiful white tree, a process that involved shaking them from the branches, when Evelyn set down her basket.

"Samuel, are you okay? You haven't been speaking."

"Yeah, just tired," I said, not liking that I couldn't tell her what was truly bothering me.

"Go lie down in the hammock. You should catch up on some sleep." She stroked my cheek. "Don't worry about cleaning up here. I'll take care of everything."

I felt so fortunate to have her. "Thank you, my love." I kissed her, but she took my arm before I left.

"And please don't blame yourself for the Luna situation," she said with a perceptive gaze. "I may not know all she's going through, but I do know she's not angry with you. She wouldn't have given you that message if that were true."

I nodded, then gave her an affectionate embrace, reminded of all I should be thankful for as I stared up at the blossoming branches of the almond tree.

Once back under the willow, I pulled the cuff from my satchel and studied it carefully.

"Okay, Luna. What are you trying to tell me?"

I closed my eyes for several minutes, waiting for an answer to surface. The gentle breeze rustled the branches, and birds sang in the distance. But in my mind, I sensed nothing except my own stubborn questioning.

This persisted until the sun began setting and the children gathered in the rose garden for the night's feast. I joined them with my satchel, planning to come clean about what was inside. After helping arrange the harvest, I sat on the ground with a welcome sense of peace. Evelyn came and sat by my side. Her siblings assembled around us, and I held her hand as I gave them all a warm smile, letting go of my mind's futile attempts to make sense of everything.

Johanna went up to give her premeal speech. Rather than commencing a prayer of gratitude, she simply stared into the crowd as we fell into silence, the waterfall the only sound.

At last, she said, "I want to tell you all a story." More than a hundred children listened attentively while their leader shared with a somber tone, "A little girl was born to a military family in a ravaged society. As soon as she emerged from the womb, they knew something was different about her. She possessed eyes as large and as bright as anyone had ever seen, which both frightened and fascinated those around her. But it wasn't until they started noticing strange happenings whenever she cried—lights blinking, objects moving on their own—that the military men took a particular interest.

"Her father was more intrigued than anyone, suggesting she be taken to a lab to be studied. From then on, he treated her more like an experiment than a daughter, performing cruel tests on her before she could even speak. Over the next several years, she lived mostly on bases, some that were underground, connected by trains, and at times she wouldn't see sunlight for weeks. She was forced to kill animals with her extraordinary abilities, made to purposefully inflict trauma to turn her into a weapon and brainwash her into being a slave. Her mother and her father disliked each other, but they had more children anyway, if only for the experiment. Both of her younger sisters were born on these secret bases, and they had it even worse than she did. Because both had the same eyes and abilities."

Johanna gathered herself while glances were shared among the crowd. Then she resumed. "At this point, the girl was older, more in control of her abilities, and she was far more powerful than any of these men. She could have done something to help her younger sisters. She could have killed their torturers if she wanted to. But her mind was so well conditioned that she just stood and watched while they had their way with them—while her sisters screamed."

Her voice cracked with emotion, and she brushed away tears.

"Eventually, the family split ways. Her mother became quite unwell mentally, and her father, well, that's a whole different story. His daughters had served their purpose, and he chose to focus his efforts elsewhere, leaving his family to fend for themselves. And though they didn't have to participate in the experiments anymore, they were in a horrible position, with broken minds and barely enough to survive.

"The girl luckily met someone, a kindhearted boy who assisted with her deprogramming and taught her about true love. Her sisters, unfortunately, fell in with the wrong crowd. The girl tried to help her family, but it was too late. Her mother was murdered, and one of her sisters was too—or so she thought. The youngest was deceived and seduced by that same group of killers, angry children who thought they owned the world, who themselves were deceived and seduced by powers unseen. The girl saw no other choice but to escape with the boy, and so they prayed to God, receiving visions of a place they came to know as Sanctuary. They were led there as if drawn by the divine. And it was at this place they had a daughter of their own, welcoming any other children who were also in need, vowing never to let them suffer like they did."

The crowd was dead quiet as Johanna finished her story. She managed a soft smile. "As you might have guessed, that little girl was me. And I've told you this so that now you understand that I am far from perfect. I've made a lot of mistakes in my life, but it is never too late to change and be redeemed. You all are everything to me.

"So, that is my story. If anyone else wants to share their own, I want to give you a chance to do so before we eat."

The children murmured while I caught Evelyn's eyes. "She never told you all of that, did she?" she whispered sorrowfully.

I shook my head, saddened that Luna had not shared with me the full story. I felt terrible for her, and the revelation led to a greater understanding of her behavior. Looking back on things now, recovering from that trauma the way she had seemed nothing short of a miracle.

We turned our attention back to the gathering, but when nobody else elected to speak, Felix stepped to Johanna's side. "For the longest time, I thought I was alone in this world. My mother died during childbirth, and my father later abandoned me, thinking I was some sort of demon. I have to admit, for a while I believed him."

Felix went on to share his story, telling of a kindly old couple who took him in, sheltering him from outside forces before they passed away.

Cyrus followed, speaking of parents who sold him to the Facility.

Finally, the younger ones had the courage to come forward, and one after another, they shared their own stories, even if they were brief. Several had been abandoned or had parents who were killed, some were abused horrifically, and others couldn't remember much of anything, not even the faces of their mothers or the comfort of their arms. Dozens of children spoke as the sun dropped below the horizon. In the crystal light illuminating the gathering, many cried tears of release. Despite everything they'd gone through, they managed to find Sanctuary, where they had learned what it was to be part of a loving family.

Just as I thought everyone was done sharing, the girl I loved stood to speak.

"My name is Evelyn Agartha," she said. "And I was lucky enough to have wonderful parents. They would always tell me how much they loved me and sang me beautiful songs when I had trouble falling asleep. Both of them died when I was young, unfortunately. It was a freak accident. A building collapsed."

Silent empathy pervaded the crowd. "I was a sick little girl with no one to take me in. Very few people could bear that responsibility. But I must have had guardian angels watching over me, because someone got word of a woman named Maggie, who was kind and honorable and raising orphans on her farm. I was taken to her village, where I was immediately adopted, meeting others who would become my siblings. Up the road was this strange facility where they were doing tests on children with funny-looking eyes."

She smiled at me tenderly, and I squeezed her hand.

"I fell in love with a boy from there who came to work with us every week, and though it took a while for him to open up, I came to realize that he also loved me. For years we stayed there, until the point came when we were forced to run away. Not long after, we were captured again, held at gunpoint as I fell into a coma. And yet the angels never left, because a courageous girl came to rescue us in our time of need, guiding us to a sanctuary led by her older sister, where I would heal and meet my family."

Johanna placed her hands over her heart, clearly touched. "Thank you so much for sharing, Evelyn. Is there anyone else who wishes to speak?"

She scanned the crowd, but no one answered. At the urging of my heart, I grasped Evelyn's hand tighter, and she helped me up to stand beside her. "My name is Samuel Helen, and I was born in a village not far from the ocean. My mother loved me despite my different eyes, and she would sing me songs from the old world. I can still remember her voice so clearly, and the way I felt when she held me in her arms. Until she died of cancer, she refused to stop singing. I was only a little boy when it happened, and it wasn't long before my father died too. Well, I killed him, accidentally, after he tried to hurt me, and I got very angry."

I sighed shakily at that confession as hundreds of compassionate, understanding eyes stared at me. "I was soon found by the military, going on to spend ten years in a place I knew only as the Facility, and for most of my life, I thought there was a monster inside me. But it has been a journey of forgiveness and self-discovery. I've met several amazing people because of these events, including a girl I came to love and a man who became my second father, who believed that there is an order to everything.

"In the process, I've also learned that there are others like me. And I'm not just talking about kids with big eyes and strange abilities but also about those who have been through *so much* in their lives, even losing their families, yet still manage to overcome and be happy. So rather than falling prey to a monster in our mind, let us find who we truly are beneath all the scars. We can do that by connecting with something deeper than the stories of ourselves."

A wave of emotion swept over the crowd. I looked down at my satchel, contemplating what I should next tell them.

In that moment I felt hundreds of invisible presences dispersed among the tearful children, some with hands on their faces and shoulders, others whispering loving messages into their ears. With conviction, I turned to Johanna. "That's how I know your sisters will return. Both of them. Because we're all pieces of the same whole. And even the broken pieces eventually find their way home."

Hope reverberated in every child while Johanna wiped fresh tears from her eyes. "Thank you, Samuel. That means so much to me. And my heart goes out to everyone who was brave enough to share this evening, as well as the others who served by listening, even if it is not yet time to tell their stories." She released a sigh. "As for my sisters, it does sting that they are not here, but I have to let them have their freedom, for however much time—and trust that everything has a purpose in the grand design."

I smiled as she said this. "There is a design," I said under my breath.

My head suddenly twisted almost of its own volition, and I found myself staring at a monarch butterfly fluttering about a rose, its orange wings visible under the light of a crystal. I thought it odd to see one at night but was reminded of a similar sight after burying Leon next to his wife. Then I recalled the one that had come to me when we arrived at Sanctuary, when I'd jumped down the waterfall for the first time; the image that formed in Evelyn's eyes while surrounded by angels, before awakening from the dream; the thought transfer Sangeetha sent us right before the argument with Luna; and what Lila had said when she tried to find her the day after—that all she saw was a butterfly.

Johanna had now called everyone up to eat, but I pondered this chain of synchronicity, convinced that it was a message. My heart confirmed the feeling as I tuned into it, summoning the memory of what Luna had advised me beneath the willow tree, before the unexpected shift in her personality. Her voice echoed in my mind: *"See the signs and know their meaning."*

"Samuel." Evelyn snapped me out of it. "Don't you want to go stand in line?"

Orderly children approached the delicious feast, but my own hunger had given way to a greater intrigue.

"I'm sorry," I told her. "I have to go check something."

Her brow furrowed in concern. "Where are you going?"

"I'll tell you afterward, but for now you'll have to trust me. I might be absent for a while, so if I'm not back until later, I don't want you to worry."

After a moment's hesitation, she nodded in understanding. I could tell she knew I was hiding something. I kissed her to make up for it, then left with my satchel. One more pair of eyes followed me as I departed—Sangeetha's, incisive and knowing.

The cave recognized me immediately, its crystals shining generously to light the way. It seemed empty, and when I reached the narrow passageway, I basked in bottomless silence before advancing toward the chamber of light.

The wheelbarrow sat at the opening; I greeted it like an old acquaintance. Then I pulled out Luna's cuff, proceeding to follow my intuition. I sat comfortably at the center of the chamber, closed my eyes, and breathed into meditation.

In the silence, I heard the chatter of my mind. Some thoughts were old programs still running, ones of uncertainty and guilt for all that was happening, while others questioned the validity of my feelings and what I was even doing. Then came the fear that I would be blocked like I was that morning, with that dreaded ringing.

"They are only thoughts," I heard Sangeetha say. *"There is nothing to fear. You are protected here."*

Although I couldn't be sure where her voice came from, this gave me enough faith to drop into my heart and relax entirely. Rather than engaging, I observed my mind as if it were a river. Finally, after easing into the tranquility of the space between, I felt a stillness that had always been there: an unadulterated consciousness cleverly disguised by a false sense of identity.

To connect with my true self, I had to surrender any construct of this identity: my role, my personal history, my life situation, and the problems it was suggesting. With another breath, a crack formed in the veil, and I broke out of character, awakening into a reality where all was one—nameless, timeless, beyond any concepts, with unity underlying all duality. That infinite moment was all that truly existed. In it I heard the song of my own soul. It was as gorgeous as the songbirds singing, for it had always known the score to everything.

I opened my eyes and realized I was levitating, but even more striking was the image of the monarch on the wall before me. I held the golden cuff against the brilliant crystal light, and as I had somehow known would happen, a hidden design appeared.

They were numbers, written ethereally, starting at the uppermost edge and spiraling around the cuff until there were dozens of them, separated by dashes. From beginning to end, it read:

377 − 233 − 1 − 3 − 1 − 1597 − 377 − 17711 − 233
− 3 − 2 − 21 − 233 − 5 − 1597 − 377 − 233 − 4181 − 377
− 5 − 4181 − 13 − 3 − 2584 − 6765 − 233 − 21 − 233 − 4181
− 13 − 3 − 2584 − 55 − 46368 − 5 − 377 − 1597 − 4181 − 13
− 377 − 2584 − 3 − 21 − 89 − 377 − 10946 − 3 − 21 − 144
− 6765 − 2584 − 4181 − 0 − 8 − 0 − 21 − 233 − 2 − 21 − 3

It was a code. *"Remember"* came a voice in my head.

I read it over and over, taking note of the recurring numbers and attempting to memorize the full sequence. I stayed there for what must have been hours, continuing until the code was burned into my mind.

By some mechanism, I found myself back under the night sky, feeling as if I had been hypnotized. I visited the willow to see Evelyn sleeping in her hammock and set my satchel nearby.

Then I walked out onto the grass and sprawled on the ground, still repeating the sequence. The stars were dazzling, and I swore some were moving—watching and communicating, traveling in a spiraling geometry.

∼

In the few hours of sleep to be had that night, I was visited in a dream by my mother. We were in the living room of my childhood home, sitting together on the sofa.

What was unique was that my father was there too, standing behind her shoulder. He was bright eyed and clean shaven, his soul as clear as I had seen in him, with a flowing white gown that matched my mother's. His trauma was gone, as were the demons that had deranged him. No words were needed as I caught his gaze. In mutual forgiveness, a cycle had been broken, and I was given back the energy taken from me.

As the dream began, I was already close to lucidity. Yet there were parts of our lives I didn't want to remember as I stared into the loving eyes of the woman by my side. "I've missed you, Mommy," I whispered fondly.

"I've missed you too, sugar bear. But in truth, I never left you. We see each other often when you sleep, even if you cannot remember in the morning."

"I know." I chuckled, and memories emerged of that plane. "Sometimes it just feels that way." I glanced at the pictures above the fireplace mantel, depicting three magnificent, celestial beings. "Are you one of the angels that have been watching over me?"

"I suppose I am." She laughed. "Your father is too. We're both so proud of you, Samuel, for everything you've come through. Trust me when I say that we love you unconditionally. We always will." She became more serious as she took my hand tenderly. "You are so strong in your heart, and that is the greatest of your abilities. There is still one more trial you must face, but you are not alone. You must remember who you are—and never be afraid of anything."

"A trial?" I frowned. "What do you mean?"

"You will know, my love. And soon, you will see."

My awareness jumped a level as I examined our hands and realized that mine were larger. Through the window I saw clouds rather than trees, like the house was floating. I gazed back at my mother with urgency. "Are you *really* here with me?"

She raised her hand to my heart. "Of course we are."

"But this is just a dream, isn't it? When I awaken, you're not going to leave me?"

My mother looked over her shoulder, and for a moment my parents stared at one another. Finally, my father stepped forward with an expression that was solemn yet loving. He caressed my cheek, then pressed his thumb firmly to my forehead.

"Open your eyes, my son. There is something you must see."

Immediately, I was struck by an energy so intense that my body began shaking. My head twisted, and I found myself staring into a large, circular mirror on a wall. In it I saw the wings of a monarch butterfly unfurling from my spine. But also reflecting back was an even greater surprise. For there was Luna, watching from the corner. She too had wings, and she winked, grinning.

With a surge of awareness, I broke out of my sleep.

And I knew without a doubt that it was more than a dream.

"That was real," I whispered with tears in my eyes. "They're really here. They're watching me." I still felt a pressure on my forehead and the power in my body. A few deep breaths calmed my heart and brought me back to my reality.

In the middle of a moonless night, I sat in the grass outside the willow tree, scattered crystal beacons suffusing Sanctuary with a soft, otherworldly light. I glanced behind my shoulder, but there were no visible wings. Yet it was such a vivid out-of-body experience that I spent the next hour pondering its meaning. Although seeing Luna there was slightly disturbing, her presence had to be connected with her cuff and the code I had memorized.

After some time, I sensed I might receive more insight if I simply went back to sleep. However, just as I was about to lie down again, I noticed a dark figure lurking near the edge of the forest. Looking closer, I detected a pair of eyes glowing in the night. The figure simply stood there, watching quietly.

It seemed to nod, and I rose hesitantly, questioning whether my mind was playing games with me. Because there was an intelligence to those eyes, a familiar one, yet I wasn't even sure if it was a human being.

"Who are you?" I whispered, my heart racing with anticipation as I thought back to the dream. "Please, show yourself."

To my shock, it obediently stepped from the forest and into the light. Though a part of me had already known what it was, my jaw dropped nonetheless. It was the doe—the very same one that had guided me and Evelyn to water when we needed it the most. Apparently, it was still watching over us. But then something inexplicable happened.

"I'm sorry" was the message it transmitted—along with a forgotten memory of me as a child, fascinated with the waves when first visiting the sea—before disappearing again into the trees.

"Wait! Don't leave!" I chased it without thinking—and had hardly stepped foot into the forest before my pounding heart reminded me of the last time I'd run after this creature and left Evelyn behind, only to be captured. It reminded me of how I thought it was my mother, and of the many ways the mind could be deceived.

After much debate, I listened to the inner voice that would never lead me astray. I let out a sigh and turned back toward Sanctuary.

Then a presence emerged behind me. There was a hand on my forehead and a sensation of heat. That was the last thing I remembered before losing consciousness.

～

"Open your eyes!" urged a male voice.

I woke for a second time just before dawn, to the sounds of helicopters overhead, followed by yelling. After a moment of disorientation, I leaped to my feet, running from the forest and into the clearing. Terror seized me as I gazed upon the scene, praying by some miracle that this was just a bad dream.

Hordes of white-armored soldiers were descending from huge, black helicopters as children screamed. I rushed toward the willow where Evelyn slept but was brought to my knees by a painful, high-pitched ringing.

CHAPTER 18

FOR AN EXCRUCIATING minute, the ringing filled my awareness, like a nail being inserted into the center of my brain.

I clasped my ears, but this did nothing. My vision was hazy, and I felt helpless and paralyzed by the horror, hearing muffled sounds of terrified children while a legion of soldiers invaded Sanctuary. Then I remembered my mother telling me never to be afraid. *Protect the children at any cost*, I prayed as rain spilled from the sky. The pain eased a little, my vision stabilized, and at the break of dawn, I found the inner strength to rise.

Helicopters were stationed around the lake, and dozens of children—hampered by the ringing—were immobilized and captured. The soldiers seemed unaffected, and a troop of them headed into the cave. I saw Ezra being dragged into a helicopter and Sidney tackling a soldier before he was overwhelmed by others. Xavier struggled as his hands were restrained, and Maya was stunned by electrical darts after attempting to run away. I wanted to help them, but it was already too late. Cyrus approached me in a panic.

"Samuel! Behind you!"

I turned to see more of them pouring from the forest, setting their sights on me. They had us surrounded, and there was nowhere to hide.

"Come on!" I shouted as I started toward the lake. "We have to find Evelyn, and we need to fight!"

The rain picked up as we dashed through the gardens, finding a path to the willow tree. Meanwhile, shock set in. Our friends had been captured, and there was little we could do. The ringing persisted. Within all the chaos, I could barely think. I just knew that if we found Evelyn, it would be all right. Through a momentary flashback to distant dreams, I found hope that there was still a reason behind everything.

Then three soldiers blocked our path, pointing their weapons straight at us.

"Surrender, or we'll shoot!" one of them yelled. But with adrenaline rising, I wasn't going to give up so easily.

I channeled my anger and unleashed it from my soul. "No!" I screamed, attempting to push them back. Yet there was no energy. It didn't do anything. After their initial nervous recoil, one of them laughed, amused by the knowledge of what I had feared—that our abilities were useless while afflicted by the ringing.

"Why are you doing this?" I asked in desperation, searching for their eyes beneath their helmets. "They're just *children*!"

In a moment of seeming conscience, they looked at each other, then all around at the kids being seized. It bought us time, but more of them approached from either side. I felt a hand on my shoulder and caught Cyrus's anguished gaze. "They've got us, brother. They must have hidden the memory." He let out a pained sigh. "Go find Evelyn."

Before I could ponder what he was saying, he charged at them. A second later, he was on the ground, shaking with the voltage long after he went unconscious. As heart wrenching as it was to witness, I was struck by intense déjà vu, along with a sudden recollection of a similar scene when we were in the labs together, and we started running . . .

"*Escape*," I heard a boy tell me telepathically.

I sprinted around the soldiers and toward the willow tree, leaving those memories behind. All the while, I braced for pain, expecting to be shot in the back and stunned. Surprisingly, it never came. They let me run all the way to the lake, then into the drooping branches of the willow.

I rushed to her hammock, but it was empty.

My satchel holding the golden cuff was gone.

I peered up through the branches shielding the rain and found no sign of the girl I loved. I couldn't believe I had left her again. I collapsed on the ground, waiting for the soldiers to take me with them, my head aching from the ringing and my heart weeping in resignation.

Footsteps came from the other side of the trunk. "Evelyn?" I questioned, crouching to look. But I was forced to step back and stand straight as General Mabus emerged from the shadows in his decorated military uniform, grinning pridefully with cold, uncaring eyes.

His face had grown more worn in the years since I had last seen him, a cap concealing his baldness, his aura radiating an ominous energy. As I gathered myself, I tried not to show emotion, but my body shook in visceral reaction to the trauma stored in memory. He was the man who first brought me in and stripped me of my humanity. He was the man who discovered that pain was the secret to bringing out my abilities, thereafter abducting other children to experiment on at the Facility.

"What have you done with her?" My voice quivered with rage. "What are you doing with all the children?"

"Samuel Helen." He smiled as he approached. "I would expect a more proper greeting from an old friend."

"Answer me!" I shouted. "Where is she? Where is Evelyn?!"

"The girl is safe with us. Don't worry. We wouldn't harm such a young, beautiful member of our own species, something that seems to be getting rarer and rarer these days. As for the others, that is up for debate. But I might consider a more favorable outcome if you behave."

I fumed. "I am no longer your experiment. I am no longer your slave!"

He laughed. "You still have that temper. It's tough to get rid of old, programmed habits, as much as you try to convince yourself you've changed. In the past, your anger was a force to be reckoned with. Yet as I'm sure you've already realized, you hold no power at this time, and *we* decide your fate."

As soldiers brushed aside the branches, I closed my eyes and attempted to breathe, yearning to ease my mind away from the ringing. However, staring again at the sneering general, I finally accepted that this was not something I could fight.

"What is it?" I surrendered. "What is happening?"

"Finally asking some productive questions!" He paced back and forth as he boasted, "What you and your friends are experiencing is an intelligent nanotechnology, one that has been carefully refined by our greatest scientists over the past decade. It is specifically designed to target those with your genetic markers—shall we say, your DNA signature. But something else is required."

He motioned behind him, and a soldier brought out a mysterious black cube around two feet in length. My pulse quickened as he placed it between me and the general, for I knew that I had seen it before.

"This right here transmits a special frequency. The frequency itself hinders your abilities, but not enough to disable them. That is where the nanites come in. They live inside the body of the subject, attaching to the pineal gland in the brain, then activate once exposed to the frequency. Any psychic functioning, telepathy or telekinesis, is rendered powerless for the time being."

"I don't understand." I had to push through pain in order to think. "How were we infected with nanotechnology?"

"You really don't remember, do you?" His eyes lit up, clearly pleased that I was at his mercy. "This is why I wanted to meet with you privately, Samuel. You were, after all, the first child at my facility and have always been my most cherished experiment. You haven't seen much of me for the past few years, but I've always been there, watching your progress. And I feel like I owe you an explanation, as hard as it might be for you to accept."

He gave a mocking sigh. "Because *you* are the source of the nanites, Samuel—at least, you spread them to all of your friends. That other boy too—Cyrus is his name? But, my dear boy, you gave us the greater contribution. You were carefully chosen to take part in this final experiment, and it ended up being such a success."

"You're lying," I scoffed. "Your experiments never worked. They were cruel and pointless. You simply tortured me and the others."

"The mind is a funny thing—its illusions so convincing, its memories so fragile and easily shaped. You believe that those ten years were for nothing because that's what we wanted you to think. You see, a weapon is only valuable as long as it's properly controlled, as long as we decide when to use it. As long as there is an off switch, so to speak. Otherwise, it presents a danger not only to our Union but to the very survival of humanity."

He snickered, his tone becoming angry. "If you want to speak about cruelty, my boy, those same great scientists who risked their lives for progress were *slaughtered* by your kind, like animals without defense. But thankfully it was not in vain, and we owe much of that to you."

I thought back to the memory of me and Cyrus running through the labs, then going through a door, but shook my head. "No. It's not true."

"Stop lying to yourself, Samuel." He nodded to the cube. "See past the illusions, and remember what was given to you."

The memory expanded suddenly, and I recalled seeing the strange holograms, as well as Luna singing behind a window. Then the scientists took me for that forgotten experiment—the injection of black goo and a high-pitched ringing. My mind had been tampered with, manipulated through screen memories. Whether it was dead rabbits, holographic projections, or vegan ice cream, I could not tell what was real anymore and what was a dream.

"But most here have never even been to the Facility," I said despairingly.

"It doesn't matter. The nanoparticles are designed to spread through the slightest touch or even breathing in proximity. Give it a few days, and it will spread to everyone in your sanctuary." His grin felt like a punch in the gut as I comprehended the depravity. "That's right, Samuel. All this time that you thought you were free, you were really just part of the final testing. Did you think that we couldn't track you? That we would let our greatest asset simply run away? Or did you think it was an accident that you happened to bump into those wretched punks who destroyed my facility?

"Oh, dear boy, you've helped us enormously. And even after the attack and that terrible slaughter, I wanted to give you the benefit of the doubt. I thought you were different, for I gave you comfort. I let you interact with normal children, from whom you found your blue-eyed lover. I even gave you another father. But it is a terrible affliction, those eyes and that power. After my lieutenant found you at that church and we saw just how much of a danger you could be, it was an easy decision to weed out all with your eyes—to let you lead us to this place where the rest of you have been hiding."

I wanted to scream at him in defiance but could no longer deny the truth. More helpless cries came from outside, and I stared down at my trembling hands in horror. Then, as I tuned into the ringing, I noticed an unusual connection with the others—some sort of artificial telepathy. Even so, I wept with grief at what they were feeling.

"Please stop," I pleaded with him. "You don't know what you are doing. All the children . . . the children are suffering."

"You know very well I can't do that, Samuel. But, hey, don't take it personally. If those punks were right about one thing, it's that you *are* a different species. Different DNA structure. There may be some sympathizers who encourage mixing, but it is the duty of the human race—"

He was interrupted by static from his handheld radio. "General, one of them seems to be neutralizing the signal. She's a little girl. It's still transmitting in here, but she is resisting."

"That shouldn't be possible. What is she doing?"

"Just . . . floating, sir. She keeps deflecting our stun guns and pushing us back. We've already urged her to surrender. This whole place is lighting up."

After a moment of conflict, he replied tonelessly, "Do what must be done." Soon afterward, sounds of gunshots reverberated from deep within the cave.

"No!" I shrieked, pouncing onto the black cube instinctively. In futility, I tried to heave it into the lake but was paralyzed by electricity. Rage boiled through my veins as the soldiers held me to the ground and cuffed my arms behind my back. Mabus strolled over, glaring down in spite.

"Poor, deluded Samuel Helen, always thinking he's the hero. I would have considered giving you the antidote, but obviously your behavior hasn't changed. Besides, the cubes are just transceivers. Do you know what that means? Trying to destroy them would be pointless. The original source of the frequency isn't even of this planet."

Through all the anger, sadness, and pain, a sense of bafflement broke through.

"What are you talking about?" I managed to mutter.

He smirked knowingly before turning his back to me. "Blind him," he ordered his soldiers, and they tied a rag around my eyes, then dragged my body from the shade. As we moved toward a helicopter, the smell of smoke stood out against the rain, and I realized that they were setting trees on fire to force out those in hiding. I heard Johanna's heartbreaking cries in the distance, mourning the loss of her gifted daughter and the capture of her children. And I was too weak to do anything.

Before they loaded me with the others, I overheard Mabus speaking: "There you are, darling. It worked like a charm."

"All part of the plan, Daddy," Luna responded wickedly.

~

The helicopter was large with no defined seating, and I sensed about a dozen children packed into the cabin, some crying, others in silent shock. Soldiers shouted at those crying to shut up.

They still sounded threatened by us, yet there wasn't much we could do. Our eyes were covered, our hands were cuffed, and even the blades of the helicopters couldn't drown out the ringing. Worse than all that, my spirit was broken. A feeling of utter betrayal overshadowed any other emotion—betrayal by not only someone I thought I could trust but also my own mind and memory. I had been used as a pawn.

The helicopter took off to follow the others to some mysterious destination, leaving behind the burning Sanctuary.

"You fooled me, Luna, but how could you do this to your family?" I gritted out under my breath, as furious as I was stunned. I combed back through time with apprehension, trying to come to terms with a harsh yet incomprehensible reality.

She had saved me and Evelyn on multiple occasions, to the point of taking a bullet in the church. She guided us along the river and taught me so much. She pulled me out of my darkest moments. She helped me believe in my abilities, miracles, and faith, yet never took life too seriously. She even warned me—soon after we first met—about the impending attack on the Facility, something that Mabus didn't seem to be aware of.

Yet all this time, she was hiding a dark secret: she was merely keeping tabs on me at his request. I was a weapon they'd planted at her sister's sanctuary, leading to our capture and the tragic murder of her niece, all for a father who tortured her and her sisters as children, just as he did to me. So many things didn't make sense.

I thought again to the day we met, when I had awoken to a fractured memory—to the absurdity of dead rabbits and vegan ice cream. I recalled all those soldiers she had eerily and easily put to sleep. Skipping forward, I thought of her rescuing me and Evelyn with such convenient timing that one could say it was a miracle. Only then did Evelyn fall into a coma, despite the lack of any apparent injury. Even the village doctor thought it was uncanny. The only solution, according to Luna, was to journey to our now-ravaged safe haven.

This realization punched the air right out of me, and I could have slapped myself for my stupidity. Her intentions had become clear; there was no more denying their cruelty. She had put a spell on the one I loved, nearly killing us in the process, only to let her awaken at the opportune time. Was this all part of her grand plan—her alleged design? Even the golden cuff and the code I had memorized could have simply been a tool to distract my mind. Then there was our kiss, her affection and apparent jealousy, yet I could not tell if they were real or staged. All this now seemed like an act, a game played by a formidable psychic. Everything became inverted. I had been manipulated like a puppet on strings.

I caught myself breathing heavily, and at my panic, more children began crying. A girl beside me spoke up. "Don't worry, everyone. Everything's gonna be—"

"No talking!" barked one of the soldiers.

I couldn't see her face, but I recognized the voice: Penelope, optimistic through seemingly hopeless times, just like Noah always was at the Facility. They had her too, even though she wasn't a new youth, and I wondered if they were also bringing Evelyn.

In rebellion, I turned to stretch my shackled hands, and she somehow knew to reach back, wrapping her fingers around mine. We did the same to the children at our sides. The crying ceased, the breathing relaxed, and as I felt the comfort of their hands, there was no more pain. The soldiers said nothing; I even sensed a shred of empathy. In that moment, I hoped they saw our shared humanity— that no matter what happened, we would remain in unity.

The ride lasted for what seemed like an eternity. I didn't want to think about Luna any longer, so I summoned the memory of the last time I had been in a helicopter, when I was seven years old and they were taking me to the Facility. Just like back then, there was a crack in the blindfold through which I glimpsed the land below. And just like back then, we were crossing vast wastelands of hazardous radiation scattered with ruins of the old world. This time, I could be sure that it wasn't an illusion. Gone was the magic of the river and Sanctuary. Maybe I had been deluded that we could do away with the past and change our reality.

Eventually, we flew over green again. Then, to my shock, we passed a city in the midst of rebuilding. I had heard about them, but this was the first time I had ever seen such buildings. I knew instantly that this was the Union's capital, not far from where I was born, though my mother never dared to take me. I could smell it in the air: we were near the sea. On the outskirts, I knew, was a military base. Surely that was where we were descending.

The pilot called back to us, "Prepare for landing."

We soon touched down on solid ground, along with the other helicopters, their blades deafening. From there, we waited as they took turns unloading. Our friends cried out as they were dragged to an unknown fate, and we all locked fingers again. Finally, we were the next to be emptied.

"You don't have to do this," Penelope pleaded with a voice of innocence.

"We don't have a choice," a man responded. "Now, this can be hard, or this can be easy."

We were led off the helicopter, and I saw no point in resisting while still blinded and impaired by the ringing. My sandals pressed against concrete, and I was handed to more soldiers, who grabbed me by the arms and took me to my destination.

"I know this kid," one of them said. "He's the freak that stopped our guns from shooting."

"Is that right?" replied the other, who sounded young. "He's not so tough now, is he?" I was shoved in the back and nearly fell but regained my balance and composure. My lack of reaction seemed to aggravate them further, so they dragged me the rest of the way. All around I heard children shouting with terror, doors slamming shut, and the rattling of chains. To my revulsion, it seemed the soldiers were keeping them caged and that we were in no ordinary base; we were in a prison.

Before long, I was led to a cell of my own.

"Here's your new home," said the one who had shoved me. "Nice and cozy just for you."

The door creaked open, but before I stepped through, I heard the familiar voice of a girl erupting out of the surrounding turmoil.

"Let us go! You don't know who you're messing with!"

"Evelyn!" I yelled. "Hold on, I'm coming!"

Only then did I struggle, and I shook one off violently. But while Evelyn shouted my name, the other struck me in the gut and pushed me to the ground through the opening.

"Like I said, you're not so tough. We'll take good care of your girlfriend. Special orders from the general."

I got up in a rage and charged at him, but the metal door slammed in my face, and I rammed against it helplessly. Suddenly, I was in total darkness. Even without the blindfold, I wouldn't have been able to see, and I felt around the tiny cell, touching nothing but cold concrete. No windows, nor any external sound, except for that frequency still blaring so loud that I thought my head would explode.

Oh God, what do I do now? I collapsed back to the ground, curling into a ball and shedding tears.

At that moment, I could have descended into a spiral of negativity, crying hopelessly with guilt, regret, and blame toward others for all that was happening. A part of me wanted to. I was so angry. But as I observed these emotions, I knew that they did not comprise who I was underneath. And there were people who needed me.

Gradually, I accepted all that had happened and all that was currently happening, even the dreaded ringing, and remembered what the old priest had told me about taking every obstacle as an opportunity. From there, another path opened up, filled with possibility.

I focused my mind on the ringing, tuning into the artificial consciousness that I had glimpsed, and sensed many dozens of children in the same position, trapped in cells, frightened and in agony. The anguish of it all was too much to handle, so I broke off abruptly.

"*Follow your heart,*" I heard Evelyn whisper, reminding me of a vision from an extraordinary little girl we had both received.

I dropped my awareness into my chest and listened carefully, feeling a more profound connection with all other beings, which predated even our individuality. There was no pain in this awareness and no further suffering. I knew intuitively that it was real—an infinite love that could overcome anything. Our minds may have been compromised, but our enemies could never get to our hearts. And I felt mine beating as one with Evelyn's.

I sensed her emotion and knew that she also sensed me. She was scared, panicky, struggling to breathe. I didn't know where it came from, but I started singing the way my mother used to sing:

> "*For you, there'll be no more crying,*
> *For you, the sun will be shining,*
> *And I feel that when I'm with you,*
> *It's all right, I know it's right . . .*"

I felt her spirit lighten and her breath soften accordingly. I didn't even think she knew the words, but in my heart, I heard her begin to sing along with me. At the same time, we relived every moment of the past decade with each other, from her first finding me and offering her hand to kissing each other when no one was watching. From washing her feet when she was in a coma to being surrounded by angels in a lucid dream. Finally, professing our love beneath the willow, evoking the experience of two souls in one body.

We continued in unison:

"And the songbirds keep singing, like they know the score,
And I love you, I love you, I love you, like never before . . ."

As we finished, a bridge of golden energy formed between our hearts, proceeding to branch out to every child in need. I breathed in gratitude as I felt the darkness driven away and the suffering cease, for together we were healed by unconditional love. I extended this to Luna, too, as well as members of the military, knowing that they were only acting out programs of a damaged upbringing.

Lastly, I felt love for myself and forgave any action that might have put us in this position. Everything in the universe flowed according to balance, and the more darkness I could overcome, the more wisdom I would glean; the more I surrendered the false prisons of my identity, the higher into the light I would ascend. I felt my inner child helping me as I did for him, urging me to laugh and smile in the face of all rationality. I was given a memory of my mother kissing me on the cheek after singing me to sleep, then of a dog licking my face with glee. In times of crisis, two paths lay before me. Which one I would take was always a choice.

My body started vibrating, and I felt a sudden quickening—a rush of energy pouring in through my head. A bright light flashed above, and from it reached an ethereal hand. I stared at it in awe for a moment; even with a blindfold, I could see.

A female voice whispered in my awareness, *"Take it when you're ready."*

I relished a long, deep breath, then reached for it without thinking, realizing that my arm was not handcuffed anymore. Grasped lovingly by the spirit, I was yanked out of my physical body.

~

I was struck by the sensation of flying in all directions, then rising through a vortex, feeling like my spirit was being stretched between dimensional planes. A nauseating uneasiness made it seem like I was dying, and for a second I feared that something sinister had taken me. But I couldn't go back. I couldn't even scream. So, I gave up all resistance and rode out the rest of the journey.

As abruptly as I flew out, my awareness stabilized—then expanded immensely. Discomfort settled into bliss, and a surreal environment came to life before me.

All around was simply light, arranging into flowing patterns of otherworldly geometry I barely had words to describe. They were colorful, dynamic, and breathing with energy, with shades of blue, gold, purple, and white—plus colors I had never seen through human eyes. For my body was also composed of pure light, and my vision was not constricted in one direction. There was a stillness around which it all danced, conscious and alive, throbbing gently like a universal heartbeat.

I felt guided by a force I couldn't see, and I continued to trust, surrendering to its lead. As the geometry moved into a certain arrangement, almond-shaped openings formed, like portals. I was led to one of them, to peer through a window in the fabric of reality.

I found myself in the sky above Sanctuary. The sun was setting, and I gazed down at all the children gathered for a feast. Then I noticed something uncanny underneath the branches of one of the willow trees. It was *me*, gaping in my direction while Evelyn rested in the hammock, on the verge of an awakening.

The window closed, and I was guided to another. Through this one I saw a gorgeous doe emerge from the forest. Yet before it stepped into the clearing, it changed its form bit by bit as if shifting its holographic blueprint. Suddenly I was staring at Luna as she had appeared when I first met her—complete with her robes, cuff, and earrings. She strolled to the top of a hill, where she gazed toward the sky, then waited until a truck sped down, heading for a tree. As this happened, she chanted a spell of protection, creating an energetic cushion for me and Evelyn that shielded us from true harm. At the same time, another was cast over Evelyn, sending her into a mysterious sleep.

The third window I was guided to was the most astonishing, for I innately understood that the scene it presented was not in the past but rather taking place currently. As a result, a heaviness dropped from my soul. For there was Sangeetha, meditating in the chamber of light, appearing full of life. Crowded around her were dozens of children, each in their own form of prayer and meditation. And circled around them were entities normally imperceptible but what could only be described as nine beings of liquid blue light, providing comfort and protection, radiating higher consciousness. Finally, standing guard at the entrance was a tenth with a defined form: the archangel Michael, with his mighty shield and fiery sword. Together they formed a barrier so strong that no bullet could penetrate.

I looked back toward Sangeetha, and as monarch wings flashed within the crystals behind her, she opened her large, brilliant eyes. I could tell that she noticed me as we gazed between planes. She nodded slowly, letting me know that all was going according to design.

Within the final window I peered through, I saw only a small corridor leading to an ordinary wooden door—one that had a certain familiarity. Then a gust of wind from behind nudged me through the opening. By the time I looked back, it had already closed, sealing off the realm of geometry. In its place was a boundless void with scattered specks of light spilling into the darkness like stars crying. Looking down, I saw that I had a body again, clothed in the white robes we wore at the Facility. There was no choice but to walk through the corridor, to the familiar door.

Instinctively, I knocked three times, the sound echoing through the immeasurable silence.

"Come in!" called a voice from the other side, causing my heart to ignite.

I opened the door and entered with disbelief, met by a dark room with no form or clarity. "Where am I?" I asked.

"A place of your choosing."

Acting on intuition, I flicked a switch to my side. Then, through the flame of creation, atom by atom, the room was bestowed with light and physicality. It was an office I knew well, shelves of records materializing on either far corner, underneath old portraits of famous musicians. Of course, there was the record player, his desk, his chair, and finally my beloved tutor with his unkempt hair, beaming at me with so much light in his eyes, still wearing his quirky monocle. He was the same as I remembered him, though exuding more youth and vibrance than I had ever seen when he was alive.

"Walter," I uttered.

"Samuel." He smiled.

I stared at my hands in wonder, then around at the environment, marveling at how it seemed more real than physical reality. All of the albums were now filed neatly with the exception of one still on the floor, displaying an image of an embryo with angel wings.

"You've cleaned up remarkably since the last time we met, kiddo," Walter observed before gesturing to the armchair facing his desk. "Please, take a seat."

I nodded, too amazed to speak, then didn't walk to the chair so much as I floated, sitting down comfortably. His desk was the same except for small details; the rainbow Buddha was laughing, and the old photograph of his wife and son now showed a young Walter standing beside them, and they were all smiling. I was thankful to see that Mabus's portrait had been replaced by a mirror. I leaned closely to Walter, scrutinizing the folds of his smile and the small hairs on his face. He seemed entertained.

"What's the matter, Samuel? You look surprised."

"I don't know if you're real or just in my mind."

He laughed. "I won't be offended either way you decide. But why does it have to be a choice? Why not cast away all judgment and experience everything as it is?"

"I saw you die, Walter," I said finally. "I saw Matteo slit your throat."

"Is that so?" He glanced at his clean robes. "Because I feel just fine." He proceeded to pull an apple from his drawer, offering it to me casually. "You want a bite?"

I paused before giving in. "Okay." As I reached for it, it levitated from his hand and hovered toward me. I accepted it and bit into it with curiosity. It was crisp and juicy, its flavor exploding in my mouth, and so I sat back in my armchair, questioning everything I knew about reality.

"So, where are we really?" I asked.

"What you perceive is the same as always, a projection of the light of consciousness, condensed to a specific density," he warmly replied. "The astral plane, a lucid dream—it doesn't matter what you call it. The experience itself is what life is all about. And I'd advise someone who is still living to be in the moment, here and now, because there is no other place to be."

I smiled, for it was definitely something the man I knew would say. But going against his wisdom, I couldn't help thinking about the difficulties on another plane.

"We're in a tough position right now, Walter. They've captured me and most of the children. We've been betrayed. I'm trying to stay positive and see the light in all this, but I don't know if there's anything I can do."

"Tell me, Samuel, do you believe in yourself?" he asked.

"Yes, but I don't think you—"

"As long as you believe in yourself and do the best you can, any action you choose is good enough. And if there is nothing left to do, then focus on being. That is often all it takes for you to find a way."

"I'm serious, Walter. I need more than just proverbs. They have us imprisoned, and they might even kill us, all because I trusted someone I shouldn't have and was too blind to see that I was being used as a weapon. I've been working on total forgiveness, but it doesn't change the fact that I did this. I may have screwed up everything."

His face grew serious. "Don't let them make you lose confidence in yourself. You are the creator of your reality, the one with all the power, and they know very well that the only way to control you is by making you believe you are controllable—to convince you to create your own chains, making you question your intentions as well as your sanity. Stop holding on to them, Samuel. You did nothing wrong. You must let go of the past and trust your intuition. Refuse to give in to these mind games."

A memory sparked—of our last conversation—and something clicked.

"Before you died, you told me to break the strings. You meant the strings of time, didn't you? Of prewritten destiny? So that I can be the creator of my reality."

His expression was beatific. "Well, when we spoke last, you said that you felt like a puppet. That you're not in control of your own fate. You still feel that way, don't you?"

I nodded. "Because I've been played."

"You continually underestimate your own power, Samuel, in spite of so much evidence. There are forces at play here greater than you can comprehend. Call it God or universal consciousness, they are working through you, even if you don't realize it. Stop insisting with the mind about how things must be and surrender to that awareness. Only then will you see that you have written all of it."

"I appreciate the kind words, Walter. But I don't have time to become one with God."

"Then do away with time. Nobody becomes one with God; you simply recognize this oneness as those great prophets and sages have recognized it. Be still and know that it is already the case. You just have to push that stubborn ego out of the way, allowing the knowing of your soul to take its place."

His eyes enlivened. "Anyway, we might as well enjoy the rest of our time here." He rose from his chair and approached the shelves of records on the Hendrix side, skimming through them until he pulled one out. "Ah, here it is." On the cover was a tall, well-dressed man holding hands with a dark-robed woman. "*Rumours* by Fleetwood Mac. It was made decades before I was even born, but it's a great, great record, and a personal favorite. Have I ever shown you this one?"

I stared at him, unsure what to say.

He smiled. "Maybe the music will awaken your memory." He levitated the record to the player. Soon, the sounds of upbeat acoustic guitars filled our awareness, and a man began singing:

"I know there's nothing to say,
Someone has taken my place,
When times go bad, when times go rough,
Won't you lay me down in the tall grass and let me do my stuff . . ."

"So, what do you think?" Walter inquired, returning to his chair.

"It's so real," I said in amazement, making out the precise layers of instrumentation. "I still don't understand how this is happening."

"Don't try to understand. Just listen." He winked. "Allow yourself to marvel at the magnificent power of your mind, as well as the dreamlike nature of the universe."

I took another bite of my apple, and together we listened, reveling in the moment until the song reached a crescendo and transitioned.

The next song was slower yet soul stirring, with a woman singing over an enchanting rhythm:

"Now here you go again, you say you want your freedom,
Well, who am I to keep you down,
It's only right that you should play the way you feel it,
But listen carefully to the sound of your loneliness . . ."

"Beautiful, isn't it?" Walter commented.

I nodded, feeling my heart wade through memory and emotion. "Walter?"

"Yes, Samuel?"

"I don't want to die alone."

He gazed compassionately, the spirit clear in his eyes. "With great wisdom comes great loneliness, and yet wise men realize they are never truly alone. There are those who lie outside of time, in touch with the light of the universal mind. You may not see them, but they are watching your every move. We are on your side, Samuel. And we simply want you to remember."

"Remember what?" I asked curiously.

"Well, I can't spoil it, can I?" he laughed. "But if I am truly a part of you, then you should know somewhere deep inside your soul. Just as you know all the music and lyrics to this album."

"I do, don't I?" My eyes watered while listening to the melody. "You know, when you were alive, I would brush off any mention of oneness with the divine. I just didn't believe it until I got a glimpse of it personally. Maybe I didn't think I was worthy."

"A balance must be struck between humility and self-love," he affirmed.

"Because there is no self, ultimately."

"Precisely, and very wise." He nodded with pride. "Does it really matter, Samuel, whether I am what you would consider real or a fragment of your mind? Everyone you meet is an embodiment of the same light, each playing their part in dreaming the world into existence. It is one big, everlasting symphony."

I took a final bite of my apple, getting to its seeds. "Thank you, Walter. Thank you for everything. I don't know what I would have done if you weren't there for me." I reached over the desk to touch his hand affectionately. "I'm sorry it had to be this way."

"Oh, death isn't so bad, kiddo." He gestured to the photograph of his family. "It just feels like a release, then a coming home, like rivers returning to the ocean. Once you get that fear out of the way, nothing can stop you." He gripped my hand, and from it flowed a familiar, loving energy. "You know, Samuel, your mother really loved this album. She would dance around the house with you to it. She would play it for you all the time."

I felt tears stream down my face, reliving joyous memories. "I know," I whispered as the ghost of Stevie Nicks sang the closing lines:

"They say women, they will come and they will go,
When the rain washes you clean you'll know . . ."

Still holding hands, Walter and I smiled at one another. In the mirror behind him, I saw orbs of light coming to take me, and after one last gaze of gratitude, I let go, falling into physical reality.

Before reentering my body, I looked down at it for a moment from the ceiling of my cell, connected by a flickering silver cord. Strangely, the lips of my physical body were moving as if channeling a silent song. That's when my mother appeared kneeling over me, illuminating the darkness with her aura alone. And I realized that she had been singing to me all this time.

She smiled up at me as she placed her hand on my heart. There materialized a shining golden key, and I was reminded that it was still within me.

Then, the spirit of my father appeared beside her. He crouched over my face and lifted my blindfold. My eyes were open, and I saw that He and I were one before he vanished with my mother.

CHAPTER 19

I woke up panting in my physical body. The blindfold was off, and despite the darkness, my mind's eye was filled with a celestial light. In the background, I heard the ringing, but it no longer pained or bothered me. I was focused on the wonderment of whom I'd just met, what I had witnessed, and what I now knew without a doubt: that our loved ones were always watching and guiding us.

Plus, that beautiful song Walter had put on was still in my head, the soundtrack of fond childhood memories. But I knew I had heard it recently somewhere else.

"There are no accidents," a voice whispered in the silence.

Suddenly, I was taken to where I first saw Luna: through the blue door before the experiment, when she was singing to me behind a window that no one else saw. She pointed to her ear, telling me to listen, and I came to realize she was singing the same song. All of it now seemed like a dream, but my intuition urged me to find the hidden meaning.

Finally, I realized she was pointing to her golden spiral earrings. My heart beat excitedly, confirming that it was an important sign.

I was reminded of a unique lesson from when I was younger, when Walter taught me about a sequence discovered by a man named Fibonacci. It began with the numbers zero and one and progressed by taking the sum of the preceding two numbers, extending into infinity. From this sequence emerged a golden ratio, drawn as a spiral when depicted mathematically. Most incredibly, however, it was a common intelligence found throughout nature— from the shapes of shells and galaxies to the unfolding of embryos and the branching of trees. Walter marveled at this miracle of design, mentioning that even in music, this ratio was utilized to establish harmony.

I followed the sequence to an epiphany: all of the numbers in Luna's code were a part of it. It was not just an accident and wasn't meant to confuse me. She had embedded a message she wanted me to receive.

So, I assigned the first number in the sequence, zero, to the first letter in the alphabet and began from there. The entire code was ingrained in my mind:

$$377 - 233 - 1 - 3 - 1 - 1597 - 377 - 17711 - 233 - 3$$
$$- 2 - 21 - 233 - 5 - 1597 - 377 - 233 - 4181 - 377 - 5$$
$$- 4181 - 13 - 3 - 2584 - 6765 - 233 - 21 - 233 - 4181$$
$$- 13 - 3 - 2584 - 55 - 46368 - 5 - 377 - 1597 - 4181 - 13$$
$$- 377 - 2584 - 3 - 21 - 89 - 377 - 10946 - 3 - 21 - 144$$
$$- 6765 - 2584 - 4181 - 0 - 8 - 0 - 21 - 233 - 2 - 21 - 3$$

I deciphered it accordingly: 377 would be the fifteenth number in the sequence, corresponding to "O" in the alphabet; 233 was the fourteenth: "N." And 1 was both the second and third numbers in the sequence, so either "B" or "C," but I felt the latter to be more fitting. And 3 was the fifth number, "E," spelling out the first word in the message: "Once." My heart leaped at this point, and the next hour was spent decoding the rest.

With three more characters to go, it read: "Once crowned in front of the sun in the sky, for those I love I must again . . ."

Before I could decipher the final word, the door opened without warning. Blinding light flooded my cell, and the footsteps of multiple soldiers drew near.

"Who told you to take off your blindfold?" one of them shouted—the same young soldier who had punched me. He angrily retied it around my eyes before he and another pulled me up and started dragging me out. "Come on, freak. It's time to meet your—"

"Leave him," ordered a commanding voice from the entrance. "Let me have a word with the boy privately."

The soldiers paused, then released their grips. "Yes, sir." They snickered as they exited the cell, and I regained my balance. I struggled to contain my emotions when their superior entered in their place, for even hearing his voice evoked a pent-up rage. A light switched on above us, and the door closed behind him.

For a moment, Lieutenant Hernandez stood quietly by the entrance, my breath becoming heavy as I relived his murderous cruelty, along with Leon's brave sacrifice. However, as he moved to stand in front of me and his aura intermingled with mine, I was struck by a remarkable transformation in his energy. Rather than arrogance, there was humility—even sorrow and remorse. What happened in the church had clearly changed him; he was regretful of the path he had chosen, yet through grace and acceptance, the light had begun to fend off the dark shadows. My heart knew all this without even looking into his eyes or hearing him speak.

"Samuel," he grunted, clearing his throat.

I composed myself before responding, "What is it you want?"

"To say that I'm sorry." His words trembled with grief. "I behaved like a monster. I should have never killed that old man. Something had taken hold of me. I just couldn't see."

A part of me still wanted to scream, but instead I chose to speak calmly.

"You're right. It was wicked and merciless." I sighed. "But I know that his soul is fine. And that he forgives you."

I felt another shadow leave as he exhaled in release. Then, I heard a rustling. "This is an antidote to the nanites and the ringing. I only have one dose in my possession, but I think you should have it. Quickly, please drink." He put something to my lips. My mind stepped in with a moment of skepticism, knowing that I'd been fooled before. "Trust me," he said, and my heart confirmed he was there to assist me, however unlikely it seemed. In my mind's eye, I saw Walter smiling.

The antidote was foul, but I swallowed it down decisively.

"Thank you," I told him.

"It may take another hour for it to kick in, but at least we got it in your system. The general is very angry over what happened. I'm sorry for the way they are treating you and your friends, but not all of us agree with these methods anymore. Take this and hold it tightly."

He moved behind me and tucked a small device into one of my cuffed hands. I wrapped my fingers around it.

"The handcuffs work according to an electromagnetic frequency. The button on this is a master key that will broadcast a signal to uncuff everyone in your proximity. All you have to do is press it, but don't do it yet. You will know when the time is right. Do you understand?"

I nodded, stunned but grateful.

"Good. Please forgive me for this." He grabbed my arm and, after opening the door with a keypad, jerked me out aggressively. "Stop your resisting!" he shouted.

I played along with him while sounds of commotion opened up around us. Countless children yelled and shrieked as we were all taken from our cells and led to the same location. I transmitted from my heart a reassuring energy, knowing that there was reason to have faith. Yet I recognized none of the voices as Evelyn's and was angrily reminded of what the soldier had said.

"Is *she* okay?" I whispered to the lieutenant, hoping for a simple affirmative. Before he could answer, I was passed to two other men.

"Let's go, kid," said one of them, whose voice I remembered from the helicopter.

"What will become of us?" I asked him.

"That's up to the general. You better hold on to whatever hope you have left."

He sounded almost sympathetic. I clutched the key behind my back while swallowing the lingering taste of the antidote. Soon we approached the center of the commotion, and I could no longer quell my anxiety. A hundred voices clamored; children cried and struggled while soldiers screamed at them to get in line. I was halted in the midst of it, my pulse racing, my cuffed hands quivering.

After an unbearable minute of turmoil, deafening gunshots blasted through the air.

"Everyone be quiet!" a soldier shouted. "Let the general speak, or be dealt with swiftly."

The crowd fell silent immediately, save for nervous breathing and children whimpering—and one who still seemed to be fighting, yelling above the ringing, "What are you doing, you cowards! I command you to resist! This is *our* revolution!"

I was astonished to recognize the voice. Matteo continued shouting, but with their abilities disabled, none of his followers dared to join him. He struggled alone. And toward the front of the crowd, a man began laughing.

"General, should we kill him?" a soldier questioned.

"Not yet," Mabus growled. "He must suffer for what he did. He must feel the torment of those unarmed scientists. And after we are done with him, he will wish he were dead."

"You will pay for this! I am enlightened! You should be bowing to *me*, you swine!"

"Is that so?" Mabus replied.

Matteo screamed in agony. Once. Twice. He kept on fighting, but his tortured wails were enough to paralyze the entire crowd. It wasn't long before he stopped struggling altogether and simply cried.

At that, the veil dropped, and I heard myself as a traumatized little boy, abandoned by his parents and abused by evil men who grinned as they shocked and fractured his mind. But Matteo didn't have someone like Walter to guide him. He didn't have an Evelyn. I could hardly believe it after all he had done, but as Matteo fell unconscious, tears filled my eyes.

"Anybody else?" Mabus demanded. I felt rows of children trembling, some softly weeping. "Now, I understand that many of you here may feel wrongfully victimized, for not all have abused their powers to the extent of engaging in slaughter. However, there is an order to this world that must be preserved. We are in the process of building back our Union better than ever. And as we have discovered through years of trial and error, any large-eyed child allowed to roam rampant is a danger to a free and safe society.

"We have already heard the reports of raids on our villages, the use of your abilities to terrorize others. You carry a sickness that has progressed to the point of murder. You view us ordinary humans as lesser and conspire to overthrow our nation and our culture. It should therefore come as no surprise that we find it necessary to take drastic measures to manage this threat, or at least to encourage those under its influence to comply to our standards.

"That is where you all presently find yourselves, for as long as you hear that ringing, your dangerous advantages are neutralized. Don't bother to fight. It is our greatest advancement in safeguarding the human race, and it is all thanks to the one who has spent the longest at my facility and was sent out like a Trojan horse to infest the rest of you with our nanotechnology."

Gasps and sharp inhales came from the crowd, and I felt the attention turn toward me. Rather than giving in to shame, I clung to internal faith, remembering Walter urging me not to lend power to divisive mind games.

"Needless to say," resumed Mabus, "we control your destiny. And several of you will fortunately learn what it's like to have discipline for the first time in your lives, instead of being treated as one with superiority. The outcomes may differ, but I might have enough grace to look past the color of your robes and previous affiliations. Because what's going to matter from here on out is whether you choose to *obey*."

He paused, and the surrounding energy was so tense it became overwhelming. Then, he let out a bitter sigh.

"Men, bring out the humans. It is time for them to pick sides."

Adrenaline surged as protesting children were led to the front of the crowd. I recognized their voices; most were Evelyn's orphan siblings. More yelling erupted all around, but gunshots silenced them.

"There's no need for alarm," Mabus insisted. "All I'm offering is a deal, and quite a generous one, I might add. Because I promise each one of you beautiful human children that once this deal is accepted, not only will you walk out of here unharmed, but a life you could not have imagined will begin. I will place you into a good, kind family, one with money to provide you with everything you ever wanted, for there are so many willing parents out there, yearning to adopt children like you. You will live in the capital, which contains the pinnacle of our technology. You will have friends of your own species and get an education paid for by our military. This is my offer to each of you. All you have to do to accept is step forward and vow allegiance to our Union."

Every child in the crowd waited with bated breath for them to accept, and I would not have judged them if they did. Yet after thirty seconds of nothing but silence, the load on my heart lightened, and I could breathe again.

Mabus sneered impatiently. "What's the matter? Don't you want a family?"

"We already have a family," Penelope declared. "It's not our fault that you screwed up your own."

I heard him huff in frustration. "Have it your way. Be treated like the rest of them. Retie her blindfold and restrain this brat again." Soldiers followed his command and led her into the crowd. Several children cheered before being forcefully hushed. "Is there anyone else? Don't be shy. What about you, little boy? You seem awfully quiet."

"*No*," replied Xavier. "They're my friends, and I love them. I don't need anything else. Even the ones in black. I think most of them just want someone to hug them."

I felt Mabus's blood boil. "You silly child. Do you know how they view us? They're different than us. They have abilities."

"We do too," he answered casually.

After a hesitation, Mabus laughed, and a few soldiers joined in. "Fine. But when you have nowhere left to go, don't say I didn't offer. Have fun being labeled as traitors to the Union."

"Unity isn't something that needs to be forced!" cried Evelyn, finally. "Let them go, or—"

"You have no powers, and you have no guns. Keep your threats. You're just a dirty cast-off."

She slapped him so hard it echoed. I felt the pain in my heart as he grabbed her and she screamed.

"Let her go!" I shouted. My rage reverberated through a moment of quiet, and the world seemed to freeze in place.

Mabus continued laughing. "I thought that might work. Always so easy to play, aren't we, Mr. Helen? Bring him up here if he thinks he has something to say."

My arms were gripped tightly, and I was escorted through the hushed crowd until I heard the general breathing nearby.

"Oh, my precious experiment. Everyone already knows what you have done. You're the reason why they are here. And as a reward to you, I will let you see."

I was turned around before my blindfold was ripped off, my eyes initially held captive by the shining sun. Then I stared at the children lined up in rows within the vast courtyard of the militaristic compound, surrounded by buildings and jail cells, black cubes set up all around us. Many wore gold; they had captured most of us from Sanctuary. But there were also several in black with shaved heads and dragon emblems, similarly blinded, handcuffed, and dejected. Despite the large number of children, there were more than enough soldiers to handle each one.

Lying unconscious on the ground was Matteo with his pyramidal amulet; beside him, Tiana exuded silent animosity, wearing Evelyn's heart-shaped locket. I saw Selena drooping sadly and her big sister, Johanna, trying to stay resolute and keep her chin lifted despite the tears streaming from beneath her blindfold. Then I noticed a little boy in black no older than three, his sobbing evoking the grief of the mother at the village and my promise to return the children safely.

To my side, Evelyn stood with her siblings; thankfully, I could see into her expressive eyes, concerned yet filled with hope. "Samuel," she whispered, but before I could smile back at her, Mabus paced between us with an arrogant smirk.

"So, Mr. Helen, what's it going to be? Will you choose to be wise and surrender to the Union, which may very well improve the rest of their fates? Or perhaps you should first take this opportunity to apologize to your friends, being that so many of them must feel so betrayed."

Unfazed, I met his glare squarely. "I just want to tell you that there's still time to change."

He snickered. "Is that supposed to be a threat or some fragile moral display? Like it or not, boy, we've known exactly the kind of person you are ever since you killed your drunk father. Not to mention being so easily led to infect everyone here with our technology by no less than my own daughter."

My hand clenched the key as I waited impatiently for the antidote to kick in. The ringing persisted. The lieutenant stood toward the edge of the crowd. His patch was gone, for his eye had healed. He shook his head as I caught his steady gaze, urging me to continue to be patient.

Mabus strolled toward Evelyn as he resumed. "I can tell you're having difficulty, so I'll make this easy for you. Submit to the Union and consent to be used for our purposes whenever needed. Say it and mean it, and you and your lover over here will make it out alive. If not, let's just say"—he glanced over Evelyn, who kept her glistening eyes on me—"you will never look into those pretty blue eyes again."

Every doubt in my mind was telling me to give in. But beneath the fear, I felt our souls' shared knowing. I turned back to Mabus with conviction.

"No," I said. "I refuse to be manipulated any longer."

He scoffed in incredulity, and a palpable shock struck every child. "Very well, then. Take the girl . . ." He trailed off as he stared into the crowd. "Those two there. What are they doing?"

I followed the direction of his glower and saw two painted boys standing out among the rest. Despite being blindfolded and having their arms restrained, through the guidance of their hearts, Ezra and Sidney had managed to find one another and were resting their heads together.

"They appear to be hugging, sir," a soldier responded bluntly.

"Disgusting." Mabus scowled. "Get them off each other."

Another pair of children followed in solidarity, then another after that, and several more. A chain reaction flowed from that one act of unity, and before I knew it, a hundred children were hugging the ones next to them, including many in black robes, the most eager being that little three-year-old. And though some of the soldiers moved to separate them, most simply watched indifferently, even as Mabus threw a tantrum.

"What are you morons standing around for? I said to get them *off!*" he screamed, storming around furiously. My eyes welled up at the heartening scene, and I gazed at Evelyn, smiling. But in that instant, I lost awareness of the device I was holding, and my grip loosened as Mabus bumped into me.

It fell to the ground, and, losing balance, I did as well, taking back attention from the crowd. For a moment the general and I watched as the device bounced on the concrete and rested face up, exposing a small button.

We glanced at each other. I lunged at it with my whole body— but it was too late. He crushed it with his boot, and as the crowd quieted, trying to figure out what was happening, he bent down to pick up the remnants, the expression on his face growing violent.

"Now!" Lieutenant Hernandez yelled, sparking a coup among the soldiers.

~

A standoff ensued between two military factions, and the courtyard became starkly divided. On one side, the lieutenant led a large group in rebellion, thankfully taking most of the smaller children with them— whom they valiantly protected behind a line of soldiers pointing guns before proceeding to remove their blindfolds and handcuffs.

The side loyal to Mabus held dozens of us as hostages, including Evelyn and the orphans, Cyrus, Felix, Tiana, and Matteo, who was still in a daze, and even the general's two present daughters. I remained frozen on the ground as Mabus himself held a revolver to my head, fury coursing through his arteries and into his fingers. I pleaded with my body to metabolize the antidote and summon my abilities, but to my frustration, I felt no psychic energy, and the ringing refused to subside.

In a malicious tone, Mabus addressed the lieutenant: "I suspected that you'd become soft for them, Jacob, but I never would have foreseen such treachery."

"The only treachery is what you're doing to these kids," the lieutenant asserted. "Let them go, or things could get ugly."

"Really? Because it appears that you're in no position. One wrong move, and we won't hesitate to kill them."

What came next suffused me with immeasurable hope. A powerful voice channeled through Lieutenant Hernandez. "You will no longer harm our children." For a second, in my field of etheric vision, the wings of Michael rose behind him.

"*Now* they're your children, after all this time? What has happened to you? Do you want them to die?"

But the lieutenant was fixated on a scene unfolding on his side of the courtyard. As his fellow rebels provided protection, a young girl in black robes was led to him.

He choked out the word "Sara!" and bent down with open arms.

"Daddy!" She ran to him.

"I'm so sorry, my beautiful child. I'm so sorry for everything."

The girl and her father embraced with tears in their eyes, and through love and forgiveness, a cycle was transcended. The lieutenant stood to implore the angry general, "George, this isn't the way. Samuel is right; there is still time to change. God knows how long it took me to see the light. Open your eyes and look at what you're doing to these kids. Look at what you're doing to your own daughters!"

Mabus seemed uneasy as he glanced through the hostages but shook his head and responded heartlessly, "There is only one daughter who has been loyal to me, who has been installed with the correct programming. The other two are failed experiments. They have done nothing but betray me."

"How could you say that!" shouted Johanna, struggling with her captor. "You tortured and abandoned us! You were *never* a father. There was no one to betray." She choked up as she wept beneath the blindfold. "And now you will never get to see your own granddaughter."

Selena too began crying, and a chord of empathy was struck throughout the crowd, one so great that even some soldiers loyal to Mabus lowered their guns in sudden clarity. The ones on the lieutenant's side took off their helmets. I could finally see into the eyes of these young men, as well as several women, and even from this distance sensed their compassion. Within each of them burned the eternal fire.

Mabus only became angrier. "All in resistance have fifteen seconds to surrender, or I'll kill him," he threatened, pressing the gun to my head before nodding toward Evelyn. "Then I'll kill her."

A countdown started before the distraught crowd, and the lieutenant looked alarmed and ready to step forward. "Don't do this, George," he urged, but Mabus did not possess the understanding to listen. The revolver rattled in his hands, and I comprehended that a mere ten seconds remained to me in this life.

Then the wind nudged my head toward Evelyn, who was whispering in prayer—and her angels heard her. Two robed figures appeared behind her, a man and a woman, but now their faces were uncovered. I recognized them from her locket. *"You are free, my sweet child,"* Evelyn's mother told me telepathically. *"You always have been."*

As Mabus counted the final seconds, and with the lieutenant about to give in, I realized that my hands were unconfined. As soon as he glanced in the other direction, I moved them to my side and batted the gun away with all my strength.

I hurled myself toward it, but Mabus tackled me with a savage snarl. Still, I stretched for it and came within inches before he drove a knife through my hand, chipping the concrete. It was a pain I had never before felt, and I wailed in agony.

Mabus retrieved his revolver and aimed it again callously. "You made this choice," he said to me. I stared up into the eyes of the man who was about to send a bullet through my skull. Then my gaze slid behind him.

By some miracle, dark clouds began filling the sky at a supernatural speed. As we froze in a violent image, the wind whipped up, and raindrops began falling.

Lightning struck a nearby building just as I heard Evelyn shriek.

All who were able to see gaped at her in disbelief. Evelyn's eyes brimmed with an inexhaustible white light as she stalked toward us, enraged—her breath the wind that pushed away the soldiers, her anger the dark clouds, and her tears the pouring rain.

"What is this sorcery?" Mabus yelled in astonishment, and as the wind ripped the knife from my hand, he fearfully backed away. He tried to steady his gun in her direction, but with another shriek, lightning hit the ground beside him, deafening and blinding.

The storm settled as abruptly as it arose. Mabus lay motionless before his stunned soldiers. Evelyn stood over me, her golden robes rippling elegantly in the softening breeze. The light in her eyes faded to crystal blue, but in them I knew was a spirit more consequential than I could imagine. After a moment of disorientation, she smiled tenderly and extended her hand to me, just as she had when we were children.

"They were listening," she whispered.

I nodded, awestruck. "Yes, and you were right. This life *is* a lucid dream." I reached up with my right hand, nearly forgetting my wound.

Then came the sounds of gunshots.

One more tear fell from her eye, and she clutched the side of her stomach, revealing blood of her own. "Evelyn!" I screamed, rushing to catch her as she collapsed in my arms, heaving.

I pressed my hands against the bullet wound beneath her robes, our blood intermingling while she clasped my arm with desperate strength. I glared up with rage, yearning to wreak vengeance on the soldier who had shot her—but it was already done. He lay on the ground in critical condition, his blood seeping onto the concrete. He removed his helmet and stared at me with his life force waning.

"Sorry, kid," he said as he choked on more blood. I realized he was the same one who had locked me in my cell, and he looked so young he could have been my age.

By now every soldier had lowered their guns. Many children were crying; they felt the sorrow in their hearts, even if they couldn't see. "Samuel." The lieutenant approached somberly with a few of his men, rifle in hand. "I'm sorry I was too late."

"You weren't." I wept as I met Evelyn's eyes, which flickered with spiritual light. "You'll make it, won't you, my love?"

She continued to gasp in distress yet had enough strength to take my hand and place it just below her stomach. *"Feel"* was the message she transmitted telepathically, together with an image of her loving parents feeding her as a baby.

I did as she asked and closed my eyes, knowing that even in crisis, I always had the ability to quiet the mind. Immediately, I sensed it—something growing inside her, something incredibly special. Luckily, by the grace of God, the bullet had missed it and her major organs. But I knew that if I didn't act swiftly, we would be in dire circumstances.

"It could have been so much easier," said a voice to my side. Mabus was clambering to his feet with the help of two soldiers, wounded yet alive. As another standoff commenced between the lieutenant's faction and Mabus's remaining supporters, he glared at me. I paid him no mind. I saw clearly that his soul was distorted, a higher awareness transmuting any anger.

"I love you," I told Evelyn, grasping her hand. "I love you so much. Please don't leave."

She managed to smile, and my heart gently opened; and from it flowed a healing golden energy that shined through my palms and into her body. Then, as I sensed the miracle of life within her and beheld all the children in need, the note of my consciousness in the cosmic symphony shifted up an octave. My heart exploded like the sun with that same aureate energy and swept throughout the base, disintegrating the nanites in the children's brains and unlocking their handcuffs with its frequency. The antidote had never been needed, nor an external key. The power existed within us all along.

A moment passed, and I rejoiced as Evelyn breathed comfortably again, the bullet emerging miraculously from her wound, before I rose with a welcome rush of psychic energy. The black cubes had been deactivated. There was no more of that dreaded ringing. And all around, the children lifted their blindfolds without resistance, as if collectively awakening from a dream.

"No," Mabus uttered in confusion. "What are they doing? Stop them!" As he realized how few soldiers were still loyal to him, he whirled to face me. "*You.*" He hobbled toward the revolver between us, but I flung it away with a swipe of my hand. He looked up desperately; then his eyes widened in terror at something over my shoulder.

"I told you that you would pay."

Matteo roared as he propelled the general through the air at speed, to land with a thud all the way by the buildings. His sister next took turns teleporting the soldiers who had flanked him, stabbing them murderously with the knife that bore my blood. Finally, the others from Mabus's faction aimed their guns, but they were quickly overcome by the formerly captive children. With a lift of her arm, Johanna disarmed twenty of them at once, her fiery eyes possessed with rage. Felix pounded the concrete and blasted them with a shock wave. Then Ezra and Sidney sent the rest scurrying in panic with holograms of giant scorpions, their tails and pincers chasing them away.

I looked at the lieutenant and gestured to Evelyn. "Take her, please." He nodded, promptly signaling his men to transport her into their protection along with the orphans and several more children.

As I gazed back at Matteo and Tiana, now huddling over dead soldiers with a dozen of their black-robed followers, I felt the anger in their hearts. It wasn't long before they turned toward me with hostile glares.

"He did this to us!" Matteo screamed. "He's been working for them! He tried to deny us our divine gifts and have us imprisoned like pigs!"

"That's not true," I contended, trying to reason with him. "I never knew about the technology. I had no idea this would happen."

"I should have killed you when I had the chance," he snarled, refusing to listen as he stepped forward and the others came abreast. "This time, I won't make the same mistake. Because now my perspective has changed, *brother.* All swine and their sympathizers must be eliminated."

"Then you'll have to go through me." Johanna appeared at my side with glowing eyes, giving me a nod of assurance and belief.

"Us too." Cyrus joined, then Felix, Ezra, Sidney, and several others from Sanctuary. A knot of appreciation formed in my throat as behind me gathered an army of light, both seen and unseen.

"This is how it's going to be? You and your band of useless hippies?" His followers cackled while Matteo sneered. "In that case, this might be a bit more fun than I expected. But don't worry." His eyes burned. "I'll still make this quick and easy."

He lunged to attack me while a battle commenced between the others, psychic energy colliding and then erupting throughout the courtyard—yet I was protected by the strength of my heart. A sphere of light shielded my body, manifesting out of inner stillness. Even as Matteo bombarded me with blasts of telekinesis, they couldn't touch me; the energy simply evaporated. I continued to step back calmly as he shrieked with irritation, imbuing his attacks with more and more anger. But nothing could get through as long as I remained in my power. In his eyes I sensed his growing confusion.

"When we met, you told me that we're not so different," I said to him. "I couldn't see it at the time, but I now know it to be true. I understand how you and your sister were treated as children. I know that they abused you instead of recognizing your gifts. And I'm so sorry for what they did."

This seemed to only trigger him. "I don't need your pity. You know nothing, you swine!" He levitated a dead soldier's helmet and hurled it at me, but it bounced away as well.

"I am not your enemy," I asserted. "Open your eyes."

"My eyes are open as wide as they've ever been," he responded with a guttural growl, and as he touched his pyramidal amulet to the emblem on his wrist, the pupils of his eyes became vertically slit. "Time to die," he hissed, and I realized then that he had fully given in to a hidden, dark power. He emptied dozens of bullets from the chambers of soldiers' guns, pointing them at me. Then, with a violent jerk of his arm, he fired them at lethal velocity all at once.

They struck my shield with such force that I fell back and hit the ground. Instead of succumbing to fear, though, I held to my faith, and as I scanned my body, I saw that nothing had penetrated its flesh. The bullets had disintegrated against the field of my aura. Clouds of metal particles floated above, which the wind then blew away.

I spotted the others amid the ongoing psychic battle. Felix and Johanna stood back-to-back, countering attacks from Tiana as she teleported back and forth, giggling as she tried to stab them. Cyrus looked bruised and battered in his duel with the boy I recognized as Aleister, yet he still gave it his all. Fighting alongside one another, Ezra and Sidney distracted some others by creating holograms of themselves that pounced from all angles, toying with the dragon children like they were in a hall of mirrors. But my friends seemed to be tiring, and I wasn't sure if they could hold them off much longer.

Then, I looked further, toward the edge of the courtyard, and saw the young children behind the benevolent soldiers. I caught the eyes of a boy who was watching me with worry: it was the three-year-old in black robes, praying for us to win against the ones who stole him from his mother.

After the dust settled, I rose reinvigorated by higher purpose, replenishing my shield as I stood to face both Matteo and the entity that possessed him, which looked on in bewilderment.

"How is this possible?" he asked, his mouth hanging open.

"Because you have been deceived into selling your soul for power," I told him. "No matter what happens, there is always a chance to grow and heal. There is always the option to choose the right path."

This time, I took measured steps toward him while he anxiously backed away, his attacks diminishing. Finally, I raised my wounded hand and nudged him to the ground. He waited, gasping, his eyes oscillating between those of a snake and a traumatized child.

Before I could draw closer to expel the entity, a voice in distress called, "Samuel! Help me!"

I turned to find Tiana glaring with devilish eyes, holding Evelyn hostage with her knife while the others wrestled nearby. And she had no regard for mercy or empathy. She didn't even give us a chance to say goodbye. While wearing the locket that carried the image of Evelyn's parents, she plunged the knife into their daughter's chest. I watched my love breathe her final breaths in anguish. My grief-stricken heart felt pierced the same way.

"No." My legs gave out, and Tiana had the depravity to giggle.

"Samuel, see through it! It's all in your mind!" yelled Ezra, engaged in a struggle.

I looked back and saw that the girl who I thought was Evelyn, even as she gasped, had no soul in her eyes. Yet as the illusion vanished, it was too late. My defenses were down, and I was left vulnerable. *"I've got you now."* Tiana grinned diabolically. With her full psychic energy, she went straight for my heart.

There was an agonizing constriction. I fell to my back and clutched my chest as her ruthless telekinetic grasp tried to force me into cardiac arrest. I became lightheaded, struck with a terrible dread. But right on the verge of losing consciousness, willpower that I didn't know I possessed activated. My valiant heart began to fight back, thumping in defiance.

I heard a deafening screech, and as my blood flowed to recover my vision, I saw Johanna coming to my aid, driving Tiana away. But Matteo quickly approached under the spell of an enraged entity, now clenching the knife.

"You may have learned a few more tricks," he hissed, "but your sympathy for them leaves you weak."

I struggled to regain my strength and get to my feet, though my muscles still felt paralyzed. He raised the knife and went to jab it into my body—only to be obstructed by an invisible barrier. As his hand rebounded, he looked around in perplexity, until his eyes narrowed at my protector.

Noah stood behind me, a fire raging in his dauntless gaze.

"Leave my friend alone," he spat at his former controller, and in the background I saw a resistance of black robes joining to help us in battle.

"You foolish, ungrateful runt." Matteo scowled. "You *dare* to challenge me?"

"Yes," Noah answered, flinging the knife away from Matteo's hand and ramming the psychic barrier into the snake-eyed leader so forcefully that he was launched fifteen feet backward.

No sooner had Noah let his guard down than he too was thrust to the ground, by Aleister, charging in to help his master. In retribution, I gathered my remaining energy and did the same to him, sending the boy tumbling on the concrete—which pained me, but it was necessary. An infuriated Matteo was already getting up, proceeding to suffocate Noah with a psychic stranglehold. But he was disrupted when Penelope hit him on the head with chains, our former restraints.

"Tell your stupid lizard friends to crawl back to where they came from!" she bravely shouted.

Matteo laughed demonically, then pulled her like a magnet until he clasped his hand around her neck. "How delightful, this little rabbit hopping into a dragon's den," the entity snarled through him. "There is fear growing inside of you. I can smell it running through your blood."

I rose to assist her, but Noah was already on it. With eyes blazing fiercely, he choked Matteo with his own amulet, pressing the edge of the pyramid firmly against his throat. Matteo was forced to release Penelope as he grunted and croaked. She stared at him as he dropped to his knees.

"Now who's the fearful one?" she taunted as he attempted to loosen the hold.

Finally, a small bald girl, previously invisible, appeared in front of him. The knife flew into her grasp as she advanced toward him and, to my horror, lunged to stab his face—stopping within inches before throwing it away. She yanked off his amulet to put him out of his misery, smashing it into pieces against the concrete. Matteo let out a hideous squeal; perhaps it was the demon withering inside him. I sensed a dark contract broken, its power drained.

"How could you, Selena?" He looked up at her with pupils shifting. "We took you in. We gave you everything."

"Yeah, and you also taught me how to read minds," Selena responded. "You killed my mother. And you wanted me to do the same to my sister." She placed her glowing hands on his head, and he fell into a deep sleep among the shattered remnants of his amulet.

Selena glanced back at me and nodded before going to assist Johanna—who seemed to have finally apprehended Tiana—while Penelope and Noah hugged each other tightly. He blushed and smiled as she kissed him on the cheek, then turned to me with his light-filled gaze.

"Thank you for saving me," I told him as my heart reopened.

"It's what friends do," he said. "Plus, it felt pretty good."

I went to embrace him for the very first time, and as he wrapped his arms around me, he began to cry.

"I'm so sorry, Noah, for leaving you behind at the Facility. You didn't deserve to go through all that."

"It's okay, Samuel," he replied. "It was tough, but I learned how to stand up for myself and others, just like you do for the people you love. I wouldn't have it any other way."

"I hope your hair grows back quickly, but I kinda dig the tattoo." Penelope grinned. "Now come on. Let's put an end to this."

After witnessing Johanna tearfully hugging her youngest sister, together we went to finish the battle. With the help of the resistance, the black-robed leaders unconscious, and the entity expelled, it turned into an easy victory. Many of Matteo's loyal followers had surrendered. Aleister was the final holdout, struggling to needlessly prolong the conflict while clutching his reinjured shoulder.

I approached him steadily while Noah held him down. He went still and glared up into my eyes. *"If you're gonna kill me, just do it, you coward,"* he said telepathically, and I recalled how I had wanted him dead after he hurt Noah, nearly getting my wish when he was shot by the lieutenant. Yet as our minds further connected and I scanned the tragic episodes of his short life, abducted at a young age, I felt great empathy for the boy. Like Matteo, he'd never had anybody to show him the way.

With this epiphany, golden light with swirling hues of pink shined from my palms and entered his chest, giving him a taste of the unconditional love he had never before experienced. I signaled Noah to let him go; no more force was needed as Aleister wept on the ground.

There was an air of celebration in the wake of the battle, with many more children running to hug one another. Several lay injured, however, including Cyrus, Sidney, and black robes who had surrendered; but children with healing abilities were coming to their aid, as well as benevolent soldiers. I rushed into the crowd to find Evelyn but was halted by a ragged voice.

"Samuel." It was Lieutenant Hernandez, approaching with a few of his men and holding the hand of his little daughter. "Great work out there. You are truly gifted. You all are. The world is very lucky to have those like you. Let's get you fixed up, and we'll take you to her."

A woman came to bandage my hand, and I warmly met the eyes of the heroic soldiers. "Thank you for protecting them." The soldiers nodded, radiating a sense of redemption, and Sara squeezed her father's arm.

From there, I was led to Evelyn. She lay on blankets, and, beautifully, healers in both black and gold were huddled around her, running their hands above her body in a coordinated dance, replenishing her vitality. Above them, I caught a glimpse of Sangeetha in her astral state, projecting her consciousness from the crystal cave. She smiled at me when she realized I could see her. She was conducting the whole thing, lending them her energy.

I knelt beside Evelyn and stroked her hair, and she turned her head and beamed. There resided her limitless spirit, whose light I could clearly recognize. No words were needed. We rested in the joy in our hearts, the stillness of God.

Her eyes widened at something over my shoulder, and I turned to find Selena carrying Evelyn's treasured locket. "I think this belongs to you." She bent down to offer it with a shy smile. "No hard feelings, I hope."

"None at all." Evelyn reached to caress her hand. "Thank you. Thank you so much." After Selena stepped back, I helped to attach the locket once more around Evelyn's neck. She took a comfortable breath. "Samuel, why don't you go talk to the lieutenant? See if they have a plan to get the children out safely."

"Of course, my love." I stood to navigate the lively crowd while Xavier, Penelope, Noah, and the orphans came to greet her.

But before I could find Lieutenant Hernandez again, I was abruptly grabbed by the arm—Maya, her eyes glowing in a trance. "Great destruction is imminent," she said. "It is coming from the sky. It is coming with the wind. A cleanse of the old ways."

She turned me to Lila, who spoke from a state of meditation: "All around the earth, they are now stationed. They are here. They are waiting."

"Who's *they*?" I asked with growing concern.

A wave of disquiet washed over the crowd before she could answer. As I peered through the masses, I saw Matteo waking from his induced slumber, seemingly disoriented yet quickly filling with anger.

"You've got to be kidding me," I muttered, making my way toward him, accompanied by several older children and soldiers.

Right as he got to his feet, however, he collapsed again as if struck by another sudden coma.

A telepathic voice resounded within the minds of everyone present. *"Hate to spoil all the fun, but this party is over."*

We gawked, startled, as a fiery-eyed Luna strode toward us in her violet dress from the side of the courtyard. She had put Matteo back to sleep with a mere wave of her hand. And she was walking arm-in-arm with her father.

CHAPTER 20

THE EARTH SEEMED to stop turning on its axis as we halted twenty feet from one another. Permeating the atmosphere of that moment was a cosmic significance. What happened next would reverberate across the planet, the fate of its children hanging in the balance.

On one side, I stood with an increasing number of psychic children and deprogrammed soldiers. Among them were the lieutenant and his daughter, gathering shoulder to shoulder with the others while Johanna and her youngest sister held each other with heartache in their eyes.

On the other side, Luna stared with an eerie lack of emotion, even as she saw her sisters. She was wearing her golden cuff again, combined with her spiral earrings, and when she met my eyes, I kept waiting for a message, a sign, one of her playful winks, or even a glimpse of her soul. Instead she paid me no mind as she supported the man who had tortured us all and imprisoned his own daughters. Mabus was bloodied and badly injured. He surely had broken bones, for he could barely stand on his own. His soldiers had abandoned him, and he was outnumbered a hundredfold. Yet he grinned.

Lieutenant Hernandez was the first to speak. "Madeleine, I can't begin to describe how sorry I am for the terrible things I've participated in. I'm sorry that I refused to see what was happening.

But your father instigated these crimes against children. You would do well to hand him over."

For a moment, I was hopeful, but then she snickered at him.

"Maddie." Johanna emerged from the crowd as she wept. "Maddie, please wake up. This isn't who you are. You're not like this."

Nothing registered in those green eyes.

"I didn't mean what I said, Maddie," Selena joined in. "I was confused and angry. No matter what happened in the past, you'll always be my sister."

Finally, I saw in Luna a trace of emotion, but she shook it away; a darker side was fighting to keep control.

"My name is *Luna*," she coldly replied. My head instinctively tilted upward, drawn to witness a spectacle in the sky: above passing clouds, the moon had begun to eclipse the sun, causing a strange twilight to descend on the earth. And I looked down to see Luna with flames burning in her eyes.

"She will not listen to you," said Mabus. "She will not listen to any of you. So many of you cowards may have betrayed me, but she was trained to be loyal. It would be my honor to now show you all the power of a *true* biological weapon once it is disciplined—no nanites needed."

"Arrest him," barked the lieutenant.

"Stop them," Mabus countered.

The soldiers had barely stepped forward before they were pushed back by a huge energetic barrier. Some of the children began attacking it psychically, but it was too strong to bring down.

Then a single item floated through. Everyone quieted as we watched it float toward Luna: a single pink rose. I caught Ezra's luminous eyes and realized that it was a hologram. Sidney, in spite of his wounds, summoned the energy to manifest birds dancing around it, singing a sweet tune before vanishing in front of her.

"You can speak to them, remember?" I called out to her. "Through their songs, we found our way along the river. I forgive you for anything else you've done, Luna, because without you I wouldn't have had the courage to face my own shadow, gaining the tools to know myself and control my abilities. I never would have talked to that wise old priest and ate spaghetti in that village with that kind woman and her nieces." As she turned those burning eyes toward me, I projected cherished memories telepathically. "Through you, I've experienced so many incredible things. So please, Luna, remember. I know there's more to who you are."

"Do you, Samuel?" Mabus laughed. "And how long have you known her, boy? A couple of weeks? Let me guess what she told you—that she put on those black robes in her spite against me. That she nearly died after being buried alive yet miraculously survived. That she lived among the trees and animals for years afterward with nowhere to go. And that all along, I was nowhere to be found, never thinking of returning to my original experiments in whom I had invested so much time."

He shook his head, and Luna's gaze dropped.

"I regret to tell you this, but ever since joining those dragons, she's been my double agent. After she tried to kill them, unsuccessfully, she came back to me. They buried her alive, yes, but who do you think dug her up? How in the world do you think she survived? She wasn't living with the birds! She was in our labs for more training. Then I sent her on another mission to keep an eye on crucial projects at my facility—such as *you*, Samuel. Along with your precious lover."

I relived the memory she'd shown me of being flooded by divine energy on the verge of death, which at the time had seemed like a spiritual resurrection.

"That can't be true," I said. The children were silent, and her sisters looked stunned.

"So young and naive," Mabus resumed. "But I don't blame you. She can be very convincing. Sometimes, she doesn't even know her own memory. The trick is to split the personality, fragment the mind. It is an operation so compartmentalized that only I know the full extent of it—the outcome being a new human more powerful than anyone who has ever lived. I call it Project Monarch. Luna, darling?"

She turned to him robotically.

"Take care of them, will you?"

"Yes, Daddy."

The barrier thrust outward in a shock wave of psychic energy. Cries sounded as we were shoved back, many of us tumbling to the ground. I regained my composure before observing in horror as Luna extended her glowing hand over the crowd. Dozens of soldiers fell into sudden comas before they had time to stand back up. Others became disoriented, walking in circles and casting away their weapons. The children were more resistant. Several erected their own shields to protect others from her influence, including Sara, who was shielding her father.

Silencing my mind, I joined in, combining my energy with Johanna's, Selena's, and Noah's to safeguard as many people as possible. In a panic, a couple of soldiers broke from our protection and began shooting at Luna and her father, ignoring the lieutenant's pleas. To my great relief, as well as astonishment, the bullets simply bent around their targets as Luna simultaneously deflected psychic attacks with ease. I could hardly believe my eyes as she put them all to sleep; I knew then that I had only glimpsed the true strength of her abilities.

"Neat trick, huh? Wonderful for manipulation." Angling her hand toward us, Luna sent me an image of her touching Evelyn's head. I was unfazed, refusing to give in to anger or vengeance. I noticed her lips curve upward as I warded off her pressing influence by resting in the power of my heart's greater awareness.

There came a familiar snarl from beside me, and I saw that Matteo had risen from his sleep to glare at Luna with fury. Levitating around him were the dozen or so deactivated black cubes, which he proceeded to hurl at her one by one. "No one controls me! No one *dares* to use dark magic against me!"

His eyes went wide in disbelief as he ran out of projectiles: with her spare hand, Luna had caught them all in a magnetic vortex. "Oh really?"

The vortex sped up, and with a flash of light, the cubes melded together, undergoing a transmutation. From them sprang a long, dark, metallic substance, which she animated with a spark of life. Before any of us had time to contemplate what we were seeing, a giant black snake was slithering toward Matteo, hissing with large, frightening fangs, resisting his desperate attacks. It lunged and wrapped swiftly around his body, swallowing him whole and cutting off a horrible scream.

Luna grinned, and the children gasped in shock and revulsion as the snake hardened into metal again, burying him within. Even Mabus hobbled back uneasily. He seemed to realize that he was no longer in control. This must have been a power he had not foreseen.

"No!" yelled a voice I had only previously heard through telepathy. Tiana appeared beside her brother to try to puncture the material, then shrieked maniacally at Luna. She teleported behind her with the knife, but Luna was one step ahead. She grabbed the bald girl psychically by the neck and held her up in the air. Any further attempts at teleportation malfunctioned.

"You were such a nasty ex-girlfriend. You always liked to fight. I'm sure you can tell that this won't be like last time." As Luna tightened her grasp, there was fear in Tiana's eyes. "And yet I suppose I should thank you, for if my former self hadn't died, I never would have known who I truly am. To think, all this time, I've been hiding my true power. Glad I don't have to play weak anymore." She tossed her former girlfriend aside effortlessly, leaving her unconscious on the concrete next to her entombed brother.

Finally, Felix stepped forward, his bright-blue eyes intensifying with an extraordinary light. He hummed a vibration that resonated through the crowd, capturing everyone's attention.

"Don't do it," Johanna urged him. "It's against our code!"

"Screw the code. She's the reason our daughter is dead." He continued humming while Johanna was struck by a heartfelt realization, tears dripping in a release of emotion.

"No. They were lying! It isn't true!"

But Felix didn't listen. The vibration grew louder and louder, the light in his eyes brighter, until it seemed that the molecular bonds of his body were breaking. He proclaimed to the universe, "I call upon my higher self, in this time of need, to replace my arms with wings, to step into this density!"

"She's my sister!" shouted Johanna, but it was too late. Before our eyes occurred a profound transfiguration: his previous form began to disintegrate, and in its place, inch by inch, rose a ten-foot-tall, flaming blue phoenix. The children backed away, then gawked in amazement as it took flight with a glistening trail. Mabus fell to the ground, his expression frozen in a rictus of fright. Yet Luna remained grinning.

After soaring incredibly high, Felix swooped down, flapping his giant wings as he unleashed an overpowering gust of blue fire. Luna expertly intercepted it, directing it in a manner such that it spiraled around her body. "You poor spirit. It seems you've picked the wrong element," she said slyly before casting it away toward some far-off buildings.

Again and again this happened with the same result: Felix couldn't even graze her as Johanna cried for him to surrender and Mabus yelled at Luna to stop redirecting the fire. But she acted in accordance with her own will, and while the moon continued its eclipse in the backdrop of the battle, the base burned all around us.

In a final effort, Felix spun in the air during his descent, sending multiple blasts of fire; Luna caught them all and condensed them around her. As she ran the fire through her glowing hands, I sensed another striking transmutation. She slowed its vibration and changed the molecular structure so that within a few seconds, the fire had turned into water. She returned it to Felix as a concentrated blast, and he screeched as it hit him square in the chest.

With his fire dwindling, he dropped out of the sky—luckily landing on an energetic cushion. Johanna rushed over with several other children as he shifted back into his human form.

The surrounding buildings were scorched, and I followed the trail of smoke to where the eclipse approached totality, sweeping waves of shadows over the horizon. But gleaming white clouds quickly emerged. From them sprang a cleansing rain. And another voice arose from the crowd.

"Luna!"

All present shifted to face her. Soldiers were awakening from their comas. Every person stood aside as Evelyn limped toward Luna, unafraid, even with her robes bloodstained, her gentle tears mixing with the rain.

"Luna, you saved me." Her words floated with the wind. "You were there, helping me. I remember it now, in the background of my dreams. You healed my sickness, and you were always protecting me. You put me to sleep, but it was all to teach me. To allow me to see my parents again, and to truly know that this life is all a dream."

Clutching her locket, Evelyn halted in front of Luna, who observed silently.

"I understand now that there is a purpose to everything, as part of God's will for us to experience and to grow. Because even as a doe, you were guiding us, weren't you?"

On the ground behind her, Mabus was about to speak, but Luna glued his lips together with a lift of her finger. She stared at Evelyn, then at me, before lifting the girl I loved into the air. The crowd gasped as Evelyn ascended eight feet. She simply breathed calmly as she remained there, levitating.

"Let her go, Luna, please," I pleaded, at last stepping forward. "You don't understand. There is life growing inside of her."

"I see." Luna glanced with interest at Evelyn's stomach. "And I suppose I should tell you congratulations. You love her, don't you?"

"Yes," I answered as I continued my slow approach. "But I also love you. And all that you encompass, even those darker aspects." I acknowledged the muted, bewildered general before turning back to the soldiers and children. "I know that everyone here can say the same."

In sequence, each of them nodded, and with gratitude I gazed upon the familiar faces: Noah and Penelope, Ezra and Sidney, Maya, Lila, Cyrus, Xavier, and finally the courageous lieutenant, holding his little daughter. And this love also extended to those I didn't know personally, for there was a recognition that we were one beneath the diminishing sun, our souls cleansed by fire and a spiritual rain.

"It's true," said Johanna, arriving back at the front of the crowd.

"Always, sister," Selena added.

"I love you as well." Felix emerged without a scratch on him, his indigo robes intact despite the transformation. "Thank you, Luna, for not letting me fall."

I smiled up at Evelyn suspended in midair, for by now everyone was awake. Even Tiana sat staring in a surrendered daze while the metal cocoon Luna had placed her brother in evaporated in the pouring rain.

Just as the rest of the crowd was about to step forward, Luna stopped them all with another psychic barrier.

"I appreciate the sentiment, but now this is between me and him." With a wave of her hand, she extended the fire from the burning buildings around us, blazing a line across the entire courtyard that separated me, her, and a floating Evelyn from the yelling soldiers and children.

Mabus tried to crawl away, but Luna blocked his path with the raging blue flames.

"Sorry, Daddy," she said. "We wouldn't want to miss all the fun, now would we?" He curled up into a ball, paralyzed by fright, while Evelyn's breath accelerated, tears coursing from her eyes.

"Luna, why are you doing this?" I asked as she turned toward me.

"You say that I taught you, so show me," she replied, her gaze reflecting fire in the twilight of the eclipse.

"I don't understand. What do you mean?"

"Show me!" A ball of psychic energy drove me ten feet back, parallel to the fire. After I rose in confusion, she forged another wall of flames between us, surrounding me so that I was now separated from all others.

I instinctively tried to part it with my mind, though this seemed to make things worse, for the fire continued raging, imperishable despite the rain. I saw no escape. I was trapped there all alone as buildings toppled to the ground, and on the other side of the wall, Evelyn dangled above encroaching flames.

"Samuel!" she called. I looked to the sky at the tiny sliver of sunlight and took a moment to pray. And I saw a brilliant-blue feather blowing in the wind.

I closed my eyes and walked by faith.

Soon, this faith turned into a knowing, for even as I sensed the heat of the fire, I experienced nothing but serenity. I had heightened my vibration to the point where it couldn't harm me. And when I opened my eyes on the other side of those flames, even my robes remained unscathed.

"Hold on!" I called up to Evelyn as the initial wall grew and widened, coming within inches of her feet. "I'll get you down. Just relax and breathe!"

With all my determination, I extended my hand and tried to will her toward me. My eyes watered as I struggled in vain, shifting between her stomach and her gaze. My mental abilities were of no use—for a greater power held her in place.

"In order to get to her, you have to get through me." Luna emerged from the flickering shadows of the flames with an aura so fierce that it seemed to bend the elements.

"Luna, please," I begged. "I still don't understand. What do you want?"

"I told you, Samuel. If you can control your abilities, if you truly know yourself as you claim, then show me!" She raised her right hand and nudged me back. I fell, panting but unafraid.

"I will not fight you," I said, surrendering completely.

"Why not?" she asked, her golden cuff glinting and a familiar image forming in her eyes.

I opened my mouth, but there was nothing to say. Despite everything going on outside, the fire raging, and the people I loved in apparent crisis, I felt as if my entire being had dissolved back into an eternal silence. In that moment, I forgot even my name. There was a harmonizing balance between light and darkness as the heavens and the earth shifted into a new state.

I looked up through the parting clouds, my breath taken away. The moon had eclipsed the sun in totality, creating a fiery corona around its dark edges and casting a shadow so encompassing that the brightest of stars could now be seen. Each one reflected our true image and likeness, for they were pure, divine light, erasing the illusory separation of all that I perceived. With this epiphany, some began rearranging. I sensed that they were watching me, waiting.

Then I looked down at my palm, where the bandage was unraveling, the softening rain washing clean my blood. I became aware of every cell in my body, yet also that I was a cell in a body much greater, expressing its glory along with every living being. For all was one with the universal mind, through which we were endlessly cocreating. An energy flooded into the crown of my head, balanced by the love from my open heart, and I gazed back at Luna as if awakening from a dream, birds singing in the background, finally answering:

"Because there is no you and there is no me. Because harming you would be like harming myself." I breathed deeply as I stared up at the sky, where the stars projected the image of a monarch butterfly. "Because *I Am* all that is written!"

I slammed my palm onto the ground, triggering a vibration that reverberated across the whole planet in an instant.

When I looked back up, time had stopped, for its strings had been broken.

CHAPTER 21

I BEHELD THE miracle before me with indescribable awe.

Thousands of raindrops were suspended in the air, some in the midst of splashing on various surfaces. All movement of the world around me had ceased, yet I was sure that I was alive. My heart was still beating. I speechlessly reached out to touch a drop, moving it around like a hovering bead.

Evelyn floated frozen above the flames. Even those fiery fingers had stilled, their blue light interweaving with the shadows cast from the sky to create a gorgeous spectral pattern.

Finally, I turned back to Luna. At first I thought that she too was frozen, but then I noticed the makings of a smile, a playful wink, and lastly a burst of childlike laughter, as if this were all one big cosmic game and she could no longer keep up the act. Her eyes shined with radiant light, reflecting the beauty of what was projected in the sky. I knew that she had also broken the strings; she was an agent operating beyond time.

"So nice of you to join me," she said with love overflowing as wings extended from each of our spines.

"What's happening?" I asked, perplexed by the sheer lucidity of what felt like a dream.

"Rise, my darling. You already know. And now, you will see."

I planted my palms to push to my feet, but no effort was needed. As time released its hold on us, so did gravity. I lost all sense of weight and levitated with wide eyes, surrounded by an egg-shaped bubble. Then, I willfully ascended until I reached Evelyn's height, spiritual upliftment pervading every molecule. There, I beheld all the soldiers and children trapped in time and confronted by fearsome flames. Beneath the illusion was a universal truth I saw clearly in each of their eyes, exposed by the soft glow of the crowned moon: they represented many forms of one consciousness interacting with itself, forgetting again and again, only to find itself once more.

Luna rose to join me, also surrounded by a shimmering bubble, visibly overjoyed. I wanted to surrender to this state of euphoria, but there were still so many questions, and all I could ask was one thing: "Luna, *why*?"

She laughed. "I suppose you're wondering why I acted that way, why I put you through all of that trouble, how the whole world is currently frozen, and why the two of us are up here together, floating above time."

"Well, yes," I said before nodding to her cuff, which contained the code I had now deciphered fully. "But the message you gave me. Why do all this, Luna, just so you can die?"

"Figured it out, didn't you?" She unveiled a blissful expression, and as her eyes became transparent, I finally saw all of who she was. Her soul was magnificent, at one with our satellite crowned in the sky and directly in tune with the universal mind. "I will answer that, Samuel, but first, I want to apologize. I didn't like behaving that way, but you must understand that I had to play a role, and make it convincing, in order to lead you down a certain path of awakening. I really did love you—and I still do. But if you were listening, you'd know that I was never really angry. I was just singing old tunes."

I was taken back to the implanted memory of stumbling through a blue door after the escape attempt with Cyrus that was only a dream. There, I saw a holographic projector that outlined my future and Evelyn's transformation while Luna sang behind a window, letting me know that there was a greater plan and through it we were always protected. Suddenly, it seemed that all I had touched and all I had seen—all the challenges Evelyn, I, and the rest of the children experienced—was an orchestrated symphony leading us to this moment. And all along, Luna had been rearranging the strings so that it culminated perfectly.

"As was spoken in poems throughout the ages, we are the music makers," she affirmed, having read what I was thinking. "We are the dreamers and the conductors of our reality, yet each of our souls emits a unique frequency to contribute to the overall harmony of the universe."

"Then aren't we all just playing roles here?" I remarked, recognizing the oneness behind every pair of eyes surrounding us.

"Yes," she responded. "Some are able to know this consciously and thus gain the ability to see and act beyond the illusion, while others have a harder time remembering, becoming disconnected from their soul and lost in their character."

She gestured to Mabus, who was curled up in fright.

"Always trust your gut instinct, Samuel, because you were right; none of what he was saying was the truth. I'm the one who manipulated his memory, not the other way around." She showed me a scene of placing her palms on his head while he slept. "It was necessary to the design, but in his pride, he cannot see it. He simply carries out his role as he dreams up an identity according to time—to illusory memory. Still, he is an important catalyst for your evolution and awakening, and that of the others, even if he doesn't know it consciously."

I thought back to the painful trials he'd put me through. In my present state, I couldn't help but feel gratitude. "What will happen to him?" I questioned.

"It might take lifetimes of experience for him to burn off his karma by means of realignment, correcting the imbalance. But at some point in the matrix of time, he will know his inner self just as we do and join us in this ascension."

"So his soul will be punished?" I stared at the fire beside him.

"His soul will take responsibility for his actions and choose to experience only what is necessary to awaken to the same realization, fanning the divine spark into a flame. We are all that is written, my darling, within the forever-evolving story of God." With the monarch in her eyes, she gestured toward everyone present, even Matteo, who had emerged from the black metal, shaken yet alive. "We are all one with the Creator and hence can rewrite time and shape our destiny. The only difference is that we know this."

With these words, my palms illuminated with pure white light before differentiating into an array of color through the unconditional love flowing from my heart, the illusion of separation slowly unraveling.

"This is all too much," I said to her, humbled at a glimpse of dimensions beyond normal understanding.

"If it overflows within you, give it to others."

I nodded to Luna, then hovered over to Evelyn, brushing aside the frozen rain and gently wiping the tears from her eyes. In them, I saw no fear but rather the birthing of a transformative light within a soul so glorious that it encompassed the whole earth. I placed my glowing hand on her womb before kissing her softly on the lips. When I pulled back my head, Evelyn inhaled as if born again, staring at me in wonder as an egg-shaped bubble brought her beyond time.

"Samuel . . ." She trailed off as she gazed around us, slack jawed. Whether it was the countless levitating raindrops, the crowd of frozen soldiers and children, the breathtaking eclipse and stars above us, or the still blue flames just below, everywhere we looked indeed revealed a miracle. She clutched her locket, and I took her hand and placed it on my chest, letting her feel the tranquil rhythm of my heart.

"It's okay," I said. "There is nothing to fear."

Her eyes widened in astonishment as a resplendent Luna floated over.

"Welcome, my love," she greeted her. "I thought you might like to hang out with us."

"Luna. This is all so incredible." Transfixed by her green gaze, Evelyn burst into a joyful smile. "I knew that there was more to you!"

Luna gave an affectionate wink. "As I was telling Samuel, not everything is as it seems. There are events that have to play out in a certain way, conspiring toward a greater purpose and design. Now it is time for you to look within yourself and realize your own soul's true vastness and beauty." She extended her hand warmly. "But as charming as the view is from up here, I wouldn't want our clothes burning off our bodies once we rejoin time. Let's get you down, shall we?"

With Evelyn in the center, the three of us glided to the ground, planting our feet in the midst of the crowd. There, we walked through the rain and quietly observed our friends, wondering if their hearts could sense us. Although some were scattered, dozens of children had banded together in the face of the fire, standing just behind the brave soldiers attempting to shield them, including the lieutenant, who clung to his daughter. Luna approached her two earthly sisters; Johanna stood by Felix and Selena, peering tearfully through the wall of flames. Evelyn went to her orphan siblings, who were huddling with some others. Penelope was hugging Noah. Beside them, Ezra and Sidney comforted the black-robed three-year-old with a hologram of an enchanting, benevolent white wolf standing guard between him and the fire. Evelyn brushed little Xavier's hair with her fingertips before turning away.

"You must have many questions," Luna observed. "But once time starts up again, I will not be here. I'm sorry to leave you so soon, but it is necessary for the greater plan—and we will forever be connected in spirit. So, I must give you this chance: is there anything you'd like to ask beforehand?"

Evelyn turned to her with damp eyes. "I just want to know that everyone will be fine."

"I give you my word," a resonant voice said, channeled through Luna's vocal cords. "No child of the earth will ever be forsaken."

"Okay," said Evelyn. "I guess I'm ready, then."

Luna went to her, smiling and holding out her palms. "The next moment you experience, I will be gone. Just know that you were never truly in danger. I did everything for you, my sweet, blue sister." Dozens of cherry blossoms emerged from her hands, multiplying into hundreds, then seemingly thousands, manifesting at an incredible speed from what surely was an infinite storehouse of energy. Evelyn gasped as the blossoms spiraled around her with a transcendent wind. A lucent image of a majestic doe became superimposed on Luna's body, and Evelyn stilled, beholding the flowers in a moment of bliss.

Luna turned to me as the doe disappeared suddenly, like a spirit returning home. "It's really true then?" I asked. "You're leaving?"

"I am," she said, and as I looked into dazzling green eyes exuding endless light, I received the vision of her former resurrection. "The inhabitant of this body has died before, and so must I die again. This was always supposed to be a temporary situation. As you have now figured out, dying to your old self is the only way you can truly live."

She gestured over my shoulder at my celestial wings.

"You, Samuel, are more powerful than you can imagine. As a true monarch, you hold the keys to time itself, of creation and destruction, to cleansing the earth of its old systems in order to bring about the birth of a new world. All I did was prepare you for this, from guiding you to that church and village to giving you a simple kiss, helping you to remember who you are in the process. And who *she* really is, as well." She nodded fondly toward Evelyn before lifting her eyes toward the eclipse. "You are the one chosen to free my soul. It has to be you. And it has to be at this moment."

"You're saying that I have to kill you?" I demanded.

"I'm asking you to help me to ascend to spirit, where I can do so much more to assist the earth. To accomplish this, however, destruction is needed, for a darkness has been hindering me. My body has been corrupted."

She removed her golden cuff to uncover the dragon on her wrist, the same emblem that each of the black robes carried. As I felt into it, I sensed a growing cancer, spreading from her skin to affect her other organs. Simultaneously, I was given another vision of strange technologies built on the surface of the moon, transmitting hypnotic frequencies that shrouded the earth. Luna sighed as she replaced her cuff.

"Now you see why this has to be done. Remaining in this body will only serve to keep humanity asleep, cycling along on the wheels of karma. But it has long been time for the children of the earth to wake from their coma. This is my mission: to awaken the planet—my true sister. Even if it means sacrificing myself."

I saw in her eyes the reflection of the eclipse. It was as if the entire essence of our lonely satellite had incarnated on this planet for a single purpose. I recalled the ending of the experiment she had tinkered with in my memory—and a blueprint activated. I, too, glimpsed through the veil, remembering who I was on a soul level and what I came here to accomplish. Nevertheless, I shook my head, not wanting it to be true.

"What about your human sisters?" I asked her. "What about those who know you by a different name and all the others who love you?"

"The one they know died years ago. Madeleine Mabus is a girl I have never met—save for a contract I made with her soul to walk into her body at the time of her death."

"It is *you* I care about, Luna." I wiped away tears as they fell undeterred by the stoppage of time. "There has to be another way. I don't want you to die."

"Remember what Walter taught you, Samuel, and, more importantly, what you have directly experienced these past couple weeks. You of all people should know that death as we see it is far from the end. Bodies come and go, but nothing real is ever threatened. You are not killing me, darling." Her expression radiated peace. "You are merely setting me free."

Energy swelled in my heart. "I love you, Luna," I said automatically.

"I love you too, Sammy. As well as everyone here. Always. Unconditionally." She went back to Johanna and Selena and placed one hand on each of their chests. "Forgive your sister for the choice she made years earlier," she said as their hearts glowed, listening. "She loves the both of you, just as I do. Nothing will be hidden in the coming age. With time, you will come to know everything."

An otherworldly light connected the sisters' hearts, then expanded suddenly to everyone on the base, illuminating the shadows brighter than the blue flames. Evelyn's womb was the last to begin shining, and we rejoiced in this sign of awakening and the evolution of the earth—a brand-new beginning.

Luna faced me again, nodding quietly, and I knew what had to be done. Golden energy was already flooding out of my palms, carried along the mystical wind to spiral around her body, sinking into her skin. She breathed in release as it healed and dissolved the cancerous cells weighing her soul down. I extended my hand toward her heart and used all my power to set it free, accessing the far reaches of my mind while orbs of light danced around me. Those orbs expanded into apparitions of my mother and father, who stood at my side to lend strength and compassion. Walter and Leon appeared next to them, evoking the wisdom of spirit, of life everlasting. And in the corner of my eye, little Sangeetha in her astral body smiled between her parents as a radiant monarch beyond the strings of time.

Once Luna was completely healed, liberated of the darkness, she could ascend into spirit. *"Thank you."* She breathed in one final breath before doing so willingly. But something monumental had happened, for an enormous force had been broken: the core of that greater entity above us.

As time moved forward and the rain resumed falling, her body collapsed.

Her sisters rushed over in shock, calling her name.

Then the earth shook mightily, and each soul looked up to see that the moon above us had cracked into three. As the shards of it separated, rays of the sun broke through from behind; we had to look away and close our eyes as it flashed with light, increasing its brightness a thousandfold. When we opened them again, there was no panic—not even a shred of fear. Rather, we came together, tranquil in our being and united in spirit, as a silent knowing arose within every soul. It was as if the whole of the earth, and each of her children, became illumined by the mind of God.

I did not expect what happened next—when the girl I knew as Luna suddenly breathed another breath. Her sisters lit up with joy, caressing her face as a soul arrived again behind her eyes. It wasn't Luna's; this was Madeleine, coming back into her body to tearfully explain her long journey to the other side and the contract she had made.

Nearby, Sangeetha appeared to everyone in her astral state. Many children gathered, and Felix wept happily as she began introducing them to the archangels and light beings who were protecting the others in the crystal cave.

Meanwhile, Matteo and Tiana sat together in contemplation, staring down at their hands, crying softly. Whatever had possessed them had fully left. The rays of higher consciousness shined upon their innermost shadows, bringing them to the surface. As Matteo glanced up and met my eyes, I saw once more that traumatized boy, a shadow we shared, triggering great empathy. He had never taken the opportunity to look within himself and do the proper healing. Perhaps now he could.

The lieutenant embraced his daughter, and his soldiers did the same to other children and to each other. To my astonishment, Mabus then came to me through the wall of blue flames—but his body was translucent, and I realized that he had passed into spirit. *"I'm sorry for everything I did,"* he whispered in my mind. *"Please let my daughters know, in this life or the next. I really do love them. I was just afraid. I couldn't see."*

I nodded, forgiving him what was mine to forgive. He reached out his ghostly hand while I reached back; as we grazed each other's fingertips, I felt the world shift into karmic balance. The earth again shuddered accordingly, and there blew a great wind. As Mabus's spirit vanished and more buildings disintegrated in the flames, I saw in the distance the tall towers of the capital toppling to the ground. Then I felt in my heart a massive wave coming in.

"Evelyn!" I shouted, looking around. "Evelyn!" But I had lost sight of her in the crowd. I closed my eyes and calmed myself before opening them into the eyes of Ezra as he embraced Sidney.

"Twist your head around," Ezra communicated.

I did as he advised, and there she was through the parting children, with Maya, Lila, Cyrus, and her siblings. Everyone was at peace, for we knew that we were protected. We felt the love of God. And as Evelyn's blue eyes shined with the soul of the new earth, she ran to hug me.

The last image I saw was of Noah, Penelope at his side, pointing up at the sky as it swirled with rainbow light. Then our souls blissfully intertwined, and I could no longer tell through whose eyes I was seeing. We found ourselves among the stars, holding each other and gracefully spinning while giant waves of cosmic energy enveloped the planet.

The next moment, we were back in our bodies, levitating with the others. As one with the rain, we cried joyously while our spirits awakened. Our collective emotion generated a force so potent that we vanished into thin air—right as the ocean waves washed over the land.

CHAPTER 0

I AWOKE FROM what seemed like a long, strange dream. It was a dream that I could suddenly recognize was illusory yet was so emotional and vivid that one could easily be convinced of its reality.

I opened my eyes under soft blue light in a pod-like apparatus, lying on a comfortable, watery material that molded to my body. I didn't immediately know where I was, but I felt uncannily at home and didn't have the desire to be anywhere else. Healing frequencies carried in the light combined with soothing sound vibrations to bathe my whole being in a holographic blueprint of harmony and perfection. The restoration soon finished, and the pod opened from above to reveal a small room with a reflective ceiling. I rose with wonder to take in my surroundings, feeling reborn from the game of existence.

"*Welcome back,*" said an inner voice as I surveyed the rounded crystalline walls situated on all sides. There were no light fixtures nor any other furniture but the white pod in the center, and the room pulsated with vibrant energy.

My attention turned to my body, which was fitted with a skin-tight, electric-blue suit. My face was clean shaven. My hand carried no scar, its wound a distant memory. As I stepped out onto the floor, my body was so insubstantial that it did not even cast a shadow; my bare feet made no sound. I was healed not only physically but mentally as well, gifted with great stillness and clarity.

Despite being alone in the room, I had the distinct feeling that I was being watched.

"Is anybody there?" I called out. The glittering walls coursed with white light, separating at intervals into a wide spectrum of color and evoking the memory of a certain cave and conscious crystals. Then I realized something concerning: there were no doors or windows. Before anxiety took hold, however, an orb of light emerged from my chest to appear directly before me.

I watched it for a moment as it flickered, communicating without words. Then it hovered to the wall, where a portion rippled until made transparent, leading to a larger, sparsely lit area. The orb floated through, inviting me to follow. But before doing so, I paused to listen to whispers of what sounded like an angelic choir backgrounded by a familiar, dreamlike drone—a sound I knew was made by playing a guitar with a cello bow. Chuckling, I stepped through the opening.

My chuckle gave way to a gulp of astonishment; there was no floor. I was suspended in the center of an enormous, empty cylinder illuminated solely by intersecting spirals of windows that extended both far above and below, including the one that contained my room. In this cylinder, there was no concept of gravity.

"Where are you taking me?" I asked the orb breathlessly; it turned bright green, and I sensed it laughing before beginning to ascend. Releasing my fear and worry naturally enabled me to rise up with it.

As we elevated, I looked through the other windows and saw that they too had pods. I wondered how many were awake and here with me and how many others were still on assignment, projecting their spirits into the dream.

We arrived at the very top portion of the cylinder, which did not contain windows. Rather, as a screen closed just below us, we were suddenly levitating in total darkness, stars in the vacuum of space. "What is happening?" I asked my orb friend. It came alight with color, excited for what I was about to see.

On the walls of the cylinder, a movie began playing. I witnessed myself as a baby, dressed in tiny pajamas, held tenderly in the arms of a woman whose perspective we were seeing through. The more I stared, the more immersed I became, until I was my mother. I felt the sheer love she possessed for me, the wonderment at my large eyes and abilities. There was a strong sense of wanting to protect me, yet she didn't care what others thought or how I might be viewed by society. I knew then that she had always loved me for exactly who I was. I gave her a reason for living and felt that I had fulfilled my entire purpose by giving that happiness to her—just by coming into the world. Just by existing.

From there, my awareness expanded drastically, and so did my vision. My present self dissipated, and I became lost in the movie of my life playing holographically in simultaneous scenes. I saw and experienced the years of my childhood and the entire decade at the Facility in one all-encompassing moment. Kissing Evelyn. Laughing with Walter. Watching my mother die as I held her hand and feeling the anger of my father as he glared into my eyes. I experienced not only my feelings and emotions but also those of everyone who had ever interacted with me, reliving every incident from their perspective.

I was shown how I had affected their lives, both positively and negatively, and the things I could have changed. I was shown my successes, where I went wrong, and places where I withheld love that I could have given more freely—which I felt was the most important thing. I became the child I was choking outside the Facility and Matteo as I tried stabbing him angrily. But there was no judgment, only lessons from experience, imbued with a love without condition. And as a final scene showed a giant wave approaching, I chose to forgive everything.

The following moment, I was back floating in space next to my orb friend, who seemed to smile while I digested the experience, processing the humbling magnificence of every event and emotion stored in the eternal memory of the universe.

The wall roiled, and a circular opening was revealed before us, leading to a light-filled corridor of the same crystalline substance. My orb friend glided through, waiting at the entrance as I steadied my breath. No longer questioning, I soared to accompany him, stepping onto a polished floor that encapsulated me in gravity once again.

"Come" was the sole word he transmitted, in a familiar and comforting voice. I followed him through the corridor, passing other openings along the way. One led to a room brimming with clear quartz crystals arranged in a geometric grid that centered on a giant levitating one, shaped like two counterrotating pyramids. As the grid pulsed with an electric current, the center crystal shined with ceaseless light, lending the feeling that it was generating energy.

Another room looked like an advanced laboratory and contained a wealth of scientific instruments along with thousands of fluid-filled vials stored in transparent cabinets. I got the impression that this lab had to do with genetics.

A little further down was the most breathtaking scene of all. I caught up to my orb friend as he waited for me at the opening, flashing rainbow light in reverence at the beauty.

I heard birds singing before I peered through.

An enormous garden with a thriving ecosystem extended as far as I could see, replete with gorgeous bioluminescent plants and trees and several animals from the earth—but also some I had never seen. Many seemed to be hybrids of creatures I was familiar with, but none appeared predatory, as the whole environment moved in unmistakable harmony, acting as one organism. Remarkably, a huge, floating ball of plasma shined over all of it, like a replica of the sun, in front of lifelike holograms of white clouds and a blue sky. I stepped into the garden to inhale the pristine air as colorful flowers bloomed around me and a rabbit hopped through the tall green grass, ignorant of fear and worry.

I caught sight of a waterfall in the distance, sparking fond memories, before the orb led me back down the crystalline corridor.

Soon, the hall opened into a large, disc-shaped area, still with no apparent windows nor furnishings of any kind. The orb floated to the center as the walls emitted shades of violet. Then it expanded into a fully formed body.

"Walter," I breathed.

He stood with elegant white robes and a luminous aura, staring at the wall with his back to me. I walked to him in amazement, and he turned to greet me.

"Welcome, Samuel." He nodded, beaming with affection. Yet as soon as I met his eyes, I realized this wasn't the same soul I had known; he wasn't wearing his monocle, either.

"You're not really him, are you?"

"Not in the way that you mean it." He gave a gentle smile. "If I deceived you, I must apologize. You may call me by his name if you would like, my child, because as you know by now, the One resides within every pair of eyes."

"But who are you, exactly?"

"I am what you might call your higher self, an aspect of your soul that has evolved to the point where it exists beyond space and time. I can take any form and be any place. In a sense, I am all that you are destined to become—and more, in our continued development."

"You must know everything about me, then."

"I have always known you, in the warmth of your mother's arms. I have watched and guided you through every moment of your life. I have been there for you in troubled times, as feelings of hope and joy in your heart and as the soft inner voice telling you that everything will be fine, even when things appeared to be hopeless and there was no escape in sight."

As he spoke, his forehead flashed with a continuum of light, corresponding with the walls around us. Underneath his words, a deeper telepathic exchange resonated within the core of my being. I found myself reliving a childhood memory of huddling in a closet, clutching my teddy bear while hearing my father scream, before looking up with a sense of comfort at a hovering orb of light.

He resumed, "As you grew older, I implanted subtle signs into the framework of your reality in order to help you to remember—as simple as sending you a pretty blue feather or whispering the words to your favorite songs along the wind and into the minds of others. Indeed, I know everything about you, Samuel. Because I *am* you. There is no separation."

"Then why take the form of Walter?" I asked, staring into his eyes and recognizing my own light.

"Because this is the form your mind is most comfortable with, as someone you view as wise and benevolent. He was, after all, the closest thing you've had to a father. His spirit lives on and has been guiding you until the end—his along with many others."

I recalled the final memory of my life review. "Am I dead?"

"Do not concern yourself with illusion," he said. "Recognize instead that your existence in this moment penetrates eternity. You have been on a marvelous journey of self-awakening. Come now. Sit with me."

I stood puzzled for a second until he manifested a sofa beside us—the same one my mother had held me on when I was a child. We sat next to each other, and it was just as comfortable as it was then. I realized—or perhaps remembered—that within the walls flowed a limitless energy with which we could consciously interact, manifesting whatever we desired. I tested this by visualizing a sweet, red apple. As soon as I asked for it, it materialized in my hand.

"Very good, Samuel." My higher self radiated a seraphic presence. "The universe is indeed at your service." He waved his hand at the wall in front of us, and an entire half of the room became transparent. Suddenly, our feet dangled over the edge of space. We observed the planet as she was bathed in light from the sun and bombarded with cosmic waves, creating a golden energetic field around her that looked like the wings of a butterfly. I sensed her being cleansed by water and wind that washed off lasting impurities and blew away the memory held by time.

Astonishingly, there were thousands of silver ships in the sky, coming and going from the surface. I knew they were assisting in her process of transformation, and as I watched with awe, I received a vision of joyful mothers and fathers reunited with their rescued children. Several of the ships were far out in space, steering away debris with their incredible technology—from a moon who, in her ascension, had cracked into three.

"So, all that actually happened," I said, thinking of the girl who had stopped time with me. "It's all real. It's not only a dream."

"The experience itself is always real, no matter the construct it takes place in. So yes, Samuel. Your actions have cosmic significance. And what you did—along with the honorable sacrifices of your wonderful friends—helped to trigger a necessary reset. It marks the destruction of illusory paradigms, the rebalancing of the earth on new magnetic poles, as well as a shift to a higher level of vibration, affecting the consciousness of all her children. Thus, you can say that as this happens and the matrix crumbles, she will become more aligned with what is truly real. Distortions of fear, greed, and violence will all but vanish, vibrationally incompatible with the new energies. For as the sun and the earth move into a portion of the galaxy with highly charged electromagnetic waves, together they ascend into a higher state."

"What about those still on the surface?" I asked. "Is it safe?"

"The ones who choose to match the new vibration are going to live through it, while the ills of the world will be washed away. It is a process, and it might take time until it is completely safe, but have faith that the earth will be repopulated in a new age. This is only the beginning, for there will come a point when all of her children will act as one race, and nothing will be restrained from them. Until then, they are protected by those watchers and stewards of the planet. This is not an accident, Samuel. This was meant to happen, long prophesied by your religions and spiritual traditions."

"You're making it sound like I was chosen to do this." I took a bite from the apple in the vague hope that it would ground me back to the planet; yet there we remained, floating in space among thousands of ark ships that were certainly not of human origin.

"You both chose and were chosen, as part of a plan beyond time itself. You volunteered to come for this mission, remember? Hence, we seeded you on the earth. You along with many others." I recalled the hundreds of pods I'd seen in the cylinder, yet there was only one person on my mind—which, of course, he picked up on. "Her soul resides with us during this process of rebirth. Do you wish to see her?"

"Really her?" I asked.

He smiled. "Really her."

We rose from the sofa, which vanished accordingly, and he gestured behind me. An elevator appeared in the wall. I turned back to him with curiosity. "Okay. But before I go, I want you to show me your true form."

"Very well." He nodded. Then, to my utter bewilderment, he shifted into a perfect image of my mother. "Within this form, the truth lies," she whispered with a hand over her heart as I stared at the gorgeous light in her eyes. Then, she morphed into my father. "In this form too, my son." He regarded me with pride before transforming into Luna exactly as I knew her, with her violet dress and golden cuff and earrings. "My true form is in the light that shines within the eyes of everyone you have ever met." She winked playfully as she suddenly became General Mabus. "Even within those who cannot recognize it."

Finally, he turned into me as a little boy, wearing the same white robes I'd worn when I first arrived at the Facility. I opened my arms instinctively, and he ran to hug me. "Everything is going to be okay," I said to him, tears falling. "I promise you. It's all for the best."

As I continued to tenderly embrace him, his form slowly shifted into Walter's again. "Do you understand now?" he said, giving me a fatherly pat on the shoulder as I released him.

"Yes. I just thought—"

"What, were you expecting an alien?" He transformed into a dazzling-looking humanoid with shining blue skin and eyes resembling small galaxies. *"In case you were wondering, in the journey of the soul, we've been that too,"* he transmitted telepathically as he condensed into an orb of pure white light, then projected into Walter. "But our *true* form is in the formless, Samuel—the unmanifested universal substance of infinite intelligence from which all life springs. And if you seek the keys to the Kingdom of Heaven, then allow this divine essence to sit on the throne of your consciousness."

I nodded in recognition. "I understand. But what will happen to you after this conversation? Will you just disappear back into it?" I let the apple float out of my grasp, and it gradually disintegrated.

"In the course of time, we will integrate into one mind, and you will regain your full memory. Until that point, however long you decide, I will stand beside you as a friend."

I hugged him again lovingly before manifesting a record player in homage to my wise tutor, whose spirit I felt was watching with a warm chuckle and a jovial smile. From it played a beautiful song I knew he loved, with the soft plucking of guitars and uplifting, rhythmic percussion. Together we listened for a few moments, reveling in the music. Then I headed toward the elevator. Its doors opened with a welcoming energy as the singer sang in falsetto:

> *"Reckoner,*
> *Take me with you,*
> *Dedicated to all human beings . . ."*

The elevator took me up one level, and soon I arrived at the upper room. There, I saw Evelyn resting in a pod of her own, although it was open. I paused while my heart expanded with a blissful feeling; a part of me wanted to be with her again in a lucid dream, under a cherry blossom tree near a lake of black-eyed angels.

I approached her and caressed her cheek, taking in her staggering beauty. She wasn't wearing a blue suit like me but rather a gown of light flowing with colors that mirrored the surrounding walls. The scar on her forehead was gone, and she breathed in peace, her heart-shaped locket glowing around her neck. As I rubbed her hand gently, she opened her eyes to stare into mine; that's when I noticed a striking detail.

They were larger, filled with even more light, the vastness of her spirit plain to see. She beamed when she saw me, then gazed around serenely. "Samuel," she whispered. "We're home, aren't we?"

"We never left," I said intuitively.

Smiling, she placed my hand on her womb, and we received a wonderful vision: one of children being raised in a better world, green and plentiful, without fear or limitation. Earth was restored to her natural beauty—her trees regrown, the toxic radiation dissipated—yet floating above the surface were magnificent crystal cities, abundant with resources and fantastic technology. Nothing was hidden, and all beings were free. Even the dead were resurrected within new bodies.

Then we were back on the ship.

"Come," I said. "There's something I want to show you."

I helped her up, and as we walked hand in hand, monarch butterflies manifested from the walls around us. While they gracefully fluttered about, I connected with the ship's intelligence so that the area we faced became transparent. Evelyn gasped in wonder as we stepped out into space. I felt her angels standing beside her while mine appeared over my shoulders. I wiped tears from her eyes, and together we gazed upon a new heaven and new earth.

I took in a deep breath, feeling unfettered by time, shedding the past, leaving my old self behind.

In transcending what is written, I create a new destiny.

Then the breath leaves my lungs, carried away through the unseen strings of the universe.

MUSICAL ACKNOWLEDGEMENTS

I would like to formally thank and acknowledge the brilliant artists and musicians whose compositions have formed the soundtrack to my life, providing inspiration for this novel. Whether openly referenced or secretly hidden, the inclusion of music lyrics has helped to make this book what it is, and below is a list of songs that were used with permission. See if you can spot them and decipher their meaning. As Walter had believed, we are living in a musical universe indeed.

RECKONER
Words and Music by THOMAS YORKE, JONATHAN GREENWOOD, COLIN GREENWOOD, EDWARD O'BRIEN and PHILIP SELWAY
© 2007 WARNER CHAPPELL MUSIC LTD.
All Rights in the U.S. and Canada Administered by WC MUSIC CORP.
All Rights Reserved
Used by Permission of ALFRED MUSIC

ASLEEP
Words and Music by JOHNNY MARR and STEVEN MORRISSEY
© 1985 MARR SONGS and UNIVERSAL–SONGS OF POLYGRAM INTERNATIONAL, INC.
All Rights for MARR SONGS Administered by WARNER-TAMERLANE PUBLISHING CORP.
All Rights Reserved
Used by Permission of ALFRED MUSIC

WELL I WONDER
Words and Music by STEVEN MORRISSEY and JOHNNY MARR
© 1985 ARTEMIS MUZIEKUITGEVERIJ B.V. (BUM/STE)
All rights on behalf of ARTEMIS MUZIEKUITGEVERIJ B.V. administered by WARNER-TAMERLANE PUBLISHING CORP.
All Rights Reserved
Used by Permission of ALFRED MUSIC

21 − 5 − 5 − 377 − 1597 − 3 − 10946 − 3 − 1597 − 46368 − 377 − 6765 − 0 − 1597 − 3 − 2584 − 3 − 0 − 1597 − 1 − 13 − 21 − 233 − 8

5 − 377 − 1597 − 4181 − 13 − 3 − 4181 − 1597 − 6765 − 4181 − 13 − 4181 − 377 − 89 − 21 − 5 − 3

46368 − 377 − 6765 − 0 − 1597 − 3 − 17711 − 0 − 2584 − 4181 − 21 − 233 − 8 − 46368 − 377 − 6765 − 1597 − 4181 − 21 − 144 − 3

5 − 377 − 1597 − 89 − 377 − 10946 − 3 − 21 − 2584 − 2584 − 377 − 2584 − 21 − 144 − 610 − 89 − 3

Made in United States
North Haven, CT
02 July 2024

54311976R00243